WHERE THE SUN DIES

FARLEIGH COLLINS

BOUNDLESS QUILL
PUBLISHING

First published by Boundless Quill 2025

Copyright © 2025 by Farleigh Collins

Cover by Felix Tidall

Edited by Brett Savory

First edition

ISBN (paperback): 979-8-9920813-1-2

ISBN (hardcover): 979-8-9920813-0-5

ISBN (ebook): 979-8-9920813-2-9

There's no place like home.

- Dorothy, The Wizard of Oz

CHAPTER ONE

Heat bore down on Elanor, oppressive and dry, unlike anything she had ever felt. She blinked her eyes open. The faintest sliver of sunlight sent sharp pain shooting through her skull. Her head throbbed with a deep, relentless ache that made it hard to think. She laid still, fingers digging into the hard, cracked ground beneath her, sensing the grit of dirt beneath her nails. Elanor couldn't quite remember where she had been before this, but it felt . . . different.

A flicker of unease rippled through her.

Am I dreaming? Am I alive?

The thoughts surfaced unbidden, sharp and cold against the heat pressing down on her. For a moment, she couldn't tell. Her body felt heavy, her movements slow, as if trapped in some half-formed dream. But the ground beneath her was solid, unyielding. The sensation of grit and dust between her fingers was far too vivid, the sunlight far too bright. It wasn't a dream. It was real—too real.

She searched her mind for what happened and how she got to her current predicament. Her memories of her life before this place were blurry, like trying to recall a dream after waking up. Her name and the feeling she didn't belong here were the only things she could cling to. But everything else—her past, her home, her family—was slipping further and further away. This feeling sent chills down Elanor's spine, unsettling and profound. The more she tried to grasp at the fading images, the more elusive they became, like shadows dissolving under the midday sun. It was as if her mind was a locked vault to which she had lost the key.

A gust of hot wind whipped across her skin, carrying the scent of dust and something earthy and ancient. Elanor blinked once more, trying to keep her eyes open this time. The bright sky was blinding—not a single cloud to block the hues of a brilliant blue. The sun was rising in the east, casting long rays across the barren landscape. To the west, a full moon hung low on the horizon. It was dropping slowly, as if unwilling to relinquish the night. Slowly, she pushed herself up on her elbows, her entire body aching as if she had fallen from a great height.

As she sat up, her hand instinctively brushed against her chest. It was then that she noticed the silver locket resting on her shirt, and despite the intense heat, the metal felt cool to the touch, its surface gleaming faintly in the sunlight. Her brow furrowed as she wrapped her fingers around it, bringing it closer for a better look. The locket was simple yet elegant, its edges worn smooth, and she felt a tiny latch on its side with her fingers.

Her attempts to open it failed. It wouldn't budge and frustration itched at her as she fiddled with the latch. It remained shut as if the secrets it held weren't ready to be revealed. She let it drop back against her chest with a sigh, and the weight of it was both comforting and enigmatic.

Elanor sat up gently, her muscles protesting every movement. As she glanced around, a surge of adrenaline coursed through her as she took in an empty street bordered by old wooden buildings, each weathered by time. "Saloon," "Bank," "Sheriff's Office"—the signs dangled loosely above doorways, their paint faded and chipped.

Her stomach churned. "What the hell?" Elanor muttered, her voice hoarse and cracking.

She looked down at herself. She wore oversized jeans and a man's button-up shirt that swamped her frame. A wide-brimmed hat sat low on her head, its heaviness unfamiliar.

2

Panic surged in her chest. This world was different from Elanor's, but she couldn't quite pinpoint why.

Dizziness washed over her, momentarily tilting the world. The boots on her feet—heavy, scuffed leather that didn't belong to her—sank slightly into the dirt road beneath her. She turned slowly in a circle, taking in the empty street and the silence that hung over everything like a thick, suffocating blanket. There was no sound, no movement—just the dry rustle of wind between the buildings.

"Hello?" she called out, her voice rough and uncertain.

The whisper of the wind was the only response for a long moment. Then came the low sound of laughter from the shadows of a nearby porch—raspy and grating, but undeniably human.

A surge of adrenaline shot through Elanor as she turned toward the sound. There, slumped against the railing of a run-down wooden building, sat a man. He was heavyset, with scruffy, unkempt hair and a thick beard, which was more salt than pepper. His clothes were filthy—caked with dust and grime—and in his hand he held a half-empty bottle that resembled whiskey. The man squinted at her, revealing the lines around his eyes, then let out another wheezing laugh.

"Well, now," the man drawled, his Southern accent thick and slow, "ain't you a sight for sore eyes. Look like you been ridin' with the ghosts."

Elanor blinked at him, heart pounding. "Where am I?" she asked, voice shaky.

The man let out a wheezing laugh, slapping his knee. "Where are ya? Hell, darlin', you're in Bodie. Finest town this side of nowhere."

"Bodie?" Elanor echoed, distant and unfamiliar. She glimpsed around again, taking in the dusty, deserted street. "Is this a ghost town?"

The man grinned, revealing a set of crooked, yellowed teeth. "Ghost town? Ain't no ghost town here, missy. Although there might be plenty of ghosts roamin' around these parts. This here's the most beautifulist town you'll ever set foot in. An' me? I'm the most beautifulist man in it."

He tilted his hat toward her, his wide smile never disappearing. Elanor's stomach twisted again. This wasn't right. Or was it? She shook her head, trying to recall memories of where she came from. Although

3

she couldn't quite pinpoint it, she knew this wasn't the place. This couldn't be real, but Elanor didn't understand why. It had to be a joke. Or a dream? Was it some elaborate prank? But everything was so vivid—the heat on her skin, the grit of the dirt under her boots, the sharp scent of whiskey in the air. This wasn't a dream. And if it were, it would be the most real dream she had ever experienced.

Still slumped against the railing, Boone laughed and quipped, "Hey, you look like you're wearing my clothes."

Elanor looked down in panic, eyes widening as she took in the dirt on her clothes. She feared she was as filthy as Boone. Realization settled in and relief washed over her; even with the dust, her outfit was still cleaner than his grimy attire. She squeezed the fabric at her waist, noting how much it wrapped around her slender frame. This confirmed her suspicion that these weren't her clothes, but she couldn't be certain whose they were.

"Very funny," she replied, and managed a small, tense smile, rolling her eyes but feeling amused in spite of her confusion.

Boone chuckled, then gestured to his own worn and filthy clothes. "Just making sure you're still with us, darlin'. Wouldn't want you blending in too well with the local dirt."

Elanor's mind spun. She was in Bodie—an unfamiliar place named as if she should know it. She turned back to Boone, trying to anchor herself with more questions. "What year is it?" she asked.

Boone raised an eyebrow, then took a long swig from his bottle. "Year? Hell, it's 1883, last I checked. Why, what year do ya think it is?"

The world tilted beneath Elanor's feet: 1883? That couldn't be right.

"Eighteen eighty-three? No. No, that's impossible," she muttered.

Boone tipped his head back and laughed, whiskey sloshing in his bottle. "Impossible, huh? Well, I reckon a lot o' things feel impossible 'til they ain't. But you're here now, ain't ya?"

Elanor opened her mouth to respond, but no words emerged. Her thoughts were spinning too fast, too wildly. She needed to wake up. She needed to get back to . . . where? Home? To when? The more she tried to concentrate, the fuzzier her memories became, slipping away like smoke.

Boone cleared his throat. "You alright there, darlin'? You look like you might topple over any second. Need me to fetch the sheriff?"

"The sheriff?" Elanor echoed, her voice thin.

Boone nodded, pointing down the street toward a building with a faded red sign that read "Saloon."

"Sheriff's prob'ly down at the saloon, like he always is. Ain't the brightest fella, but he might be able to help you figure out where you're s'posed to be."

Elanor's head was spinning again. The sheriff? A saloon? This had to be some kind of joke. Or . . . maybe she had bumped her head somewhere, and this was all some strange, vivid hallucination. But no matter how hard she tried to convince herself, everything felt too real. Too solid.

"I need to get home," she said.

Boone shrugged, taking another swig of whiskey. "Well, home's a long way from here, I reckon. But if you're lookin' to get somewhere, the sheriff's your best bet. Unless you wanna keep wanderin' 'round like a lost calf."

Elanor peered down the street toward the saloon. Wooden buildings reached over her; their square shapes cast long shadows under the morning sun. A growing sense of unease coiled in her stomach, and a chill swept over her, despite the heat. What choice did she have? She had no idea where she was, how she had arrived, or how to return home. She wasn't even sure where home was. The sheriff, whoever he was, might be the one who could provide her with some answers, and she needed to explore every option.

"Thanks," she muttered, turning away from Boone and starting down the road.

"Hey!" he called after her, his voice slightly slurred. "You ain't even gonna ask my name?"

Elanor stopped, glancing over her shoulder at him. "What's your name?"

He grinned wide, raising his bottle in a mock salute. "Name's Boone. Mayor of this here town, if you ask me."

A small smile tugged at the corner of Elanor's mouth. "Very kind of you to help me, Boone."

He let out another laugh, slapping his knee. "Anytime, darlin'. But, uh—word of advice? Don't get too attached to leavin'. This place don't let go easy."

Was he playing with her? Or was he serious? The way he said it, as casually as asking for more whiskey, sent chills down her back.

Elanor's gut twisted tighter, but she didn't waver. She struggled to regain her footing on the desolate street leading to the saloon. Her boots scraped against the dirt as the sun rose higher in the sky. The moon stubbornly clung to the horizon as if it refused to fade away, exuding an odd and timeless feeling.

She still heard Boone's laughter echoing in the distance as she approached the saloon, where the faded red paint peeled from the walls like old skin. Her pulse thundered in her ears, and her hands shook as she reached for the swinging doors.

She didn't know what was waiting for her inside, but she was certain this was not your typical dream.

The saloon doors groaned loudly as she pushed them open. She stepped into the dimly lit room, air was heavy with the scent of stale whiskey and sweat. Clinking of glasses, soft murmur of conversation, and the distant twang of a poorly tuned piano filled the space.

Elanor blinked to adjust her eyes to the dim light as she stepped farther inside. Her boots echoed on the hollow wooden floor. She drew the attention of a few men seated at a nearby table, their eyes narrowing slightly as they assessed her strange and unfamiliar appearance. Their stares were fleeting as they reverted to their drinks and cards, displaying no interest.

A long, wooden bar spanned the wall at the far end of the room, lined with half-empty bottles of whiskey, gin, and other spirits. Behind it stood a heavyset woman with wild red curls, polishing a glass with a rag that looked dirtier than the glass itself. She was broad-shouldered, her freckled face displaying a no-nonsense expression, and when her eyes fell on Elanor, she raised an eyebrow.

"You lost, honey?" the woman asked, loud enough to cut through the background noise.

Elanor swallowed hard, making her way toward the bar. Her legs were still unsteady, the surreal nature of everything pressing down on her. "I— Uh, I'm looking for the sheriff," she said, her voice shaky but firm enough to be heard.

The woman snorted, setting the glass down on the bar with a thud. "Sheriff? That fool's probably sittin' in the back room of my bar, losing his money at cards, like usual. What d'ya want with him?"

Elanor hesitated, unsure of how much to reveal. She had no idea where she was, how she had gotten there, or why this was happening. Admitting this to a room full of strangers was sure to lead to disaster. "I just . . . I need to talk to him," she said vaguely.

"Say," the woman started, pausing to reach for Elanor's hair. "Fancy hair you got there."

Elanor blinked, momentarily thrown by the question. "My . . . hair?"

"Yeah, them curls. So tight an' smooth. Mine? Looks like a damn bird's nest every mornin'." The woman grinned while tossing her hair. "You got a secret? Some fancy cream from wherever you came from?"

Elanor smiled weakly. "No secrets. Just genetics . . . I think?"

The woman squinted at her, her grin widening. "Well, I reckon we could be twins, then. 'Cept my skin ain't as dark as yours; you got them golden eyes. Ain't never seen eyes like that before. Oh, and I got the body men want. You're too skinny for their tastes."

Elanor's throat tightened. Nora's words were casual, yet they reminded her of how out of place she must appear here. Even though she couldn't recall any memories of this, she sensed her mixed-race heritage had always made her stand out, but in this unfamiliar place, it made her feel even more like an outsider.

"I'm just passing through," Elanor said, trying to steer the conversation away from herself. "About the sheriff?"

Nora barked a laugh, tossing her rag over her shoulder. "In the back. Don't expect too much, though. Man's about as useful as a screen door in a dust storm."

Elanor nodded her thanks and made her way toward the back room, her stomach churning with nerves. She approached the saloon's back room, passing a dusty mirror hanging crookedly on the hallway wall. She paused as the reflection of a woman with hazel eyes stared back at her. Her eyes lingered on the high cheekbones and sharp jawline framed by black, curly hair that rested just above her shoulders. Her plump lips, slightly parted, seemed to echo a question she couldn't quite voice.

She stared at her reflection. She searched for a glimmer of recognition, a hint of memory in her features. The understanding, the familiarity she longed for didn't come. It left a hollow feeling in its wake.

Who am I?

The question worried her. Her reflection offered no answers and only deepened the mystery of her identity.

Elanor took a steadying breath to calm her nerves and tore her gaze from the mirror. She walked toward the door at the end of the hall and pushed it open. She stepped into the small, dimly lit room, shadows dancing along the walls, illuminated by the faint flicker of an oil lamp. Four men were engrossed in a card game, and the air was thick with the scents of cigar smoke and liquor.

Her eyes adjusted to the dim light, scanning the rough expressions and hardened features of the men seated at the table. Then, her gaze settled on the man with a silver star pinned to his vest, and for a fleeting moment, a heavy weight pressed against her chest.

The sheriff was young—much younger than she had expected for someone in his position. He appeared to be close to the age Elanor thought she might have been in the mirror, maybe late twenties, early thirties. His short, black hair was neatly combed—a stark contrast with the messy styles of the others. Hints of stubble framed his defined jawline, giving an air of ruggedness that softened the otherwise clean-cut distinctness of his appearance. His sharp, discerning brown eyes caught the low light, their intensity indicating that he missed nothing.

His clothes were what caught her attention the most. Like his beard, the vest and trousers were unnervingly clean, with sharp creases. It was as if he had stepped out of a catalog, rather than a dusty town in the Wild West. Even his tan cowboy boots shimmered in the dim light. The contrast made him stand out against the backdrop of the gamblers around him, giving him an air of authority that suggested it was more expected than earned.

The sheriff's wide-brimmed hat was shifted low over his brow, concealing his expression as he studied his cards. The sound of Elanor's presence in the room drew his attention, his head lifting slightly. His eyes locked onto hers. The room stilled, the air thick with unspoken weight as he leaned back in his chair, his fingers drumming a measured rhythm on the table.

"You look lost," he said, his voice low and steady, with a hint of dry humor. The faintest trace of a smile touched the corner of his mouth, though his eyes remained sharp and unreadable.

Elanor straightened, determined not to let her unease show. "I'm exactly where I'm meant to be," she replied, voice steady even with the nervous flutter in her chest.

She walked closer, a rush of nervous energy building with each step. The man lifted his head as she neared, his eyes squinting under the brim of his hat.

"Well," the sheriff drawled, his voice slow and measured. "What brings you to Bodie, then, missy?"

Elanor swallowed, feeling the pressure of the world crashing down around her. "I . . ." she began, confidence wavering. "I don't belong here. I need help."

The sheriff reclined, crossing his arms as he observed her. "Don't belong? Nobody comes to Bodie by accident. If you're here, it's for a reason. What's your story?"

Elanor tensed.

What's my story?

She wasn't sure anymore. Her memories felt like fragments, pieces of a puzzle that just wouldn't fit together. Everything seemed so distant, like another life entirely.

"I don't know how I got here," she admitted, her voice soft but steady. "One minute I was in . . . somewhere, and the next I woke up here, in . . . in 1883, apparently."

The sheriff raised an eyebrow. "Somewhere, huh? Well, missy, you sure ain't there no more."

"I know that," Elanor snapped, her frustration boiling over. "I'm not stupid. I just . . . I don't know how any of this is possible or how to get back."

The sheriff sighed, tossing his cards onto the table. "Ain't nobody left this town in a long while, especially if you don't know where you're goin'. Bodie's got a way of holdin' onto folks. Once you're here, you're here for good."

Something heavy settled in her chest. "What do you mean?"

"I mean," the sheriff said, his voice low and ominous, "people who try to leave? They don't make it. This place doesn't let go easy."

The room closed around Elanor, the sheriff's words settling with a heaviness in her chest. Dizziness hit her, her feet unsteady. "There has to be a way," she said, trembling. "I can't be stuck here. I don't belong in this time. I have a life back home."

"Might work out better if you knew where home was first." The sheriff gave her a long, measured look, his stare unwavering. Then, slowly, he nodded toward the door. "If you're lookin' for answers, you might wanna see Tawa. Some folks say he knows things . . . things most people can't understand. Lives out by the river, up in the mountains."

Elanor latched onto the name like a lifeline: Tawa. "Who is he?"

The sheriff leaned farther back in his chair, crossing his arms again. "Old Indian fella. Says he sees things. People 'round here think he talks a lotta nonsense, but he's got a way of knowin' things that most folks can't explain. Might be your best shot if you really are from somewhere . . . else."

Her mind raced. This was the first glimmer of hope she'd received since waking up in this strange place. Could that be it? Could there be some explanation for how she had ended up here—some way to return?

"How do I get to him?" she asked, desperate for any details.

The sheriff's lips twitched into a slight smirk. "You don't. Not alone, anyway. Ain't no safe path for a woman out there by herself—especially with the bandits and coyotes runnin' 'round. Best get yourself some company and a horse."

Elanor's heart sank. She had no horse, no money, and no one to help her. The sheriff's words felt like another door closing, the way out slipping further from her grasp.

She opened her mouth to respond, but no words emerged. The burden of it all—being trapped here, being alone—settled on her like a lead blanket. She found herself in the middle of nowhere, in a time that wasn't hers, with no clear path forward. How was she supposed to reach Tawa if she had no way to travel?

Sensing her hesitation, the sheriff stood from the table and walked toward her. "Look, missy, I'm not here to tell ya how to live your life. But if you're serious about gettin' outta here, you'll need help. This town's got a few folks who might be willin' to lend a hand if you ask nice enough."

"Any ideas of who to ask?" Elanor said.

"Ask around until you get a yes, I suppose."

"Don't suppose you could help, Sheriff?"

He didn't speak, just shook his head. "Most I can give you is some directions," he said. "Head east on the main trail. After a few miles, you'll come to a fork—take the left path. Follow it until you hear the river. Once you're near the water, keep heading upstream. You'll find Tawa's place in a clearing not far from where the river bends. Shouldn't take more than a day's ride to get there."

Elanor nodded, her mind spinning. "Thanks," she managed to say, her voice barely a whisper.

The sheriff gave her a friendly tip. "Good luck. You're gonna need it."

Elanor returned to the main room of the saloon. She had a lead now —*Tawa*—but she also had no way to reach him. She was alone in this world without friends, family, resources, or any knowledge of how to navigate the dangerous lands beyond Bodie. The reality of her isolation settled in with each passing moment.

Nora glanced up from behind the bar as Elanor emerged from the back room. "Well? Sheriff give you anythin' useful?"

Elanor paused, then shook her head slightly. "He told me about someone—someone who might be able to help. But I have no way of getting to him."

Nora raised an eyebrow. "You mean Tawa? That ol' fool? Ha, if anyone's got answers 'bout weird things 'round here, it's him. But he ain't exactly next door."

"So the sheriff says." Elanor sighed, glancing out the saloon windows to the empty street outside. "And I don't have a horse. I can't get out there alone."

Nora snorted, wiping her hands on the rag slung over her shoulder. "Well, ya better find yourself some company, then. Ain't nobody gonna let ya wander off into the desert by yourself—unless you're Boone, but he's crazy as a rattlesnake."

Elanor thought of Boone and his wild laugh, the way he'd grinned at her as if this were all some big joke. He may have been insane, but at least he had been more empathetic toward her than anyone else so far.

Nora must have noticed Elanor's expression, as she burst into laughter. "Oh, hell, girl. You thinkin' 'bout askin' ol' Boone for help? Ha! You'll be lucky if he don't fall off his horse 'fore you get halfway there. He's always quick to offer help, but being much use is another story."

Elanor's lips twitched into a faint smile in spite of the overwhelming situation. "I don't exactly have a lot of options."

Nora leaned back against the bar, her sharp gaze flicking to Elanor. "Before you rush out there and get yourself into God knows what kind of trouble, you want a drink? Might do you good to settle your nerves before you go runnin' off with the likes of Boone."

Elanor instinctively shook her head. "I don't drink," she replied, the words escaping her lips as naturally as breathing. It wasn't something she needed to contemplate, just a part of who she was—or had always been.

Nora raised a brow, the corners of her mouth quirking into a small, knowing smile. "Suit yourself. Water, then? Can't have you droppin' dead from thirst before you even get halfway up the trail."

The offer felt like a lifeline, though Elanor couldn't quite understand why. "Water would be great," she said quietly, hoping this pause might allow her a moment to clear her head. Perhaps the cool drink would fully wake her, shaking her out of the haze that had clouded her mind since she'd arrived in Bodie.

Nora reached behind the bar and poured a glass from a metal pitcher, the water catching the dim light as it splashed into the glass. "Here you go, princess," she said, sliding it across the polished wood. "Fresh from the pump. Best you'll find in this town."

Elanor wrapped her hands around the glass, the coolness seeping into her palms. "Thanks," she murmured, taking a small sip and letting the crisp water wash over her parched throat.

Nora leaned her elbows on the bar, studying Elanor with curiosity and mild amusement. "You're not from around here. That's clear enough. What's draggin' you out to see Tawa? Most folks steer clear of the river, especially with all the talk of curses and ghosts floatin' around."

Elanor contemplated Nora's question, swirling the water in her glass as she chose her words. "It's . . . important. Something I have to do."

Nora's expression softened. "Well, if you're settin' off into the wild, you're gonna need more than just determination. Luck, for one. And maybe a bit of sense to go with it."

Then the saloon doors creaked open, catching the room's attention. A young blonde woman sauntered in, her dress a deep crimson that shimmered softly in the dusty light; the skirt was hitched high on one side to reveal a shapely leg clad in black stockings. Her confident smile drew the attention of the few men scattered at the round card tables.

Nora snorted, glancing toward the piano in the corner. "Looks like Molly's decided to grace us with her talent—or somethin' close to it."

Molly's heels clicked against the wooden floor as she approached the piano, fingers trailing along the top before she sat down with practiced elegance. She played a few lively chords. The notes were harsh yet cheerful, drawing whistles and cheers from two nearby men. Elanor did not quite understand why.

Elanor's eyes lingered on the scene as she absorbed the subtle details of the saloon. Hanging lanterns cast warm, amber light, leaving a glow about the room that softened the rough edges of the wooden tables and scuffed floorboards. The scent of aged whiskey mingled with the strong zest of cigar smoke. As the whistles settled, the low hum of conversation resumed to provide a backdrop to Molly's spirited playing.

"Don't let her distract you too much," Nora said, her voice cutting through Elanor's thoughts. "Molly's good at what she does, but she's better at causin' trouble when she's in the mood."

Elanor smiled softly as she sipped the last of her water. The saloon buzzed with a comforting yet disorienting energy. It displayed a world of vibrancy even amid her uncertainty. She set the empty glass on the bar and locked eyes with Nora.

"Thank you for this," she said. "For the water and the . . . talk."

Nora waved dismissively, though a flicker of warmth crossed her face. "Don't go gettin' sentimental on me now. Just make sure you get where you're goin'. And if you find yourself in need of a drink—or a reason to laugh—come on back. This place'll still be here."

Elanor nodded. Rising from her stool, she cast one last look around the saloon. Molly sang softly and her fingers danced over the piano keys, the tune tripping and sad.

Elanor pressed the doors open and stepped into the midday sun. A pang of longing for the fleeting warmth of the saloon struck Elanor as sweat formed on the back of her neck. But there was no time to linger. She had a journey ahead, and needed to get back to . . . back to herself.

The sheriff's words still lingered and weighed on Elanor. She was stranded, yes, but at least she had something to work with. If she convinced Boone to help her, maybe she'd have a chance to make it to Tawa.

As quick as she thought it, though, doubt crept in. The journey ahead was filled with impossibilities. The idea of relying on strangers in a world she didn't understand made her uneasy. However, she had no choice. If she wanted to get back—if there was even a chance of returning home—she'd have to take it.

Alone in the dusty street of Bodie, Elanor took a deep breath, allowing the dry air to fill her lungs. With a determined set to her jaw, she began walking, the weight of her journey ahead pressing down on her like the sun's relentless heat.

CHAPTER TWO

Elanor hesitated before taking another step toward Boone. Her boots scuffed against the dusty road, but she stopped short, a knot tightening in her chest. Was she really about to ask the town drunk to help her? The thought was ridiculous the more she lingered on it.

She scanned the town again, looking for anyone who might be a better option. But the street remained empty, the faded wooden buildings sagging in the oppressive heat.

Boone was sprawled on the porch of a run-down building, still clutching his whiskey bottle like it was his only possession in the world.

Her mind raced, desperately trying to come up with an alternative. She couldn't stay in Bodie, that much was true. This wasn't her world, and the sheriff's cryptic words echoed in her head: *Once you're here, you're here for good.*

Elanor's stomach churned. She couldn't afford to be picky about who helped her—not when every second in this ghost town was a slow descent into madness. But relying on Boone? The man could barely stay upright, let alone guide her through the dangers that surely awaited outside Bodie.

She shook her head, pinching her arm to wake herself up. Nothing happened outside of slight pain from her nails digging into her skin.

Elanor hit herself in the head repeatedly with the palm of her hand, hoping for something to happen, anything . . . but nothing did. She was still faced with the Wild West street before her, Boone in her sights.

"God, this is insane," she muttered, rubbing her forehead. She took a deep breath and forced her feet to move. She didn't have time for doubts. There was no one else.

Boone was humming some off-key tune, eyes glazed over as Elanor approached him again. His boots were still propped up on the railing, and he was oblivious to her presence until she cleared her throat.

"Boone," she said, forcing her voice to stay calm, "I need your help."

Boone blinked slowly as it took him a second to register what she'd said. "Help? Well, now, that's a funny thing to be askin' me for," he slurred, a lazy grin spreading across his face.

Elanor bit her lip and held back a sigh. "You're the mayor. You should help people in need."

Boone squinted at her. "Mayor? Now, that's a mighty fine title, but I reckon we ain't got no mayor in these parts." He chuckled as though she'd just told the funniest joke he'd heard all day. "Lost the title to my brother, but he's long gone. So, guess I'm the stand-in, huh?"

She rolled her eyes. Of course he wasn't the mayor. However, her options were limited. "Look, I just need someone who knows the area. I'm trying to find someone named Tawa, and I need help getting there. I don't have a horse or any supplies. You know the area, don't you?"

Boone's grin widened. "Well, ain't that the truth. Can't nobody find their way 'round Bodie and the desert like me. But you'll be needin' more than just my company. We're gonna need another hand. Good thing I know just the man."

Elanor asked, "Who?"

"Ah, everybody knows ol' Weston," Boone said. "Man's got a way with horses. Strong as an ox. He's rough 'round the edges, but he's good folk."

Weston. Hearing the name triggered something in Elanor's mind, a faint tug of familiarity she couldn't quite place. She frowned, trying to grasp the fleeting memory, but it slipped through her fingers like smoke. Why did the name sound so familiar?

Her chest constricted with frustration. "Fine. Let's go see him."

They walked in silence at first, heading toward the outskirts of town where Boone claimed Weston lived. The buildings grew more dilapidated the farther they went, windows boarded up, roofs sagging, like the town itself was slowly sinking into the dust.

Elanor stared at Boone, who was humming again, clearly oblivious to her mounting anxiety. She couldn't help but wonder if she'd made the wrong choice. This man lacked mental clarity—how could he provide the guidance she required?

"You ever hear 'bout the time I ran this whole town?" Boone said suddenly, breaking the silence.

Elanor arched an eyebrow. "You said you weren't the mayor."

Boone waved his hand dismissively. "Details, details. Back in my prime, I was the one everyone came to. Had my finger in every pie, so to speak. People trusted me. They still do, I reckon. Just 'cause I like a little whiskey now and then don't mean I'm useless."

Elanor glanced at him, unsure whether to believe a word of what he was saying. His words were slurred, and he stumbled a little as they walked, but there was something oddly endearing about him. At least he was eager to help, even if his methods were questionable.

As they passed the last few buildings on the edge of town, Boone pointed toward a small stable. "There's Weston tendin' to his horse. Let me do the talkin'—he ain't always the friendly type."

The sight of Weston caught Elanor's breath in her throat. He was crouched beside a large, muscular horse, his broad frame moving with quiet confidence as he gently wrapped a bandage around the animal's leg. His medium brown hair was slightly messy, damp from the heat, the strands catching the sunlight in a way that made them almost shimmer. A short beard framed his strong jaw, accentuating the sharp lines of his face and the striking blue of his eyes—a shade so vivid, it caught and held the light.

The collar of his shirt was open, revealing the strong curve of his chest, his skin glistening faintly with sweat. The muscles of his forearms were exposed by the roll of his shirt sleeves to his elbows. They flexed with each precise movement as he worked with a focused intensity, his hands both careful and steady, a contrast of strength and tenderness that made Elanor's breath hitch again. There was something captivating about how he moved, a hint at years of hard work and discipline.

Elanor watched Weston tend to his horse. A fleeting thought crossed her mind about her clothes—they were baggy and had a rugged, practical style that, for some reason, reminded her of Weston. She didn't know why she thought of him specifically—perhaps it was the way he carried himself, or maybe just a random connection made in the whirl-wind of unfamiliar faces and places. Her eyes shifted briefly to her attire, pondering the possibility before dismissing it as another unexplained mystery in a day full of them.

Boone, oblivious to her distraction, called out, "Hey there, Wes!"

Weston looked up, and his face hardened when his eyes settled on Boone. "What do you want, Boone?" he said, his voice low and firm.

The hint of a Southern accent in his words caught Elanor's atten-tion, though it wasn't as pronounced as the others she'd came across since she woke up. It sounded practiced, like something he'd picked up rather than being natural. She tilted her head slightly, curiosity forming beneath her otherwise cautious observation. There was more to him than met the eye—that much was clear.

She stared momentarily, caught between curiosity and the unwel-come tug of attraction. She blinked, quickly shaking her head to clear her thoughts.

Get it together, Elanor.

She had more significant problems than being distracted by some guy's physique—no matter how beautiful he might be.

"Well, now that you ask, I got a little favor to ask ya." Boone grinned, swaying slightly as he leaned against the stable door. "This here's Elanor. She's got herself in a bit of a pickle, an' I reckon you'd be just the man to help her out."

Weston stood slowly, eyes narrowing as he looked Elanor up and down. "Help her with what?"

Elanor stepped forward, trying to steady her nerves. "I'm trying to find a man named Tawa. I need to . . . get back to where I came from, and he might know how. But I don't know the area, and I don't have a horse. Boone said you could help."

Weston turned away. "I don't do favors for people I don't know."

A wave of heaviness settled over her, but Elanor refused to give up. "Please. I'm not from here. I don't even know how I got here. I just need to find a way back. Boone said you were good with horses, and I can't do this without someone who knows the land."

Jaw set, arms crossed, Weston spoke plainly: "Sounds like you've got more problems than I'm willing to take on."

Elanor's desperation surged. She opened her mouth to speak again, but Boone interrupted, his grin widening. "Now, now, Wes, don't be so quick to turn us down. I reckon I got somethin' that might sweeten the deal." He patted his coat pocket, where the outline of a flask was barely visible. "You help us out, and this here flask of the good stuff is yours."

Weston's eyes flicked to the flask, then to Elanor, and for a moment, she thought she witnessed a flicker of interest. He let out a slow breath, shoulders relaxing slightly. "Whiskey's not enough to convince me to go on some wild goose chase, Boone."

Boone chuckled, pulling the flask from his pocket. "Oh, but it ain't just any whiskey, Wes. This here's the finest in town. Hard to come by these days."

Weston hesitated, looking at Elanor again, taking her in longer than expected. A sense of sadness rested on his face before speaking. "You really think this Tawa guy can help you?"

Elanor nodded. "I'm not certain, but it's the only lead I have. Please, I need help to get through this."

He looked back and forth at Elanor and Boone, his face giving nothing away. After a moment, he let out a sigh. "Fine. But don't think this is gonna be easy. The desert's unforgiving. We have little to no idea what we'll encounter along the way."

"Thank you."

"Just don't expect me to play babysitter," he said, waving her off.

In town, the group gathered supplies for the journey ahead. Weston's movements were precise and efficient as he gathered food and water.

Elanor felt a mix of awe and frustration as she observed him. He had a smoothness in everything he did.

Meanwhile, Boone fumbled with his saddlebags. He nearly dropped the few items they had managed to scrounge together. "Got it under control," he muttered through his struggles.

Elanor scanned the small town square, wondering how they would gather enough supplies for the journey. A few townspeople's gazes surveyed them from afar. Although she was unfamiliar with the workings of the Wild West, she understood that nothing was easy, and certainly not without a cost.

As Boone stumbled, nearly dropping a bundle of blankets, a woman emerged from the doorway of a nearby shop. She had curly blonde hair tied up in a loose bun, and her sharp gaze landed on Boone with a mix of curiosity and disapproval.

"Well, well," the woman said, crossing her arms. "Boone, what are you up to now? You plannin' on takin' a trip, or are you just wanderin' around town drunk again?"

Boone straightened with a grin. "Clarabelle, darlin'! Now, don't be so harsh on ol' Boone. I'm just gatherin' a few things for a little journey. Nothin' too serious."

Clarabelle's gaze narrowed as she eyeballed Elanor and Boone. "Who's the girl, then? You sure look cozy for someone who's always runnin' his mouth 'bout how he don't need nobody."

Elanor shifted uncomfortably as Clarabelle's eyes lingered on her.

"This here's Elanor," Boone said, waving his hand dramatically. "She's in a bit of trouble, so I'm takin' her on a little adventure. Thought you might help us with some supplies, seein' how you and I go way back."

Clarabelle let out a snort. "Boone, you always come around when you need somethin', don't ya?" She glared at him before turning to Elanor. "You sure you trust him? I've seen him promise the moon to people before, and all they get is disappointment."

Elanor opened her mouth, but Boone cut in with a wide grin. "Now, now, no need to scare the lady. I'm a changed man, Clarabelle! We've got a real purpose this time, and I'd be ever so grateful if you could spare a few supplies for the road."

Clarabelle looked Boone up and down, her eyes softening slightly as she sighed. "You're lucky we've got a history. Careful who you go beggin' to around town, though. Word's gettin' around that you can't follow through with your promises anymore." She turned and called into the shop. "Johnny, get a couple of those bags we got in the back. We'll lend 'em to Boone and his friend here."

A slim young man stepped out from behind the counter with two large bags, which he handed to Elanor and Boone.

"Don't think I ain't keeping tabs on these," Clarabelle warned. "You'd best return 'em when you're done."

Boone winked at her, slipping an arm around her waist. "You're an angel, Clarabelle. You'll always have my heart."

Clarabelle shoved him off, laughing. "You say that to all the girls, Boone."

Elanor watched the interaction with amusement and embarrassment but mostly relief. They were one step closer to being ready, and Boone's charm—however sloppy—was at least working in their favor.

With the bags from Clarabelle in hand, they moved on to their last stop—guns and ammo.

A small shop was nestled in the corner of the street, its windows dusty and cracked, with a barely legible, faded wooden sign that read "Graves & Sons General Store." Inside, the air smelled of gunpowder and sweat, and rows of shelves were stacked with various supplies—though not many looked well-stocked.

Following Boone and Weston inside, the floorboards creaked beneath Elanor's boots. Behind the counter stood a tall, wiry man with sunken eyes and a weathered face. His hands were calloused, and he was busy polishing a rifle, though he paused when the group entered. His eyes lingered on Elanor, then shifted to Weston with a raised brow.

"What do you need?" the man asked, voice gruff and impatient.

"Guns and ammo, Graves," Weston said flatly, stepping up to the counter. "We're heading out and need enough to handle any trouble."

The shopkeeper snorted, setting the rifle down with a thud. "You ain't the only ones lookin' for extra firepower these days. Lot of folks comin' in askin' for the same thing. Prices are high, and I ain't in the business of givin' discounts."

Elanor glanced at Weston, her heart sinking. She had no idea how they were going to afford weapons. She had nothing on her, and she doubted Boone was better off. Her eyes flicked to Boone, leaning against the counter, looking like he was on the verge of dozing off.

Weston crossed his arms. "We don't need much. Just enough to keep ourselves safe from Merrick's men."

At the mention of Merrick, the shopkeeper's eyes narrowed, his expression hardening. "Merrick's been stirrin' up trouble for everyone, but that don't mean I can go around handin' out guns for free. You want 'em, you pay."

Seemingly roused by the tension in the room, Boone stepped forward with a crooked grin. "Now, now, Graves, let's not be too hasty. You and I go way back, don't we? Remember the time I helped you haul that shipment of rifles when your son ran off to chase some girl?"

Graves scowled. "That was years ago, Boone, and I ain't runnin' a charity."

Boone wobbled slightly but kept his grin intact. "True, true. But how 'bout this? You give us what we need, and I'll owe you one. A big one. You know I'm good for it." He pulled out his flask, waving it like it was part of the deal.

Graves eyed the flask, then shifted his positioning to Weston. "You got anythin' better to offer than this drunk's promises?"

Weston stepped forward, voice low and steady. "Look, we're not askin' for charity. We can trade. I've got a spare saddle and a couple of good tools I don't need anymore. You can have them."

Graves considered this for a moment, rubbing his chin thoughtfully. "A saddle, huh? What kind?"

"Solid leather, hardly worn. You won't find better around here," Weston said.

Graves mulled it over, clearly not thrilled but tempted by the offer. He eyed Elanor, then Boone, before sighing heavily. "Alright, fine. You bring me the saddle, and I'll give you two pistols and enough ammo to last you a few days. But after that, you're on your own."

Weston nodded. "Deal."

As they left the shop, Elanor released a breath she hadn't realized she'd been holding. "I didn't think that was going to work," she admitted.

Boone patted her on the back, his grin wide and triumphant. "See, darlin'? All it takes is a little charm and some well-placed favors. Stick with me, and we'll get through this just fine."

Elanor wasn't so sure, but at least they had the weapons they needed. For now, that was enough.

Elanor and Boone continued preparations at the stables as Weston returned from a nearby shop with a few sacks of food slung over his shoulder. He moved with purpose, avoiding the idle chit-chat Boone thrived on. Elanor tried to help where she could, but she was one step behind Weston every time she reached for something.

She walked over to him as he secured the bags to his horse. "You don't have to do everything yourself," she said.

Weston looked at her with a neutral expression. "Just trying to get things done right."

Frustrated, Elanor crossed her arms. "I'm not completely useless, you know."

His face softened. "Didn't say you were. But this ain't the kind of journey you can take lightly. You've got a lot to learn," he said.

She couldn't argue. She experienced a sense of alienation and isolation in this challenging world, but she wouldn't let that stop her from succeeding in getting her memories back.

"Maybe," she said. "But I'm here, and I'm trying."

"That's good enough for now. But once we're out there, things get dangerous. We don't have time for mistakes," he said.

Elanor swallowed hard. "What kind of danger?"

"Merrick's gang," he said bluntly. "They've been getting more aggressive. Stealing supplies, attacking travelers. We'll have to stay sharp."

The name sent a chill from the top of her head down the length of her back. It reminded her of Nora's warning at the saloon. Weston displayed a steeled resolve compared to how Elanor felt, his work wrapping up with the tightening of the straps on his saddle bags.

With supplies gathered and horses saddled, the group stood at the edge of town, ready to set out. Boone had somehow managed to hold onto his flask through the entire process, though Elanor noticed it was now nearly empty.

"Alright, team!" Boone announced, throwing his arm casually over Elanor's shoulder with a crooked smile. "We've got ourselves a fine crew here. What could possibly go wrong?"

Elanor winced, glancing at Weston, who rolled his eyes. "Famous last words," he muttered.

She paused at her horse, taking it in. Sunlight seeped in through the stable's doors and window, framing it in a gleaming light and highlighting the rippled muscles of the dusted chestnut horse. Each movement exuded strength and grace. Elanor's gaze lingered on the peculiar white marking encircling its left eye. The irregular shape gave the animal a unique, almost mystical quality. She reached out and ran her fingers over the velvet-soft muzzle. The horse snorted softly, its dark eyes meeting hers with an intelligence that connected with her.

For a moment, Elanor stood still, marveling at the sheer beauty and presence of the creature, before gathering her resolve to swing herself up into the saddle. While she wasn't sure how it came quickly to her, mounting her horse wasn't completely foreign.

The sun hung high in the sky, and the burden of the unknown pressed down on her.

They began the long journey, the town of Bodie shrinking behind them, the wind kicking up dust that blurred the edges of the horizon. There was no turning back now.

Blood pumped in Elanor's ears as she looked back at the fading town. Her future lay somewhere in the vast, unforgiving desert ahead. With every step their horses took, Elanor felt uneasy, her past slipping further and further away.

CHAPTER THREE

The sun beat down relentlessly, the heat shimmering off the dry, cracked earth that stretched endlessly before them. Elanor wiped the sweat from her forehead, squinting against the glare of the unforgiving desert landscape. Her skin was taut and gritty from the dust swirling around them, and every breath she took was laced with the dry, earthy scent of the arid ground. The horizon was impossibly far, a wavering line of heat with no sign of respite. Bodie was already a distant memory, swallowed up by the vast expanse of nothingness behind them, and ahead lay only more of the same—a barren, desolate world with no shelter.

Elanor glanced down at herself, frowning in frustration at the oversized men's clothes she still wore. The heavy, dusty shirt clung to her back, soaked with sweat, and the jeans—far too big for her frame—rubbed uncomfortably against her legs with each step her horse took. She shifted in her saddle, annoyed by how ill-fitting the clothes were. Every movement reminded her of being out of place in this strange world. She longed for a comforting familiarity in her clothing, which didn't make her feel like she was drowning in fabric, but she couldn't be sure what familiarity would feel like be.

Ahead of her, Boone swayed lazily in his saddle, humming an off-key tune as though the heat and dust were just a minor inconvenience. His shirt was untucked and half-open, revealing a stained undershirt, and his battered hat sat crooked on his head. Despite the sweat that gleamed on his skin, he looked utterly unfazed by the oppressive sun. The carefree way he rode—occasionally tipping his hat back to wipe his brow—grated on Elanor's nerves. She hadn't seen him take a sip of water since they left, and the fact that he treated this journey like a casual ride through town made her throat feel even drier.

And then there was Weston.

Weston, who had spent his entire life in the saddle, rode confidently ahead of her. Like Boone's, his shirt was open at the collar, but it didn't hang loose or sloppy on him. It clung to the muscles of his back and arms, the thin fabric darkened by sweat in places and outlining the hard lines of his shoulders. Elanor's eyes lingered on him momentarily, watching how his back muscles flexed beneath the fabric as he guided his horse through the desert. The sun glinted off the light sheen of sweat on his skin, making the contours of his body all the more noticeable.

For a moment, she found herself staring, her thoughts drifting in a direction that had nothing to do with their difficult journey. The strength in his frame and the quiet confidence in how he rode made her feel . . . something. But then she shook her head, mentally scolding herself for getting distracted. This was no time to be ogling the cowboy. She had far more significant problems than the way his shirt fit him.

She sighed and refocused on the endless expanse ahead, but her frustration with everything—the heat, the dust, the uncomfortable clothes, and Boone's reckless attitude—gnawed at her. If she didn't exercise caution, she could find herself as uncomfortable in this desert as she was in her clothes.

"How long do you think this is gonna take?" Elanor asked, wiping sweat from her brow and glancing toward Weston as she caught up beside him.

Weston's eyes were fixed ahead, scanning the horizon like he was waiting for something—or someone. His jaw was set in a firm line, his eyes unreadable beneath the brim of his hat.

"Depends on how fast we move," he finally said, voice low and steady. "And what kind of trouble we run into along the way."

Elanor swallowed hard, mouth dry. "Trouble?"

He didn't elaborate, and the silence that followed made her even more uneasy. She watched Boone, who was still humming as if the world around him wasn't slowly trying to bake them alive.

As she was about to ask Weston for more details, Boone reached into one of his saddlebags and pulled out a familiar flask. Elanor's stomach tightened as she watched him uncork it with a flourish and tip it back for a long, hearty swig.

"Whiskey?" she asked incredulously. "You're drinking whiskey out here?"

Boone wiped his mouth with his hand, beaming with joy. "Why not, darlin'? A little whiskey helps keep the spirits high on a long, dry day like this."

Elanor shook her head, her patience waning. "We need water, not whiskey, Boone. You can't just—"

But then she stopped, a horrible realization dawning on her. Her eyes flicked from the flask to the bulging saddlebags on Boone's horse.

"Wait," she said slowly, narrowing her eyes at him. "Boone . . . did you switch out your water for whiskey?"

Boone chuckled, clearly pleased with himself. "'Course I did! I figured we could use some of the good stuff on this trip. Keeps the spirits up and the worries away. Ain't nothin' wrong with a little drink, especially when you're stuck out in the desert."

Elanor felt a jolt of dread as the color drained from her face. "Boone," she said, voice taut with disbelief. "That's all you brought?"

Boone blinked at her as if the concept hadn't fully sunk in. "Yeah," he said, shrugging. "I mean, I thought—"

"You what?!" Weston's voice cut through the air, sharp and angry. "You brought whiskey instead of water? Are you out of your damn mind?"

Boone waved him off. "Relax, Wes. It's not like we're out here forever. Just a little trip, that's all. A few swigs of whiskey, and you'll be feelin' better in no time."

Weston's eyes flashed with barely restrained fury. "We're in the desert, Boone. You think we're going to make it without water? What the hell were you thinking?"

Panic rose in Elanor's chest. She hadn't realized how much she'd relied on the idea that Boone and Weston were prepared for what they were doing. They were in serious trouble, and the journey had barely begun.

"Do we have enough water?" she asked.

Weston's jaw clenched as he glared at Boone, who was still sipping his whiskey like this was a joke.

"Between the two of us," Weston said, his voice low and tense, "we have some water. But not enough if things get tough. We were counting on Boone to carry his share."

Elanor had no idea how dangerous this situation could get, but his expression made it clear—this wasn't just a minor inconvenience. This was bad.

Boone, however, didn't seem concerned in the least. "Come on, Wes," he said with a lazy grin. "You know I've been out in the desert plenty of times. A little whiskey never hurt nobody."

Weston didn't answer, but the look he shot Boone could've cut through stone. He turned back to Elanor. "We'll have to make do with what we've got. But this changes things. We'll need to be extra careful from here on out. No unnecessary stops. No wasting time."

She nodded and tried to shake off the fear that gnawed at the edges of her thoughts. They hadn't even left the safer parts of the desert yet, and already they were running low on water.

Boone had returned to humming and sipping from his flask like nothing was wrong.

She wanted to scream. Instead, she forced herself to focus. They'd get through this. They had to.

Beginning its slow descent in the sky, the sun cast long shadows across jagged rock formations that loomed on both sides of the narrow pass. The light dulled into a reddish hue. It rendered the terrain ominous and strangely beautiful. The rigid set of Weston's shoulders and the way his eyes flicked to every shadow in the narrowing canyon revealed his unease. His vigilance was so intense that Elanor could almost feel the weight of it, a palpable pressure that seemed to echo in her own chest.

"Keep your eyes open," Weston muttered, his voice barely audible over the wind that whistled through the narrow pass. His hand hovered near the gun strapped to his hip. "We're in prime territory for bandits."

Boone sobered up as much as he could in that moment; his usual humming faded into silence. His eyes darted, and Elanor noticed his knuckles turn white as he gripped the reins tighter. The sight of Boone looking genuinely uneasy sent a shiver up her spine. She grabbed her own horse's reins more firmly as a wave of unease washed over her.

The towering rock formations loomed above them like ancient sentinels, casting deep shadows that made it difficult to see much of anything beyond the narrow trail. It was a perfect spot for an ambush. The silence was deafening now—no birds, no rustle of wildlife, just the sound of the wind howling through the rocks and the occasional clink of their horses' hooves against the hard ground.

They were halfway through the pass when it happened.

"Well, well, what do we have here?"

The voice rang out from above, sharp and mocking. Elanor's gaze shot upward, and her stomach twisted with fear. Two men stood perched on the rocky ledges above them, rifles in hand. The setting sun cast their figures in silhouette, but she saw their wicked grins even from this distance.

One of the men—a wiry figure with a filthy bandana tied around his neck and a crooked grin that looked more like a sneer—crouched lower, his rifle aimed directly at Weston. His teeth flashed yellow in the fading light.

"Looks like a couple of lost sheep wandered into the wrong pasture," the man sneered, voice dripping with cruel amusement.

Weston's hand twitched near his gun, but he didn't draw. His voice was steady. "We don't want any trouble. We're just passing through."

The bandit's grin didn't falter. He adjusted his grip on the rifle, looking down the barrel as if lining up a perfect shot. "Oh, I don't think so, cowboy. You're in Merrick's territory now, and nobody passes through without payin' their dues."

Boone, of course, chose this moment to speak up. "Now, fellas," he slurred, trying to sound smooth, though his voice wobbled with the whiskey still swirling in his system. "I'm sure we can come to some kind of arrangement. No need to get all . . . gun-happy." He lifted his flask, offering it up with a wide grin. "Care for a drink?"

The bandits erupted into laughter, the sound echoing off the canyon walls, cruel and mocking. The second man, bulkier with a scruffy beard, leaned forward from his rocky perch, his rifle also trained on the group below. He spat into the dirt and grinned. "Whiskey, huh? That all you got to offer, old man?"

"Plenty more where that came from," Boone began, still holding out the flask as if it were the grand prize in some ridiculous game.

Weston's patience snapped. "Shut up, Boone," he growled, voice low and dangerous. His fingers hovered near his gun, every muscle in his body drawn tight, ready to explode into action at the slightest provocation.

But the bandits noticed, too.

"Uh-uh, cowboy," the wiry one called out, wagging a finger from his perch. "You go reachin' for that gun, and you'll be dead before you clear the holster."

Elanor's breath hitched in her throat. She felt her pulse thrumming in her ears. Her mouth was dry, fingers trembling as she clutched the reins, trying to remember how to breathe. The two men above had the height advantage and looked far too comfortable with their guns trained on them.

And worse still, they were encouraged.

The bandits glanced at one another, their confidence growing. From their vantage point, they saw three easy targets: an unarmed woman, a drunk, and a cowboy who appeared to be just a few seconds away from being shot.

"What'll it be?" the bearded bandit called out, grin spreading wider. "Hand over whatever you got, or we take it from your dead bodies."

Weston remained frozen, the air around them thick with an unbearable weight. A shiver ran down Elanor's spine as sweat slicked her skin, her thoughts spiraling. Fighting back felt like a death sentence, but surrendering seemed no less perilous.

Her eyes darted toward Weston, looking for a sign of what to do, but his stare was still locked on the bandits. For all his bravado, Boone shrunk slightly, his hand lowering the flask as he also understood just how much danger they were in.

The bandits were starting to grow impatient.

"Last chance," the wiry man called out. "Make it easy on yourselves, or we'll make it real hard."

Weston's fingers twitched toward his gun, and Elanor's pulse quickened, her eyes widening. Any sudden movement and the bandits would fire. She saw it in how their hands gripped the rifles, their fingers itching to pull the trigger.

When Elanor felt the situation couldn't worsen, a new sound filled the canyon—the thunder of hooves. Elanor whipped her head around, pulse quickening as two riders approached fast: Nora, her wild red hair blazing in the wind, and the sheriff, gripping his reins tightly with an expression that showed more resolve than confidence. Dust billowed up from the dry earth in their wake, the sound of the hooves reverberating off the canyon walls.

"Well, ain't this a party. Mind if we join in?" Nora called out, pistol ready, lips turned up at the corners.

The bandits exchanged anxious looks and hesitated, their postures stiffening. One's hand twitched near his rifle with a curse, and the leader's crooked grin faltered. He observed Nora and the sheriff, his badge gleaming in the fading sunlight.

"You really wanna make this difficult?" Nora asked. "I'd think twice before pullin' that trigger if I were you."

The two bandits exchanged nervous looks. Their confidence faltered. The slender one changed his stance, his hold on the rifle loosening slightly, and then, without saying anything further, they withdrew, vanishing like shadows into the canyon.

Once the dust settled, Elanor recognized she'd been holding her breath. She exhaled slowly, the knot in her chest loosening. Nora swung off her horse with practiced ease, dusting off her pants before striding over with a knowing shake.

"Should've known you lot would get yourselves into trouble," Nora said, her sharp gaze landing squarely on Boone. She crossed her arms, eyes narrowing as she took him in from head to toe. "And let me guess— Boone thought whiskey was a better travel companion than water?"

Boone held onto his flask. He rubbed the back of his neck, flashed a sheepish grin, and shrugged, resembling a guilty child. "Now, Nora, I thought we could all use a bit of cheer out here. The desert's a dry place, after all."

Nora's lips curled, and she seized the flask from his iron fist. She brought it to her nose and grimaced in distaste before shaking her head.

"You'd be dead in two days if we hadn't shown up. Water's what you need out here, not this poison," she said and threw the flask at him.

Nora's straightforward, practical demeanor dispelled some of the tension, alleviating the anxiety that had gripped Elanor. However, her nerves remained on edge from the whole ordeal. The idea of being stranded without water made her stomach churn.

"Thanks," Elanor said as she approached Nora. Her hands continued to shake slightly, despite the reprieve of immediate danger. "I didn't know what we would do if you hadn't shown up."

"Well, that's why I'm here." Nora gave Elanor a firm, reassuring pat on the shoulder. "I figured you'd run into trouble sooner or later. Took some convincing to get the sheriff onboard, but I wasn't about to let you wander out here unprepared."

After dismounting, the sheriff awkwardly fidgeted with his hat and stepped forward. His face was flushed with a firm smile, either from the heat or nerves. "Nora's the one who recognized what you'd be up against. I . . . well, I thought we'd better bring some extra supplies just in case." His hands shook slightly as though he hadn't recovered from the confrontation.

Nora eyeballed him, unimpressed with his hesitance, but she gave a curt nod. "Least he's here, I'll give him that. Brought extra water and food, too. You lot are lucky you've got me looking after you."

Weston stepped forward, silently watching the scene play out, his usual stoic expression softened by a hint of relief. His shoulders relaxed, though his eyes remained wary. "Appreciate the backup," he said calmly, measuredly, giving Nora a brief nod.

Nora lifted an eyebrow, examining him briefly before a sly grin appeared on her lips. "I had a feeling you'd be the one keepin' these two out of the fire."

Weston let out a shrug, briefly tightening his jaw before averting his eyes. There was something in his expression, something unspoken, that passed quickly before he hid it behind his usual calm mask. Elanor couldn't quite place it—was it relief? Gratitude? Or something deeper?

Weston stared out at the rock formations. "Alright, let's take a moment to regroup," he said, voice returning to his commanding tone. "We've got a long way to go, and with Merrick's men lurking around, we can't let our guard down."

Elanor nodded in agreement, her heartbeat finally beginning to ease. They weren't out of the woods yet, but the odds suddenly were a little less bleak with Nora and the sheriff here. The danger was far more accute than she had anticipated, but now they were better equipped to handle it.

Elanor observed the sheriff with a mix of sympathy and amusement as he clumsily handled the water canteens while the others collected their supplies. His hands were trembling. She gratefully accepted one; the cool metal felt refreshing against her warm skin. She relished the refreshing liquid, lifting it to her lips and gulping deeply. It felt like a lifeline, her first genuine breath since the ambush.

"Feels good, doesn't it?" Nora asked, her smile keen as Elanor eagerly drank the water. "Better than that whiskey Boone's been lugging around, I bet."

Elanor nodded as she wiped her mouth. "Definitely."

With a chuckle, Nora cast a sidelong look at Boone, who was occupied with examining the dirt on his boots, evidently still nursing his wounded pride. "I figured the sheriff and I had better come along to keep things from goin' completely off the rails. I've got my cousin lookin' after the saloon while I'm gone, and I reckon you'll need a person who manages herself confidently in a fight. Sheriff's deputies will oversee the town while we're out."

Boone, who had been quietly sulking since Nora took his flask, perked up, his voice defensive. "We would've been just fine! I had everything under control." He puffed out his chest slightly, though it was clear to everyone that his confidence was more for show than substance.

Nora let out a bark of laughter. "Sure you did, Boone. Just like you always do, right?"

Weston tentatively scanned the surroundings. His eyes glided over the canyon walls like a hawk while Elanor sat near Nora. Elanor felt reassured by another woman's presence. With Nora there, a feeling of safety enveloped her—a sense that everything might be okay.

CHAPTER FOUR

The late afternoon sun hung low in the sky, casting long, jagged shadows across the barren landscape. The heat, which had been relentless all day, was finally beginning to fade, but a growing sense of unease came with it. The rocky terrain they had been navigating for hours showed no signs of familiarity—at least not to Elanor, who couldn't make sense of the endless expanse of rock and sand. But the farther they went, the more she noticed the subtle changes in Weston's demeanor. His back, once relaxed and sure in the saddle, had grown rigid, and every so often, she caught him glancing over his shoulder, his brow furrowed in frustration.

"We should've seen that ridge by now," Weston muttered, more to himself than the others.

As he followed behind, Boone adjusted his collar and gave Weston a curious side-eye. "Wes, you sure we're headed the right way? This place don't look familiar."

Weston's jaw tightened, his silence stretching as his eyes darted across the horizon. The unease rippled from him, seeping into Elanor and setting her nerves on edge.

"Keep drinking, Boone, and maybe the path will start to look familiar," Weston said. He flicked the reins of his horse with more force than needed, urging it forward. "We're following the directions the sheriff gave us."

Elanor's stomach churned at the thought of being lost. Her eyes shifted to the sheriff for confirmation that Weston was right and that they were following the correct path. The sheriff remained silent, avoiding eye contact.

Boone, riding beside Elanor, broke the silence with a chuckle. "Seems like we're discoverin' new lands, eh? Might even name one of these hills after me."

Nora, riding just ahead, shot him a glare over her shoulder. "Now's not the time for jokes, Boone," she said sharply. "We need to find somewhere to settle before dark."

Boone just shrugged, his lopsided grin still in place, but he fell silent after Nora's sharp tone.

The sheriff, too, wasn't convinced by Weston's words. He pressed his horse closer to Weston's side and muttered, "I don't recognize any of this. We're supposed to be heading west, but this looks more like the south foothills. You sure we didn't take a wrong turn?"

Weston exhaled through his nose, clearly irritated by the sheriff's question. He didn't respond immediately, his eyes locked on the terrain ahead. "We took a wrong turn," he admitted, his voice low enough that only those nearby could hear. "We're too far south, closer to the foothills than I'd like. If we keep going this way, we'll wander all night."

Elanor's pulse quickened. Getting lost in the desert was bad enough during the day, but at night? Without knowing what dangers lurked nearby—wild animals, bandits, or even just the sheer drop in temperature—her imagination ran wild with possibilities.

"What do we do now?" she asked, trying to keep the rising panic out of her voice. She felt her throat closing, the weight of their situation pressing down on her.

Weston straightened in his saddle, his voice firmer this time. "We head toward the mountains. There's enough cover to hide a fire and keep us from being spotted. We'll rest and figure out where we went wrong come morning."

The sheriff sighed, clearly unhappy with the answer but resigned to the fact that there was no other option. "Well, I don't like being out here all night with our backs to the foothills, but I guess we ain't got much choice."

Boone, ever the optimist, tipped his hat. "See? No need to worry. A nice mountain camp sounds cozy, don't it?"

Nora didn't bother responding to Boone's inane comment, her jaw set as she urged her horse forward. "Weston's right," she said, eyes scanning the horizon. "We need to be somewhere the fire won't give us away."

The group continued onward in silence as the sun sank lower, casting the rugged landscape in deep amber hues. After riding all day, Elanor's body ached, but she didn't dare voice her discomfort. Her mind swam with nervous energy as she watched Weston and his fixed gaze on the terrain ahead. He now carried an air of determination, even though the slight stiffness in his shoulders still hinted at his earlier mistake.

"Let's just hope we don't run into anything worse than a wrong turn," the sheriff muttered.

The horses carefully navigated between jagged stones as the trail became rockier in their ascent into the foothills. The temperature dropped as they climbed, and a brisk wind swept through the canyon, carrying the scent of dust and sage. Elanor took her jacket from her pack and wrapped it firmly around herself. She was thankful that the oppressive heat had finally given way, though the cold bite in the air was a stark reminder of their exposure.

Steep walls and large boulders provided a narrow path through a ravine as Weston led the way. The enclosed space also provided the protection they required. The last rays of sunlight flickered out of sight, plunging the canyon into twilight. The sheer height of the rocks around them meant their fire would be hidden from prying eyes. It wasn't ideal, but it was the best they could do.

"We'll set up camp here," Weston said, dismounting and tying his horse to a nearby smoketree. He glanced up at the darkening sky. "Looks like we've got a clear night ahead. No storm, but it's going to get cold fast."

Boone swung off his horse with a groan, stretching his back as he landed. "Ain't nothin' wrong with a cool night under the stars. Adds a bit of adventure, don't ya think?" He chuckled, but his voice lacked its usual bravado.

The sheriff didn't look convinced, eyes darting toward the darkening sky as he fidgeted with his hat. "Yeah, well, let's just hope the 'adventure' don't involve any trouble we can't handle."

Elanor slid off her horse, legs aching as they hit the ground. She stretched her back, the strain from the ride still lingering in her muscles. As the group began to unpack their supplies, the first tendrils of real worry began to creep into her thoughts. They were lost in the wilderness with night rapidly approaching—and tomorrow, they'd have to retrace their steps in an unfamiliar and potentially dangerous landscape.

The hidden area they found offered a slight sense of security. Sheltered by the towering rocks and out of the open desert, Elanor relaxed—if only a little. It wasn't much, but it was better than exposure to the wilderness. Despite their secluded spot, she couldn't shake the worry gnawing at the back of her mind.

As Weston knelt to gather brush for the fire, Elanor watched how he moved with practiced efficiency, the muscles in his arms and back flexing beneath his shirt. Unlike her awkward fumbling, he was entirely at ease in the wilderness, every motion deliberate and sure. A strange sense of comfort fell over her while watching him work, even though the questions swirling in her head refused to quiet down.

"How safe are we out here?" she asked, her voice low but laced with concern.

Weston looked up briefly from his task, his expression calm but serious. "Safer than we would be in the open. But it's not foolproof. We'll need to keep watch tonight—take shifts, make sure no one sneaks up on us."

Elanor nodded, her stomach knotting at the thought of someone creeping into their camp in the dead of night. But at least there was a plan. It made her feel better knowing they'd take turns on guard. "Who's taking the first watch?" she asked.

Weston tossed the brush into the makeshift fire pit and shrugged. "I'll take it. Then we'll rotate. No one's getting a full night's sleep, but we'll be safer for it."

Boone, who had been untying his bedroll with much less grace than

Weston, groaned loudly. "Ah, come on! Ain't we earned a bit of shut-eye after the day we've had?"

"You want a bandit's bullet in your back?" Weston shot back, his tone curt but controlled.

Boone raised his hands in mock surrender, a lazy grin spreading across his face. "Alright, alright, you win. But don't go expectin' me to be too sharp on my watch."

Setting down the extra bags she'd brought from her horse, Nora eyed them, her eyes intent but silent. She hadn't said much since they'd made camp, her no-nonsense demeanor intact as she worked to organize their supplies. She was the type who wasn't easily rattled, but Elanor could tell by the way she scanned the area that she was just as aware of the potential dangers as Weston.

Awkwardly fumbling with his saddle, the sheriff looked up nervously. "I— I can take a watch, too," he said, voice wavering slightly. "Nora brought me along for a reason, after all."

Nora glanced at him, lips twitching into the barest hint of a smile, though she quickly masked it. "Yeah, you're here, alright," she muttered, not unkindly—there was a glint of humor in her eyes.

Elanor watched as everyone settled into their roles: Weston focused on the fire; Boone grumbled as he untangled ropes from his pack; and Nora worked quietly but efficiently. Despite the strain of the journey and Elanor's unease, the routine of camp life provided a strange sense of normalcy. It wasn't home, but at least there was order here, a plan.

The flames flickered to life as Weston struck a match, the fire casting a warm, golden glow across the rocks. The shadows danced and shifted with the crackling flames, and a small measure of comfort ran through Elanor's body in the soft warmth of the firelight. The darkness beyond their camp, however, was still vast and unknowable.

The scent of something cooking drifted in the air, and Elanor's stomach grumbled in response. She hadn't recognized her hunger until Nora set to work over the fire, preparing a simple but hearty meal from the provisions she'd brought.

The group gathered around, their faces illuminated by the golden glow of the fire, and for the first time since the ambush, a sense of calm settled over them. The tension from earlier ebbed away, at least for now, as the crackle of the fire and the soft clinking of metal pans replaced the silence that had hung over them during their journey.

Nora stirred the pot with practiced ease, her movements smooth and efficient. "Ain't much, but it'll fill your belly," she said, glancing around at the others. "Could've made something fancier if Boone had brought more than just whiskey."

Boone chuckled from his spot, reclining comfortably against his bedroll. "Whiskey's a meal in itself, Nora. Warms you up from the inside out."

Nora shot him a glare, but there was a faint smile on her lips. "I'll take real food over your liquid diet any day."

Seated across from Elanor, Weston nodded in agreement, though his eyes were still focused on the fire. "We'll need our strength. Food, water, and rest are more valuable out here than any alcohol"

Sitting awkwardly on a rock, the sheriff looked relieved when Nora handed him a plate. His nervous energy had calmed since they'd stopped, though he still fidgeted occasionally, glancing at the shadows beyond their camp as if expecting something—or someone—to leap out at them.

Elanor accepted her plate with a grateful nod, the food's warmth in her hands a welcome contrast to the growing chill in the night air. As they ate in relative silence, she couldn't help but marvel at how quickly the day had turned. The looming dangers of the desert and the bandits still lingered in the back of her mind, but the simple act of sitting around the fire and sharing a meal created a momentary sense of normalcy.

When everyone finished eating, Boone broke the quiet. "You know, this reminds me of the time ol' McGregor got himself lost in the mountains. Fella thought he could outsmart the terrain, but nature had other plans."

Nora smirked, shaking her head as she passed around a second serving of food. "You've told this story more times than I can count, Boone. And it gets more exaggerated every time."

Boone grinned, undeterred. "Ah, but it's a good one, ain't it? Besides, these young folk need to hear how we survived the wilderness back in the day."

The sheriff raised an eyebrow, glancing between Boone and Nora. "I've heard about McGregor. Wasn't he the one who got chased by a bear and ended up in a tree for two days?"

Weston snorted softly, shaking his head. "If you believe Boone's version, sure."

"Well," Boone jumped back in, "I've got plenty of stories to tell . . . like when I lost a bet to Gregory Washington down in the swamps of Georgia. Girls down there real pretty, know what I'm sayin'? Anywho . . ." He hesitated, searching for the words. "Well, anyway, don't be lettin' people use your money to bet on alligator fights in Georgia."

"What?" the sheriff asked.

"They'll eat you right up, they will," Boone smirked.

Elanor smiled at the banter, a light filling the camp that hadn't been there earlier. Though simple, the shared stories and jokes made her feel more connected to the group—like they were more than just travelers thrown together by circumstance. It was comforting, even if only for a little while.

"Alright, enough stories," Weston said. His tone shifted to a more serious note. "We've got a long way ahead of us, and we'll need to be ready for whatever comes."

Elanor settled a look upon Weston as she finished eating. His commanding attitude hadn't faded, but how he interacted with the group—balancing humor with a quiet authority—made her feel safer than expected. Despite their danger, she couldn't deny that something was reassuring about his presence.

Boone stretched lazily, letting out a long sigh. "Guess I'll take the second watch after Wes does the hard work of the first shift."

The sheriff hesitated, then nodded slowly. "I'll . . . I'll take third. I might not be much in a fight, but I can keep an eye out."

His comment was strange to Elanor; the tough sheriff she'd met in Bodie was different in the desert. She wondered if the tough exterior was more of an act than a defining character trait, but she hoped it wouldn't come back to bite the group later when they needed strength the most.

Nora shrugged, wiping her hands on a cloth as she stood up from her spot by the fire. "Looks like I get the last watch. Fine by me—gives me more time to sleep."

The group settled into a quiet rhythm as they finished their food, the fire crackling steadily in the background. The looming night was less intimidating now, though Elanor still felt the darkness of the wilderness pressing in on them. As they discussed the details of the watch, the reality of how much they were relying on one another settled in.

Elanor shifted uncomfortably in her spot by the fire. She hadn't been assigned a shift, and it dawned on her that she was the only one left without a turn. A mixture of guilt and uncertainty bubbled up in her chest.

"I didn't get a shift for the night watch," she said quietly.

Nora, who had just finished checking her pistol and stowing it near her bedroll, looked up. She waved a dismissive hand. "Don't worry about it, Elanor. You'll take the first shift tomorrow night. Consider this a free pass for tonight."

Nora cut her off with a firm look before Elanor could protest. "We've got it covered. You'll be more useful with some rest under your belt. So, relax."

Elanor sighed. She was still adjusting to how things worked in this world—how easily they fell into their roles, how naturally the others handled every situation.

Nora settled down next to her, her usual stern demeanor softening slightly in the fire's dim light. "You've been through the wringer, haven't you?"

Elanor studied her, unsure of how to respond at first. "I guess you could say that," she said after a beat, her voice barely above a whisper. "I still don't know how I ended up here . . . or why."

Nora nodded, her expression thoughtful as she poked at the fire with a stick. "Life's funny that way. You can think you've got everything figured out, and then—bam—it knocks you flat on your back, leaves you wondering how you got there."

Elanor smiled faintly at that, feeling a bit of the tightness in her chest ease. "That's definitely what it feels like."

There was a brief silence as the two women watched the flames dance, the crackling of the fire the only sound between them. The others were scattered nearby—Boone had already started to snore softly from his spot by the fire while Weston was ensuring the camp was secure before he took the first watch. The sheriff sat quietly, fiddling with his hat again, his stare distant but alert.

Nora turned her attention back to Elanor, her eyes flicking over the oversized clothes that Elanor still wore. "You know," she started with a half-smirk, "I brought something for you. I had a feeling those clothes weren't exactly doing you any favors."

Elanor blinked, glancing down at the baggy shirt and loose jeans she'd been stuck in since she arrived. "I didn't exactly have time to figure something out," she muttered.

Nora chuckled. "No worries. Most women around these parts wear dresses, but I figured that wasn't quite your style." She rummaged through her pack, pulling out a bundle of clothes and tossing it to Elanor. "Here. They're more fitted. Should make you feel a little more like yourself."

Elanor caught the bundle, her fingers running over the fabric. The clothes looked practical and modern for a woman in this period—pants and a shirt that would fit her properly. Touched by the gesture, she let out a chuckle. "Thank you," she said with warmth and gratitude.

Nora shrugged, leaning back against her bedroll. "Don't mention it. Figured you'd need 'em."

Elanor smirked. "You figured right."

The air between them lightened as they shared smiles. It was a rare moment of connection—Elanor hadn't had time to bond with anyone in this strange world since she'd arrived. Everything had been about survival, about getting through each new challenge. But now, in this quiet moment by the fire, an unexpected but welcome sense of camaraderie with Nora brought warmth to her chest.

After a moment, Nora eyed her sideways. "You remind me of someone. A woman who didn't take crap from anybody, always ready to fight her way out of a tight spot."

Elanor's eyebrows lifted in surprise. "Oh?"

Nora's smile faded slightly, and she looked back into the fire, her expression more guarded now. "Probably much the same now," she said. "Made her own way, out of this place, despite everything stacked against her. You remind me of her 'cause you're a fighter, too, Elanor. That's how I know you'll figure out a way to get to where you're meant to be."

Elanor didn't know what to say. The idea that someone had escaped this world gave her a sliver of hope, but it also raised more questions. "Did she ever . . . find out why she was here? Do you know how she got out of here?"

Nora poked at the fire, looking off into the distance. "Some questions don't have answers. Sometimes, all you can do is move forward."

Elanor thought about that. She was searching for answers, yes, but maybe it wasn't about the why. Perhaps it was about how she handled the situation she'd been thrown into.

The fire crackled softly between them, grounding Elanor a little more—whatever happened next, she wasn't as alone as she had felt.

After a quiet moment, Nora nudged her. "Go on, try the clothes. You'll feel better without all that extra fabric hanging off you."

Elanor nodded, standing up and heading toward the edge of the camp where she could change in privacy. As she pulled on the new clothes—pants that fit snugly at the waist and a shirt that hugged her frame instead of swallowing her whole—a strange sense of comfort washed over her. She looked down at herself and, for once, she felt a little more like . . . her.

When she returned to the campfire, Nora gave her a nod of approval. "Much better," she said with a grin.

Elanor settled back at the campfire, the warmth of the flames now a welcome comfort against the cool night air. Nora had already finished cleaning up after dinner, clinking dishes fading into the background as the camp grew quiet. The fire whispered, casting flickering shadows over the group as they began to wind down.

Elanor scanned the camp and settled on Weston as he finished tying down the packs by the horses. His shirt, damp with sweat, clung to his muscular frame, and as he straightened, stretching his back, Elanor caught herself staring at the way the firelight highlighted the sharp lines of his body.

Their eyes met, and for a moment, the world slowed. Weston lingered on her, his expression unreadable, but there was something there—something unspoken, something simmering beneath the surface. Elanor's breath caught as the connection between them held, an invisible thread tugging at her, drawing her in.

Weston then quickly averted his eyes, as if he realized he had been caught, returning to the horses. The spell dissipated, yet the moment remained, filling Elanor with a warmth in her chest unrelated to the fire.

She adjusted her position on the ground, unexpectedly feeling self-aware as her mind swirled with unanticipated thoughts. What drew her attention to him? Was it merely the intensity of their predicament, or was there something deeper?

Elanor shook her head, determined to concentrate. The stakes were too high to be swayed by brief glances and unspoken gestures. Still, as she pulled her blanket around her shoulders and lay beside the fire, her thoughts drifted back to Weston's lingering gaze and the questions it raised.

The camp had grown quiet, the soft crackling of the fire the only sound breaking the stillness of the night. Elanor rolled onto her side, pulling her blanket closer, but sleep didn't come quickly. This was the third time she'd flipped over to find comfort in her position. The day's events swirled in her mind, along with the lingering tension in the unspoken exchange between her and Weston. She closed her eyes, willing her mind to settle, but the faint sound of hushed voices reached her ears.

Elanor opened her eyes and saw Nora and Weston speaking quietly near the horses. She remained quiet, hesitant to interrupt, yet their conversation intrigued her. Their voices were gentle, drifting with the breeze, but she caught enough to grasp the significance of their discussion.

"I don't like it, Wes," Nora murmured, edged with concern. "Merrick's men aren't the type to back off after one little scare. If they've gotten wind of us headin' toward Tawa, you know they'll be waiting. They've been gettin' bolder, more reckless."

"I know," Weston replied, his tone heavy. "We'll need to be extra cautious from here on out. Can't take any chances. They'll be lookin' for easy prey, and we've already been slowed down after takin' that wrong turn."

"We've been lucky so far. But luck only lasts so long. I don't want to see anyone end up like you did when the last girl got outta Bodie."

Elanor's brow furrowed as she lay still. *Last girl?* The way Nora mentioned this person, with a mix of regret and sadness, made Elanor wonder what had happened to the girl—and why Nora cared so much.

Weston was silent for a moment before he spoke, his voice quieter, almost resigned. "It wasn't meant to be, Nora. It wasn't my place to stop her."

"I know you think that," Nora said, her tone softening, "but that don't mean it wasn't hard on you. You don't have to pretend it didn't leave a mark."

Elanor's heart fell. Was this girl someone from Weston's past? Someone he had cared for? The pieces didn't quite fit together yet, but there was a heaviness in Weston's silence that told her the topic hit closer to home than he let on.

"I'm not worried about the past," Weston said, his voice rougher now, as if he were trying to shake off the conversation. "I'm focused on what's in front of us. Merrick's the threat we must deal with now, not old . . . situations."

Nora didn't press further, but the heaviness of what was left unsaid settled heavily between them. Whatever had happened with that girl had left a scar on Weston, one he wasn't ready to discuss. But the threat of Merrick lingered over the conversation like a dark cloud, pulling them both back to the present danger.

"You get some rest, Nora. We'll need to be sharp tomorrow," Weston said after a pause.

Nora sighed again but didn't argue. "Fine, but don't go thinkin' you can handle everything on your own. We're in this together, Wes. Remember that."

"I haven't forgotten," he muttered.

Elanor kept her eyes closed as the conversation ended, her mind buzzing with more questions than before. The mention of Merrick's men only brought reminders that the journey ahead would be more dangerous, but the cryptic exchange about the girl from Bodie stuck with her the most. Who had she been? And what was her connection to Weston? The idea that there was something personal he wasn't sharing, gnawed at her thoughts as she finally drifted into an uneasy sleep.

CHAPTER FIVE

Elanor stirred awake to the faint crackle of the campfire and the gentle murmur of voices. The first light of dawn peeked over the mountains, casting long shadows across the rocky ground. Her body was stiff from sleeping on the hard earth, but a slight sense of security—though fragile —washed over her, knowing the night had passed without incident.

The smell of something cooking over the fire pulled her further from sleep, and she pushed herself up, rubbing her eyes. Looking tired but still alert, Nora sat near the fire, stirring something in a pot. Her red hair, usually wild, was now braided back, though a few stray curls had slipped loose. Elanor scanned the area and noticed Boone snoring lightly a few feet away, curled up with his hat pulled low over his eyes, the sheriff nearby fiddling awkwardly with his gear.

Weston was already up, checking the horses, his movements deliberate and calm, as always. His expression was unreadable, but Elanor noticed the way his eyes flicked toward the horizon, his unease evident in the tightness of his movements. The memory of last night—the bandits, the close call—still hung in the air, making it hard to completely relax.

"You're up early," Nora said, her voice low as she watched Elanor, offering a slight smile. "Got some breakfast going if you're hungry."

Elanor nodded, stretching her sore limbs. "I'll take anything, honestly." She moved closer to the fire, the warmth a welcome contrast to the cool morning air.

As she sat down, Elanor noticed the sheriff was quiet—too quiet. There was a heaviness hanging over him, and it didn't take long to realize why. The sheriff, nervously packing his things, was particularly uneasy this morning. He was quiet for much of last night, and his lack of eye contact with the others was concerning.

A troubling sensation settled in the pit of Elanor's stomach. She moved closer to the fire. "Everything okay?" she asked, her eyes flicking between Nora and the sheriff.

The sheriff paused and looked up, then quickly turned away. His hands fumbled with his canteen, dispelling any doubt Elanor had about the awkward silence.

"Sheriff?" Weston's voice cut through the quiet, calm but direct. He was watching the sheriff closely. "You seem off. What's going on?"

The sheriff sighed heavily, finally looking up at the group. His face was flushed from embarrassment or frustration—it was hard to tell. "I . . . Well, even if we regroup and head west, I'm not certain we're heading the right way."

Nora stopped stirring the pot, narrowing her eyes at him. "What do you mean you're not sure? You were the one who gave us the route to Tawa."

The sheriff's shoulders slumped, and he wiped his brow with the back of his hand, clearly uncomfortable under their scrutiny. "I only know what I've heard from others," he admitted, his voice low. "I've never been to Tawa's camp myself. I just . . . I thought we were heading in the right direction, but now . . . I don't know. The instructions I heard aren't as clear as I thought they might've been."

Silence fell over the group like a heavy blanket. Elanor's chest tightened as the reality of the situation set in. She had trusted the sheriff's instructions and passed them on to Weston to follow. The group believed they could be guided through the harsh desert by his words. Now, however, that trust had proved to be misplaced.

Weston tensed and stood. He dusted off his hands and fixed his eyes on the sheriff. "So, we have no idea where we're going?"

The sheriff opened his mouth and shut it. His silence was answer enough.

Nora muttered under her breath and shook her head. "Unbelievable."

Elanor watched Weston, wanting to gauge his reaction. He stared into the distance, narrowing his eyes as if searching for direction among the endless mountains. The frustration was written plainly on his face, but he didn't lash out. Instead, he muttered something under his breath —something Elanor couldn't catch, but it sounded like, "Been here before."

Before she could ask, Boone let out a loud snore, drawing everyone's attention. He jerked awake, blinking groggily and looking around with bleary eyes. "What'd I miss?"

Nora sighed, clearly unimpressed, but Elanor couldn't help but chuckle. "Nothing, Boone. We're just . . . trying to figure out what to do next."

Boone stretched, yawning widely. "Well, I say we just keep goin'. Ain't no point in worryin' about it too much. We'll get to where we're headed eventually, right?"

As Boone reached down to pull on his boots, a sudden shriek split the air. He jumped back, nearly tripping over a log as a snake slithered out of one boot and disappeared into the underbrush. The group erupted into laughter at the sight of Boone's wide-eyed panic.

"I swear it was gonna eat me!" Boone exclaimed, his voice still shaking, which only made the group laugh harder.

Nora, wiping tears from her eyes, managed to jest, "Sure it was, Boone. That snake just wanted a warm place to sleep, not a meal! 'Bout time something sobered you up."

Their laughter echoed across the desert, lightening the mood. As it faded, the reality of their situation settled back in.

Weston's frustration softened at Boone's carefree attitude, though his tone remained firm. "No, Boone. We need to backtrack and figure out where we went wrong. We can't just wander around aimlessly out here."

Boone shrugged, nonchalant. "Suit yourself, cowboy. I'm just along for the ride."

The seriousness of the situation settled on Elanor again. They were lost, and she was disheartened by the poor directions the sheriff had provided. The desert was vast and unforgiving, but despite the frustration and uncertainty, there was something about how Weston handled it—collected and determined—that made her feel a little more secure.

She took a deep breath to shake off the creeping sense of dread. They weren't out of the woods yet—not by a long shot—but at least they were together. That had to count for something.

"We'll figure it out," Weston said. "But we need to stay sharp. There's more than just the desert to worry about out here." Weston's voice lingered, grounding the group.

Nora stood up from the fire, dusting off her hands and giving the sheriff a hard look before turning to Weston. "Well," she said, her tone sharp but not unkind, "if we can't rely on the sheriff's directions, what's the new plan?"

Weston crossed his arms, deep in thought. "We'll head back to that ridge we passed yesterday—get a better view of the terrain. From there, we'll figure out the right direction. We'll see something if Tawa's camp is where the sheriff first thought it might be. It's not so far that it will cause an issue . . . not unless the camp isn't there."

Elanor watched as the others listened intently to Weston, but she couldn't shake the unease gnawing at her. They had already wasted time heading in the wrong direction. They might run into more trouble if they didn't find their way soon—not just from the desert.

Now fully awake and brushing dust off his clothes, Boone chimed in, "Ah, we ain't that lost. Just took the scenic route, is all. Maybe Tawa's waitin' for us to make a grand entrance." He winked at Elanor as if he were completely unfazed by their situation.

The sheriff seemed eager to vanish, his face flushing as he fidgeted with his canteen strap. "I'm sorry," he mumbled, glancing at Nora. "I thought I had it figured out. . . ."

Nora dismissed him with a wave. "Don't beat yourself up 'bout it now. It's done. Let's just get this thing sorted before any more problems find us."

Weston adjusted the strap on his saddle and nodded. "Exactly. No use pointing fingers now. We need to make the most of daylight. Everyone ready?"

The group began packing up the camp, and Elanor couldn't help but feel a little more grounded by their quick return to routine. There was a strange comfort in the mechanical actions of saddling horses, rolling up bedrolls, and gathering supplies. It reminded her of how far she'd come in such a short time—adapting to a world that she instinctively knew was different from hers.

Still not accustomed to the tight fit of her new clothes, Elanor rearranged her shirt and tucked it into her waistline. While she fastened the belt, she noticed Weston watching her from the corner of her eye. He held his gaze, lingering momentarily, then swiftly turned away, feigning a check of his saddle straps.

Elanor's pulse quickened as a flicker of interest grew inside her. She turned away before he could catch her staring back, her mind racing with thoughts she didn't have time to entertain.

As they prepared to move out, Weston climbed onto his horse first, his usual focus returning. He scanned the horizon again. A flicker of unease crossed his face for just a second before it vanished. "We'll move fast," he remarked, eyeing the sheriff, who was having difficulty mounting his horse. "Sheriff, you'll ride in the middle. Nora, keep an eye on him."

Still feeling the sting of his earlier mistake, the sheriff nodded briefly, shoulders slumped.

Boone trotted over to Elanor with a grin. "Guess it's me and you ridin' at the back, then. You keep watchin' my back, and I'll keep watchin' yours."

Elanor rolled her eyes but couldn't help smirking at Boone's unshakable optimism. "I'll be sure to keep an eye on you, Boone."

With that, the group set off again, retracing their steps toward the ridge Weston had mentioned. The sun was already climbing higher, casting long shadows across the rocks and making the heat rise in shimmering waves from the ground. The tension from the morning still clung to them, but there was a renewed sense of purpose as they rode together.

As they made their way toward the ridge, the heat became more oppressive. The air was thick and heavy, and the silence among the group only amplified the potential danger of the journey ahead.

Elanor focused on the rhythm of her horse's hooves hitting the rocky ground, trying to ignore the ache in her legs from riding for so long since leaving Bodie.

Weston rode silently, his gaze sweeping the landscape with a sharp, watchful intensity. His fingers flexed on the reins, every movement hinting at a readiness for whatever might lie ahead. The unease radiating from him made Elanor's pulse quicken, though she kept her thoughts to herself.

Nora, the sheriff, and Boone rode in silence, their earlier chatter fading.

The sun was nearing its highest point in the sky when Boone broke the silence with a lighthearted chuckle. "Well, ain't this somethin'," he said. "Out here in the middle of nowhere, ridin' like we're outlaws. I reckon I've been in worse places, though. Like that time I ended up in a barrel 'cause the sheriff back in Texas got a little too serious 'bout his card games."

Elanor arched an eyebrow at Boone. "You ended up in a barrel?"

Boone grinned, tipping his hat. "Oh yeah. Got myself in a heap of trouble over a hand of poker. Sheriff didn't take too kindly to me winnin' his money. Threw me in a barrel and sent me floatin' down the Mississippi River." He let out a boisterous laugh, clearly pleased with his own story.

The sheriff chuckled. "The Mississippi isn't connected to Texas."

"Well, that's because it wasn't the Mississippi," Boone said matter-of-factly. "That's 'cause it was in Memphis. If you ask me, though, city life never was quite what I thought it would be."

Nora side-eyed Boone over her shoulder. "How much of that's true, Boone?"

Boone shrugged with a mischievous glint in his eye. "Does it matter? It's a damn good story, ain't it?"

Elanor couldn't contain her laughter. She admired Boone's knack for discovering humor in even the most unexpected circumstances. The strain in her chest relaxed, and the burden of the journey felt somewhat lighter thanks to his wit.

At the front, Weston remained quiet, not joining in the laughter. His jaw was taut, head on a swivel, scanning the horizon. From her position at the back, Elanor observed him with an intensified curiosity. There was an aspect of him—something he concealed. It transcended his merely stoic nature. He seemed to be withholding something significant, and Elanor couldn't shake the sense that it mattered greatly.

Her eyes drifted over his broad shoulders, his back tensing every time the wind shifted or a shadow passed over them. Weston had been quiet most of the day, even more silent than usual, and though Elanor had gotten used to his silence, today it was heavier—like he was carrying a burden none of them understood.

She was about to ask him what was on his mind when Nora spoke up from the front. "Think we're headed in the right direction, Wes?" she called out, her voice laced with concern and impatience.

Weston remained quiet, fixed on the horizon, deep in thought. After a long pause, he finally spoke, his voice low and guarded. "We'll find it," he said. "Just keep moving."

Boone shifted in his saddle. "You sure? I mean . . . if Tawa's camp is this far out, and it's not where we think it is, how are we goin' to find it?"

Weston shot him a look, lips pressed into a thin line. "We have no choice but to figure it out. If we had better information that didn't lead us astray, we wouldn't be having this conversation."

The sheriff's face paled at the implication, and he mumbled something no one heard. Nora let out a sigh, shaking her head as she continued riding.

Elanor couldn't shake the nagging suspicion that Weston was holding something back. His words were deliberately vague, his demeanor guarded, and the way he carried himself suggested he had no intention of sharing his secrets. She considered pressing him for answers, but an instinct stopped her—a sense that the moment wasn't right.

Instead, she watched the sheriff, who was still riding beside her, jaw clenched.

"You ever regret leavin' a place behind?" the sheriff asked softly, as if the question had slipped out unintentionally.

Elanor blinked, surprised by his tone change. "I . . . I don't know," she admitted. "I don't really remember much of what I left behind."

The sheriff nodded, his face contemplative as he looked ahead. "Funny thing, ain't it? Leavin' places, leavin' people. Sometimes you don't realize what you left until you're miles away."

Elanor didn't respond. She wasn't sure how to. She didn't remember what she had left behind—at least, not clearly. The reminder of that feeling of loss sent a chill down Elanor's back.

Weston's voice cut through the silence once more. "We're close. Keep your eyes open."

Elanor's stomach tightened as she scanned the rocky terrain, the shadows growing longer as the sun slowly descended. She wasn't sure what they would find when they reached Tawa's camp, but something told her this journey was far from over.

Elanor felt sweat trickling down her neck, and the ache in her legs from hours in the saddle had become a dull, constant throb. She lifted her head to the sky, frowning. It had been hours since they'd set out in the morning, yet the landscape looked eerily familiar.

She wasn't the only one who noticed.

Nora pulled her horse up beside Weston. "That ledge should've appeared by now," she muttered, her voice low but tense. "It wasn't that far. Two hours, tops."

Weston clenched his jaw as his eyes searched the horizon, feeling increasingly uneasy. "We're going the right way," he said, though a note of uncertainty had crept into his voice.

"The hell we are," Nora shot back. "We've been riding all morning, and we're no closer than we were yesterday."

Elanor felt her stomach churn. She had thought Weston knew their destination—he was the one guiding them, after all. But now the doubt in his voice was unmistakable. They were supposed to be heading back to the ledge they had passed the day before, but something was wrong.

Riding silently at the back of the group, the sheriff cleared his throat nervously. "You sure we didn't miss a turn somewhere?"

Weston shot him a piercing stare. "There weren't any turns to miss."

Riding ahead with his usual carefree attitude, Boone slowed down and peered over his shoulder. "Well, it's a big desert. You reckon we're just goin' in circles?"

"Don't say that," Elanor muttered, voice tinged with worry. "That's the last thing we need right now."

Weston's grip tensed around the reins as he exhaled sharply through his nose. "We're not going in circles. We'll hit the ledge soon. Just keep moving."

But the frustration was spreading through the group, despite his attempt to maintain control. The hours dragged on, and the heat became oppressive as they continued through the same barren landscape, the rocky outcrops becoming more familiar with each passing mile.

By midafternoon, even Weston's stoic demeanor began to crack. He pulled his horse to a stop and dismounted, pacing a few steps away from the group as he scanned the terrain again in frustration. "We should've been there by now," he muttered, loud enough for Elanor to hear. "Something's not right."

Elanor felt her heart drop as she observed the tightness rising in Weston's shoulders. If he was unaware of their destination, what hope did they have of navigating? She shifted restlessly in her saddle and glanced anxiously at Nora, who remained notably quiet.

"Are we lost?" Elanor asked, her voice taut and anxious.

Weston didn't answer right away. Instead, he kicked at a rock on the ground, his expression dark. "I don't know," he admitted after a moment. "We should've been back at that ledge hours ago."

Boone, who had been listening quietly for once, leaned forward in his saddle with a playful grin. "Well, at least we ain't runnin' into bandits again. Could be worse."

Nora shot him a glare. "That's not helping, Boone."

Boone shrugged, unaffected by her biting tone. "Just sayin'. It could always be worse."

Weston let out a long breath, frustration boiling over. "We need to stop for the night," he said, glancing at the sky. "It's too late to keep pushing forward. We'll figure it out in the morning."

The sheriff nodded, relieved. "Best we don't ride through the dark," he mumbled.

A surge of frustration warmed Elanor's cheeks, but she kept it to herself. They had been riding for hours, and now they would stop. She scanned the landscape; the sun was already starting its descent. Something was unsettling about the idea of camping out here again, especially when they didn't even know where they were.

"We'll make camp up ahead," Weston said. "There's a clearing not far from here."

The group moved quietly, anxiety thick in the air. As darkness fell, they arrived at the clearing—a tiny, protected space encircled by low shrubs and rocks.

But as soon as they dismounted, realization hit them.

Elanor felt a sinking sensation as she saw the remains of the campfire from the previous night. The way the rocks were arranged and the flattened areas of dirt where they had rested were stark reminders of their previous night there.

"We were here last night," Nora said flatly as she looked around.

They hadn't merely lost their path—they had been trapped in a loop.

"We're lost," Elanor whispered.

Weston didn't respond, his jaw set in a grim line as he looked out into the fading light. The others were also silent, the realization settling over them like a dark cloud. They had no idea where they were going, and night was falling fast.

Boone, ever the optimist, broke the silence with a chuckle. "Well, at least we know this spot's a good one. Reckon we'll just set up here again."

Elanor wanted to scream, but she could only stare at the familiar clearing, her mind racing with uncertainty. They were lost in the desert, without clear direction or sign of Tawa's camp.

As the sun set, its rays casting shadows over the landscape, the difficulty of their situation became harder to overlook.

The evening shadows stretched across the camp as the group settled in for their second night. Frustration hung heavily in the air. Nora's sharp, clipped movements spoke of her simmering anger, while Weston's deliberate silence and tightly controlled gestures hinted at his mounting annoyance. Even Boone's usual easygoing demeanor seemed forced, his jokes quieter and less frequent. As expected, the sheriff's restless fidgeting and frequent glances toward the darkened treeline betrayed his unease as if he expected danger to emerge from the shadows at any moment.

Weston knelt by the fire pit. His face was concentrated as he worked to reignite the flames. The dry brush caught quickly, and soon the flickering light danced across their faces, highlighting the weariness etched into their expressions.

Nora crossed her arms. "We'll have to backtrack tomorrow," she said bluntly. "We can't keep wandering around in circles like this."

Elanor nodded, yet the knot of anxiety in her chest remained tight. "Do you think we can find our way?" she asked.

Weston looked up with a grim expression. "We don't have a choice," he said. "We'll backtrack and try to pick up the right trail. One wrong turn could've thrown us off. We have to stay sharp."

The sheriff shifted uncomfortably, pulling his hat down lower over his brow. "I still say we could've missed a landmark or somethin'," he muttered, primarily to himself. "This desert all looks the same to me."

Nora shot him a sharp look. "We're not lost because of landmarks, Sheriff. We're lost because you gave us bad directions to begin with."

The sheriff's face flushed, but he didn't argue. He looked down at his boots, clearly embarrassed.

Sitting near the fire, flask in hand, Boone chuckled lightly. "Well, sounds like a good time for a good ol' sip of whiskey. I call that a win."

Nora gave him a piercing look, though a small smile tugged at the corners of her lips.

With the fire crackling, an uneasy silence enveloped the group. They felt exhausted, both mentally and physically. They were lost in an unforgiving desert with no clear path forward. It was hard to feel hopeful. But still, they had to move on and not look back.

"We should eat and get some rest," Weston said. "Tomorrow's gonna be a long day."

Nora retrieved a small pot and began cooking a basic meal over the fire. The aroma of simmering beans and dried meat permeated the air, and while it was a modest offering, it satisfied Elanor's hunger.

During their shared meal in quiet companionship, Elanor noticed her thoughts drifting. She couldn't help but contemplate the journey ahead, feeling a blend of excitement and uncertainty about what awaited beyond the vast desert. A slight worry nagged at her, wondering if they would ever find Tawa, if she would ever find her way home. But even more than that, her mind drifted back to moments from her past—those memories just out of reach. The harder she tried to grasp her life before Bodie, the more it slipped through her fingers, like fine sand. It was as if she were gazing into a soft, swirling fog, aware that something meaningful was there but unable to bring it into focus.

When the meal was done, and the fire had burned lower, Weston stood and stretched, his movements slow and deliberate. "I'll take the first watch again," he said, glancing around the clearing. "We don't want any surprises during the night."

Nora nodded. "I'll take the second."

Elanor shifted, feeling the influence of guilt settle over her. "I didn't take a turn last night," she admitted, her voice quiet. "I can—"

"You'll take first watch tomorrow night," Nora cut her off gently but firmly. "We need everyone rested, and you'll have your turn. Don't worry about it."

Elanor wanted to argue but acknowledged Nora was right. She was exhausted, and the day's tension had drained whatever energy she had left. She glanced at Weston scanning the darkened landscape with the sharp focus of someone who wouldn't let anything slip by.

As the others began to settle in for the night, Boone sprawled out near the fire, already snoring softly, and Nora pulled her hat down low as she leaned against her bedroll, closing her eyes but still alert. The sheriff sat with his back to a nearby boulder, nervously fidgeting with his pistol before setting it aside.

Elanor lay down on her bedroll, staring up at the night sky. The stars above were bright, scattered across the velvet expanse like diamonds, and for a moment, the vastness of it all made her feel incredibly small.

She gently closed her eyes, hoping the soothing sounds of crickets chirping and the wind playfully rustling through the sparse brush would lull her to sleep. However, no matter how hard she tried, her mind seemed to resist the calm. Thoughts about their journey, the mystery surrounding Tawa's whereabouts, and the nagging uncertainty of what awaited them danced in her head.

Tomorrow brought the promise of further exploration as they revisited their earlier route, each moment imbued with the hope of finding the correct path forward. But for the time being, all they could do was accept the necessity of rest.

After turning the thoughts over in her head more times than she could count, the soft crackling of the fire got to Elanor as she drifted into a restless sleep, her dreams weaving together fragments of forgotten memories mixed with the intriguing shadows of the desert.

CHAPTER SIX

The early morning sun peeked over the horizon, casting long, pale shadows over the camp. The air was cool and still. Elanor stretched her aching limbs, wiping a bit of dust from her face, and looked around at the others. Boone was sprawled near the fire's dying embers, snoring softly, his hat pulled over his eyes.

Nora, already awake, was repacking her bags, her movements precise and practiced. She didn't speak, but Elanor noticed the look of slight consternation on her face. Weston was off to the side, leaning against his saddle, arms crossed, and the sheriff, though trying to appear calm, fidgeted with his holster.

Elanor frowned. Something was wrong. She reflected on the stress of the previous morning. Her eyes shifted around the group until Weston broke the silence. He sighed, half to himself. "Should've brought a damn compass."

At that, Boone stirred, tipping his hat up lazily. "Oh, I've got one," he said with a calm grin as if this revelation wasn't about to send the entire group into a frustrated uproar.

The air in the camp shifted in an instant.

"You've got a what?" Weston growled, turning sharply toward Boone.

Boone sat up, stretching like he hadn't a care in the world. "A compass. You know, one of those fancy things that point north?" He chuckled, clearly unaware or uninterested in the rising tension around him.

Elanor's eyes widened, and Nora's head snapped up from her pack. "Boone, why the hell didn't you mention that yesterday?"

Boone blinked innocently, scratching his head as if the thought had only just occurred. "Didn't think it was important. Figured we were fine just followin' the horizon."

Weston took a deep breath, trying—and failing—to stay calm. "Boone. The one thing we needed, and you didn't think it was important?"

Boone shrugged. He stood up and brushed the dust off his clothes. "We weren't *lost* lost—just a little turned around. Lemme grab it for ya." He strolled over to his horse, reaching for his saddlebag.

The group watched in disbelief as Boone rummaged through his bag, his movements slow and casual. It was as if he were searching for a lost pair of socks instead of a critical navigation tool. After a moment, he pulled out a nearly empty bottle of whiskey.

He grinned sheepishly. "Oops, must've switched the bags. That's the good stuff." He chuckled to himself as if that made it all better.

Nora rolled her eyes and muttered something, clearly trying to keep herself from throwing something at him.

Boone rifled through another bag. With a triumphant grin, he pulled out a small brass compass. "There she is!" He tossed it to Weston, who caught it midair, his expression dark but grateful.

Weston turned the compass over in his hand, muttering something as he tried to shake off his anger. Elanor couldn't help but notice how quickly the tone shifted within the group due to just one small object. It wasn't a solution to all their problems but a step in the right direction—literally.

"Least now we won't keep retracing our steps," Nora said, standing and brushing the dust off her clothes. She eyed Boone. "Next time mention when you've got somethin' useful, will ya?"

Boone gave her a half-salute, grinning like a fool. "Anything for you, Nora."

The sheriff, however, looked pale. His hands shook slightly as he tucked his holster into place and cast a nervous look toward the horizon. "This compass . . . it doesn't change that we still don't know where Tawa is."

Studying the compass, Weston gave a terse nod. "No, but it means we won't keep walking in circles. We'll head north and adjust from there." He eyed the sheriff, his patience wearing thin. "If there's anything else you're not sure about, now's the time to speak up."

The sheriff shifted uncomfortably, his face falling to the ground. "I — Well . . . it's been a while since I've actually been out this far. I was just going off what I'd heard from some of the old-timers." He swallowed hard. "I thought we could find it, but . . . I didn't know it'd be this difficult."

Weston shook his head, but Elanor stepped forward before the frustration could bubble over. She cast a glance at Weston. "It's fine. We'll figure it out."

The tension eased, if only slightly. Weston exhaled through his nose and nodded, eyes softening just a little. "Let's get moving, then."

They packed up their camp in relative silence, but as they mounted their horses and began riding north with the compass guiding them, Elanor couldn't shake the feeling that something was still off. It wasn't just the landscape or the uncertainty of their journey—it was the way the sheriff's words lingered, like a warning she couldn't quite put her finger on.

For now, though, they had a direction, and that was enough to keep them moving.

The sun rose higher, casting long, golden rays over the barren landscape. Elanor kept her eyes on the horizon, muscles tense from days in the saddle. The land around them was still the same—dry, unyielding, and endless—but something about how they moved was different now. The compass gave them a renewed sense of hope, even if the uncertainty of their final destination still lingered like a shadow over the group.

They rode in relative silence for a while, the only sounds being the rhythmic clop of their horses' hooves and the occasional rustle of wind through the dry brush. Nora rode close to Elanor, eyes scanning the horizon with practiced precision. Now and then, Nora peered back at

Weston as if silently gauging his mood, but she kept her thoughts to herself.

For her part, Elanor couldn't shake the growing feeling of unease gnawing at her. They had a compass now, but their path to Tawa was no more apparent. She wanted to trust in Weston's confidence, but the sheriff's admission earlier still rattled her. If he didn't know precisely where Tawa was, how long could they wander out here before something went terribly wrong?

She wasn't the only one with doubts.

"This don't feel right," Nora said under her breath, not loud enough for the whole group but loud enough for Elanor to hear. Her voice was laced with frustration. "We should've seen something by now."

Elanor turned to Nora, worry prickling at her. "What do you mean?"

Nora shifted in her saddle, pulling her hat lower over her face. "The desert's deceptive, but I've traveled these parts before. Even if we don't know where Tawa's camp is, we should've hit some landmarks by now. A clearing, a rock formation—something. Feels like we're ridin' through the same bit of mountain, just over and over."

Elanor glanced over at Weston. He was a little farther ahead, shoulders set in a rigid line. Even from a distance, she saw the tightness in his back.

"Do you think . . . Do you think we're lost again?" Elanor asked quietly.

Nora snorted softly. "We were never not lost, sweetheart. The compass helps, but without a map or some proper directions, we're wanderin' blind." She eyed the sheriff, hanging back near the group's rear, his gaze cast down, clearly avoiding everyone's looks.

Elanor followed Nora's gaze and sighed. The sheriff hadn't spoken much since that morning. His silence was heavy, guilty. She wondered how much of their current predicament was weighing on him, but at the same time, she couldn't afford to feel pity for him now.

Ahead, Boone was riding lazily. He was humming some tune again, hat tipped low as if he didn't have a care in the world. Occasionally, he'd pull out one of his remaining whiskey bottles, swig, and mutter something about "desert dust." It grated on Elanor's nerves, but strangely, Boone's lightheartedness kept the group from completely falling apart.

As if sensing the rising unease, Weston slowed his horse and fell back toward the middle of the group, pulling up next to Nora and Elanor. At first, he didn't say anything, but Elanor noticed how his eyes darted between them, reading their expressions.

"We'll get there," Weston said, his voice lacking its usual confidence. "Just need to keep moving. This place plays tricks on you."

Her raised eyebrows accentuated Nora's side-eye. "You sure we're on the right track, Wes?"

Weston's jaw tightened. With a slight, almost imperceptible nod, he muttered, "We're not going in circles anymore. That's a start."

A pang of sympathy for him filled Elanor, but it didn't stop her growing concern. "It just feels like . . . something's off," she admitted, her voice soft. "Like we're being pulled in the wrong direction."

Weston's eyes flicked to her, then back to the horizon. He didn't deny it.

Overhearing the conversation, Boone piped up with a carefree grin. "You lot worry too much. We'll find our way. Ain't nobody ever gotten lost forever, right?"

Elanor wasn't so sure, but she forced a weak smile. Boone's oblivious optimism, though misplaced, was almost comforting in its way.

Riding at the back, the sheriff finally spoke up, his voice wavering slightly. "Maybe we should stop again. Look at the compass, recheck the directions . . ."

"No," Weston said sharply, not even looking back. "We've lost enough time as it is. We keep moving."

Nora shot the sheriff a look that said everything she was thinking. Elanor caught it out of the corner of her eye—Nora wasn't exactly forgiving the sheriff for leading them astray, and now that they were depending on Weston, any wavering confidence in him could cause the fragile balance of the group to unravel.

Elanor adjusted herself in her saddle and firmed her grip around the reins. The desert stretched endlessly around them, yet its vastness didn't evoke a sense of freedom—it felt like a trap.

The relentless heat bore down on the group as the day dragged on.

The sun hammered them mercilessly, and sweat trickled down Elanor's back. Her throat was parched, despite the sips of water she took now and then, and every muscle in her body ached from hours in the saddle. Ignoring the growing sense of unease gnawing at her insides was getting more complicated. They'd been riding for what felt like an eternity, yet the landscape around them *still* barely changed.

The silence among the group was heavy, each rider lost in their thoughts. Boone's usual humming had faded into quiet, and even Nora, who often had something sharp to say, was unusually quiet as they pushed forward into the unknown.

Exiting the mountains dragged, but they did it, now faced with the open desert again. They traveled through the barren lands through the evening, and as the sun began its slow descent toward the horizon, casting long shadows across the desert, Weston pulled his horse to a stop and looked around. He swept over the terrain before finally landing on the group.

"We're not making it to Tawa today," he said bluntly, his voice cutting through the oppressive silence.

Elanor wasn't surprised by the declaration, but hearing it out loud made her stomach twist with disappointment. "What do we do, then?" she asked, shifting in her saddle. "We can't keep going, can we?"

Nora nodded, her face flushed from the heat. "We'll have to stop soon. Find some cover, make camp again before it gets too dark."

Weston looked around again, scanning the horizon for any sign of shelter. "We're not far from the mountains," he said calmly. "We'll head that way and find a spot similar to the one from the last two nights. If we're lucky, we'll find something close to water."

"More mountains!" Boone exclaimed, drawing a short laugh from Elanor.

The mention of water brought a warm flicker of hope in Elanor. They were running low, and the thought of being out here without enough to drink was terrifying. "Do you think there's a stream nearby?"

"Maybe," Weston replied. "It's not guaranteed, but either way, the mountains are our best bet for cover."

The sheriff, who had been quiet most of the day, cleared his throat.

"I think it's the right call. We don't want to be in the open when night falls."

Nora raised an eyebrow but said nothing. Her silence was enough to convey what she thought of the sheriff's sudden input—he had lost the right to offer much advice after his poor directions that had gotten them lost in the first place.

Elanor eyed Weston, who curtly nodded, indicating they should keep moving. She saw the strain in his eyes now, the responsibility of leadership bearing down on him. He was doing his best, but Elanor couldn't shake the feeling they were no closer to finding Tawa. Still, Weston's quiet determination gave her a strange sense of comfort, like he wouldn't let things completely fall apart—even if they'd already begun to.

They rode on in silence, the light fading, until they reached the foothills of a new set of mountains. The terrain shifted slightly, the rocky ground offering some respite from the flat, featureless desert. Weston led the group toward a small clearing between two ridges where they'd be well-hidden from passersby but still able to keep watch.

"This'll do," Weston said, pulling his horse to a halt. "We can set up camp here."

As they dismounted, Elanor stretched her aching legs, her muscles protesting the long ride. The coolness of the mountain breeze was a welcome change from the searing heat of the desert, but the chill that came with the setting sun made her shiver. She wrapped her arms around herself, glancing around as the others unloaded their supplies.

Always lighthearted, Boone took a moment to stretch dramatically, joints popping. "Well, well, ain't this a lovely spot," he said with a grin, plopping himself down on a nearby rock. "Almost makes me forget how lost we are."

Nora glared at him but didn't say anything. Elanor noticed the bags under her eyes, the strain of the day's fruitless journey wearing on her, a reflection of the entire group.

Weston, however, was already moving with efficiency, setting up the campsite with practiced ease. He tethered the horses to a nearby desert willow and began arranging a small circle of stones for the fire. Elanor couldn't help but watch him, admiring the quiet strength in his actions. Even when the group was ready to unravel, Weston held it together.

Nora gathered wood for the fire and motioned for the sheriff to help. He moved quickly to follow her lead.

Elanor, in contrast, felt an unsettling sense of inadequacy creeping in. Unlike Weston or Nora, she lacked the practiced skills of survival, and though she tried to help, it often seemed like she was more hindrance than help. As she hesitated, unsure of her next move, she caught Weston's gaze. Their eyes met for a fleeting moment, and the heaviness in the air seemed to lighten, if only briefly.

"You alright?" Weston asked.

Elanor nodded, but the truth was, she wasn't sure. "I'm just . . . tired," she admitted, glancing at the others already busying themselves with camp.

Weston gave her a slight nod of understanding. "We'll rest tonight. Things will look better in the morning."

Elanor couldn't be so certain. But as the sun dipped below the horizon and the darkness began to creep in, they didn't have much choice. They'd make it through another night—if only by sheer determination.

As the fire crackled softly, casting flickering shadows on the rocks around them, Elanor found herself sitting next to Weston, the warmth of the flames providing a welcome reprieve from the cooling night air. The camp had settled into a quiet rhythm, and a hint of security filled Elanor's mind, though unease still gnawed at the edges of her thoughts.

Weston was methodically cleaning his gun, his strong hands working with precision. The others were scattered around the camp, Boone already snoring lightly in the background, Nora across from them, her back turned, focused on her task.

Elanor shifted, glancing at Weston. She had been thinking about everything they had been through, and more than once today, she had caught herself watching him. Something was steadying about him, even when he wasn't saying much. Now, with the quiet wrapping around them, she had an urge to speak, to ask him something that had been circling in her mind.

"Do you ever get tired of it?" she asked softly, breaking the silence. "Of all this?"

Weston paused momentarily, his hand stilling on the pistol as he looked at her. His eyes caught the firelight, flickering with a warmth contrasting their surroundings' harshness. "Tired?" he echoed. "Of the journey?"

Elanor shrugged, feeling a little self-conscious under his gaze. "Yeah. The journey . . . the danger . . . not knowing if you're going to make it."

Weston's lips quirked into a small smile, but there was something deeper behind it—a trace of understanding, that he knew exactly what she meant. "Every damn day," he admitted. "But this is all I've known for quite some time now. It's how you keep going, even when you don't know what's coming next. What about you? You regret any of your past?"

"I guess I don't know how to keep going. Not with everything being . . . this confusing."

Weston looked down briefly, fingers tracing his pistol, before looking back at her. "I shouldn't have asked about your past," he said, his tone soft but filled with regret. "I forget sometimes that you don't have your memories."

Elanor smiled gently. "It's okay. It's not like you meant anything by it." She paused and noticed a subtle shift in the air between them. "It's strange, though. Not knowing who I was . . . am. I can feel parts of me coming back, but . . . everything else? It's like something in me doesn't want me to remember."

Weston studied her for a moment. "Must be hard, not knowing what you're fighting for," he said quietly, his voice softer than she'd ever heard.

Elanor nodded, her chest tightening. "Yeah. It's . . . hard." She looked at him while trying to express her swirling emotions. "But you're right. We keep going, don't we?"

Something unspoken passed between them during a brief silence. Weston lingered on her, and Elanor's pulse quickened. There was a warmth in his eyes, something she hadn't noticed before—or maybe she had, but now it was impossible to ignore.

"Guess we don't have much choice," Weston said, his voice almost teasing now. "But you seem to be handling it better than most."

Elanor raised an eyebrow, a small smile tugging at her lips. "You think so?"

"Yeah," Weston replied, the corner of his mouth twitching into the faintest of smiles. "I've seen people lose it over less. But you—you're different. You're still standing."

Elanor's breath caught at his words, and warmth crept up her neck she couldn't suppress. She shifted slightly, brushing a strand of hair behind her ear, her eyes never leaving his. "Well, maybe I've had good company."

Weston chuckled softly, his eyes dropping to the ground momentarily before meeting hers again. "Maybe," he said, his voice quiet and sincere.

The air between them was charged now, a subtle tenseness hanging in the space that neither acknowledged outright but couldn't deny. Elanor wasn't sure what to say next, but it didn't matter. Weston's eyes had softened, the hard edges of his usual expression giving way to something gentler. For the first time, Elanor saw him not just as the stoic cowboy leading them through the wilderness but as someone with his own doubts and struggles.

Before she could say anything more, Weston shifted slightly, his gaze flicking over her, lingering a little longer than usual. His eyes swept over her figure, the firelight casting a warm glow on his face, and Elanor suddenly became aware of how her clothes fit now—thanks to Nora's more form-fitting outfit. They weren't the bulky, oversized clothes she had been wearing before, and for a brief second, she wondered if Weston noticed.

He did.

His stare moved quickly from her eyes to her waist, then back up again, but he didn't look away this time. There was something there—something she couldn't quite place, but it made her breath catch. Her heart thudded in her chest, and when their eyes met again, the moment lingered, stretching between them like a taut string waiting to snap.

Weston cleared his throat, suddenly aware of the silence between them. "You should get some rest," he said softly. "We've got a long day ahead tomorrow."

Elanor nodded and smiled faintly while her heart still raced. "Yeah, you're probably right."

For a second, it was like he was about to say something else, but Boone's voice cut through the quiet before he could. "Ain't this cozy?" he drawled, voice thick with humor as he sat up from where he had been pretending to sleep. "Our little lovebirds, sittin' by the fire."

Elanor's cheeks flushed instantly, and she saw Weston shift slightly, his jaw tightening. But as she looked at him, she caught the faintest flicker of a smile on his face, as if Boone's comment hadn't truly bothered him.

Nora snorted from across the camp, shaking her head. "Leave 'em alone, Boone. You're just jealous."

Boone grinned, clearly enjoying himself. "Maybe I am, Nora. Maybe I am."

The group shared a small laugh, the tension easing, but even as the laughter died down, Elanor and Weston exchanged one last look. His eyes lingered on hers, and for a moment, the world around them faded, leaving just the two of them in the glow of the fire. It was fleeting, but its weight settled in her chest, warm and undeniable.

Boone yawned, dramatically stretching as he lay back down. "Goodnight, lovebirds," he mumbled before drifting off.

Weston sighed, shaking his head with a slight smile before glancing at Elanor one last time. "Guess we'll both need that rest now."

Elanor chuckled softly, feeling the lingering warmth between them as she settled down, her fingers instinctively reaching for the silver locket resting against her chest. The memory of that look stayed with her, filling the quiet as the fire crackled beside them.

Elanor blinked awake, her body stiff from the uneven rocky ground, the morning sun already creeping over the jagged peaks above them. For a brief moment, there was peace—the quiet stillness of dawn. But then she noticed Weston, already sitting up, his expression rigid and tense.

Something was wrong.

He swore under his breath, and the strain in his voice made her stomach drop. "Damn it," he muttered, rubbing a hand across his face.

"What is it?" Elanor asked, her voice thick with sleep but edged with concern.

Weston narrowed his eyes as he scanned the camp's surroundings. "We didn't take shifts. No one kept watch last night."

The realization hit Elanor like a punch to the gut. She shot upright, her pulse hammering. How could they all have slept through the night without someone on watch? The mountains were hardly a secure spot to relax, particularly with Merrick's men possibly hiding close by.

Boone stretched lazily, sprawled out on his bedroll. He yawned loudly. "Well, I'd say that's a win. Nothin' came for us, right? No harm, no foul."

Elanor shared a glance with Weston, who appeared anything but reassured. He stood, moving quickly to pack up his things.

"We can't afford to be this careless," Weston said, his voice sharp.

A wave of guilt washed over Elanor. She hadn't even thought about her turn to stay awake. Had they all been so exhausted that they forgot?

Nora stirred next, rubbing her eyes as she looked between them. "What's goin' on?"

Weston diverted his attention to the rocky landscape around him. The mountains stood tall and formidable, scattered jagged boulders and sparse brush covering the landscape. It wasn't a place that offered easy cover, so any movement—whether animal or human—would stand out starkly against the barren backdrop.

That's when Elanor heard a faint scraping noise echoing in her ears, like stones shifting off in the distance. At first, it was easy to dismiss it as natural, just the wind moving through the rocks. But it came again, louder, more deliberate, like something—or someone—was out there.

Nora's face hardened immediately, her hand instinctively reaching for her pistol. "We got company?"

The sound grew closer. The mountains were quiet, and every shift of a rock now was an impending threat.

Elanor shot a look at Weston, who had already moved to gather the horses. "We need to get out of here," he said.

Boone, still half-asleep, finally sat up, a lazy grin on his face. "Aw, come on now, what's the rush? Ain't no need to—"

Another sound cut him off, a distinct crack, like stones breaking underfoot, echoing across the canyon.

Even Boone's grin faded then, his eyes narrowing at the rocks above them.

"I'd get up if I were you," Nora said, already on her feet. "I don't like the sound of this."

The sheriff, who had just woken up, fumbled to get his gear in order, hands shaking as he grabbed his hat. "What's out there?" he asked, his voice strained.

"I don't know," Elanor whispered as she sighted the distant cliffs. "But we shouldn't wait to find out."

Everyone hurried, the air heavy with urgency as they broke down the camp. The horses stomped anxiously, their hooves echoing on the rocky ground.

Weston mounted his horse swiftly, his eyes never leaving the distant ridges where shadows shifted unnervingly. Whatever was out there, it was too close for comfort.

Boone, still looking unconvinced but no longer laughing, mumbled, "Maybe it's just some critter or—"

Another crack echoed across the canyon, louder this time, and even Boone stopped talking.

"We're leaving," Weston said, his voice brooking no argument.

Elanor didn't need to be told twice. She hurried to mount her horse, her pulse pounding in her chest as they kicked into motion, leaving the rocky clearing behind. But even as they moved, Elanor couldn't shake the feeling that they were being watched from the shadows of the mountain peaks.

CHAPTER SEVEN

Elanor swung herself onto her horse, heartbeat pounding in her ears as low, rumbling sounds echoed through the mountains. Dust swirled in the air, kicked up by the sudden movement of the group as they hurried to escape whatever was coming from above. She peered up at the jagged cliffs; her stomach churned as the noise's source became clear—loose rocks began to tumble down the mountainside.

"Let's move!" Weston shouted. He spurred his horse forward, leading the way. "Stick close, and keep your heads down!"

Elanor urged her horse to follow, her pulse racing with the urgency in Weston's voice. Nora and the sheriff trailed closely behind her, Boone trailing behind, silently muttering as they broke into a gallop down the narrow mountain trail.

The ground shook beneath them, and the sound of falling rocks grew louder. Elanor peered over her shoulder just in time to see a large boulder crash into the trail they had just passed, sending a plume of dust and debris into the air.

"Rocks are coming down fast!" Nora shouted.

Weston's eyes darted up toward the mountainside, his expression stern. "We need to pick up speed. Stay tight to the ledge."

A loud crash echoed behind them as another boulder slammed into the trail, too close for comfort.

Riding at the back, Boone let out a nervous laugh, his usual bravado failing to mask his unease. "Maybe next time we pick a route with fewer falling mountains?"

"Not the time, Boone!" Weston snapped, his eyes narrowing as the path grew steeper and more treacherous.

Ahead of them, the trail curved sharply to the left, but just as they rounded the bend, the ground shook violently. A loud crash followed the rumble, and Elanor watched in horror as a massive boulder tumbled down the cliffside, slamming into the path ahead and blocking their way forward.

"We're trapped!" The sheriff yanked his horse to a halt, eyes wide with panic.

Weston cursed under his breath, mind racing as he surveyed the blocked path. The mountain was still shifting, more rocks dislodging from the cliffs above, threatening to rain down on them at any moment.

"We'll have to go higher!" he shouted, steering his horse toward a narrow ridge that cut across the mountainside. "Stay close, and don't lose your footing!"

Elanor's horse scrambled to find solid ground on the rocky ledge. The wind whipped through the canyon, carrying the sound of more falling rocks. She glanced back, her chest taut with fear as another section of the trail collapsed under the weight of the boulders.

The ridge they followed was barely wide enough for the horses, and the drop to the valley floor below was dizzying. One wrong step and they would fall—Elanor tried not to think about that as they pressed on, the rocks shifting ominously overhead.

Weston led the way, his jaw set in grim determination. He looked back at the group every few seconds, making sure they were keeping pace. Despite his usual flippant attitude, Boone was uncharacteristically silent, his eyes wide as he focused on the path ahead.

With a mask of focus on her face, Nora rode right behind Weston. The sheriff, however, was clearly rattled, and his horse was having trouble navigating the rough ground. "We need to find a way out of here," he muttered, voice laced with fear.

"We will," Weston said. "Just stay close."

Elanor's hands were slick with sweat as the rocks continued to fall behind them.

The sound of stone scraping against stone reverberated through the canyon. The narrow trail twisted ahead, and with every step, the horses teetered on the edge of disaster. Elanor's legs hurt from keeping her horse steady while pushing it ahead at the same speed as the others.

With his head spinning frequently and his eyes searching the cliffs above for any indications of another collapse, Weston's figure remained tense.

A sharp crack reverberated from behind, sending a stream of loose boulders falling down mere feet behind Boone's horse.

"Move!" Weston barked, spurring his horse forward.

The path narrowed again, sloping upward as the ridge shrunk beneath them. The horses stumbled on the loose gravel, their hooves clattering dangerously close to the edge. As they ascended, Elanor forced herself to maintain her concentration by holding her breath, heart thumping in her ears.

The air was thick with dust, and the sound of the rocks behind them began to fade, but the path ahead offered little respite. Another rock tumbled down the mountainside, and the sheriff's horse reared up, nearly tossing him from his saddle.

"Hold on!" Nora shouted as she fought to keep her horse steady on the uneven terrain.

Elanor's chest tightened as she watched the sheriff struggle to calm his mount, but Weston's voice cut through the rising panic. "Keep pushing forward—we're almost there!"

There was no time to question how close "there" really was. Elanor's legs burned with each squeeze of the horse's side, and her horse's labored breathing mirrored her exhaustion. The ridge began to widen, and though the trail was still treacherous, the cliffside sloped away slightly, offering a glimmer of hope.

Squinting through the dust, Elanor saw a little plateau in front of them, where the rocks suddenly tapered off. Although the footing remained rough and rocky, it appeared stable.

Weston pulled his horse to a stop, his chest heaving as he scanned the cliffs one last time, ensuring no more dangers lurked above.

Elanor followed, her muscles trembling as she dismounted, legs weak from the strain of the ride. She felt adrenaline still coursing through her veins as she stepped onto the ground. They'd had made it—but only just.

"We'll need to find another way down," Weston said. "We can't go back the way we came."

Nora nodded, wiping sweat from her brow. "That was too close."

Boone dismounted, his legs shaky as he stretched. "Next time, we take a route that doesn't involve playing chicken with a mountain, yeah?"

Elanor released a breath she had been holding

The eerie calm of the mountains enveloped the group as they gathered their breath on the little plateau. Feeling the grit on her skin, Elanor wiped dust from her face and collected her composure.

Weston scanned the horizon. He made deliberate movements, making sure everyone was okay while he inspected the horses. Although Elanor sensed the stress in his shoulders, he was clearly composed under pressure.

"We need to keep moving," Weston said. "This plateau is stable for now, but we can't stay here long."

Nora, her hair wild and streaked with dust, nodded. "Where do we go from here?" she asked. "We've obviously got to get out of these mountains, but I'm not liking our options."

Weston paused momentarily, his gaze flicking back to the narrow trail they had just come up, now blocked by the fallen rocks. "We'll have to head farther up, find a safer path down."

Still gray from the experience, the sheriff shifted uncomfortably in his saddle. "Farther up?" His voice wavered, clearly unsettled by the prospect. "How can going higher make sense when we're trying to get out of these mountains?"

Boone, who had been stealthily searching his saddlebags, sighed loudly and shook his head in a disproportionately frustrated gesture. "Oh, come on, Sheriff. Haven't you heard? The only way out is up!"

Though his usual boldness was slightly deflated after their brush with disaster, he grinned.

Boone's attempt to lighten the mood made Elanor smile faintly

Elanor kept looking at Weston as he bent forward to examine the trail ahead. He took command in a reassuring way, as though he made every choice with precision, even when under pressure. Even in the craziness of their predicament, she felt more grounded because of his quiet strength.

"What do you think, Wes?" Nora asked, moving closer to stand beside him. "What's our best bet?"

Weston pointed to a narrow path that cut through a steeper section of the mountain, its jagged edges hidden in shadow. "That trail there," he said. "It's a gamble, but it'll take us higher and away from the worst of the rockfalls. From there, we might be able to find a clearer way down."

Elanor's stomach churned at the thought of going higher, but she trusted Weston's intuition. Even though her voice was harsher than she had wanted, she said, "It's better than sitting here waiting for more boulders to fall."

The sheriff groaned softly, his unease palpable. "I'm not much for gambling," he muttered.

"The hell you ain't," Nora shot back.

Having finished his rummaging, Boone pulled out a flask and gave the sheriff a playful nudge. "Come on now, Sheriff, what's life without a little risk? Besides, we've survived worse, right?"

Weston shot Boone a look. "Put that away," he said sharply. "We need to stay focused."

Boone shrugged, though he obliged, tucking the flask back into his saddlebag. "Just trying to keep things lively," he said with a wink, though more subdued than usual.

Elanor swung back into her saddle, ready to follow Weston's lead. Her body ached, and the fear still gnawed at her, but they couldn't stay on this plateau for long.

Weston mounted his horse again, eyes still scanning the rocky cliffs above them, ever alert. "Let's move out," he said. "Stay close, and watch your footing."

With the sun casting long shadows across the cliffs, they set off once more, their path treacherous but obvious—for now.

Elanor's horse skidded on the loose gravel as they neared the top of the ridge, her muscles aching with the effort of holding steady. The rumbling beneath them grew louder, each shift of the ground sending more rocks cascading down the mountainside. Dust swirled in thick clouds, stinging her eyes and coating her throat with grit.

Weston urged his horse harder forward, looking around at the perilous road ahead. Elanor's horse's feet scrambled frantically as they crawled over the uneven terrain. Only a few feet separated them from the ridge—each step could be their last.

A sharp crack echoed from the cliffs above as a boulder the size of a cartwheel tumbled down the mountain, crashing into the path behind them. The sheriff let out a startled shout, his horse rearing up in fear.

"We're going to be alright!" Weston's voice cut through the chaos, firm and commanding. "Not much more to go!"

Elanor clenched her teeth, pushing her horse forward, every nerve on edge as the mountain shook. The ground was unstable beneath her, as if at any moment it would open up and swallow them whole. But Weston pressed on, leading them closer to the top, and Elanor forced herself to follow.

As they reached the top of the ridge, the wind struck her forcefully, infusing her with the aroma of dust and rock. But there was no time to catch her breath. The ground beneath them trembled again, a low growl reverberating through the mountain.

"We have to get down the other side!" Weston shouted, glancing back at the group. His eyes flicked over the precarious path descending into the valley below. The mountain continued to shift, and remaining here would mean certain death.

Elanor steered her horse toward the narrow trail on the far side of the ridge. The path ahead was steep and treacherous, but it was the only way down. The rumbling from above had grown more erratic, and every step was another gamble with the mountain.

"Stay close to the cliff's wall!" Weston called over his shoulder as he started down the slope, his horse kicking up loose rocks with every step.

Elanor followed, breathing in ragged gasps as she tried to keep her horse steady on the narrow path. The rocks beneath them shifted dangerously. The sheriff muttered nervously, and Boone let out a string of curses as he struggled to keep pace at the back of the group.

Another deep rumble rolled through the mountain, and a cascade of rocks tumbled just feet from where Elanor rode. Her horse whinnied in fear, but she kept it moving, clenching the reins as they navigated the unstable ground.

The descent was steep, each step threatening to send them careening over the edge. However, Weston persisted, his expression grimly determined, eyes darting back and forth between the cliffs above and the path ahead. The landscape leveled out beneath them as they eventually arrived at another little plateau. However, the urgency remained.

Elanor gripped the reins as her horse stumbled over the loose rocks, its hooves skidding against the narrow trail. Breathing didn't come easy, her chest tight as the ground trembled beneath them again. The air was thick with dust, making it hard to see more than a few feet ahead. Weston was just a silhouette in the haze, guiding them down the risky path.

Every stone crack was a potential attack, and the rocks that had fallen behind them were still too close for comfort.

"We need to get down, fast," Weston called. His outline shifted, steadying his horse as it descended the unstable ground.

Elanor barely heard him, her focus entirely on keeping her horse upright. The descent was worse than the climb. The cliff edge was impossibly close. She heard the sheriff muttering behind her, his voice laced with panic, as Nora urged him to keep moving.

Another rumble echoed from above, and Elanor's horse shied away from the noise, its hooves slipping even more dangerously close to the edge. Her breath caught in her throat, fear settling into her chest, but she held firm to the reins, forcing the animal back onto the narrow path.

"Steady," she whispered. "Just a little more. We can do this."

The trail narrowed even more as they descended, the cliff face looming on one side, the sheer drop on the other. The constant shifting of the rocks beneath them made every step a struggle for balance and willpower.

She looked at Weston his shoulders set, his figure high on his horse.

He moved with a studied confidence that was hard to overlook, even in the midst of the commotion. But something in his posture—something rigid and strained—told her he was just as worried as the rest of them.

Another tremor shook the ground, and the sheriff's horse stumbled, nearly sending him over the edge. Nora cursed under her breath, reaching out to steady his horse as rocks clattered down behind them.

"Keep moving!" Weston yelled. "We've got this!"

The ground leveled out, the trail widening slightly, but Elanor couldn't relax. Not yet.

"Move, move!" Weston urged, his voice hoarse from the grit and from shouting over the wind.

The rocks were still coming down behind them, but they were out of immediate danger. Elanor sucked in a shaky breath, adrenaline still coursing through her veins as they continued onward.

When they reached a flatter area of the mountain, Weston pulled up, and Elanor finally released her held breath. Her legs trembled as she slid off her horse, body aching from the stress.

She saw the same exhaustion on everyone's faces. They didn't speak, each lost in their own thoughts as they caught their breath. The sheriff was pale, hands shaking as he dismounted. Nora gave him a stern look, her expression filled with equal parts annoyance and relief.

Boone let out a breathy laugh. "Nothin' like a shaky morning to get you goin', huh?"

Nora shot him a glare, but even she couldn't hide the slight curve of a smile.

Weston wiped the dust from his brow, his face set in a frown as he surveyed the path ahead. "We're not safe yet. We need to keep moving."

Elanor nodded. Ahead of her, Weston's jaw was set with determination, his eyes flicking between the group and the path.

As they mounted and continued, the faint crunch of gravel beneath the hooves should have been an ordinary sound—a reminder of the treacherous path. But this time, it was different. Elanor's horse shuddered beneath her, its muscles tensing, a tremor rippling through its frame as its front legs skidded.

There was no warning. The loose gravel shifted like sand under the pounding force of hooves. The ground dropped beneath them. Panic exploded in Elanor's chest. The horse's eyes were wide, rolling back in fright as its hooves scraped and scrambled for grip on the unstable edge of the narrow ledge. Rocks scattered and tumbled down the slope into the deep ravine below.

"Steady! Easy!" Elanor's voice cracked with urgency, but fear had already overtaken the animal. The horse reared slightly before pitching sideways. Elanor jerked back on the reins, her arms straining with desperate strength, but momentum was already against them. The ledge was too narrow, and gravity was merciless.

The ground shifted again—this time more violently. The horse let out a panicked, high-pitched whinny as it lost its footing completely. Gravity fully took over, a terrifying force dragging Elanor forward. Her stomach lurched. The world blurred.

Not like this, she thought, her mind a whirlwind of dread as her fingers burned from the strain on the leather reins. But there was no stopping the fall. Hooves thrashed in a helpless, frantic dance before the horse slipped over the edge, pulling her with it.

Elanor's arm shot out instinctively, reaching for anything that could anchor her to the world above. Her fingers grazed jagged rocks, ripping at her gloves and skin before latching onto a rough, gnarled branch. The impact wrenched her shoulder with such force, she thought it might tear free, but she held on, her breath escaping in a strangled gasp. Below, her horse vanished into the abyss with a sound that would haunt her— the final, echoing scream of a loyal companion lost to the void.

Time stretched and compressed at once. The drumming of her heartbeat blended with the roar of the wind in her ears. Elanor dared not look down. Every muscle strained as she dangled, the rough bark biting into her palm. Her legs swung, weightless and useless, over the abyss, and for a breathless moment, she was only a heartbeat away from the same fate as her horse.

Elanor closed her eyes and focused, forcing the panic down. She couldn't fall apart—not now. She pressed her forehead against the rock, feeling every grain of dirt and every painful scrape, anchoring herself in the raw reality of the moment. She was alive. But the margin for error had shrunk to the width of a single branch.

Her grip faltered—just for an instant—but it was enough to send another surge of terror through her veins. She clenched her teeth, resisting the urge to scream. Somewhere far below, the ravine's depths beckoned coldly. She wouldn't go down like that. Not yet. Inch by inch, she began to pull herself up, muscles screaming in protest.

"Elanor!" Weston's voice mirrored the panic of the situation.

Her grip faltered on the branch, fingers trembling. "Weston, help!" she gasped, fear choking her voice.

Weston appeared over the edge, pain and fear laced within his eyes.

"Grab on!" He reached down and closed his hand around her wrist as the branch began to crack under her weight. His grip was firm and steady, pulling her up with a force she didn't think was possible. With one hard pull, he dragged her back onto the ledge, his arm wrapping around her waist as he lifted her to safety.

Elanor collapsed against him, her chest heaving from the sudden shock of the moment. The ground was solid beneath her again, but her mind spun as she tried to process how close she'd come to falling.

"You're alright," Weston murmured. His arms were still around her, holding her firmly against him, and for a moment, she couldn't move— she didn't want to move. She was too shaken, too overwhelmed by the adrenaline.

"I . . . my horse . . ." she breathed, her eyes wide with disbelief as she glanced down the mountainside, but all she saw was the vast drop below.

Weston didn't let go. His chest pressed against hers, and she felt the rise and fall of his breath, grounding her in the reality that she was safe. "I'm sorry," he said softly. "But we need to keep moving."

Elanor's heart ached at the loss of her horse, but before she could respond, she recognized just how close she and Weston were. His face was inches from hers, their breaths mingling in the cold mountain air. She saw the concern in his eyes, the way his brow furrowed with worry, and the world narrowed to just the two of them for a moment.

She couldn't look away. There was something unspoken in the air between them, something neither of them was quite ready to acknowledge, but it was there all the same—a connection, something that had been building since Elanor's first day in Bodie.

Weston's stare flickered to her lips for just a fraction of a second, but

Nora's voice broke through the moment before anything could happen. "Well, I hate to interrupt your little romance, but we should hightail it outta here before this mountain swallows us up."

Elanor quickly pulled back, cheeks flushed as she steadied herself. Weston cleared his throat, his expression shifting back to its usual seriousness as he looked away, though his hand lingered on her arm for a moment longer.

Nora wasn't wrong—the rocks were still shifting above them, and the danger wasn't over yet. But Elanor's legs shook—not just from the near-death experience, but from the way Weston had held her, from the way their eyes had locked in that brief, electrifying moment.

"We need to keep moving," Weston said, his voice firm as he released her. He turned to Nora with a curt nod. "Let's get down from here."

But with Elanor's horse gone, they faced a new problem.

"Looks like you'll be riding with me," Weston said as he gestured to his horse.

Elanor hesitated, her emotions still swirling from everything that had happened, but she nodded. She wasn't about to slow the group down; with Weston, she'd be safe.

Weston mounted his horse and reached down, offering her a hand. She took it, and he pulled her up effortlessly, settling her in front of him on the saddle. The warmth of his chest pressed against her back as he wrapped one arm around her waist, his other hand holding the reins.

"Hold on tight," Weston said, his breath warm against her ear.

She did as he said, her hands gripping the saddle as they descended the mountain again.

The rest of the descent passed in tense silence, the group navigating the rocky path with focused determination. Elanor's thoughts were a jumble of emotions. The shock of losing her horse gnawed at her, the image of the animal slipping over the edge replaying in her mind. Guilt and sorrow coiled in her chest—a kind and loyal creature, and now it was gone. But realizing how close she'd come to falling herself was even more overwhelming. The terror of dangling on the cliff's edge, knowing that only a fragile branch had stood between her and the end, sent a shiver through her.

But then there was Weston.

The memory of his strong hands pulling her to safety, of how he'd wrapped his arms around her, lingered in her thoughts. His body was pressed against hers as they descended the mountain, arm wrapped securely around her waist. It should've been uncomfortable, but an odd sense of safety allowed her to relax her shoulders. She leaned deeper into him, trusting him fully in that moment, and her heart quickened once again.

The mountain continued to rumble behind them, but she focused on the steady rhythm of the horse beneath her and the warmth of Weston at her back, grounding her in the here and now. After minutes that felt like hours, they reached the base of the mountain.

Elanor let out a long breath of relief as they reached flatter ground. The tension that had gripped the group during the dangerous descent slowly ebbed away. They had made it—barely. Her legs shook, weak, as she sat in front of Weston, still adjusting to the loss of her horse and the chaos they had just survived. The steady presence of his arm around her had been a physical and emotional lifeline, though she wasn't ready to fully confront the complexity of those feelings just yet.

His voice uncharacteristically subdued, Boone said, "Well, we made it, by the skin of our toes."

Elanor nodded, finally sliding off Weston's horse. Her legs wobbled, and for a moment, the ground swayed beneath her, the lingering adrenaline from her brush with a terrifying fall making her feel unsteady. She glanced back at Weston, a silent dialogue unfolding between them, filled with relief and gratitude.

Just as the group started to collect themselves, the sheriff, who had been scanning the horizon, suddenly straightened in his saddle.

"Hold up," he said, pointing toward the distance. "Look over there."

Elanor followed his gaze, squinting against the late afternoon sun. She spotted it—a small town nestled at the base of the valley. The buildings were faint but unmistakable.

"There's a town," the sheriff said, voice laced with hope. "We're not far now."

Nora clapped Weston on the back, a wide grin spreading across her face. "Looks like we might get outta this mess, after all. Let's hope that town's got some answers—and a stiff drink to settle the rest of my nerves."

Boone, ever the opportunist, grinned widely. "If there's whiskey, I'll have two bottles before the rest of you can find the front door. Call it . . . motivation."

Nora rolled her eyes. "More like you'll be too drunk to walk out the door."

Boone tipped his hat, completely unbothered. "Then I'll just sleep there 'til the next bottle shows up."

Elanor smiled. The sight of the town ignited a tiny spark of hope.

"We're almost there," she murmured, more to herself than anyone else.

Her eyes drifted back to the mountain that had nearly claimed her life. Its jagged peaks rose against the fading sunlight, indifferent to the chaos it had unleashed. The scars of their struggle—the loose gravel, the collapsed trails, the scattered boulders—were invisible from this distance. It looked unchanged, as if her near-death escape had been a fleeting whisper in its ancient, unyielding presence. The mountain stood timeless and unmoved, while the memory of dangling on its edge lingered sharp and raw in Elanor's mind. It was a humbling reminder of how fragile she was, how fleeting her battles were against the world's immensity.

She pressed her hand against her chest, feeling the faint thrum of her heartbeat, and let out a slow, shaky breath. The mountain might not bear the weight of her story, but she would carry it with her—etched into her soul alongside the gratitude for another chance to move forward.

The group began their push toward the town, faced with challenges to come. Elanor couldn't shake the feeling that whatever awaited them there would change the course of their journey.

CHAPTER EIGHT

Hooves thudded softly against the rocky ground as the group rode toward the distant town. Elanor sat in front of Weston, still feeling the tight grip of his arm around her waist, steadying her in the saddle. She shifted slightly, but the ache in her muscles from the strain on the mountain made it hard to relax fully.

Weston had saved her. The thought lingered, and she found herself glancing at the arm that rested across her. He had been calm and focused, just like always, but there had been something different this time. For a brief moment, as he pulled her up, their faces inches apart, a spark ignited between them, a warmth unrelated to the danger they had just escaped. Now, as they rode, her thoughts couldn't escape it.

"What are you thinking about?" Weston's voice broke through her thoughts, soft near her ear.

Elanor hesitated for a moment. "About what happened."

"With the mountain?" he asked, his grip tightening slightly as they rode over a patch of uneven ground.

She nodded again. "I guess it shook me up more than I realized. Losing my horse, the way everything just happened so fast. I thought I was done for." She swallowed, her throat dry. "Thanks, by the way. For saving me back there."

Weston's voice softened even more. "You don't need to thank me. I wasn't about to let you fall."

Elanor allowed herself a small smile, her heart still fluttering slightly at the memory of his hands gripping hers, pulling her back from the edge. She hadn't experienced such a lack of control since arriving in Bodie, so close to a moment of finality. The severity of that moment still pressed on her, but she also couldn't shake the warmth blossoming when she'd looked into Weston's eyes after he'd saved her.

The silence between them grew comfortable, but her thoughts remained jumbled. How had she ended up in this strange place with these people? She couldn't remember her past, and every time she tried to focus on it, it drifted even farther away. All she had was now—and right now, she was wrapped up in something much bigger than herself.

"How are the rest of you holding up?" Weston called out.

Behind them, Nora laughed, though it was a bit more forced than usual. "Well, I still have all my limbs, so that's a win."

Boone chimed in, "Next time, let's bypass the scenic route and opt for the express slide." He chuckled tiredly, exhaustion evident beneath the thin veneer of humor.

The sheriff, riding in the back, remained quiet. He had been shaken back on the mountain, and though he tried to hide it, Elanor had seen the uncertainty in his eyes when the rocks had blocked them in. Now, he simply muttered, "Let's just keep moving. I'm not keen on hanging around here any longer than we have to."

The group continued in relative silence. The sun lowered, casting long shadows over the trail as they approached the town. It was close enough now to see the outline of the buildings nestled in the valley ahead.

Elanor leaned back slightly into Weston's chest, feeling the steady rise and fall of his breath—a sense of security. Maybe it was because they were out of immediate danger, or perhaps it was because Weston's presence made her feel like she wasn't alone. Either way, she wasn't ready to let go of that feeling.

The town loomed closer, and with it, the promise of answers—or perhaps more questions. Either way, it was a step forward, and that was enough for now.

The town sprawled before them, smaller than Bodie but alive with activity. Dusty streets were lined with buildings worn by time but which stood firm—housing, shops, saloons, and homes. Horses clopped along the road, and people milled about, some casting curious glances as Elanor and the group rode in.

Elanor scanned the scene, the sight of civilization bringing a flicker of relief. They had made it here, and there was a chance to regroup, resupply, and get real answers about where to find Tawa.

Nora rode beside her and Weston, nodding toward the general store on the left. "We should start there. If this town's got anything worth taking on a journey, that's where we'll find it."

Weston nodded, steering his horse toward the store. "Let's split up. We'll cover more ground. Sheriff, Boone, why don't you see if anyone's heard anything about Tawa?"

Boone smiled and tilted his hat. "I'll sniff around, see what I can dig up. Maybe make a stop at the saloon while I'm at it." His usual humor had returned, though Elanor saw the exhaustion lingering in his eyes.

The sheriff shifted uncomfortably in his saddle. "I'll— Yeah, I'll ask around," he muttered, barely making eye contact with anyone.

Elanor watched him, sensing something off in his demeanor, but before she could ask, the sheriff turned his horse down the street, trailing after Boone.

As they approached the general store, Elanor stayed close to Weston, who dismounted and turned to help her down from the horse. His hands lingered for a moment longer than necessary.

From a distance, a raised voice caught their attention. Down the street, near the entrance of the saloon, a man called out, "Well, I'll be damned. Ain't that the sheriff?"

Weston's expression darkened as he turned toward the voice, and Elanor followed his gaze. The sheriff had frozen mid-step, his hand hovering near the saloon's door. The man who had called out strode toward him, a grin splitting his weathered face. He looked rough—grizzled beard, sunburned skin, and eyes that gleamed with recognition.

"Hold on a minute," the man said, clapping a hand on the sheriff's shoulder. "Don't I know you from somewhere?"

Elanor couldn't hear the sheriff's reply from where she stood, but something about his body language made her uneasy. His shoulders tensed, and he didn't turn to face the man. Instead, he muttered something under his breath and tried to move away.

"What's going on?" Elanor asked as she looked at Weston.

"Nothing good," Weston replied. "Let's monitor this closely."

Elanor followed him toward the saloon.

The man laughed loud enough for the whole street to hear. "Still shy, huh? Thought you'd come back to settle old scores. Figured you'd be a little braver by now, Sheriff."

Nora, who had been tying up her horse near the store, drew her focus toward the scene, her eyes narrowing. "What's his deal?" she asked.

Elanor flinched as she watched the exchange, sensing something bigger going on beneath the surface—something about the sheriff's past he wasn't sharing with them.

Boone strolled back from the saloon just as the agitation in the air grew thick. "Looks like ol' Sheriff's got himself a fan," he quipped, though his light tone couldn't quite mask the concern in his eyes.

Weston remained silent, his eyes fixed on the sheriff as the man from the saloon continued to talk, loud and animated. Elanor felt the unease ripple through the group, but no one moved yet. Whatever the sheriff was hiding, it was clearly something that couldn't stay buried much longer.

The sheriff's body remained stiff, his every movement laced with unease. The man who had recognized him from the saloon kept talking, his words slurred from drink, but there was a sharpness to them—something that made it clear he wasn't just making casual conversation.

"Well, well, I'd know that face anywhere," the man slurred, clapping the sheriff on the back with far too much familiarity. "Never thought I'd see you again after what happened back in Leto."

The sheriff's face tightened, his hand twitching near his gun, but he didn't respond. Elanor's stomach flipped.

Leto? What had happened there?

With the sheriff on edge, ready to act, Elanor, Nora, and Weston closed in on the group outside the saloon.

The strange man, seemingly oblivious to the tension radiating from the sheriff, continued, his grin widening. "Thought you got outta the law game after that mess. Can't say I blame you—things got pretty ugly."

Before the sheriff could respond, Weston stepped forward, his expression neutral but his posture radiating authority. "Everything alright, Sheriff?" he asked.

The sheriff shot Weston a look of relief, though his voice was strained when he finally spoke. "Fine," he muttered. "Just a misunderstanding."

The man from the saloon wasn't so easily deterred. "Misunderstanding, huh?" His grin turned sly. "You always were good at those. Folks back in Leto still talk about you, you know. Can't forget a man who—"

"That's enough." The sheriff's voice cut through the man's words, cold and commanding.

Nora stepped in with a forced smile. "Well, we've got business to attend to, so if you don't mind, we'll be on our way."

The man raised his hands in mock surrender, his grin never faltering. "Whatever you say, missy. But you might wanna ask your sheriff friend here about his time in Leto. Got a real interesting history, this one."

Elanor exchanged a glance with Nora and Weston, the unspoken question hanging between them: What was the sheriff hiding?

Boone, ever the one to diffuse tension with humor, sauntered over, his usual lazy grin in place. "Come on now, folks. Let's focus on the present. A stiff drink, no talk of the past— you catchin' my drift?"

The man sneered but backed off, shooting one last look at the sheriff before heading back into the saloon. "We'll see how long you can keep runnin' from it," he muttered, just loud enough for the sheriff to hear. Louder: "Hell, I think Cletus is inside somewhere. We both know he don't like you as much as I do. Maybe he'll have you singin' like a canary."

The sheriff didn't respond, his body rigid as he watched the man disappear into the saloon. His hand finally dropped from his gun, but the stiffness in his shoulders betrayed his lingering unease. "Let's just get what we need and move on," he muttered.

Elanor peered at Weston, who clearly shared her concern. Whatever had happened in Leto, it was obvious the sheriff wasn't keen on sharing. And now that his past was catching up with him, the group had more to worry about than just Merrick's gang.

Weston broke the quiet first, turning toward the general store. "We'll deal with it later," he muttered. "For now, let's get what we came for."

The group followed him into the store, where the atmosphere was markedly calmer. The musty smell of dry goods and leather greeted them as they stepped inside, shelves lined with supplies they sorely needed after their trek through the mountains.

Nora promptly assumed responsibility, meticulously examining the shelves. "We're low on everything," she said, grabbing a basket. "Food, water, ammo. Let's stock up on enough to get us to Tawa."

Elanor nodded, though her mind was still spinning with the sheriff's strange behavior. She tried to focus as she moved through the store, grabbing essentials, but she couldn't shake the run-in at the saloon.

Weston moved in silence, his sharp eyes scanning the shelves, but he was distracted.

When Elanor caught up to him near the back of the store, she hesitated before speaking. "You think the sheriff's okay?" she asked softly, low enough that the others couldn't hear.

Weston's eyes flicked toward the door, where the sheriff stood outside, his back to the group, keeping watch. "He's not telling us everything," Weston said after a beat. "But we'll have to let him handle it. For now, we stay focused."

Elanor nodded, though the unease lingered. She wondered how deep the sheriff's past went and whether it would eventually become their problem.

Boone sauntered over with a grin. "You know, after a day like this, I could use a bottle of whiskey. Who's with me?"

"Maybe later," Elanor said, her voice soft, appreciative of his humor.

Boone winked. "I'll hold you to that."

Supplies gathered, the group headed back outside, the sun casting long shadows over the town. The sheriff hadn't said a word since the encounter, his eyes fixed on the saloon. Weston paid for the supplies, and the group stepped back into the sunlight.

Nora, ever pragmatic, took charge once again. "Alright, let's get a plan together. We're not staying here any longer than we need to."

Elanor eyed the sheriff, who remained silent and tense. Whatever was haunting him, it wasn't going away anytime soon.

The group exited the town quickly, weaving through the sparse afternoon crowd and skirting the bustling marketplace as they made their way toward an area where they could mount their horses. Elanor noticed the sheriff hanging back, keeping close to the edges of the street, head low. He wasn't the only one on edge—Nora's sharp eyes scanned the faces around them, her jaw set as if bracing for something.

As they reached the outskirts of town, a lanky man sitting outside a low, unmarked building leaned forward, squinting as he watched them pass. "Hey," he called, nodding at Weston, who stopped and gave the man a cautious look. "You folks lookin' for someone?" the man asked, adjusting the brim of his hat. "Word spreads quickly in these parts, and I understand you're searchin' for Tawa."

The sheriff tensed, his hand inching closer to his side, but Weston answered calmly. "That's right. We've got business with him but haven't had much luck with directions."

One by one, the man looked them over, his eyes lingering a little longer on the sheriff before he turned back to Weston. "You'll have better luck in Leto," he said, scratching his chin thoughtfully. "Tawa don't linger in these parts often, but folks in Leto'll know how to get word to him—or maybe even where he's headed next."

Elanor glanced at the sheriff, who looked away, hands clenched at his sides as if he were just barely holding something back.

Nora kept her tone neutral but curious. "Appreciate the help. Any idea who in Leto we oughta speak to?"

The man gave a low chuckle, his eyes twinkling with a hint of mischief. "Leto ain't exactly known for its helpful citizens, but there's an old scout by the name of Cole. People say he can find anyone or anything in those parts." He looked back to the sheriff, narrowing his eyes slightly. "Not everyone takes to strangers easily down there, though. Best be prepared."

Boone huffed, oblivious to the sheriff's unease. "If it's drinkin' and cards, I'm prepared as anyone, friend."

Elanor suppressed a smile, but her attention was drawn back to the sheriff, whose face had gone pale. He hesitated as if he wanted to turn around and ride back into the mountains, rather than head in the direction this conversation was leading.

Weston thanked the man with a nod, then turned to the sheriff, his voice measured. "Leto it is, then."

The sheriff hesitated, and Elanor caught a glimpse of something—fear, or maybe shame—flash in his eyes before he straightened and gave a reluctant nod.

"Guess we'll see what Leto's got to offer," he said, though his voice lacked confidence.

Nora's gaze shifted back to the man, who told the group about gaining information to find Tawa in Leto. She cleared her throat and approached him again, her hand resting casually on her hip.

"Before we go, think you could point us in the right direction?" Nora asked. "To Leto, that is."

The man cocked an eyebrow, eyes flicking to the sheriff before giving a sly grin. "Well, Leto's quite a ways off. Ain't the easiest place to get to, either." He hesitated, glancing at the group with calculating eyes. "Be worth somethin' for me to share that kinda knowledge, don't you think?"

Nora's jaw clenched. She looked at the sheriff, who met her eyes with a sheepish expression. "I, uh . . . don't actually know the way to Leto from here," he admitted, scratching the back of his neck. The group's frustration was palpable, a murmur passing among them.

Boone stepped forward, uncorking his flask with a practiced flick of his wrist. "How about this for a start?" he said, extending it toward the man with a mock-serious expression. "A taste of the finest—my own collateral for some directions."

The man hesitated, eyeing the flask with surprise and reluctant amusement.

Before he could respond, Nora cut in, digging into her pocket and pulling out a few coins. "This enough to loosen your tongue?" she asked with a knowing smirk.

The man's grin widened as he took the money, tucking it away. "Head south till you hit the dried riverbed, then follow that westward. You'll see a ridge when the sun's just about to set. Leto's on the other side. But watch your backs—money and supplies like you got draws attention."

Nora nodded, her expression as guarded as ever. "Thanks for the tip," she replied before stepping back toward the group.

They exchanged glances, the reality of the journey ahead sinking in. A mixture of apprehension and determination settled over Elanor as they prepared to leave.

Leto held answers—but it was clearly more than that for the sheriff. She exchanged a look with Nora, who shared a look of curiosity and concern.

They accelerated their horses, departing from the town and focusing their attention on Leto. The sheriff rode just ahead, shoulders tense, and Elanor couldn't shake the feeling that whatever lay beyond in Leto would unravel more than just the mystery of finding Tawa.

CHAPTER NINE

The group rode out of the town in tense silence. Elanor was nestled in front of Weston on his horse, the warmth of his arm steady around her waist as the afternoon sun beat down on them. The direction toward Leto was clear, but unease sat heavily on the group as if the dust trailing behind them carried an echo of what laid ahead.

Weston glanced down at her. "How you holding up?"

Elanor managed a small smile, though the lingering effects of her near-death experience on the mountain still left her unsettled. "I think . . . a little better. At least we're not aimlessly wandering anymore."

Ahead of them, Nora kept her gaze to the horizon, glancing back occasionally. "Good to know there's a direction, but it sounds like Leto's not exactly where you want to be caught off guard." She shot a look at the sheriff, raising an eyebrow. "Not like Bodie. Not at all."

The sheriff shifted uncomfortably in his saddle, glancing to the side, avoiding her look. He cleared his throat, his voice tense. "Leto . . . it's not like Bodie, no. Rough town. Plenty of folks who wouldn't hesitate to cause us trouble. Maybe we oughta . . . rethink going there."

Boone let out a loud laugh from the rear, slapping his thigh. "Oh, come now, Sheriff! Didn't take you for the nervous type! Thought you were the kind to go charging into any ol' place."

"Maybe not this place," the sheriff muttered, glancing nervously over his shoulder. "There are people there who . . . remember things differently than I'd like." His tone softened, almost pleading, "It's just . . . not the safest place. Even for our kind of trouble."

Nora shot him a skeptical look. "What're you hiding, Sheriff? Sounds like you got more than just a few skeletons in that ol' closet."

The sheriff opened his mouth, hesitating, fingers clenching around the reins. "Look, Leto isn't kind to those with . . . mistakes in their past. I did the best I could back then, and now folks there don't see it the same way."

Elanor spun slightly to look at him, noting the crease of tension in his brow. "What are you saying? We're trying to find Tawa, but we need to know what we're walking into."

The sheriff's jaw tightened, his eyes still averted. "Let's just say I'm not the man they'd want to see walkin' back into town." He paused, voice barely above a whisper, "Or . . . if they do, it'd only be to settle an old score."

"Good ol' unfinished business," Boone said with a laugh, though it had a nervous edge. "Guess I was right, huh? Seems like there's more to you than that star on your chest."

The sheriff gave him a withering look but didn't reply.

After a beat of silence, Weston finally spoke. "We're all carrying something, Sheriff. No one's asking for perfection. But if there's anything you can share to help us avoid more trouble, now's the time."

The sheriff hesitated, then sighed, his shoulders slumping slightly. "I'll do my best to keep us under the radar. But just . . . keep a low profile once we're there. And if I say we need to leave, don't ask questions."

Nora shook her head, lips pursed. "All this mystery don't sit right. But if that's the price, we'll have to pay it. Just hope it's worth it."

Boone piped up: "So, Sheriff," he drawled, "you ever gonna let us in on the real name they know you by in Leto? I reckon it ain't just 'Sheriff,' right?" He waggled his brows at the others, casting a cheeky grin.

The sheriff scowled, the corners of his mouth pulling tight. "Names don't matter as much as you'd think, Boone. Not out here." His face darkened, a flicker of something painful in his expression. "You folks wouldn't know me by it, anyhow. And that's for the better."

Shaking her head, Elanor said, "I think names can be significant. It's the only thing I can remember right now. I'd hate for it to lose its importance."

"Fine, fine," Boone replied, clearly undeterred. "I'll just call you Mr. Mysterious. Seems to suit you." He snickered, but when no one laughed, he shrugged and let the silence fall again.

Elanor took a steadying breath and leaned slightly back into Weston, feeling his warmth through her back. The sheriff's story tugged at her, a growing curiosity bubbling up within her. She wasn't sure why she cared so much; maybe it was how he'd looked—almost haunted—when he'd spoken about Leto. Or perhaps it was because the sheriff, for all his bluster, was familiar in a way she couldn't explain.

Weston broke the quiet. "We'll handle whatever's waiting in Leto. Just maintain your composure, Sheriff. We've all got our reasons for being here."

The sheriff gave a short nod, his face betraying a mixture of gratitude and guardedness. "Guess you're right," he said quietly. "I appreciate it. Just . . . let's keep things as quiet as possible."

The rest of the group murmured in agreement, though Elanor couldn't shake the feeling that they were heading straight into a storm they were unprepared for.

As they rode, Nora pulled her horse alongside Elanor and Weston's. "You alright, Elanor?" she asked, eyes keen as they searched Elanor's face. "You don't look too comfortable there."

Elanor managed a small smile, brushing her fingers across the reins. "I'm alright. Just . . . a little uneasy about what's waiting for us in Leto, I guess."

Nora nodded, glancing toward the sheriff. "Well, whatever's there, it's bound to bring more answers than questions—if he'll open up, that is." She paused, then gave Elanor a reassuring look. "Just stick close. We're in this together, no matter what lies up ahead."

A strange warmth touched Elanor's cheeks at Nora's words, and as she looked forward at the sheriff riding, shoulders slightly hunched, she understood that, for better or worse, they were becoming a kind of makeshift family.

The group rode under the harsh afternoon sun, its relentless heat beating down as they followed a meandering trail through the desert. The ache in her muscles quivered from days on horseback, a dull reminder of how far they'd come. But as they traveled, a niggling feeling crept into her mind—a sense of something missing or overlooked.

Elanor shifted slightly in the saddle, glancing back at Weston. "Why didn't we stay longer back in that last town? We barely rested."

Weston glanced at her, his brows knitting as he thought about it. "Would you want to stick around for more people to come after the sheriff and, by relation, us?"

The sheriff looked down, avoiding eye contact with the others.

"With the interruption with the sheriff, we couldn't resupply properly," Weston added, "and time hasn't been on our side."

"Time?" Elanor repeated, confusion coloring her voice. "How do you mean?"

"It can't be good going a long time without your memory. The sooner we get that worked out, the better."

"It's only been a few days, hasn't it?"

Weston's gaze lingered on her, something flickering in his eyes. "El . . . it's been over two and a half weeks since we left Bodie."

The words struck her deeply. "Two and a half weeks?"

Weston nodded slowly, concern etching into his features as he watched her, gauging her reaction. "You didn't realize?"

Elanor looked down at her hands, feeling the weight of time slipping through her fingers. Her mind raced, trying to recall each day, each night spent under the stars. But there were gaps—moments that were disjointed, as though pieces had vanished, leaving only fragments of memory in their place.

"I . . . I thought it was just a few days," she murmured, her voice barely a whisper. "I can't remember some of it . . . my memory is slipping away from me again."

Weston's hand gently rested on her shoulder, grounding her as her thoughts spun. "It's alright," he said softly. "You've been through a lot. Just focus on what you need to right now."

Elanor met his eyes, searching for reassurance, but found something else there that made her feel he understood more than he let on. She held his gaze for a beat longer before looking away, her mind buzzing with questions she couldn't quite form.

Nora, still nearby, broke the silence. "Don't let the past muddle things too much. We've got enough on our plates just figuring out how to make it to Leto in one piece." She shot the sheriff a sidelong glance, her expression unreadable. "Though I suppose the sheriff knows Leto well enough to get us there."

At the mention of Leto, flashes of something dark crossed the sheriff's face—an unease he quickly masked as he straightened in his saddle.

As they rode farther, the sheriff's face grew grimmer, the strain beneath his composed exterior becoming harder to conceal. Elanor noticed his grip on the reins tighten each time Leto came up in conversation, his jaw clenched as though he were holding back something heavy.

Nora turned to him, eyebrows raised. "Anything else you'd like to share with us before we march into Leto, Sheriff?"

He looked away, his eyes fixed on the rugged horizon, his voice defiant. "Leto's got parts of my life I'd rather leave in the past."

Boone chuckled. "Sounds like a place with plenty of stories—most likely the kind you don't share."

The sheriff's expression hardened, but he didn't argue, his silence seeming to confirm Boone's speculation.

A flicker of sympathy and something else filled Elanor—a strange familiarity that tightened her chest. She couldn't pinpoint why his words resonated with her, but they stirred an unease deep within as if his past somehow intertwined with a part of her own she couldn't quite reach.

Nora tilted her head toward him, and her voice softened. "Everyone's got shadows, Sheriff. If you're runnin' from yours, you're not alone. But the sooner we know what's lurking in Leto, the better."

The sheriff's shoulders slumped slightly, his eyes shifting toward Elanor before quickly looking away, his expression pained. "Guess you're right. Home's got a way of bringing back things you thought were buried."

Elanor's eyes lingered on him, her questions about the sheriff growing with each mile. And yet, her sense of time slipping was still more unsettling—of losing memories she hadn't even made. This disorienting discovery shivered through her spine. Her mind raced, trying to piece together the fragmented memories that drifted away like sand in the wind. The sunsets she couldn't recall, the starlit nights that were gone from her mind—how many had she lost? It was as if whole experiences had been plucked from her consciousness. This jarring realization made her question her memory and her very perception of reality. How much more had slipped away without her notice?

The group slowed as the trail opened to a narrow stream, the sound of running water an unexpected balm amid the dry, endless desert. The stream wound through a shallow, rocky basin, flanked by clusters of scrubby bushes and low, wiry trees that clung stubbornly to life despite the sun's relentless heat. Patches of sagebrush dotted the banks, and the air held the faint, earthy smell of damp soil—a rarity out here.

An odd sense of relief as they approached the water relaxed Elanor's tense muscles, and as Weston helped her down from the horse, she crouched beside the stream, dipping her fingers into the coolness, savoring the contrast. The sound of the trickling water calmed her buzzing thoughts, the ripples and eddies mesmerizing as they flowed over smooth stones. She caught her reflection in the water's surface for a moment—a wavering image framed by her black curls, now wild and tangled from days in the desert, streaked with grit and clinging sweat. Her skin, sun-darkened and marked by the harshness of their journey, was more worn than before, the hollows of her cheeks pronounced.

Next to her, Nora's reflection appeared equally worn. Their faces shared a layer of dirt and fatigue, their hair similarly unkempt and wind-tossed. There was a strange kinship in that fleeting image—two women molded by the same unforgiving terrain, standing side by side against whatever laid ahead.

Nora knelt beside her, glancing at her with a sidelong look. "You look like you've seen a ghost, Elanor," she said with a half-smile, her tone softened by genuine concern. "What's on your mind?"

Elanor hesitated, watching the water ripple between her fingers. "I don't know, Nora. It's like . . . things are slipping or blurring. I remember leaving Bodie, but the rest feels like flashes I can't piece together."

Nora's face softened, her hand resting on Elanor's shoulder briefly. "The desert here has the ability to deceive. Plays tricks on your mind." She paused, searching Elanor's face. "You're not alone, though. We're all in this together, alright?"

Elanor tried to smile, her chest easing just a little. "Thanks, Nora. It's just strange, feeling so . . . lost."

Nora gave her a reassuring nod. "I get it. Just stay grounded. You're stronger than whatever doubts are tryin' to creep in."

Elanor looked back to the water, the steady rhythm of the stream lulling her frayed nerves. The thin ribbon of water here was a lifeline in the desert, an oasis in the barren terrain surrounding them. With Nora's words and the grounding presence of the stream, a renewed resolve to keep moving forward with the group and focus on what she *did* have filled her mind: her companions by her side.

As the horses drank deeply from the stream, Weston moved to the water's edge and looked back at the group. He rubbed the back of his neck, his gaze lingering on Elanor longer than the others, a hint of worry in his eyes.

"We're pushing too hard," he said. "A rest here will do us good." He didn't wait for anyone to argue, untying a bedroll from his horse and tossing it to the ground.

A sense of relief that he had noticed her weariness reassured Elanor. Her legs were leaden, and her mind still buzzed with the unsettling realization that time had slipped from her without notice. She sank onto a patch of soft grass by the stream, watching the sunlight play on the water as it wound through the stones.

Nora dropped down beside her, rolling her shoulders with a sigh. "Well, the cowboy's right about something for once," she said with a wry smile. "No point getting to Leto half-dead."

The sheriff, however, remained standing a few paces back, his posture stiff as he scanned the surroundings. He'd been dismissive since they'd left the town, and now, with the opportunity to rest, his tension only grew. His face was lined with worry, eyes narrowing as he peered back toward the distant horizon.

"What's got you so nervous?" Boone asked, raising an eyebrow as he took a long drink from his canteen. He tilted his head at the sheriff, curiosity sparking on his face. "You actin' like we're ridin' into a trap or somethin'."

The sheriff didn't respond immediately, walking to the edge of the water. His eyes dropped to the stream, where he stared at his reflection for a long moment. "It's nothing," he muttered, though the edge in his voice betrayed him. He cleared his throat and adjusted his hat, but he couldn't mask the hint of fear that had crept into his expression.

Glancing from Elanor to the sheriff, Weston didn't let the moment pass. "You've been skittish since we left the last town," he said bluntly. "And not just because we're headin' to Leto."

For a moment, it looked as though the sheriff might brush off the comment, but something in Weston's steady look—or perhaps the exhaustion in the group's eyes—made him pause.

"It's been a long time since I set foot anywhere near Leto," he admitted quietly, his attention still fixed on the water. "Let's just say I hesitate at digging up the past."

Elanor listened closely, her curiosity piqued by the sheriff's unease. There was something oddly familiar about the way he spoke, a strange familiarity that stirred at the back of her mind. "A lot of questions around Leto and your connections to it," she said.

The sheriff shot her a brief, guarded look before shrugging. "Everyone has a past, Miss Elanor. And sometimes, it's better to leave it buried."

But Elanor couldn't shake the feeling that his past held something significant—something that tugged at her like a half-remembered dream. Her attention drifted back to the sheriff's reflection in the water, his face partially obscured by the rippling surface, and for a fleeting moment, a pang of recognition lingered. But the feeling slipped away as quickly as it came, leaving her with more questions than answers.

Most of the group settled into a tense silence, each lost in their thoughts. Weston, however, continued to watch Elanor, his expression unreadable but concerned. After the group set up camp, he broke the quiet again. "Get some rest while you can. Tomorrow's gonna be rough."

Elanor nodded, her eyes lingering on the sheriff for a moment longer before she closed them, letting the sounds of the stream fill the silence. Her mind spun with questions she couldn't yet answer, the pieces of her memory and the mysteries around her refusing to fall into place.

Elanor opened her eyes as evening settled around them; the warm glow of the setting sun bathed the group in amber light. They had set up makeshift spots for the night, each person close enough to the stream to feel its coolness but spread out to give one another space. The quiet had softened them, allowing Elanor a moment for some of the strain in her chest to ease.

Leaning back against a fallen log, Elanor watched as Weston tended to the horses, his movements deliberate and calm. She'd grown to rely on his quiet strength, though she hadn't meant to; he was steady, grounded in ways she felt like she was only pretending to be. He caught her eye as she watched and gave a slight nod, a reassuring look that made her feel safe and oddly vulnerable.

But as her eyes drifted away from Weston, her mind tugged her somewhere deeper. A small, unbidden flash—a scene she couldn't place —surfaced in her mind. She looked out at the water, just like this, though it wasn't a stream. A lake, maybe? No, the water was too vast, too endless, stretching out in every direction under an expansive, gray sky.

She stood on the shore, arms wrapped around herself as a cold wind blew. Beside her, the hazy outline of someone—someone familiar. Elanor blinked, and for a second, the figure's face sharpened: dark hair, a strong profile, a voice saying her name so gently, it made her heart ache. Then the image vanished, leaving her with only the echo of that voice and a coldness that was out of place in the warmth of the desert evening.

Her hand went to her chest, feeling the quick, heavy rhythm of her pulse, the memory's intensity still gripping her. Her fingers brushed against the silver locket, its cool surface grounding her amidst the storm of emotions. "Weston," she whispered without meaning, the name slipping out like a reflex as if she'd known it long before she'd met him here.

"Hmm?" Weston's voice broke into her thoughts, and she looked up to see him watching her with quiet curiosity.

She hesitated, the memory fading too quickly to grasp. "Nothing," she said, shaking her head. "I think . . . I think I just remembered something. It's hazy, though."

He took a step closer, curiosity flickering in his eyes. "What'd you remember?"

She attempted to articulate her thoughts, yet the specifics were swiftly vanishing. All that remained was the feeling—like a yearning, a sense that whoever had been beside her in that memory had once meant everything. "I don't know," she said quietly, frustration edging her voice. "The memories slip away before I can grasp them."

Weston's eyes softened, and he crouched beside her, placing a steadying hand on her shoulder. "What about when you do get your memories back—what do you plan to do?" he asked gently.

Elanor paused. "I'm not sure," she admitted. "I haven't put too much thought into it because my plan has always been to go home. But I don't know where that is." Her words floated in the cool night air, reflecting her deep-seated confusion and longing for answers.

Weston's expression shifted subtly, a flicker of sadness crossing his features, though he said nothing more about it. His touch remained comforting as he added, "Sometimes the memories that matter come back in pieces. Just give it time."

Elanor nodded, appreciating the reassurance, despite the inexplicable sense of loss tugging at her heart. She leaned into the quiet around them, the sound of the stream nearby lulling her back to the present. The others around the campfire hadn't noticed her brief unease, and she was grateful for that.

As she lay back down, her eyes drifting closed, she tried to hold onto the feeling from her fleeting memory—the warmth of a familiar presence beside her. But just like the fading light, it slipped away, leaving her wrapped in the silence of the night.

Elanor stirred awake, her back aching as she shifted on the rough ground. She blinked, disoriented, realizing she was wrapped in her bedroll, lying a few feet away from the log she'd been leaning against earlier. For a moment, she tried to piece together how she'd ended up here. Had Weston carried her over? Or had she somehow moved herself, then forgotten it? The haziness of her memory gnawed at her, leaving her uneasy.

As she adjusted, a murmur of voices drifted over from the other side of the camp. She recognized the low, gravelly tone of the sheriff. His voice was laced with something sharper than usual. Curiosity tugged at her, and she propped herself up quietly, careful not to make a sound as she angled herself to listen.

". . . shouldn't be going to Leto," the sheriff was saying. "There's no good reason for it; the fewer questions we ask there, the better."

Nora's response was calm but firm. "You're hiding somethin', Sheriff. You've made that obvious." She let out a humorless chuckle. "Hell, even Boone's noticed, and he spends half his days pickling his brain with whiskey."

The sheriff exhaled sharply, his voice dropping so low, Elanor had to strain to hear. "It's not somethin' I can just explain. There are things linked to my name—things that don't belong to the man I am now."

"Or the man you're pretending to be?" Nora shot back. "I don't get it, Sheriff. Why'd you come along if you're so scared of what might catch up to you?"

There was a long pause, and Elanor held her breath, waiting.

"Because I owe it to . . . someone." The sheriff's voice was barely audible, his words laced with regret. "Someone I couldn't save back then. Going to Leto means risking everything, but if it'll help her . . ."

"Her?" Nora's curiosity was piqued. "Who are we talkin' about?"

"It's not . . . it's not something you'd understand." The sheriff's tone turned defensive, and Elanor almost felt the pain he was holding back.

Nora didn't press further. Instead, she said softly, "Look, whatever you're holdin' onto, it's eatin' at you, Sheriff. We're all runnin' from somethin'—maybe that's why we ended up together. But whatever this is, maybe it's time to face it."

The sheriff sighed, his voice wavering as he said, "I tried to forget it all, you know. The person I was. But sometimes . . ." He paused, almost as if speaking more to himself than to Nora. "Sometimes, when I look at Miss Elanor, it's like I'm lookin' at someone else from my past. Someone I let down."

Elanor's pulse quickened, a shiver prickling up her spine. Had she understood him correctly? The sheriff thought he recognized something about another person in her. She leaned in, straining to hear more, but her elbow slipped on the bedroll, causing her to stumble forward slightly. She froze, hoping neither of them had noticed.

After a pause, Nora spoke again, her tone softer. "Maybe that person you lost is still with you somehow, giving you another chance to set things right."

The sheriff didn't respond, but Elanor sensed his hesitation, as though he was turning Nora's words over in his mind. Eventually, he muttered, "Maybe. Perhaps it's just my imagination playin' tricks."

Their conversation tapered off, the night settling into silence once more.

Elanor lay back on her bedroll, her pulse quickening as she tried to make sense of what she'd overheard. It was as if puzzle pieces were beginning to surface, fragments of something she didn't yet understand.

But one thing was clear—whatever lay ahead, she wasn't the only one haunted by the past.

CHAPTER TEN

Pale hues of dawn slowly illuminated the camp, revealing the group as they began to stir. The chill of the night still lingered in the air, a sharp contrast to the heat that would soon bear down on them, and a slight shiver ran down Elanor's spine as she stretched, brushing the remnants of last night's strange memories from her mind. Around her, everyone was moving with purpose, packing up gear with a quiet intensity.

Already awake and moving, Weston glanced over to where Elanor was rolling up her bedroll. "You sleep alright?" he asked, keeping his tone casual though his eyes lingered on her, searching.

Elanor gave a slight nod, though her thoughts were jumbled. "I think so. Just . . . didn't feel like enough." She met his gaze briefly, finding comfort in his steady expression before returning to her task.

Nora, gathering her belongings briskly, spoke to the group, saying, "We'd better get moving before the sun decides to scorch us," as she watched the eastern horizon. Her commanding presence set the rhythm for everyone, and soon, they all moved in step, preparing to leave.

Despite the early hour, Boone rubbed his eyes and muttered as he stumbled around his horse, still having an air of barely contained mischief about him. He nudged Elanor with a grin, holding up a tin cup half-filled with something he must've kept from the night before. "Last sip of courage?" he asked, raising his cup with a wink.

Elanor rolled her eyes, smiling despite herself. "That won't get you to Leto any faster, Boone."

"Only makes it seem that way," Boone shot back with a grin, downing the last drop, then packing his things with a flourish.

The sheriff moved silently, carefully loading his bags onto his horse with a closed off and guarded expression. Elanor noticed that he kept his focus away from the group, his jaw taut.

Weston nodded as the sun rose, casting a golden light over the land. "Alright," he said, "let's keep the pace steady. We've got a long way yet."

They mounted their horses, and as Elanor settled in front of Weston once again, the familiar strength of his arm nestled against her. It was a small gesture, but his presence and focus kept her grounded. She couldn't help but feel a flicker of gratitude as they began to ride.

As they continued along the winding path toward Leto, the morning sun climbed higher, gradually burning away the last traces of coolness lingering from the night. The group pressed on under a sky that shifted from soft pastels to a vivid blue, the air warming with every step. Hours slipped by in steady progress, marked only by brief pauses to adjust packs or exchange a few words.

By midday, the heat had settled in, pressing against them. The sun arced overhead, casting sharp shadows and drawing beads of sweat along their brows. As the day wore on, the brightness began to mellow, bathing the world in a golden hue as the light softened.

The others gradually drifted ahead, leaving Weston and Elanor in a small, quiet pocket of space. The landscape stretched out around them, rough and open yet gentled by the warmth of the afternoon light. The sway of the horse beneath them matched the gentle rhythm of their breathing, settling Elanor's thoughts.

Weston broke the silence: "Have you ever thought about where you'd go if you could pick anywhere in the world?"

She was taken aback by the question. She considered it momentarily, a little smile tugging at the corner of her mouth. "Anywhere?" she repeated, tilting her head. "Honestly, I haven't really thought about that before . . . but I think somewhere far from all of this." She gestured at the vast desert with a small laugh. "Maybe somewhere green, with water —a place where everything isn't trying to kill you."

Weston chuckled, his arm around her waist squeezing slightly, pulling her closer. "You and me both," he murmured. "Though, knowing you, you'd probably get bored of somewhere safe and quiet in no time."

She turned slightly in the saddle to look back at him, catching his faint smile and the sparkle in his eye. "You think I'd get bored?" she asked, raising a playful eyebrow.

"Oh, I know it," Weston replied, teasing but soft. "You'd have a campfire started by the end of the first night and a whole adventure planned by morning. You're not the kind to sit still for long."

A light blush warmed her cheeks at his words, surprised by how well he understood her. "Maybe you're right," she admitted. "I do like a little bit of excitement."

"A little?" He let out a soft laugh, the sound vibrating through her back. "You're halfway across a desert, running from bandits and whatever else this land decides to throw at us. I'd say that's more than 'a little' adventure, wouldn't you?"

Elanor smiled, the edges of her nerves softened by his warmth. "Guess I like to live on the edge."

He squeezed her waist, his touch sending a gentle thrill up her spine. "You're full of surprises, El," he said, his voice softer, almost reverent. "Every time I think I've got you figured out, you turn around and prove me wrong."

Something fluttered inside Elanor at his words, a feeling both thrilling and terrifying. She hadn't expected him to see her this way— hadn't expected anyone to. But before she could respond, Weston went on, his tone thoughtful again.

"How's the memory coming along?" he asked, his voice tinged with a hint of something unreadable. "Anything of note?"

The question lingered between them, sending a chill through her, despite the day's warmth. "I try pushing against my mind every day," she murmured. "It's like trying to fit together pieces of a puzzle that refuse to connect." She exhaled, a trace of frustration woven into her breath. "I just want to understand where I came from—who I was before all this.

But whenever I try, it slips away. Even as I explain it, it feels familiar, like I'm repeating myself."

Weston's leaned forward, his breath warm against her ear. "Maybe you're exactly where you need to be right now," he murmured.

Elanor's heart skipped at the closeness, the warmth of his hand, the softness in his voice. She turned her head slightly, meeting his gaze as best she could, their faces close enough to see how his eyes softened as he looked at her.

For a long moment, they stayed like that, wrapped in a quiet understanding. She felt her pulse quicken, her breath catching at just how close they were, how natural it was to be in his arms like this.

A faint smile tugging at his lips, Weston said, "Guess we make a pretty good team, don't we?"

"Yeah," she said, her voice softer than she intended. "Yeah, we do."

He chuckled, the sound humming through her like a familiar melody. "So, what's next for Elanor the adventure-seeker?" he asked, his tone light but carrying an edge of something more profound.

Elanor gave a little shrug. "Guess I'll just keep going wherever this journey takes me," she said, glancing up at him with a small, genuine smile. "As long as you're there, I think I'll be alright."

Weston's hand tightened gently at her waist again, his expression warm. "Then I'll be right here every step of the way."

They lapsed into a comfortable silence, and something settled inside Elanor—like a piece of herself she hadn't understood to be missing. She held onto that feeling, letting it carry her forward as they continued their journey, the sun casting long shadows on the path behind them.

The trail grew rockier as they continued, with stretches of rough ground requiring a slower, more cautious pace. The horses' hooves clattered against loose stones, and Elanor leaned into Weston. They had been riding in relative silence when a distant figure appeared on the horizon, moving swiftly along the trail ahead.

As the group paused to assess, the figure drew closer, dust billowing up behind his horse, the sun glinting off something metallic on his saddle. Elanor caught a glimpse of a lean man dressed in worn leathers, his face partially hidden beneath a wide-brimmed hat, eyes sharp and fixed on them intensely.

Weston's arm instinctively tightened around her as he greeted the newcomer. "What brings you out here in a hurry?"

The man's focus swept over them, assessing, before settling back on Weston. "Name's Deangelo," he introduced himself, voice rough and dusty like the terrain. "I've been sent with a message—a message that couldn't wait."

Nora shifted in her saddle, crossing her arms with a skeptical look. "Sent by who?" she asked.

Deangelo dismounted and reached into his coat pocket, drawing out a folded paper. "The man who sent me knows you're trying to reach Tawa. Thought you'd need a bit of guidance, given the . . . complications on your trail."

Elanor caught Weston's questioning look as Deangelo held out the paper to him, fingers lingering on it. "Be warned—the path to Tawa isn't a straight line. Merrick's men are moving faster than you think. They sure wouldn't mind cashing in on the trouble."

A chill ran through Elanor at his words. Merrick's gang had already proven their danger, and the idea of others lurking made her grip the saddle a little tighter.

Weston unfolded the paper with a wary glance at the man. His jaw tightened as he read, then he passed the paper to Nora, who skimmed it with narrowed eyes. "It's a warning, alright."

Boone piped in with his usual casual tone. "So, this friend of yours —is he our friend, too? Or just someone looking to make us lose sleep?"

Deangelo's expression softened slightly. "'Friend' might be stretchin' it. But he's no enemy. He wants you to make it. There's a guide waiting for you by Leto to help. If you can reach it."

The sheriff, who had been silent until now, looked uneasy. He shifted in his saddle, avoiding Deangelo's gaze. "And what exactly would this 'friend' be looking to find in Leto?" he asked, voice laced with caution.

Deangelo looked at him, eyes lingering with recognition. "Maybe the same thing you're wantin' to avoid."

The sheriff scowled, his usual guarded expression replaced by something slightly more vulnerable. He held back as if on the verge of saying something, but instead, he looked away.

"So," Nora broke in, "we follow the trail and trust this 'friend' is doing us a favor." She arched an eyebrow. "Any other warnings you'd care to share?"

Deangelo nodded, serious. "Just what the note says—Merrick's men are tracking you. But they're not the only ones. Stay sharp."

With a final nod, he mounted his horse. Not waiting for a reply, he nudged his horse forward. Deangelo disappeared down the trail, leaving the group to process his warning.

For a moment, they all sat in silence. Deangelo's words lingered like a shadow.

"Well," Weston said, his voice cutting through the silence, "we always knew trouble might follow us. We'll head to Leto, but we better be ready for anything."

Elanor took a steadying breath. The trail toward Leto loomed, filled with unknowns.

With a silent exchange of looks, they urged their horses forward.

As the group rode on, the intensity of the afternoon sun began to wane, casting long shadows over the rugged landscape. The recent warning from Deangelo played heavily on everyone's mind, and a sad quiet fell over the group as they pressed forward.

As they passed a particularly steep section, a wave of dizziness overcame Elanor. The landscape blurred, and her vision tunneled, drawing her away from the present.

Elanor was no longer on horseback but standing on a bustling city street, the noise and energy of a distant memory pulling her in. Elanor looked around, heart racing, as flashes of a past life engulfed her senses: tall buildings, taxis honking, and the sound of laughter nearby. Warm fingers intertwined with hers, a smile tugging at the edges of her lips as she looked up to see a man's face, his light eyes filled with adoration. It was . . . it was him.

She whispered softly, "Weston?" She saw him as if he were actually right there, his hand gently brushing a lock of hair from her face.

But then the memory shifted. She was in a small, familiar apartment. There was a framed picture on the table beside her: her and Weston, standing arm in arm, radiant and laughing, against the Grand Canyon. She felt the love, the happiness of that moment—until an overwhelming sadness washed over her. She felt the loss of him. She felt grief, raw and cutting, and a pain that had stayed with her long after he was gone.

The memory faded as quickly as it had come, leaving her breathless. Elanor blinked, disoriented, as the desert landscape swam back into view. She was back on Weston's horse, his arm still around her, steady and unwavering.

"You alright, El?" Weston's voice was soft and concerned as if sensing the shift in her.

She struggled to find her words, heart still pounding with the aftershocks of what she'd just seen. "I . . . I think I just remembered something."

She didn't elaborate, and the words were still too fragile on her tongue, but Weston's arm tightened slightly around her, his steady presence grounding her as she wrestled with the fragments of her past.

"Take your time," he murmured reassuringly. There was a tenderness in his tone that was familiar, comforting in a way that went beyond their short time together on this journey.

Elanor nodded, swallowing hard. She wasn't ready to share the details—not yet. But a piece of her past returned, pulling her closer to something she had once known, something precious that laid hidden beneath the surface of her fractured memories.

The group continued, unaware of the storm of emotions raging inside her. As the shadows grew longer, Elanor couldn't shake the feeling that this journey was leading her not only to Tawa but perhaps to answers she didn't even know she was searching for.

As dusk settled over the desert, Elanor volunteered to gather kindling for the fire after the group settled down and set up camp. She needed a moment to breathe after the day's tensions, to feel helpful in some small way. She wandered just beyond the camp's edge, her arms gathering a few brittle twigs as she listened to the wind rustle through the sparse brush.

She was bent over, reaching for a bundle of sticks near the tall shadow of a cactus, when a low murmur of voices drifted her way. She recognized Nora's tone, sharp but with an edge of warmth. Elanor turned, glancing toward the campfire where Weston was quietly tending to the flames, and then noticed Nora and the sheriff standing a little apart, just behind a line of scrub.

"You know, Sheriff," Nora said, her voice carrying through the quiet. "Every time we talk about Leto, you go stiffer than a church bench." Elanor stifled a chuckle, wondering if anyone was immune to Nora's teasing. "I've given you grace up until this point, but if there's somethin' about that place we need to know, now's the time to lay it out."

Elanor crouched down, adjusting the pile of sticks in her arms, telling herself to turn back toward camp but feeling the pull of their words too strongly. She carefully stepped closer, keeping her distance but close enough to hear.

The sheriff hesitated, his voice dropping to a near whisper. "I've got my reasons to avoid Leto," he said thickly. "It's not just a town to me; it's . . . it's the place where I failed someone I cared about. Someone I promised to protect."

Nora's voice softened slightly. "What happened?"

The sheriff's tone grew heavy, every word loaded with the weight of a buried grief. "She was young. So full of life, Nora. But she didn't fit in there, and people . . . they can be cruel to what they don't understand. I tried to get her away from it, to keep her safe, but I wasn't enough. And when she died —" he broke off, his voice shaking slightly, "—they blamed me."

Elanor felt a strange, distant ache tighten in her chest, resonating with the sheriff's words. She couldn't explain it, but something about how he described the girl stirred a deep sadness within her, like an echo of a memory just out of reach.

Nora's face was unreadable. "So, they chased you out?"

The sheriff nodded, distant. "A few of the men, they made sure I knew I wasn't welcome. Said if I showed my face there again, I'd be lucky to walk out alive. It's been a long time, Nora, but some ghosts don't let go."

"Sometimes, it's not about letting go," Nora said, placing a hand on his shoulder. "Sometimes, it's about facing what haunts you, reckonin' with it." She looked back toward the campfire, lingering on Elanor. Elanor turned in the hope Nora hadn't noticed her eavesdropping. "Maybe someone's here to help you do just that."

The sheriff was quiet for a moment. Elanor almost felt his eyes following Nora's onto her. "You think it's possible?" he murmured.

Nora nodded in agreement. "I think we all got reasons for being here, one way or another."

Elanor quickly turned, returning to camp, the sheriff's words and Nora's last remark playing over in her mind. She settled down by the fire, setting the twigs beside Weston, who gave her a curious look. But as the others gathered close, she lingered on the sheriff, piecing together the fragments of his story and wondering just what ghosts were shadowing their steps.

The group huddled closer to the crackling fire, its orange glow casting warm shadows across their faces as the desert's night chill crept in. After the long day, they each wore an air of exhaustion mixed with quiet relief, thankful for a rare moment of peace. Elanor settled onto her bedroll beside Weston, feeling the warmth from the fire seep into her bones.

With a hint of mischief in his eye, Boone surveyed the others, his gaze lingering on each, as if assessing them. "Well," he began, clearing his throat dramatically, "we could sit here like a pack of coyotes licking our wounds, or I could tell you a story. And not just any story—this one's about the time I turned down royalty."

Nora rolled her eyes, but a grin tugged at the corners of her mouth. "Go on, Boone. Let's see how you wriggle your way into the good graces of royalty this time."

"Oh, ye of little faith," Boone said with a mock frown. He leaned forward, elbows on his knees, gesturing animatedly as he began his tale. "There I was, a young man with an honest job in the bustling town of Crater Falls. You know, catching wild stallions, breaking horses—the usual cowboy business. But one day, out of nowhere, this fancy stage-coach pulls into town. Turns out it's a lady—a duchess—who's on the run. Now, she was calling herself Miss Daisy O'Connor, but I could tell right away she was hiding something."

Elanor smirked, indulging his tale. "So a duchess came to Crater Falls . . . for a change of scenery?"

"Precisely, Miss Elanor! The lady had run afoul of some nobleman back in Europe—something about a stolen crown and scandalous secrets. She'd fled across the ocean, disguised, hoping to disappear for a while." Boone's voice took on an air of mystery as he continued. "Well, it wasn't long 'fore she caught sight of me. And I'll tell you, she was positively enchanted. Said I was 'a man of raw charm, unpolished but pure.'"

Weston chuckled, shaking his head. "You, Boone? Pure?"

Boone placed a hand to his chest, feigning offense. "Now, Wes, she didn't say innocent, just pure. Anyway, Miss Daisy—that is, Duchess Whoever—nearly begged me to run away with her. Promised me a palace somewhere in the French countryside. Said she'd make me a prince if I'd just leave the dusty trails and ride off into the sunset with her."

Nora snorted, shooting Elanor an amused look. "And yet, here you are, no prince, no palace. What happened?"

Boone took a thoughtful sip from his flask, eyes glinting with the satisfaction of a storyteller. "Well, I thought about it. But in the end, I told her I couldn't leave behind the simple life. Couldn't turn my back on the freedom of the open land for any throne. She cried, of course. I was nearly moved to tears myself."

Elanor laughed softly, picturing the whole outlandish scene. "So, a duchess offered you a kingdom, and you chose . . . Crater Falls?"

Boone raised his flask, nodding solemnly. "I chose Crater Falls, the town, and the adventure. A man can't be tied down, not even by a duchess."

The group chuckled, the firelight reflecting off their faces, softening the hard lines left by their journey. As Elanor's laughter faded, a strange pang struck her—a flicker of something profound, like a half-remembered melody. Boone's tale, absurd as it was, stirred something in her, an unnameable ache that lingered just below her understanding.

She gazed at Weston, catching his eye momentarily, finding that same gentle humor reflected back at her. It was as if they shared an unspoken appreciation for Boone's antics, an inside joke neither had to voice.

Boone shook the flask, his expression turning serious—or as serious as he could muster. "So, let this be a lesson to you all: Never give up the open range—not for anything. Not even for a throne."

The group laughed, Boone's ridiculous story lightening the mood of the past few days. As the fire crackled and they each settled down for the night, the memory of his tale lingered, a small comfort in the quiet darkness of the desert.

The fire had burned low, its warm glow casting long shadows across the ground as the group settled into a quiet calm. The conversation had waned, each traveler succumbing to a reflective silence as they stretched out by the fire, gazing up at the starlit sky. Deep, calming stillness seeped into Elanor, and her mind drifted between relaxation and exhaustion.

But just as she began to close her eyes, a distant sound snapped her back to attention—a faint, rhythmic thumping that cut through the stillness of the night.

Elanor sat up slowly, straining her ears. The sound grew louder, unmistakable now: the beat of hooves pounding against the earth, echoing ominously in the open desert night. She glanced around at the others, her unease mirrored in their expressions as they all turned toward the sound.

Weston rose, eyes sharpening as he peered into the darkness, gaze trained on the horizon. "Remain silent," he whispered. "There's more than one of them."

Already clutching her pistol, Nora scanned the surrounding terrain with steely resolve. "Whoever they are, they're coming in fast."

Boone's face turned grim as he listened. "We should douse the fire," he said. "No sense giving them a beacon."

Weston kicked sand over the remaining embers without a word, plunging them into near-total darkness while their eyes adjusted to the lower light. The only light left was the faint glow of the moon casting eerie shadows around the camp.

Elanor's pulse quickened as she crouched low beside Weston, gripping her bedroll firmly, heartbeat nearly drowning out the approaching hooves. The riders were so close now, she could almost make out individual hoofbeats, hear the jingling of bridles, the murmur of voices.

Weston's hand settled on her shoulder, steadying her as he leaned in close. "Stay quiet," he whispered. "We'll wait for them to pass."

But as the riders drew closer, it became clear they weren't merely passing by. They were slowing down, voices carrying on the wind—low, guttural laughter mixed with tense whispers.

Weston's grip on her shoulder tightened, body taut like a coil. *Get ready,* he mouthed, his expression hardening in the moonlight.

The shadows of the riders stretched across the ground, inching closer and closer until Elanor could make out the faint glint of metal— the outline of guns in the hands of dark figures on horseback.

And then, with a sudden clarity, she acknowledged that they weren't just strangers passing by in the night. They were looking for something —or someone.

And they had found them.

CHAPTER ELEVEN

The sound of approaching riders echoed down the narrow canyon, tense and measured until the dust settled and a small group came into view. The leader—a slight, wiry man with sharp, cunning eyes—wore an amused and predatory smirk. Behind him loomed a hulking figure, wide as he was tall, face shadowed beneath the brim of his hat. He looked intimidating but kept a few paces behind, deferring to the more petite man with quiet loyalty.

"Merrick," Nora muttered under her breath, her jaw tight. "And he's brought Judah along."

A chill crept down Elanor's neck at Nora's words. Merrick's name was familiar enough from whispers and warnings along their journey, but seeing him in person was different. As Merrick and Judah approached, she had more time to scrutinize them, and the details intensified her heartbeat.

Merrick's wiry frame spoke of quickness rather than strength, his every movement sharp and deliberate. His narrow face was angular, and his hawk-like nose and sun-darkened skin gave him the appearance of a predator always watching for the slightest weakness. With every passing second, his smirk deepened. His cunning eyes flicked over each group member with the precision of someone noting every quality and weakness. Despite his slight build, he wore a dangerous confidence that challenged any weapon.

Judah was a stark contrast behind him. The hulking man looked older, with deeply set eyes beneath a heavy brow and a face carved with the hardness of a life lived in brutal terrain. His broad shoulders and thick arms were corded with muscle, his movements slower but deliberate, like a bear stalking its prey. His expression was stern and unreadable, his square jaw set in a perpetual scowl that revealed nothing of his thoughts. Though he walked in Merrick's shadow, there was a quiet menace to him, as if he needed no words to make his presence felt.

Merrick approached their group directly, sharp eyes finally focusing on Elanor. His smile widened into something more sinister, curling with unsettling satisfaction, as if he'd found exactly what he was looking for.

"Look what we have here," Merrick drawled, his voice high and nasal. "Thought you could just wander into my part of the desert, huh?"

Sitting next to him, Judah remained silent and vigilant, his size alone causing unease among the group. Though his posture was submissive to Merrick, the gazes from Merrick's men showed they took their actual cues from the quiet giant.

Nora's eyes narrowed, and she stepped forward. "Ain't nobody scared of you, Merrick."

"Oh?" Merrick's eyebrow lifted mockingly. "Maybe not me, but I think they'd be a little worried 'bout my boys here." He gestured to his men, who spread out in a show of force, guns drawn but still at their sides.

The sheriff stared at Judah, visibly wary as he edged closer to the group, hand resting on his holster. Weston, standing protectively near Elanor, kept his expression calm but watchful.

"Just passin' through, are you?" Merrick asked, his focus returning to Elanor with a look that made her skin crawl. "Well, I hear you're on a little mission to find Tawa, and I'd hate for you to waste your time. I'll save you the trip 'cause I can offer the same thing he can."

His words drew a harsh glare from Weston, who stepped forward and positioned himself more firmly in front of Elanor. "We're not interested in trouble, Merrick. Let us be."

Elanor threw a questioning look at Weston, curious about Merrick's promise to give her what she wanted— her memories.

Merrick laughed, a thin, mocking sound that echoed off the rock walls. "Trouble's what you walked into, cowboy. Though I'd be inclined to let the rest of you off easy if you just leave the girl with me." He gave Elanor a slow, unsettling once-over, a grin spreading across his face. "You don't belong here, sweetheart."

Elanor swallowed hard, feeling Weston tense beside her. Before she could respond, Boone spoke up, his usual humor tinged with nervousness. "Now, Merrick, let's be reasonable here. No need for all this unpleasantness."

But Merrick's attention shifted to the sheriff, his smile lifting with recognition. "Sheriff," he sneered, his tone mocking. "Leto's got plenty to say about you. They remember exactly what you let happen back there, and they won't be so welcoming when you come back around."

The sheriff's face paled slightly, hand tightening on his holster. Nora shot a quick, alarmed look his way, lips pressed into a thin line.

Elanor thought perhaps at the mention of an unwelcome return home, the blood was leaving her face, too.

"Enough, Merrick," Weston said. "We're not turning her over."

Merrick's smile flickered, irritation flashing across his face before he regained his composure. He nodded to Judah, who shifted slightly, his eyes cold and steady.

"Have it your way," Merrick said, his tone darkening. "But if you thought I was going to let you just ride off easy, you're even more foolish than you look."

Merrick signaled his men, and they spread out, flanking the group, positioning themselves for a standoff.

A heavy silence settled over the camp as Merrick and his men closed in, forming a loose circle around the group. She sensed a slight tenseness in Weston's arm, as his protective stance was clearly focused on her. Her heart pounded, aware that this wasn't the first time they'd encountered danger, but Merrick's presence was colder, more calculating, as if he was already a step ahead of everyone else in a game they weren't aware they were playing.

Merrick's smile twisted as he shifted his focus to Elanor, speaking as though to an old friend. "You're a long way from home, aren't you?" he said with a mock sweetness that made her stomach churn. "Seems to me you don't quite fit out here. Probably don't even know why you're here at all. I can help with that, just as well as Tawa, but with much less boring puzzles."

The proposal came again and piqued Elanor's interest in knowing more. If Merrick could follow through on his proposal, could he, indeed, be that bad?

Weston stepped forward, voice dripping with disdain. "Whatever you want, Merrick, you ain't gettin' it here."

"Oh, Weston," he replied, and chuckled dismissively. "You may have slipped away from my grasp, but I'm afraid I've already got what I want." He turned back to Elanor, eyes narrowing with intent. "All I need is for you to come along quietly, and I'll let the rest of this sorry bunch go free."

Elanor took an instinctive step back, feeling the fire's warmth against her heels as Merrick's words sank in. Similar threats had been mentioned on this journey, but this was more targeted, more personal, as though Merrick knew something about her she didn't.

Before she could speak, Weston's voice cut through the silence. "You're not taking her, Merrick. Not now, not ever."

Merrick's smile faded, and a glint of irritation flickered in his eyes. "That so? Well, I wasn't really askin'." His eyes shifted to the sheriff, a cruel light sparking as he leaned in, savoring the tension. "But I can't blame you for putting up a fight. After all, she's got no one else lookin' out for her—least no one that can stop me. Just like down in Leto, ain't that right, Sheriff?"

The sheriff's face turned to stone, but a flicker of pain crossed his eyes, barely hidden under his hat's shadow. Nora shot a quick, questioning glance at him, her lips pressed.

Merrick chuckled. "Oh, you never told them, did you?" he sneered, circling the sheriff as though he were prey. "Or did you forget how you stood back and watched? Maybe you think folks back in Leto forgot the little incident with that poor girl. Left her to die while you just watched. Not exactly sheriff material, wouldn't you say?"

Elanor's breath caught, and she looked at the sheriff, questions crowding her mind. He looked away, jaw taut, refusing to meet anyone's eyes.

Nora stepped in. "What he did or didn't do in Leto's none of your business, Merrick."

"Oh, it's everyone's business, Nora. You're all followin' a coward. He abandoned a girl and, unable to cope with the repercussions, fled to Bodie in an attempt to begin anew." Merrick gave a mocking shake of his head. "He froze up and ran off, leaving that poor girl with no chance."

Weston's eyes narrowed, his expression unreadable as he shot a hard look at the sheriff, waiting for a response. Face ashen, the sheriff finally met Merrick's gaze with a flicker of resolve. "It's easy to say that now, Merrick. But you and I both know the choice I had wasn't much of one."

"Oh, sure," Merrick said, voice dripping with sarcasm. "It's a good excuse if you can live with it. But I bet your friends here didn't know they were followin' a man who'd run from his own mistakes."

The sheriff clenched his fists, and Elanor saw the load of guilt in his expression. The group's attention was on him now, questions in their eyes. But before anyone could press further, Merrick turned back to Elanor, voice taking on a low, menacing tone.

"Look, sweetheart, this doesn't have to get ugly. Just come along, and I'll spare the lot of them. I'll make sure you're well taken care of."

A chill ran down Elanor's spine, but Weston's hand in hers steadied her, grounding her against Merrick's chilling words.

She shook her head, voice firm despite the fear swirling in her chest. "I'm not going anywhere with you."

Merrick's smile disappeared, replaced by a cold, steely glare. He took a single, deliberate step forward, signaling his men to close in, and the atmosphere grew heavier, charged with unspoken menace.

The standoff grew taut as Merrick's men tightened their grip on their weapons, eyes darting between Merrick and the group. Weston shifted slightly in front of Elanor, a silent but unmistakable warning that he would defend her with his life if necessary.

Nora was locked on Merrick, her posture defiant, and there was no trace of fear in her stance.

Standing just off to her side, Boone laughed, breaking the tension like a hammer shattering glass. "Guess it's true what they say—nothing like an overgrown rooster in a henhouse to keep the rest of 'em clucking."

Merrick's face darkened, and without a word, he raised his gun and fired. The shot cracked through the air, and Boone staggered, clutching his arm as a dark stain blossomed across the sleeve of his shirt. He dropped to his knees, his grin fading into a grimace of pain.

"Boone!" Elanor cried, lunging forward instinctively. Weston's arm shot out, holding her back, his jaw clenched as he stared Merrick down.

Boone, grimacing but defiant, forced himself upright, his voice strained as he muttered, "Guess I've still got my charm." He pressed a hand to his arm, his breathing shallow.

Nora dropped beside him, her face a mix of worry and exasperation. "You always have to go mouthin' off, don't ya?" she muttered, but the edge in her voice couldn't hide the protective note beneath it.

Merrick's men watched with smug grins, clearly reveling in the chaos. Merrick looked pleased as though Boone's suffering was nothing more than a sideshow for his amusement.

Elanor took a shaky breath, trying to steady herself as she looked into Merrick's cold eyes. "Fine," she said, her voice cracking slightly but resolute. "If you leave them alone, I'll go with you."

Weston turned to her, eyes blazing with disbelief and anger. "No," he said fiercely, his hand tightening on her arm. "We're not doing this."

"It's the only way," Elanor insisted, but Weston shook his head, face clouded with frustration.

Nora stepped forward, her voice hard as steel. "We'd rather go out in that desert without water than hand her over to the likes of you."

Merrick's eyes narrowed, but one of his men spoke, his tone chillingly calm. "That can be arranged." This drew a sharp eye from Judah.

The threat lingered in the air, heavy and unmistakable. Elanor swallowed hard, pulling herself free from Weston's grip. Seeing the hurt and desperation in his face, she whispered, "I can't let anyone else get hurt because of me."

Weston's expression softened, but the fire in his eyes didn't waver. "Elanor, please—"

She had already made her decision. She stepped forward, hands raised in surrender. "Let them go, and I'll go with you."

Merrick's eyes glittered with triumph. "Smart girl." He gestured to Judah, who approached her with a satisfied smirk. "We'll take good care of you. No harm done to the others, as long as they don't get any bright ideas."

Judah reached out to pull her toward him, and a surge of bile rose in Elanor's throat. Weston's hand shot out as she took a reluctant step forward, grabbing her arm one last time. She was taken aback by the intensity in his eyes.

"Don't do this. He's not what you think he is," he whispered fiercely, his voice full of helpless anger. She gave him a look that told him there was no other way, her hand resting briefly on his, and he reluctantly let go.

Nora's glare didn't waver as she locked eyes with Merrick. "If anything happens to her, you'll answer to me."

"Oh, I'm sure I will," Merrick sneered, unconcerned. He gave a quick nod to his men. "Let's move."

A cold, sickening fear coiled in Elanor's stomach as Judah hoisted her onto his horse. The solid strength of his arm gripped her too firmly, a reminder of how little control she had left in this situation. She settled uneasily in front of him, her body rigid as he tightened his arm around her waist, holding her in place as the horse began to move.

Her mind reeled, each hoofbeat echoing the questions racing through her thoughts. Had she done the right thing? Was surrendering the only choice she had, or had she just condemned herself—and perhaps the others? A sense of guilt settled inside her, heavier than Judah's grip, as she imagined Weston's face, the raw anger and desperation that had flashed in his eyes when she'd pulled away.

But under the fear and doubt was simmering anger, a steady burn that kept her spine straight and her jaw firm. Merrick thought he could just take her? That he could threaten her, her friends, and expect her to stay quiet? She felt her resolve harden. She wouldn't let them break her spirit, no matter what awaited her at the end of this ride.

Glancing over her shoulder, she saw the tiny figures of Weston, Nora, and the others standing firm in the distance, a small cluster of defiance against the desert landscape. She sent up a silent wish—no, a promise—that she would survive whatever laid ahead and find a way back to them.

CHAPTER TWELVE

The horse's rhythm beneath Elanor was jarring, each step sending an uncomfortable jolt through her body as she clung to the saddle in front of Judah. His large frame behind her was as solid and unmoving as a wall, his silence equally unyielding. The ride through the dry, rocky terrain only deepened her sense of isolation. She tried to focus on breathing steadily, forcing herself to keep her hands from trembling as they held the rough leather.

Merrick rode just ahead, glancing back with an infuriating smirk. He lingered on Elanor, and every time their eyes met, his confidence pressed down on her—a man who had her right where he wanted. The contrast between Merrick and Judah was stark; where Merrick was smaller in stature but domineering and calculating, Judah was massive, reserved, and far less eager to flaunt his power. She studied their dynamic silently, trying to glean any weakness in their unspoken bond.

"You got something on your mind, Elanor?" Merrick called back to her, his tone laced with amusement.

Elanor bit back a retort, knowing he'd only take her anger as confirmation of his control over her. She forced herself to look away, focusing instead on the darkened landscape around her—the dry, barren expanse stretching endlessly under a moonlit sky, offering no promise of refuge or escape.

"Trying to figure out what I'm going to do with you?" he continued, his voice sing-song, like he was entertaining a small child. "Don't worry. You'll find out in time. But let me just say, it's been a long time since I've had someone like you in my camp."

His words sent a chill down her spine. She was only trying to find Tawa—to get back to her friends. How did she fit into his schemes?

"You think you're some kind of genius, don't you?" she finally snapped, unable to resist.

Merrick simply chuckled, a noise that strained her nerves. "It's not me that's the genius here. That'd be Tawa."

"I thought you said you could do what he could do— like get back my memories," she said, forcing her voice to stay steady.

"Details, details," Merrick replied smoothly, his grin widening as he tilted his hat back. "We can get to the magic voodoo later. For now, I've got business to tend to."

Her stomach twisted. He was using her as a pawn in his scheme. But why her? The question nagged at her, stirring a faint, hazy image of a face blurred by time but unmistakably familiar. Someone held her hand, saying something she couldn't quite make out.

The memory slipped away, leaving her feeling lost, like she'd almost grasped something but couldn't hold onto it.

Merrick smirked, clearly enjoying her unease. "Don't try to fight it, Elanor. The answers you're looking for? You'll find them soon enough. Or maybe you already know more than you think."

A bitter defiance simmered within her. She refused to allow him the pleasure of witnessing her doubt.

Elanor scanned her surroundings, pulse quickening as they rode deeper into the rugged landscape. She tried to memorize every outcrop and pathway, each bend in the dusty trail, hoping she might use it to find her way back. But Merrick and Judah understood this terrain too well, and the land quickly turned into a maze of jagged rocks and narrow passes.

They crested a hill, and the hideout came into view below—a collection of makeshift tents, a rough wooden building, and a pen filled with restless horses. The hideout was cleverly nestled between two rocky outcroppings, nearly invisible from any distance unless you knew where to look. A single, winding path led down to it, threading carefully through the boulders.

As they descended, Elanor froze.

Standing near the pen, among a dozen other horses, was her horse. The one she'd watched plummet off the cliffside. Elanor's breath caught as she stared, her mind racing. *It can't be.* Yet there it was—a distinctive white marking around the left eye, a patch of mud covering its flank, just as before. It even wore the same saddle, slightly frayed on one side, that she'd been using since they left Bodie.

How could it be here, unharmed? The thought made her shiver. Had Merrick's men found it and somehow brought it back to health? Or was it . . . something else? She forced herself to look away, shaking off the eerie feeling crawling up her spine.

As they reached the bottom of the slope, Merrick attempted to swing himself off his horse with a swagger he hadn't mastered. His foot caught in the stirrup, and he stumbled, nearly falling to his knees. Several of his men smirked, stifling laughs quickly silenced by Judah's icy glare. At once, their expressions hardened, and they straightened up, wiping the amusement off their faces.

Red-faced, Merrick shot a nasty look at his men, then his eyes pierced through Elanor with a sneer. "Well, Missy Elanor, welcome to Merrick's hideout." He gestured with a sweeping arm, though the effect was spoiled by his attempt to appear unaffected by his stumble. "Not much out here, but there's no way out unless I say so."

Elanor refused to let him see any hint of fear. "I've handled worse than you, Merrick," she replied, her voice steady, despite her racing heart. "You don't scare me."

He chuckled, though there was a nervous edge to it. "Oh, is that right?" He turned to his men, a forced grin stretching across his face. "Lady thinks she's got a spine on her. Maybe we'll see how much spine soon enough."

Judah stayed back, observing the exchange quietly, his expression unreadable. But Elanor noticed how the men cast glances his way, almost like they were looking to him for direction. His broad shoulders were hunched slightly, eyes sharp and assessing. For a moment, Elanor caught a flicker of discomfort there, as if he didn't fully support the plan —but it vanished as quickly as it appeared.

Her focus drifted to the pen again, her horse still standing there, its eyes watching her almost knowingly. The sight made her stomach churn; the horse looked untouched, calm, and aware in a way that shouldn't be possible. *It's here for me.* She shivered at the realization, her mind racing as she tried to puzzle out what it meant.

But Merrick was still talking, his voice a scratchy drone as he rattled on about his "operation." She forced herself to pay attention, but all she could think about was the pen, her horse standing there, and the faint glimmer of hope it might represent.

As Merrick strutted off to rally his men, leaving Elanor with her hands bound behind a post near the pen, she noticed Judah lingering nearby, his eyes on her in a different way. It wasn't predatory, nor was it entirely sympathetic. Instead, it was . . . curious.

Elanor shifted uncomfortably under his stare, trying to maintain her composure as she looked back at him. "You don't have to stand there and stare, you know," she said, her voice a forced calm, hoping to mask the nerves bubbling up inside her.

Judah tilted his head, his expression softening, though he didn't respond immediately. Finally, he said, "Not every day we get a woman as tough as you out here."

Elanor almost snorted. "If that is your interpretation of a compliment, you are less adept at small talk than I anticipated."

His lips quirked in a small, almost hidden smile as though he were amused despite himself. "I didn't mean anything by it. Just . . . noticed. You've got more grit than some of the boys around here." As he watched Merrick's men, who were busy tending to the horses and setting up supplies, he paused, the faint smirk fading. He watched them with weary resignation, the flicker in his eyes betraying a tired familiarity —a man who lingered on the edge of a world he didn't entirely embrace but couldn't seem to leave.

Elanor took a careful breath, trying to steady herself. Judah was Merrick's second, yet he acted less invested in this setup than his title implied. She thought about what she'd noticed before—how the men watched him for cues, how they quieted at his unspoken command. Merrick might've been their leader in name, but Judah's quiet authority cast a larger shadow.

She looked him over carefully, noting the subtle strength in his stance and the way he shifted back to her, steady and grounded. "Why do you follow him?" she asked quietly, unable to stop herself. "Seems like you don't belong here, with all this. . . ."

Judah's eyes flickered with something she couldn't quite name— regret, maybe, or something far older and more profound. He sighed, folding his arms as he looked at her with a distant, thoughtful expression. "We all have our reasons for being where we are," he said finally, his voice gruff. "Sometimes we don't get to choose who we ride with." There was a long pause, then he added, almost an afterthought, "Merrick . . . he ain't always right. You should know that."

A glimmer of hope sparked in Elanor, fragile but undeniable. She wasn't sure what Judah was trying to tell her, but she sensed he was offering her something—a truth hidden beneath layers of loyalty and silence.

"What if I told you I need to leave?" she asked, her voice barely more than a whisper. "What would you do then?"

Judah's eyes held hers, steady and intent. He didn't answer right away, his expression unreadable. After a long moment, he glanced around to make sure they weren't being watched, then leaned in just enough for his voice to reach her ears alone. "Keep that grit of yours, and don't do anything foolish," he murmured, his voice so low it was almost inaudible. "You might need it soon enough."

Before she could respond, he straightened up. He stepped back, his expression hardening once again as he turned his attention to Merrick, now barking orders at his men with exaggerated confidence.

Elanor's pulse quickened, her thoughts swirling. Judah's words lingered in her mind, a quiet promise woven into a warning.

As the sun dipped lower, casting an orange glow across the hideout, Merrick approached Elanor with a smug expression, clearly savoring his power over her. He paced slowly in front of her, his small stature contrasted by the exaggerated swagger in his step, his eyes gleaming with a demented satisfaction.

"So, Miss High and Mighty," he drawled, leaning in close. "Think you're better than us, don't ya?" He gave a sly grin, his face inches from hers. "But here you are, tied up like a calf at auction. No fancy city folk and no god to save you now."

Elanor straightened as much as her bindings allowed, meeting him with steely resolve. She refused to flinch, even as his breath brushed against her cheek. "Is that why you brought me here?" she challenged, steadying her voice. "Just to feel big for a change?"

Merrick's face shifted slightly, irritation flashing in his eyes, but he quickly masked it with a smirk. "You've got a sharp tongue. Careful where you wag it, or you'll find out how easy it is to lose it."

She held his stare, her expression unyielding. "Why don't you quit the games, Merrick? I already know I don't belong here. What is it you want with me?"

His grin faltered, and he leaned back, crossing his arms. "Oh, you don't belong here, huh?" He looked her up and down, mocking. "That's right, little miss. You're a stranger in my world. No roots, no place . . . but maybe that's where you and I aren't so different."

Elanor's brow furrowed, her resolve unwavering. "I'm nothing like you," she said firmly.

Merrick laughed, low and mocking. "That's what you think now." He stepped back, gesturing grandly at the vast desert beyond the hide-out. "But once you're out here, away from everything you thought you knew, well . . . people like us? We have the ability to establish our own set of rules." He turned back to her, his eyes glinting with something dark. "And out here, my rules say you're coming with me. I could use a bold one like you in my herd."

"And why would I do that?" she shot back, defiant.

"Because you don't have a choice." He leaned in close again, his voice a near whisper. "See, you might think you're free to make your own choices, but that's just a sweet lie. And if it's not me controlling you," he looked around thoughtfully, "it'll be the next big wolf who catches you stumbling in his territory."

She clenched her teeth, anger simmering beneath her calm expression. "Whatever you think you're going to get from me, you're wrong."

Merrick raised an eyebrow, amused by her resistance. "You'll see soon enough. Like I said . . . out here, it's my rules." His voice dropped lower, his tone colder. "And my rules say that you either do as I say, or I'll make sure you never get those memories back in your pretty little head."

A surge of determination rose within Elanor. She refused to give Merrick the satisfaction of witnessing her fear, nor would she show him any signs of dominance. Eyes unwavering, she held his stare, her voice steady. "You'll get nothing from me."

A flicker of frustration crossed Merrick's face, causing his veneer of control to falter for a brief moment. But then he let out a cold laugh, shrugging nonchalantly. "Suit yourself, darlin'. It's a long journey ahead. Memories have a funny way of disappearing forever here if you don't get to where you need to in time. Maybe you'll come around."

He spun on his heel and sauntered away, his ego bruised but his ambition undeterred, leaving Elanor with a cold sense of foreboding—and a growing determination to find her way out of his grasp.

Despite Merrick's danger, the tantalizing possibility of reclaiming her past haunted her. Every instinct warned her against trusting a man who could betray so casually, who had already demonstrated his capacity for cruelty. Yet the stakes were her identity, fragments of her life she desperately needed to piece together. Could she bear the risk of rejecting his offer?

Her mind raced with doubt and confusion. To yield to Merrick might be to condone his actions, to compromise her principles irrevocably. How could she forgive herself if she submitted to his rule, knowing his willingness to manipulate and harm? However, the alternative could be even more devastating: a future clouded by amnesia, lost and disconnected from her past self. This tormenting dilemma gnawed at her, the desire for answers clashing with the imperative to remain true to herself.

As Merrick's retreating figure merged with the shadows of the desert, a hardened resolve settled deep within Elanor. Somehow, she must navigate this treacherous moral landscape, clinging to her integrity while chasing the elusive promise of a restored memory.

As evening settled over the hideout, the men began to relax, gathering around fires and passing bottles back and forth in small groups. The murmur of conversation and occasional laughter filled the air, creating a false sense of camaraderie among Merrick's gang.

Elanor, still tethered to a post and masking her fatigue, maintained a low profile, her eyes half-closed, seemingly resigned to her fate. But her ears were alert, catching snatches of conversation around her. She heard Merrick holding court near the central fire, bragging loudly about his control over Bodie and his planned future control over Leto.

In contrast, Judah was stationed a little ways off, watching Merrick's performance with an unreadable expression. Nearby, two of Merrick's men were talking in hushed tones, their voices barely audible over the crackling fire.

"Think it's wise, takin' her to Leto?" one of the men muttered. "We're bound to attract attention, and that sheriff's got friends out that way."

"Merrick thinks he can handle it," the other replied, clearly skeptical, "but you know how Leto gets. Too many folks with eyes on strangers, and it ain't like we're all inconspicuous types."

The first man grunted. "Maybe. But I heard Merrick saying something about a contact over there—someone he's meeting who wants to help gain more territory and take power away from Tawa."

Elanor's heartbeat quickened. Her thoughts raced, questions swirling about what Merrick wanted with Leto and Tawa and why she, specifically, had become included in his plans.

"But what's Merrick planning to do with the broad once he gets what he wants?" the second man asked in a near whisper.

The first shrugged, his tone carrying an edge of dark humor. "Merrick? Probably sell her off to the highest bidder or keep her around to clean his boots." The two men snickered, but their laughter died quickly when Judah's shadow loomed over them.

"What's so funny?" Judah's voice was low, his massive frame casting a long shadow over the men.

"Nothin', Judah, just talkin'," one of them stammered, looking away nervously.

Judah's eyes narrowed. "Keep your mouths shut unless you've got something useful to say." He cast a quick, assessing glance toward Elanor before stepping away, leaving the two men silent and looking at the ground.

As Judah walked off, Elanor let her breath out slowly, the pieces of the overheard conversation tumbling through her mind. Leto and someone waiting there who brought risk to her and her friends—there were far too many mysteries to ignore. However, one certainty was that Merrick's intentions for her extended beyond mere confinement.

A spark of hope flickered within her. Perhaps she could uncover the truth if she could somehow reach Leto herself. For now, however, she would have to patiently wait for any additional hints that might guide her toward a solution.

As the fires in the camp burned low, casting long shadows across the rough-hewn ground, the sounds around Elanor faded into a distant hum. A chill crept over her, the night air settling deep into her bones and making her shiver, despite her efforts to stay still. She leaned back against the post, shoulders stiff, muscles aching, but her mind was sharper than it had been in days. The snippets of conversation she'd overheard replayed in her mind, each word sparking questions, feeding her determination.

She clenched her hands behind her, the coarse rope biting into her wrists, but the pain was a grounding reminder of her purpose. The sheriff's past, Merrick's schemes, Judah's simmering resentment—they were all linked. And somehow, in the middle of it all, she was the key.

Lifting her gaze to the dark, star-strewn sky, she slowly exhaled, attempting to calm the raging storm within her. There was a deep, instinctual part of her that sensed she had been here before, entangled in a fight to find her way out of something impossible. The urgency of that feeling pulled at her, whispered to her of a promise she'd made to herself once before. *To survive. To understand.*

"Whatever it takes," she whispered, her voice almost lost in the night's quiet. "I'll find the truth."

The stars twinkled, distant and silent, watching her from another world. She closed her eyes, steadying her heartbeat, and made a quiet vow to herself: She would reach Leto. And once there, she would learn everything—about Merrick's plan, the sheriff's past, her identity, and why this screwed up journey had begun.

A flicker of courage surged through her, warming her against the night's chill. Alone and bound as she was, Elanor's resolve was never stronger.

She thought, *One way or another, I'll find my way back—no matter what awaits me in the shadows.*

CHAPTER THIRTEEN

As dawn broke over the camp, Elanor was awake, watching the soft sunlight filter through the cracks in the hideout's structure from the post to which her hands were bound. The cold morning light washed over the rough earth, but there was no warmth, only a stark reminder of where she was and who held her captive. She hadn't slept, her mind circling her situation, Merrick's motives, and the stories she overheard from those who passed by.

Rumors floated through Merrick's camp, whispers and speculations far more personal and immediate. They spoke in hushed tones of destiny, fate, and the harnessing of souls. The vague, ominous mentions of an "ultimate power" caught her attention. She didn't fully understand, but the whispers she overheard sounded like a bunch of crap they were using to scare her . . . or the whispers were the delusions of her sleepless night.

She stretched her sore muscles, careful not to draw attention. Her wrists stung from the rope burns, and her shoulders ached from having her hands tied behind the post, but in her pain was also anger. The whispers of Paradise and Tawa weren't just mysterious—they were driving Merrick and his men hard, and she was caught in the middle of it. She promised herself she wouldn't stay passive.

Nearby, Judah's voice rolled out in low, soft waves, his tone wrapping the harsh surroundings in a protective blanket of sound. As he leaned over Merrick, who was casually propped against a wooden post, Judah's hand absentmindedly played with Merrick's earlobe, a gesture intimate and full of quiet affection. Merrick responded with a sharpness that cut through the murmur, yet his words fell with an unusual gentleness, his eyes softening—a flicker of warmth out of place against his usual stern demeanor. This striking contrast offered Elanor a rare glimpse of something resembling happiness in the otherwise severe atmosphere of Merrick's camp. Watching this brief, tender exchange, a spark of curiosity ignited within her, revealing a layer of their relationship she had never seen before.

Elanor scanned the camp, taking in the men who stirred to tend to the fire and check supplies. The previous day had worn them out, but none showed any sign of backing down from this mission. Her thoughts turned back to Nora, Boone, the sheriff, and Weston—their faces flickered in her mind, grounding her. They were her only hope, her allies, yet she was miles away, left to figure out her escape.

If she learned more about Merrick's plans, she could use that knowledge to her advantage. For the time being, she would assume the role of a cooperative captive, waiting patiently. But her resolve had strengthened, and one thing was for sure: She would find a way out.

Near the post, Merrick and Judah moved behind a tent to hide from Merrick's men, who were only a few paces away from Elanor. Their faces were close together in a conversation as tense as it was secretive. Their voices drifted toward her, their quiet murmur just loud enough for her to catch most of the conversation.

"We can't just keep her here indefinitely, Merrick," Judah said, his tone strained, an undercurrent of moral conflict evident in his words. "It's not right. We've done enough of this—it has to stop."

Merrick's gaze cut sharply toward Elanor. "She's different, Judah. This isn't just about collecting—it's been a while since I've had someone like her. Someone who can get others to follow. Someone like you."

Judah's face was a mask of inner turmoil, his eyes flickering with unease. "And what if this is the one that turns against us? We've been down this road, Merrick. It never ends well."

Merrick's expression remained impassive, his resolve clear. "This time is different. And it's not about what she wants. She won't even know what's happening until we have what we need."

Running a hand through his hair, Judah looked back at Elanor, conflicted. "Dragging her deeper into this without her knowledge . . . it's not just risky—it's wrong."

Merrick let out a slow breath, his demeanor calm yet firm. "She doesn't need to understand her role—not if it complicates things. We keep her under the radar and make her feel safe. When the moment is right, we move. We're not giving her a choice in this."

Judah's expression hardened, reflecting a mix of resignation and defiance. "And if she fights back? If she realizes what's happening?"

Merrick's smile was cold, devoid of humor. "Then we ensure she doesn't get the chance. We've managed before, we'll manage now. Just keep her quiet and close. We control the situation, we control her."

"She's not yours to collect, Merrick," Judah said, his face stern.

Merrick smirked. "Not the first time I broke Tawa's rules. Just need her to go willingly and all will work out just fine and dandy."

Elanor felt an unease growing within her as she listened, Merrick's veiled words carrying a gravity that grew heavier with each passing moment. She sensed they had a specific use for her, something enigmatic and sinister, though the full intent remained beyond her grasp. Frustration and fear simmered within as she slumped to the cold ground, the rough rope binding her wrists chafing painfully.

As Merrick and Judah approached, a determined resolve took hold. Although she could not fully understand their plans, she was more than a mere piece in their cryptic scheme. Her mind raced, bracing for any opportunity to defy whatever Merrick thought he could extract from her unwillingly. She was not about to let his dark ambitions go unchallenged.

The midday sun cast harsh light across the camp as Merrick neared Elanor, an unsettling smile curling his lips. He stopped before Elanor, crossing his arms as he looked her over, seeming almost amused. "You think just staring me down is gonna change things?" he said, voice dripping with condescension.

Elanor held his gaze. "Dragging me out here for some cryptic purpose makes you the fool, not me."

Merrick's eyes narrowed, his smile morphing into a cunning smirk. "You think it's just folly, but there's something here that's powerful, something you don't understand yet."

Elanor's fists clenched, not from the mention of some mythical power or place but from the vague and ominous way Merrick spoke. Her mind raced, yet she masked her growing curiosity and fear. "What do you think I can do for you here, exactly?" she pressed, trying to glean more about his intentions without revealing her apprehension.

Merrick stepped closer, his presence overbearing. "It's not about what you can do; it's about what you have—something invaluable, yet you're completely unaware."

Judah shifted beside him, his discomfort clear as he avoided looking at either of them. "We should keep moving," he interjected softly, almost apologetically.

Ignoring Judah, Merrick's remained fixed on Elanor. "Cooperation would be wise. It could make things smoother for everyone."

"And why would I do anything for you, knowing you've only brought harm?"

Merrick's sneer deepened. "Because if you don't, the consequences won't just fall on you. I'm sure you're not willing to risk others for your defiance."

As he turned to walk away, Elanor felt a surge of desperation and resistance. Without thinking, she gathered a mouthful of saliva and spat directly at his face. The spit landed with a satisfying splat against his cheek.

Merrick halted, his expression initially twisting into a furious scowl. But almost as quickly, it shifted into a crooked smile as he wiped the spit away smoothly with his hand. "That's the spirit that attracted me to you," he said, low and menacing, yet with a disturbing warmth. "Keep that up, and you'll be just what I need." His laugh was cold, echoing slightly as he walked away, leaving Elanor shivering with rage and a chilling realization of his intentions.

Judah, who had lingered behind, looked from Merrick to Elanor, his expression troubled. He looked around the camp, then crouched down, eyes level with hers, a complex mix of emotions playing across his features. "Listen," he muttered. "I don't agree with all of this. You have no reason to trust me, but maybe . . . maybe there's a way this doesn't go down the way he's planning."

She narrowed her eyes, barely believing what she was hearing. "Why should I believe anything you say?"

Judah let out a small, strained laugh, his attention flicking toward Merrick's distant figure. "I didn't sign up to hurt people. I'm in it because . . ." He hesitated, almost as if confessing something. "Because some things are more complicated than they appear on the surface. Merrick . . . he's got his ways of drawing me in, but he doesn't always have the best judgment."

Elanor took a deep breath, hoping he couldn't see the spark of hope in her eyes. "If that's true, then help me."

Judah ran a hand over his face, clearly wrestling with his thoughts. "I can't just let you go." That'd be the end of both of us." He leaned closer, lowering his voice further. "But . . . if there's ever a chance for you to escape, I'll look the other way. If it's a choice between your freedom and what he wants . . . well, let's just say I don't need it like he does."

Elanor's heart leaped at his words, though she kept her expression steady. "Why tell me this?"

Judah's jaw clenched as he eyed her bindings. "Maybe I just needed someone to see . . . that I'm not just his shadow. Maybe it's something else." With one last conflicted look, he walked away, his shoulders tense as he left her alone.

The day stretched, the sun climbing higher as Elanor watched the camp stir around her. Her only chance of getting out of this would come when they were on the move—if she could trust Judah's word. But if there was any truth to his offer, she would take it, and she would be ready.

The sun lifted higher, making the ropes around Elanor's wrists feel even tighter as her arms strained against the post. Her skin was raw from the rough fibers, and the heat only intensified her thirst. She closed her eyes briefly, trying to calm her mind, when she sensed a presence nearby.

"Hey," a quiet voice whispered.

She opened her eyes to see a young guard standing before her, his expression hesitant. He looked over his shoulder, glancing toward Merrick's tent, then turned back to her with an awkward smile.

Elanor narrowed her eyes, instinctively pushing back against the post. "What do you want?"

The boy raised his hands in a gesture of peace. "I'm just here to help. Judah sent me. Said you could . . . use a helping hand." He pulled a canteen from his belt, uncapping it. "You look like you could use some water."

She hesitated, observing him. "Why are you doing this?"

A flicker of something softened in his eyes, and he looked around again, his voice barely above a whisper. "Not all of us are here for the reasons you think. Some of us . . . well, let's just say we don't all agree with everything Merrick does."

Her suspicion lingered, but the boy's words hinted at more than he was willing—or able—to share. With a cautious nod, she leaned forward, allowing him to lift the canteen to her lips. He tipped it gently, letting a cool stream trickle into her mouth. She drank gratefully, savoring the relief from the scorching dryness in her throat.

"Thank you," she said softly, swallowing the last dribble of water.

The boy gave a quick nod, his gaze flickering toward her bonds. "Don't mention it. Just try not to get yourself in more trouble than you already are. If Merrick knew I was over here . . ."

Elanor looked closely at his face, noticing the fleeting expression of uneasiness there. "You appear to have a strong relationship with Judah," she guessed, smiling.

A faint smile tugged at his lips. "You could say that. Judah . . . he looks out for us, even if Merrick's the one in charge." He shifted uncomfortably, clearly torn between his duty and something else lingering beneath the surface. "Judah's got his reasons. He's . . . complicated."

She nodded, carefully considering his words. Judah's loyalties might not be as clear-cut as they appeared. However subtle, this young guard's quiet defiance hinted that maybe there was a crack in Merrick's grip.

The guard capped the canteen and tucked it back on his belt. "Hang in there," he murmured. Before he turned to walk back, he leaned close and added, "I'm around if you need anything. I'll pass by as much as I can without raising suspicions. Just . . . be careful, alright?"

With that, he slipped back into the shadows, his watchful eyes keeping their silent promise. Elanor's mind raced, her hope rekindled at the thought that there might be more allies among Merrick's men than she'd first thought.

As the young guard disappeared into the camp, Elanor leaned back against the rough post, her mind racing with thoughts of her friends and everything they'd endured together so far. She pictured them vividly —Nora's fierce, unyielding courage; Boone's wry humor that always surfaced at the right moments; and the sheriff's quiet nature, always tinged with a shadow she hadn't fully understood until recently.

And then there was Weston.

A warmth bloomed in her chest as she thought of him, remembering how he'd pulled her up to safety on that mountain ledge, his face inches from hers, a mixture of worry and relief flickering in his eyes. He'd been there through every step of this twisted journey, his steady, comforting presence a constant she didn't realize she'd needed so much.

She wondered what they were doing right now. Had they figured out how to find her? Were they devising a plan to break her out of this miserable camp? She could almost see them gathered around the fire, their usual banter replaced by a determination that came only in moments of danger. The thought stirred something within her—a spark of hope and a longing she didn't quite know how to place.

Her thoughts turned to Weston again, and a pang of something deeper surged in her, something that went beyond simple gratitude. Somewhere along the way, her admiration for his courage and loyalty had shifted, becoming richer and more tender. The memory of the feel of his arms around her as they rode together—his gentle, protective grip —crossed her mind. It had been a comfort unlike anything before.

Elanor reached for memories beyond Bodie and what past she might have had before her current journey. She swore she recalled something . . . someone important, but the memory was unreachable. Elanor dug her boot into the dirt in frustration, her mind refusing to cling to the information she desperately wanted.

There was a shadow over her hope, a question that lingered unbidden: Was it worth pressing on to find Tawa? She didn't know Merrick's plan but was sure it would end in chaos, especially if he got whatever he was after. Tawa might be her best hope of returning to whatever her life had once been—or at least discovering more about herself. But part of her wondered if that was the path she wanted to take, especially when Merrick could offer the same thing.

What if she just . . . stopped? Would it be so bad if she didn't pursue Tawa and left the quest for this mysterious Paradise? She saw it: a life beyond this desperate, dangerous quest—a life where she wasn't constantly running or looking over her shoulder.

A life with Weston, both of them free from this turmoil.

However, as the concept solidified, a hint of uncertainty began to surface. If the rumors about Tawa were true, he possessed knowledge and power beyond her comprehension. If she ceased her search and succumbed to Merrick's demands, could she ever truly be free? Or would Merrick relentlessly pursue her, pulling her back into the darkness she desperately tried to escape?

Elanor exhaled slowly, feeling the burden of the decision she would have to make soon. Either way, her path was a gamble. But one thing was clear: she wasn't about to give up—not when her friends were fighting for her, and certainly not when her feelings for Weston gave her a reason to hope for something beyond the danger.

A resolve settled in her chest, quiet but steady. She would find her way back to them, no matter what. And when the time came to face Tawa, she would have to decide where her true path lay.

The sounds of the camp around her shifted. Men gathered supplies, saddled horses, and readied themselves for the journey ahead. Elanor craned her neck to see beyond the movement, curiosity mingling with dread as she wondered what Merrick's plan for her entailed. The young guard from earlier approached, his face set with an apologetic expression.

"They're putting you in a carriage for the trip to Leto," he muttered, not quite meeting her eyes. His voice was edged with something she couldn't quite place—regret, perhaps, or a hint of shame.

"A carriage?" Elanor's heart sank, imagining what that might mean. She'd expected to be tied up and forced to ride along, but a carriage meant something more ominous.

She didn't have to wait long for confirmation.

The guard led her to the edge of the camp, and there it stood: a small, darkened carriage with bars welded along the square openings, thick and cold-looking like they were meant to hold a wild animal. Inside, she could barely make out a narrow bench against one side, but the interior was shadowed, casting an eerie sense of finality over the whole setup.

The guard paused as they reached it and, glancing over both of his shoulders, leaned close. "Sorry for this," he murmured as he untied her restraints. He gestured toward the open carriage door, nodding for her to enter. "But wait."

Elanor hesitated, glancing between him and the cage-like carriage.

He quickly glanced around again, then slipped something cool and small into her palm—the jagged edge of a key. "For when the time's right," he whispered, his eyes meeting hers for a fleeting moment before he looked away, urgency written all over his face. "Wait for the right moment to use it, and keep it hidden. They'll be watching."

Elanor swallowed hard, clenching her hand around the key as if it were her lifeline. The boy ushered her inside and closed the door behind her, his face a mask of reluctant obedience as he slid the bolt shut. The loud click of the lock echoed in the still air, sending a shiver down her spine.

As he stepped back, Elanor saw Merrick, Judah, and a few others casting looks her way, and she forced herself to look anywhere but at the guard who'd helped her. The bars between her and freedom were impenetrable, but the key pressed firmly in her hand was a glimmer of hope she hadn't expected. She leaned back, pulse racing, determination strengthening her resolve.

Outside, Merrick shouted commands to his men, preparing to lead the way to Leto. But inside the cage, hidden from their sight, Elanor's fingers curled tighter around the key.

A window for her escape would come, and when it did, she would be ready.

CHAPTER FOURTEEN

The journey toward Leto was endless, each hour blending into the next as the carriage rattled over rough trails, jostling Elanor in her cramped prison. Her arms ached from being bound, and her muscles were sore from sitting for so long without being able to properly stretch. With little food or water offered, a dull hunger gnawed at her, the dryness in her mouth a constant reminder of her captivity. She swallowed, feeling the sandpaper-like scrape in her throat, each breath more challenging than the last as the day's heat bore down on her through the iron bars.

The relentless rhythm of the carriage wheels was almost hypnotic. Elanor found herself drifting in and out of a light, uncomfortable sleep, jerking awake whenever the carriage struck a deeper rut or bounced over loose stones. The sparse bits of food she'd been given had done little to satisfy her hunger, and the small, begrudging sips of water were nowhere near enough to ease her thirst. She couldn't remember ever feeling so weak, so stripped of her autonomy.

Through the gaps in the cage, Elanor peered at the men on horseback around her, clutching her locket in her hand over her chest. Most of the men had a hard, stoic look, accustomed to this kind of life. Some looked disinterested, occasionally turning to chat with each other, their laughter harsh against the quiet landscape. A few shot her wary glances as if to remind her of her place—helpless, captured, and outnumbered.

But as she looked closer, she saw more than the surface expressions: a young man at the edge of the group had worry etched on his face, casting furtive eyes toward Merrick and Judah, especially whenever Merrick's tone turned harsher; another one rode with slumped shoulders, murmuring to himself like he was trying to calm some private, anxious thought. They weren't all as hardened as they pretended. Then again, no one was entirely unaffected by their actions.

Her eyes drifted toward the front of the group where Merrick and Judah rode close together, their silhouettes contrasting sharply against the dusty horizon. Merrick's commanding presence overshadowed his small stature on his horse. Though his shoulders were squared and his chin high, Elanor noticed how often his head swiveled, watching everything as though his men might turn on him at any moment.

Judah, in contrast, held himself with a relaxed confidence, his large frame shifting comfortably with the horse's stride, one hand lightly resting on his thigh. The men clearly respected him more than they did Merrick, even if they wouldn't say it outright.

The sight of them stirred something bitter within her. They were dragging her toward Leto for some dark purpose, forcing her into a fate she hadn't chosen, and yet the memory of her friends lingered. The endless ride left her far too much time to think of them.

She pictured Nora's steely confidence, Boone's humor, the sheriff's silent determination—even his hesitance made sense in a way now that squared with his background. And then there was Weston. Her mind flashed to his face, and her stomach churned with the thought of how worried he'd be right now, how hard he'd be working to come after her. It almost hurt to think of him. Their last exchange was a simple look that said much more than she'd let herself feel.

Elanor's thoughts looped endlessly, circling back to the same faces, the same moments, until a sharp unease crept over her. Hadn't she already been here in her mind? Hadn't she already thought about Weston's worried expression, Nora's unshakable courage, and the sheriff's uneasy quiet? The details were too vivid, yet oddly distant like a memory rehearsed too many times. Or was she forgetting things in pieces, losing chunks of time without realizing it?

She tried to grasp the thread of her thoughts, but it slipped away, leaving her stranded in the present, uncertain if her memories were crumbling under pressure or if her mind was manipulating her. How much had she already forgotten? She shivered, her exhaustion making the edges of her reality blur. Was this the desert's doing, or was something far worse unraveling inside her? For the first time, she wondered if she'd even recognize herself when this was over—if she'd make it far enough to try.

The rumbling sound of the carriage wheels on the rocky ground shifted, and a change in the air, a kind of thickness, made her sit up, gripping the bars. They were nearing Leto; she sensed it.

The dirt path to Leto stretched before them, winding like a dry, unending riverbed under the relentless sun. Elanor's fingers clutched the bars of her cage, the hot metal searing against her palms as the carriage jolted forward. Each bump sent a jarring reminder of her confinement, and the rhythmic sway of the wagon mixed with the murmur of Merrick's men riding alongside.

As they neared Leto, the landscape shifted. Dry hills gave way to clusters of weathered buildings rising in the distance, their worn, cracked facades and faded signs of a life toughened by the desert. The whole town braced itself as they entered, doors shutting one by one, shutters pulled closed, hinting at a long-held familiarity with such intrusions.

Elanor's throat tightened as she looked through the bars, eyes scanning the empty streets. Not a soul moved, yet she felt hidden eyes watching, people concealed behind curtains and shadows. The only movement came from Merrick's men, whose horses kicked up dust clouds as they rode, their faces set with anticipation.

She caught a glimpse of eager smiles that hinted at a taste for the power their presence exerted over these townsfolk. But beneath their confidence, an unspoken anxiety rippled through the ranks, a sense of unease they couldn't quite mask.

Two guards broke the silence from the front of the carriage with a quiet conversation.

"So, you reckon she's really that important? Sounds like a tall tale Merrick spun to keep us on a leash," one muttered, shifting uncomfortably in his saddle and casting a wary look back at Elanor's cage.

The other shook his head, his voice tinged with doubt. "Don't know. We've been running circles for weeks now, and all we got is a caged girl who doesn't even know why she's here. Just can't see what makes her worth all this trouble."

Before they could continue, Judah turned sharply in his saddle, fixing them both with a cold glare. "You boys got nothin' better to jaw about?"

Immediately, the two men straightened, swallowed their words, and directed their attention forward, the hard edge of Judah's stare a reminder of who was keeping them in line.

Silence reclaimed the space between them, broken only by the clop of hooves and the rattle of the carriage wheels. Elanor's eyes shifted to Judah, noting his unyielding presence. She could tell he commanded more than loyalty; he commanded a quiet, simmering respect that even Merrick struggled to muster. Judah was the anchor holding the group steady, a silent force steering them down the road.

As they moved deeper into town, Elanor's unease intensified. She forced herself to breathe slowly, counting her breaths to steady her rising dread, hands gripping the bars until her knuckles turned white.

The main street was vast and empty, lined with darkened storefronts and vacant windows, resembling a stage set for an uncertain drama. The silence was occasionally pierced by the murmurs of the men around her, each whisper more indistinct than the last, weaving a tapestry of apprehension and respect. Their conversation drifted back to Elanor's ears, each word steeped in a cautious ambiguity that revealed nothing explicit, yet suggested much. This atmosphere of mystery was enough to bring them here, enough to keep them bound in a collective, nervous loyalty.

Elanor's mind raced, piecing together the scant hints in their guarded tones. There was no clear mention of her role or any explicit agenda, yet the seriousness with which they approached their task was palpable. The men's cautious glances and the enthusiasm of Merrick's directives pointed to a profound yet undisclosed significance tied to her presence.

As she was mired in thought, the procession abruptly stopped. Her head snapped up, and a surge of adrenaline coursed through her as she spotted a figure emerging from the shadows at the far end of the street.

A woman with a sheriff's badge gleaming on her chest stood, arms folded, flanked by several deputies. Her stance was steady, gaze unwavering as she looked over Merrick and his men with disdain and caution. Elanor squinted, trying to take in more of the scene, her pulse quickening.

One of the men at the front of the carriage turned halfway around, his hand resting on the grip of his pistol. "Best keep quiet back there, miss," he drawled, a faint threat lacing his tone. "Would hate to have to use this to keep the peace."

Merrick dismounted with a dramatic flourish, giving the sheriff a mock bow. "Well, if it isn't the sheriff of Leto," he said, his voice oily with false charm. "How long has it been, Angelina? I half expected you to throw us a parade."

Sheriff Angelina's expression remained steely, unimpressed. "Nobody's throwing you a parade, Merrick. Leto's a decent town—we plan on keeping it that way. That means keeping your kind out."

"Oh, come on, now." Merrick straightened, lips curling into a sly smile. "Don't act like you're not a little glad to see me. We go back, don't we?"

Angelina stepped forward, her deputies mirroring her movement. "Yeah, back far enough to know you're not welcome here anymore."

The smile on Merrick's face faltered, and something darker flashed in his eyes. "Seems you've changed, Sheriff. I remember when you'd ride with me just about anywhere."

Angelina's expression softened for the briefest of moments, though her stance didn't waver. "I didn't change, Merrick. You chose your path, and it's been nothing but trouble ever since."

"Come, now," Merrick drawled, shrugging. "You know, we all do what we have to do to survive. Some of us just don't get the luxury of playing hero."

Angelina's face hardened, her fists clenched at her sides. "Don't fool yourself. What you do has nothing to do with survival—it's destruction."

Merrick's face darkened further, a flicker of bitterness crossing its contours. He looked toward his men, who were tense but held their ground. Just as Merrick was ready to shoot back a retort, Angelina's attention shifted, her eyes catching on something behind him.

Her eyes narrowed as they landed on the barred carriage that held Elanor, and her brows pulled together in disbelief. "Really, a caged cart? She isn't yours to hold onto."

Merrick followed her glare, the smirk returning to his face. "Oh, that? Just holdin' on 'til she's ready to give in, you might say."

Angelina stepped closer, her expression hardening when her eyes locked on Elanor behind the bars. She met Elanor's wide eyes with a flash of anger before returning to Merrick. "This is low, even for you, Merrick. She's not some toy for you to play with."

Merrick's expression hardened. "I don't know about you, Angelina, but I'm having the time of my life. And just so you know, she'll be fine if nobody gets in my way."

Angelina's voice lacked warmth. "Let her go."

Merrick let out a laugh that echoed down the street. "Careful, Angelina. Not everyone can live up to your high moral standards. Besides, I wouldn't want to deprive you of the show."

Seeing a flicker of anger among Merrick's men, Angelina's deputies readied themselves, but she held up a hand to keep them steady. Her attention flickered briefly to her deputies and then back to Merrick, fury simmering beneath her calm facade. "I'll give you one warning, Merrick. This world isn't your playground, and it's not for you to bring your petty schemes through."

Merrick smirked, waving his hand dismissively. He raised two fingers, signaling his men to move Elanor's carriage out of sight. They obeyed instantly, steering it away from the main street and down a narrow alley. Elanor watched Angelina's look of disdain settle on Merrick with a fierce intensity.

As Merrick's and Angelina's voices faded, Elanor strained to hear the last few words exchanged.

"This isn't over, Merrick," Angelina called, her voice echoing faintly. "You'll pay for this."

Merrick's laughter floated back, cruel and hollow. "Save the righteous talk, Angel. Some of us live in a world worth fighting for."

Elanor's view of the main street finally disappeared as she was drawn further from the standoff, the carriage rattling over the uneven road. Angelina's fierce, determined voice was the last sound she made out, leaving her with a glimmer of hope.

Elanor leaned back against the bars, her thoughts swirling with what she'd just witnessed. The exchange between Angelina and Merrick replayed in her mind, each look and tense word between them filling her with a deeper unease. She hadn't missed how Merrick's grin had hardened, and Angelina's face had flickered with something like anger—no, disappointment. It was as if a story between them had twisted and soured over time, leaving only a bitter rivalry in its place.

Merrick had spoken to her with such open disdain, almost flaunting Elanor's captivity as if to prove something to the sheriff. The idea that she was being used as a pawn in this game grated against her, spurring the growing need to escape. But the sheriff's confidence had lingered with her, too—Angelina hadn't backed down. It felt like she was one of the few people capable of facing Merrick without fear, a reminder that Elanor wasn't alone.

Her eyes wandered to the two men on the bench at the front of the carriage.

"Think we'll have time for some fun tonight in Leto?" one asked, his voice slurred with the confidence of someone who believed he had all the time in the world.

"Dunno, depends on Merrick," the more prominent man replied, scratching his beard. "But hell, we deserve it, don't we? Been traipsin' around this godforsaken desert for weeks now."

"Sure do," the wiry one agreed, casting a backward glance at Elanor with a grin that made her shudder. "Maybe even get some time to ourselves while Merrick and Judah deal with this 'chosen one' business. What do you say?"

His companion chuckled, shaking his head as he spit to the side.

"Let's just rise up the ranks and keep outta their way. Last thing I want is to get tangled up with all this voodoo nonsense."

Elanor's grip tightened on the key. Their conversation made it clear how little they cared about her beyond the promotion they'd get for hauling her in. She eyed the men, their backs turned, caught up in their jokes. This key could potentially be her sole opportunity, but she would need to patiently wait for them to completely let down their defenses. If she could find the right moment, the briefest lapse in their attention, she might be able to unlock the door and slip away. But it had to be perfect —one wrong move, and they'd catch her, crush her only chance.

A small rock rattled against the cage's metal bars, drawing her focus down. Her heart pounded, eyes widening as she traced the stone's path back to the shadows near a building's corner.

Weston.

Standing partially hidden, he gave her a quick, subtle nod, his eyes sharp with reassurance. Relief washed over her, and her chest tightened as she held the key harder. Merrick, Angelina, and their rivalry faded into the background. Weston was here—and with that, her one chance at freedom was suddenly, thrillingly within reach.

Weston sent her a quick gesture to stay quiet. He held her gaze for a fleeting moment, his eyes conveying reassurance and determination before he slipped back into the shadows, his movements swift and practiced.

The edges of the key cut into her palm, the two guards at the front of the carriage oblivious, their laughter and offhand remarks drifting back toward her without concern.

As Elanor steadied her breathing, prepared to make her move, the sudden, sharp crack of gunfire erupted in the distance. Her blood ran cold; the sound was too close, too real—her chance at freedom was now punctuated by the echoes of shots ringing from around the corner where Weston had just hidden.

CHAPTER FIFTEEN

The gunfire continued, a rapid succession of shots that shattered the quiet of Leto's main street and made Elanor press herself instinctively against the bars of her cage. Her eyes scanned the shadows frantically, searching for any sign of Weston. Had he been caught? Was he responsible for the gunfire? Panic prickled at her senses as she struggled to piece together the chaotic sounds surrounding her. With each shot, her hopes of escape mingled with a deepening fear of the unknown dangers now erupting around her.

The two guards stationed at the front of the carriage had jolted to attention. The wiry man with a scar across his cheek nervously looked toward the main street. His eyes darted from Elanor to the street and back again, his fingers twitching as they hovered near his pistol.

"What's going on out there?" he hissed, leaning toward his companion.

The larger guard, seemingly more seasoned, shrugged, though his hand drifted instinctively to the gun on his hip. "Whatever it is, sounds like Merrick might need an extra set of hands."

The wiry guard squinted at Elanor, scratching his head as he mulled it over. "Should we check it out?"

The big guard hesitated, glancing back toward the bars behind him. "We can't just leave her," he muttered. "Merrick'll have our heads."

"But she's locked up tight," the wiry one reasoned, his attention fixed on the action at the other end of the street. "She's not going anywhere."

Beyond the men, Nora's voice rang out from around the corner, bold and taunting. "Hey, fellas! Lookin' for a real prize? Thought you'd want to try your luck with someone who'll give you a real fight!"

Both guards whipped their heads toward the sound.

The wiry guard smirked, nudging his companion with his elbow. "Think we should teach her some manners?"

The big guard peered back at Elanor one last time as if weighing his options before nodding. "Merrick'll have a fit if she slips away, but we can't let that one go, either." He looked at Elanor, his expression cold. "You stay put, girlie. Don't make me use this." He patted his pistol.

Without another word, the two men leaped down from the bench, their footsteps echoing as they rounded the corner in pursuit of Nora.

Elanor watched them disappear, heart thundering. This was her chance, but her pulse pounded with fear and anticipation—every instinct urged her to move while their backs were turned. She took a shaky breath, eyes darting around as she gathered herself, knowing she couldn't afford to waste a second.

She gripped the bars tightly, her breath shallow as she strained to hear any sound hinting at what was happening beyond her view. Just then, a faint whisper reached her ears.

"Elanor."

She whipped her head around, and there moving quickly and silently through the shadows was Weston. Relief washed over her so swiftly it almost stole her breath. He hurried to the back of the carriage, his eyes fixed on her with an intensity that melted every lingering shred of fear.

"Weston," she breathed as everything—the journey, her capture, the uncertainty—fell away for that brief, electric moment between them.

He reached through the bars, his hand grazing her cheek as his eyes searched hers. "You alright?" he asked, his voice filled with a worry that made her chest tighten.

"I . . . I think so," she managed, her words catching as she tried to take him in. "But Merrick . . . they're planning something awful, and—"

"Let's get you out of here first," Weston interrupted softly. He reached for the lock on the cage door, but his hands stilled when Elanor lifted her palm, revealing the small key she'd been clutching tightly.

Weston took the key from her with a soft, relieved chuckle and fit it into the lock. A moment later, the door swung open, and he reached in, sliding his hands under her arms to help her down from the carriage. The feel of his steadying grip sent warmth radiating through her. She stumbled slightly, weakened from her time in captivity, and he pulled her close to steady her, his arm instinctively wrapping around her waist.

"We have to move," Weston said. "Can you walk?"

Elanor nodded, though her legs still trembled from fatigue. Weston kept his arm around her as they moved away from the carriage, guiding her toward the shadows of a nearby building. She leaned into him instinctively. Around them, the sounds of gunfire from the main street continued.

Weston's gaze flickered over her face as they moved. "Think you can keep up for a bit longer?" he asked, encouraging gently.

"I'll manage," she replied, though the effort to stay upright made her every muscle ache.

With one last glance over his shoulder, Weston guided her behind the cover of the building, each step a reminder of the urgency that drove them.

The sounds of gunfire cracked through the air, echoing off the buildings as Weston and Elanor slipped through the narrow alleys behind the main street. Weston kept his arm securely around her waist, steadying her when her legs wavered while he carefully scanned their surroundings, his every movement deliberate, protective.

Elanor gritted her teeth, her steps faltering as exhaustion clawed at her, the faintness that had been creeping up on her since her time in the carriage finally starting to take its toll. She blinked hard, trying to shake the fogginess clouding her vision, but Weston sensed her weakness, adjusting his hold to keep her upright.

"You're doing fine," he murmured, his voice reassuring as he urged her forward. "Not much farther, I promise."

Despite the strain, Elanor couldn't help but feel a surge of determination. She'd made it this far—Weston had risked everything to get her out, and she couldn't let them fail now. She straightened her posture, matching his pace as best she could.

Together, they navigated the narrow, dimly lit side street, slipping behind crates and barrels as faint shadows danced across the walls. Every crunch of gravel underfoot or creak from a distant door sent a jolt through Elanor's chest, her nerves stretched taut, anticipating the shout of Merrick's men at any moment.

They rounded a corner and stopped abruptly as two of Merrick's men appeared a few paces before them, running toward the main street. Weston quickly pulled Elanor down behind an overturned wagon, his hand tightening on her in a silent signal to stay low.

Elanor held her breath, listening intently as the two men stopped near them.

"You sure you heard something?" one of them said, chuckling lazily, then some banter about being on edge while the gunfight continued on the main street.

Weston shifted slightly, his body a shield between Elanor and the two men. His hand slipped from her waist to her shoulder, a silent assurance as they waited for the men to move on. After what felt like an eternity, the footsteps faded, and Weston exhaled softly, giving her a brief nod.

"We need to keep moving," he whispered. "Let's head around the back alley, just a bit farther."

She nodded, and they continued their careful journey through the winding streets, darting through alleys and dodging the glimmers of light reflecting from nearby windows. The gunfire on the main street continued, but there was a noticeable shift in its intensity—it was like Angelina and her deputies were holding their ground against Merrick's men, which brought a surge of hope to Elanor's chest.

Finally, they reached the alley's edge near a dimly lit shop with a wooden sign creaking in the breeze. Weston paused, his grip still firm around her waist, and he tilted his head toward a side door partially obscured by a few barrels and crates.

"In here," he whispered. "Nora and the others should be close by."

They slipped inside, closing the door quietly behind them. The interior was shadowed, and there was only a faint glow from a single lantern hanging in the room's far corner. The front windows were boarded up. Elanor's eyes adjusted quickly, and a flicker of relief coursed through her as she spotted Boone and the sheriff in a small loft, their figures blending with the shadows.

"Over here," Boone hissed, waving them forward with a grin. "Looks like you both managed to escape in one piece."

The sheriff looked around as if unable to contain himself. "Imagine that," he said, a hint of pride in his voice. "Never thought I'd start a gunfight. But we needed to stir up some chaos, and, well, it sure did the job."

Boone snorted, stretching out his freshly bandaged arm with a proud wince. "Ain't no one the wiser it was us. Think they figured it was just another old-town brawl." He gave the sheriff a conspiratorial wink. "'Course, they'd never suspect a straight-laced sheriff, and his good friend Boone would be the ones lightin' up the street."

Weston helped Elanor up the stairs to the loft, his hand never leaving her side as they climbed. Once they reached the top, the anxiety started to loosen slightly as Elanor took in her friends' faces, a flicker of relief lightening her fatigue.

Below, the door creaked open, and Nora slipped in, shutting it softly behind her. She looked up. Relief was evident when she locked in on Elanor and Weston. "Glad to see you made it," she whispered, her voice filled with genuine warmth and urgency. "But we need to stay quiet and keep out of sight. They'll know she's free soon enough."

When she reached the loft, Nora leaned over, pulling Elanor into a sudden, warm hug. "Missed you, twin," she said with a teasing grin, releasing her with a wink. "Nora and Elanor reunited against the madness of the Wild West."

Elanor laughed softly, feeling a warmth she didn't think she needed.

A sheriff's friend allowed the group to shelter in a small, cramped crawl space in the loft. Their breaths held as they listened for the sounds of Merrick's men outside, and they hid behind a cleverly disguised wall panel the sheriff had slid back into place with practiced ease.

Elanor settled herself against the rough wooden planks of the loft, her eyes adjusting to the dim light and tight quarters. The space was little more than an attic tucked above the main room, the angled beams pressing down from above, making it impossible to stand upright. Rusted tools dangled from nails hammered into the beams, their silhouettes jagged and eerie in the faint streaks of sunlight filtering through a narrow window near the ceiling. Dust motes danced in the air, illuminated by the light and the faint smell of sawdust mixed with the musty scent of old wood.

A narrow bedroll was tucked into one corner, flattened and faded with use, while crates and sacks of long-forgotten supplies lined the opposite wall, some spilling over with rotting burlap. The floor creaked ominously with each slight movement, making everyone cautious to shift their weight. The space was cramped, forcing the group to huddle close, but there was a strange comfort in their proximity—a fragile sense of safety bolstered by the shared knowledge of the secret entrance.

Elanor's fingers brushed the rough edge of the wall panel beside her, its grain worn smooth in places where hands had frequently pulled it shut. Her breathing slowed as she traced the grooves, grounding herself in the small details. The thick, stale air pressed in around them, amplifying every muffled sound from outside. She peered toward the others, their faces drawn taut with exhaustion but unified by the same unspoken determination.

Curiosity tugged at Elanor, and she turned to the sheriff. "So . . . how did you all manage to get here so quickly?"

The sheriff exchanged a look with Boone before clearing his throat. "After Merrick's men left with you, we swiftly made our way to Leto. Boone here needed a good patch-up." He gestured toward Boone, who held out his arm, proudly displaying his fresh bandages.

"Got myself fixed up right proper," Boone said proudly, wincing slightly as he adjusted his shirt sleeve over the bandages. "But I told the doc to hurry—I wasn't gonna to let some gunshot keep me from gettin' back to you all."

"And the town?" Elanor asked, looking pointedly at the sheriff. "Did anyone react to seeing you?"

The sheriff's expression shifted, a flash of regret darkening his face. "They haven't seen me . . . yet." He nodded to the hidden space they were tucked into. "Been holed up here thanks to an old friend who still believes in me—one of the few who didn't fall for the rumors. She's riskin' plenty by hiding us here."

Elanor's focus lingered on the sheriff. His quiet admission resonated deeply with her. The idea of being cast out, of no longer belonging in a place that once felt like home, was uncomfortably familiar. She couldn't quite place it, but the thought of existing on the fringes—seen but unseen, tolerated but not embraced—tugged at her in a way that made her throat tighten.

She pressed her hand against the splintered wood beside her, grounding herself against the sharp edges. Why did his words sting like a truth she'd already lived? A fragment of something—something important—teased the edges of her mind, but her thoughts were too clouded by exhaustion to pull it into focus.

The sensation left her unsettled, as though the sheriff's struggle mirrored a wound in herself she hadn't known was there. The sensation of being on the outside, scrutinized by whispers and half-truths, unsettled her. She tried to brush it off, but the ache lingered, a quiet reminder of a past she couldn't reach, no matter how hard she tried.

The sheriff looked up, his face softening as he locked on Elanor. "Well," he said with a small, genuine smile, stretching his legs. "It's good to have you back with us, Miss Elanor."

A warmth spread through her as she looked at each of them, feeling the comfort of belonging—even here, in the quiet shadows of a loft above a town of strangers.

Sitting close beside her, Weston nodded. "The sheriff's right," he murmured, his attention holding hers. "It's not the same without you, El. Feels right, having you back."

A gentle smile crossed Elanor's face as she met his eyes, her heart lifting despite the dangers still lurking. For a moment, the chaotic world around them faded, and she could only feel the warmth of their closeness.

But then Boone grinned and joked. "Alright, now," he drawled, winking at Weston, "as much as I hate to interrupt a tender reunion, I'd say we save the love letters till we're well outta this place. There's only so much mush I can handle before breakfast."

Nora gave him a sidelong look. "Boone, it's the afternoon."

He remained unfazed. "What? You never have your breakfast whiskey for lunch before?" Boone tipped an imaginary hat, his grin widening. "Keeps the day consistent, no matter the time."

The group laughed collectively, the tension easing as they shared the moment.

The echoes of gunfire ricocheting down the main street finally died away, leaving an eerie silence.

Elanor took a deep breath, her nerves tingling from the sudden quiet.

Boone shifted, craning his neck as though he could see through the wooden walls. "So, reckon it's over?"

The sheriff gave a thoughtful nod, though his face was wary. "If it's quiet, it probably means they're regrouping. Merrick won't be inclined to overlook matters, particularly when he discovers Elanor's absence."

Nora crossed her arms. "When he realizes she's out of his little cage, he's going to turn this town upside down."

Elanor steeled herself. "So, what do we do, then?"

"We wait." The sheriff leaned forward. "We wait until nightfall to avoid as many eyes as we can, then head for the stables by foot. They're on the edge of town, so we'll need to keep low and out of sight."

Nora nodded, voice steady. "The horses'll get us out quicker than anything else, but the stables will be watched, no doubt. We move as one, keep it quiet, and once we're on the move, we don't stop."

Boone gave Elanor a playful nudge. "Just picture it: We'll sneak right by, saddle up, and be halfway to freedom before Merrick even knows what hit him."

The sheriff chuckled softly, but his expression was serious. "No mistakes, no extra risks. Where possible, we will navigate through the back alleys. Just stay sharp. It's gonna be tight, but we'll make it."

Elanor frowned. "And what if they spot us? Or if the stables are more heavily guarded than we think? Do we have a backup plan?"

Nora's eyes met hers. "It's a risk, Elanor. But the horses are our best chance to put distance between us and Merrick's men. Without them, we will find ourselves in a precarious situation."

Boone gave a casual shrug, though his tone held more sincerity than usual. "Ain't like we've got a stack of options here. Unless you fancy waiting around for Merrick to gift us a free pass, this is it."

The sheriff nodded, his expression serious. "It's not perfect, but it's what we've got. The longer we stay here, the greater the chance they'll find us. Moving at night gives us the best shot."

Elanor hesitated, her attention shifting to the narrow window where faint streaks of daylight filtered in. Despite her desire to argue and challenge the plan, the determination on their faces provided her with all the necessary information. It wasn't about whether the plan would work—it was about having no other choice.

Finally, she exhaled. "Alright. Let's hope it's enough."

With their plan set, a quiet unease settled over the group. There was nothing left to say, nothing to do but wait and hope. Minutes ticked by in tense silence, each of them stealing glances toward the crawlspace's entrance, alert for any sounds from below.

Below, a door flung open, slamming against the wood siding, and footsteps echoed from the shop floor. Everyone froze at the sound of footsteps, followed by the heavy shuffling of boots as Merrick's men fanned out through the shop.

Elanor held her breath, every nerve tense as one of them spoke, his voice rough and impatient. "Be vigilant. If they're hiding, they'll be holed up in a place like this."

"Boss'll have our heads if we miss 'em," another muttered.

The sheriff's eyes flashed, and he motioned for everyone to stay perfectly still, his hand tightening around the handle of his revolver.

"Check those stairs," one of them said.

The sound of a boot landing on the first step splintered the wooden stairs, piercing the tension like a knife. The group exchanged looks, fear flashing as they recognized how close they were to being found.

One slow, creaking step after another, the boots ascended. Elanor squeezed Weston's hand as the footsteps neared, her pulse pounding as she braced for the worst, the shadow of the approaching figure inching its way up the ceiling toward the loft.

CHAPTER SIXTEEN

Elanor held her breath, her heart hammering as the sound grew closer. She felt Weston's hand in hers, steady and reassuring, though she could tell by his tight expression that he was just as tense as she was. Across from her, Nora scrunched her face with each of the man's steps just outside their hiding space, her usual confidence giving way to focused stillness. In contrast, Boone's usually relaxed face had gone rigid, his eyes fixed on the hidden door.

The man reached the top of the stairs, footsteps shifting onto the creaky floor of the loft. His movements were loud and aimless, each slow step sending a shiver of anxiety through Elanor as he paced around the space, poking through the boxes and barrels stacked against the walls. Every sound was magnified, each step closer to their hiding place causing her breath to catch in her throat.

From below, a voice echoed up the stairwell, sharp and impatient. "You findin' anything up there, or just gettin' cozy?"

The guard outside their hiding spot snorted, footsteps pausing outside the wall concealing them. "Hold your horses, I'm lookin'." He knocked something over, and it crashed to the floor with a thunderous slam. The sharp, splintering sound of glass shattering inside the crate echoed through the loft, scattering a chilling wave of tinkling shards across the floor. Elanor tensed, but he merely kicked it aside with a muttered curse. Everyone was silent as they strained to listen, hoping he'd turn back toward the stairs.

He paused again, the heavy scuff of his boots stopping near the wall Nora and the sheriff had their backs to. The silence stretched painfully until he finally called down, his voice louder this time: "Hold on a second. Think I might've found somethin'."

Elanor's stomach twisted with dread, her attention darting to the others. Nora's face was grim, while Weston's eyes were fixed sharply on the floor, as if willing the man to move away.

The voice from below was eager. "What is it?"

The man upstairs gave a short laugh. "Looks like a crate of whiskey! Let's say we make ourselves a little richer for all this trouble, huh?"

Laughter erupted from the man below, and the impatient voice replied, "Well, don't dawdle! Haul it down and save some for me."

Relief washed over Elanor as the footsteps began to retreat, each creak of the stairs carrying the man—and the prize whiskey—back to the main floor and out the back door to the alley. The loft fell silent again, save for the soft, collective exhale of the group. Elanor's shoulders finally dropped, though her pulse still raced from the close call.

Boone was the first to break the silence, a mock look of horror on his face. "They took my whiskey!" he whispered with dramatic devastation, shaking his head.

Nora shot him an exasperated look, though there was the faintest hint of a smirk on her lips. "Good riddance if it means they're out of our hair."

The group exchanged a look, knowing this brief relief was temporary. They'd evaded discovery this time, but it wouldn't be long before Merrick's men regrouped—and the risk of being found again would only grow.

The group settled again in the crawlspace, the shadows growing longer as the daylight faded.

The plan was simple, but the reality of executing it weighed on them as they went over it one last time. They'd sneak out the back, follow the alley to the stables on the outskirts, and make a swift departure under cover of darkness.

"Once we're at the stables, stick close. We're not out of this until we're back on the trail," Weston murmured, his focus shifting to each group member.

Boone leaned against the wall, nodding as he added his usual lightness. "Reckon they'll hear the horses, so let's make it dramatic, yeah? A grand ol' dash out of this charming place."

Elanor's eyelids growing heavier with every word. The warmth and exhaustion from the day caught up with her, and though she tried to fight it, she found herself sinking against Weston's shoulder. His arm wrapped around her instinctively, steadying her as she drifted off, the low rumble of their voices fading into the background.

When she opened her eyes, it was to the gentle press of Weston's hand on her shoulder.

"El," he whispered, his voice barely audible. "It's time."

Blinking, she peered around. The room was cloaked in shadows, the faint glow from the moon filtering through the small window above them. She straightened, rubbing her eyes as she registered the energy shift. They were ready to move.

The others gathered their things in the dim light. Nora gave her an encouraging nod.

Boone leaned over to Elanor, giving her a quick wink as he slung a bag over his shoulder. "Gonna miss this cozy little hideout," he whispered.

Nora rolled her eyes, muttering as she tiptoed toward the door. "You're about the only one missing it, Boone."

The group moved toward the rear exit. Elanor stuck close to Weston, who led the way with a quiet assurance, his gaze sharp as he scanned the path ahead. They navigated around the stacked barrels and crates, going to the back of the shop, where three narrow steps descended to the alley.

Nora reached the door first, pressing her ear to it before carefully opening it just wide enough to peer outside. She waved the others forward, gesturing for silence, and they slipped through the door and down into the alleyway.

They were halfway to the end of the alley when Elanor noticed two of Merrick's men slumped against the wall. Their hats were tipped low as they rested, empty whiskey bottles clutched in their hands. She shot Boone a wary look as he glanced longingly at the bottles, a grin already forming.

Boone, catching her eye, gave her a hopeful shrug. "Seems a waste, don't it? Just sitting there, calling my name."

Nora reached over and nudged his shoulder. "Unless you want to wake them, I'd leave it."

Boone pouted. "Alright, alright," he muttered, casting one last sad look at the stash. "Guess some sacrifices must be made."

The group moved past the two unconscious men, their footsteps muffled on the dirt-packed ground. They crept down the alley, pulses racing, fully aware they were just a few blocks from the stables.

The group pressed forward through the dim, candlelit alley, each step slow and deliberate to keep their movements nearly silent. The walls on either side closed in as they approached intersections with side alleys connected to the main road. Every few steps, they froze, pressing themselves into shadows when the distant crunch of gravel or low murmur of voices signaled someone nearby. Elanor held her breath each time, heart pounding as shadows passed along the connecting paths.

Ahead of her, Nora peered back, her expression tense but determined. She raised a finger to her lips, urging silence as they waited for two men to stroll by at the next junction. One of the men was laughing, his loud, gravelly voice cutting through the night air. They all froze, backs pressed tight against the wall, as the sound grew louder, the men stopping right at the mouth of the alley.

". . . and then he tried to tell me that Merrick actually knew what he was doing," one of the men said, snorting, sending his companion into a fit of laughter.

Boone smirked, but the sheriff shot him a warning look, eyes narrowed as they all waited for the men to pass, barely breathing.

The laughter faded as the two continued, and Nora exhaled, her posture easing as she gave a slight nod. "Keep close and watch the edges. We're not out yet," she whispered.

They crept forward again, navigating the shadows as the stable loomed just beyond the alley's end. Elanor's pulse quickened with relief at the sight of their escape in reach, and renewed anxiety as her eyes settled on the lone guard pacing by the stable's entrance. He was distracted, glancing idly up and down the road, his rifle dangling lazily at his side. But a moment's lapse wouldn't stop him from raising the alarm if he discovered them.

The group ducked back, pressing close to the stable's outer wall. Weston leaned in, his voice barely a whisper. "We'll need to get him away from the door without alerting anyone else. If we split his attention, one of us can get close enough to take him down."

Boone grinned as he picked up a small pebble, tossed it in his hand, and raised an eyebrow. "One distraction, coming right up."

He tossed the pebble across the road, where it clinked against an overturned crate. The guard's head snapped toward the sound, and he squinted. He took a few steps toward it, fingers tightening on his rifle.

Nora moved like a shadow, slipping behind him as Weston circled to intercept his path. Just as the guard turned, Nora clamped a hand over his mouth, stifling any sound while Weston relieved him of the rifle. The guard's eyes widened as he struggled briefly, but Nora's grip and a reassuring murmur quieted him.

She whispered to him, "Take it easy. We're just here for the horses."

With a nod to Boone, they quickly bound the guard's hands, stuffed his mouth with a handkerchief, and stashed him inside the stable, tucking him behind a pile of hay bales.

"Now, the horses," Weston said quietly, leading the way inside.

They moved swiftly through the stable, their practiced silence broken only by the soft metal clinks and the horses' quiet snorts. As Elanor scanned the rows of stalls, her attention landed on a bay mare, its sleek, black coat gleaming even in the low candlelight. Nora, busy securing the saddle on her horse, glanced Elanor's way with a small smile.

"We got you a new horse," Nora murmured, nodding to the bay.

Elanor blinked, surprised. "What?"

Weston stepped over, the hint of a smile touching his lips. "Thought you might want your own again." He paused, glancing down at his hands before meeting her eyes. "I'll miss having you close, but I figured you'd be much more comfortable with one of your own."

A pang shot through her chest at his words, and she reached out to place a hand on the mare's neck, feeling the warmth beneath her fingertips. She gave Weston a soft smile, letting the moment settle between them. "I'll miss it, too," she admitted, her voice barely above a whisper.

He nodded, a subtle understanding passing between them before he returned to the task at hand, checking his saddle straps. The bittersweet feeling lingered with her as she adjusted the reins, taking a deep breath to steady herself. This horse, though unfamiliar, was a new beginning and a reminder of her independence. Yet the ache of not riding with Weston wasn't so easily dismissed.

Her fingers trailed along the mare's neck, a subtle ache forming as she took in the sight of her new mount. Her old horse—the one she'd ridden with Weston for the last stretch of their journey—had become familiar and safe, symbolizing her closeness with him. She swallowed, thinking of how much she'd missed sitting right beside him, the reassurance of his steady arm around her as they rode together.

Catching her lingering look, Weston furrowed his brow as he studied her face. "You okay to ride alone?" he asked, his voice soft but edged with worry. "You still look pale, and we don't know how far we'll need to go tonight."

The concern in his eyes stirred an ache within her, but she mustered a reassuring smile, lifting her chin to meet his eyes. "I'll be fine," she murmured. "The nap helped, and I . . . I can manage. This isn't exactly the best time to slow down, right?"

He gave a brief nod, though he still looked unconvinced. "If you need anything, you tell me."

Elanor's fingers wrapped around the reins as Weston helped her mount the mare. Elanor took a moment to find her balance, reminding herself of the independence this brought. Weston's presence was close enough to reassure her, yet the thought of not riding with him made the tiny flicker of separation feel sharper than she'd anticipated.

As the others finished saddling up, a distant shout broke through the night, echoing from the end of the road. Each second stretched as the shout grew louder, a ripple of urgency moving through the group as they mounted.

With a last, brief look, Weston reached out and gave her hand a small, grounding squeeze. "Stick close," he said.

Elanor nodded, gripping the reins tighter, blood thrumming in her ears from the danger and feeling that, with each passing second, they were a step closer to leaving Leto—and Merrick—behind.

The group urged their horses out of the stable, moving quickly but as quietly as possible down the shadowed back alleys. The buildings offered brief cover, their dark shapes blending with the night as Elanor's new mare shifted nervously beneath her.

As they neared the main road, Nora signaled for them to halt. She dismounted and crept to the edge of a building, peeking around the corner before stepping back to join them. "Merrick's men are just down the street," she murmured. "They're hanging around the saloon, but it won't take long for them to hear us once we're on open ground."

Weston nodded, his focus intense as he surveyed the street. "As soon as we head for the trails, they'll pursue us."

Boone gave a low whistle, adjusting his hat with a grin that didn't quite reach his eyes, the tightness in his movements betraying his unease. "Good thing we've got a head start, then. Let's make it a run they'll remember."

Weston turned to Elanor, his eyes lingering momentarily. "Stay close, El. Once we're out in the open, keep your horse to the side of mine. We'll break left toward the desert trail as soon as we pass the town's edge."

She swallowed, feeling her pulse quicken but giving him a determined nod. The group gathered their reins tightly, ready to immediately break into a full gallop. The air around them was charged, the quiet night thick with anticipation.

And then, they were off.

The horses bolted forward, hooves pounding against the packed dirt road as they surged past the last few buildings in Leto. Elanor gripped her reins with all her strength, keeping pace with Weston, heart racing as fast as her mare's strides. The wind whipped past her, but just as the thrill of freedom began to settle in, the shouts of Merrick's men sounded from behind them.

"There they are! After 'em!"

The shout carried through the night, followed by a scattering of hurried footsteps and the clang of saddles as Merrick's men scrambled to mount. Elanor risked a glance over her shoulder, her stomach churning at the sight of the dark figures readying for a chase, their silhouettes stretching across the road beneath the flickering lamplights.

"Faster!" Weston shouted, his voice cutting through the chaos as he urged them on.

Riding at the front, Nora veered left, her horse kicking up dust as they broke from the road onto the rocky desert trail. The transition was jarring, but they pushed forward, the uneven terrain doing little to slow them down. Their horses' hooves struck against rocks and gravel, their breaths coming in sharp, rapid bursts as they fled into the open desert.

But the voices behind them didn't fade; if anything, the sound of the pursuit grew louder, closer.

Elanor's pulse pounded in her ears as she kept pace with Weston, focusing on the rhythm of her mare's hooves and the dust swirling around them. She looked at him, a spark of determination in his eyes that steeled her nerves.

"We've got to shake 'em!" he shouted, his voice fierce. But the confidence in his voice was cut short as a gunshot cracked through the night air, the sound echoing off the rocks around them.

Elanor flinched, ducking instinctively. Another shot rang out, closer this time, and panic rose within her.

Ahead, Nora's horse stumbled slightly but recovered, and she yelled back at them, "Keep going!"

They pushed on, the relentless pursuit closing the distance, their breaths quickening in rhythm with the pounding urgency of their escape. With a final surge of strength, they accelerated farther into the desert, fully aware that the night was far from over and Merrick's men were rapidly approaching.

CHAPTER SEVENTEEN

The group urged their horses through the moonlit desert, racing past the edge of town as the landscape opened into vast, shadowy expanses. As they neared a massive rock formation jutting out against the night sky, they guided their mounts behind it, finding momentary shelter and a chance to catch their breath.

In the dim light, the sheriff pointed toward the faint outline of distant mountains to the west. "We split up here," he said, glancing between them, his expression taut with urgency. "Weston, Elanor—you come with me. We'll head west. Nora, Boone, you take the eastern route toward the dry ravine. When it's safe, we'll meet up at the Joshua tree grove five miles west, just past the bluff."

Boone snorted, casting a side-eye at the sheriff. "Last time we followed your directions, sheriff, we were more twisted around than a tumbleweed in a dust storm."

The sheriff's lips twitched, though his eyes stayed sharp. "Trust me this time, Boone. I know these parts better than any of us, and splitting up is the only way we'll shake them."

Nora gave a firm nod. "East it is, then. Boone, keep up, would you?"

Boone acknowledged Elanor and Weston with a half-grin. "Guess we'll see who ends up with the better scenery."

The group exchanged one last look before veering off in separate directions, hooves stirring up dust and the distant echoes of shouts drifting on the wind. Elanor leaned low over her horse, pulse quickening as they disappeared into the shadows to the west, following the sheriff's lead.

The chill of the night air bit sharply at Elanor's cheeks as they galloped on, the vast stretch of desert around them turning rugged and unpredictable with each stride. She felt the relentless pounding of her heart, each beat echoing the steady thud of her horse's hooves on the rocky ground. Despite the darkness, Elanor sensed the presence of Merrick's men somewhere behind them, trailing just out of sight. Occasionally, the moonlight caught on a distant glint of metal, causing her nerves to fray.

As they reached a narrow, winding passage between jagged walls of rock, the sheriff took the lead. His silhouette cut a determined figure against the terrain. The path was a maze of jutting stones and narrow turns, and every corner seemed to lead to another dead end.

"Stay close," Weston called to her. He rode just behind, guiding his horse carefully as his eyes darted between Elanor and the sheriff, alert to every sudden shift in the path.

The sheriff gestured ahead, toward a shadowed rise just visible in the moonlight. "We'll head for that bluff," he said. "It's narrow, but it might give us enough cover to lose them."

Elanor urged her horse forward, maintaining a tight grip on the reins as they navigated the uneven trail. Every step was precarious. The rocks were loose and jagged, and her horse stumbled now and then, making her grip the saddle with renewed focus. Her muscles ached as the path grew steeper, a dull reminder of how worn down she was from lack of food and rest.

They pushed on, weaving around low-hanging branches and dodging sharp rocks that jutted into the path. The desert opened before them with each wind and turn, revealing deeper shadows and craggy rock formations. She had to press her body close to the horse, narrowly avoiding the stones that scraped her boots and grazed her arms. Her left shoulder brushed painfully against a sharp edge, leaving a shallow scratch and making her wince, but she pushed the discomfort aside. They couldn't afford to slow down.

"Almost there," Weston said.

Elanor saw the faint outline of the bluff just ahead. The sheriff slowed briefly to check the terrain, his face pale in the moonlight but his eyes sharp as he surveyed the path. "We'll take a tight turn around that corner," he said, pointing ahead. "From there, we'll have enough cover to move quietly."

The distant sound of hooves still echoed faintly behind them, a reminder that they weren't in the clear yet. But, for the first time since the chase began, hope flickered within Elanor. They were out of the open desert, and the rocky landscape might finally allow them to slip out of sight, even if only for a while.

The sheriff led them up a winding trail, veering toward a cluster of large boulders nestled against the bluff. Shadows pooled heavily between the rocks, offering a brief respite from the open ground. He motioned for them to stop, his eyes flicking down the trail to ensure no one was in sight. One by one, they dismounted, leading their horses into the deeper shadows.

Elanor let out a shaky breath, grateful for the pause. Her legs trembled, barely steady, as she leaned against the rocky surface behind her. Weston's hand rested briefly on her arm, grounding her, and she looked up to find his gaze steady on her.

The sheriff peered around, his focus sharp and cautious. "Let's keep our voices low," he murmured. "If we're lucky, they'll ride past us."

Elanor settled against the rock, closing her eyes to steady herself, feeling the rough, cool surface pressing into her back. Her mouth was dry, her body weak, but there was no time to dwell on it.

The silence stretched, broken only by the quiet sounds of their breathing and the occasional shift of a horse's hooves against the gravelly ground. Weston stood beside her, eyes alert as he scanned their surroundings, hand resting on the grip of his pistol.

Minutes ticked by, each second feeling like an eternity. Elanor's muscles were taut, and every sound was amplified in the silence of the night. She glanced over at the sheriff, who was peering down the trail, his face set in concentration.

Then the faint sound of hoofbeats echoed from the direction they'd come, growing steadily louder. Elanor's breath hitched as she pressed farther back into the shadows. She felt Weston shift beside her, his body rigid as he listened intently.

The hoofbeats grew closer, and the sheriff gave a silent signal for them to stay still. Elanor's pulse raced as the sounds grew nearer, the distinct voices of Merrick's men breaking through the quiet. They were close enough now that she could make out their conversation.

"Think they took this path?"

"Wouldn't be surprised," another voice answered, rough and impatient. "Boss said to search every inch, and that's what we'll do."

Elanor held her breath, every nerve in her body on edge as the men rode by, their shadows shifting against the rocks. She dared not peek in their direction, afraid the slightest movement might catch their attention. Her fingers curled into the rocks behind her, anchoring herself as she waited, the sound of their voices fading but still too close for comfort.

One of the men slowed his horse, the sound of hooves pausing as he surveyed the area. She caught a glimpse of his silhouette just beyond the rocks, his posture tense as he scanned the surroundings. Panic rose as she realized how close he was—so close that he could have seen them if he had chosen to look a little harder.

But after a long, agonizing moment, he nudged his horse forward, his shadow merging with the others as they moved down the trail.

Elanor let out a slow and unsteady breath, glancing at Weston, who gave her a quick nod of reassurance. The sheriff waited a few more seconds, listening intently until the hoofbeats faded into the distance, leaving only the soft rustle of the desert night around them.

Elanor's breathing finally began to steady. Exhaustion washed over her.

Cool rocks prickled under Elanor's hand as she leaned against them. The sting in her arm was sharper now, and she glanced down, realizing just how much her sleeve had darkened with blood. She tried to brush it off, but the pain flared, pulling her out of her exhaustion.

Weston's attention drifted to her, narrowing as he noticed her discomfort. Without a word, he moved closer, his fingers gently tugging at her sleeve. "That looks bad," he murmured, concern etching his face.

Caught off guard, Elanor looked down at her arm, feeling slightly embarrassed. "I didn't think it was much. . . . It's just from scrambling through the rocks back there."

He shook his head, pulling a cloth from his pocket, and began to wipe the cut clean, his movements gentle and unhurried. His hand lingered on her arm briefly before he wrapped the cloth snugly around the top, just above the cut. "That should do," he said softly, the warmth of his words settling over her.

She glanced up, meeting his look, and for the first time in days, the rush in her chest wasn't solely from fear.

Before she could find the words to respond, a sound came from the shadows nearby—a heavy tread on the rocks. Weston shifted instinctively in front of her, his stance protective. The sheriff, too, stepped forward, his face hardening as a figure emerged from the darkness.

Elanor's breath caught. The stranger was tall, his wiry frame seeming both weathered and resilient, like a man who had spent a lifetime enduring harsh conditions. His salt-and-pepper hair, a mix of black and white, was cut just long enough to cover his ears, framing a face lined with age and experience. A short beard of the same mottled color outlined his strong jaw, adding to the impression of someone who had lived through countless trials. His stare was piercing, sharp with anger but carrying a shadow of something more profound—a haunting regret that weighed him down.

There was something unsettlingly familiar about him, though Elanor couldn't quite place where she'd seen him before. His presence tugged at the edges of her memory as if she had known him long ago, in another life. His voice was deep and thickly accented when he spoke, its cadence deliberate and rough, each word tinged with bitterness. His focus landed squarely on the sheriff, and he spat his words scornfully.

"Well, if it isn't Foster," he sneered, his eyes narrowing. "Thought you could just pass through without stirrin' up memories? It was all too easy to follow you to your old hiding places."

Elanor's attention shot to the sheriff, the name ringing in her ears.

Foster? She'd never heard anyone address him by that name before. Even though they'd traveled together for weeks, he had only been "the sheriff" to her, a distant title she hadn't questioned. Now, his real name echoed in her mind, adding another layer to the mystery of his identity.

The sheriff's face tightened, his jaw set. "I didn't come here to bring up the past, Simon," he said, his voice low. "We're just passing through."

The man—Simon—scoffed, glanced between Weston, Elanor, and the sheriff. "Passing through, are you?" His eyes darkened, the lines of his face casting harsh shadows in the moonlight. "Seems like you're always passing through when trouble follows."

Elanor felt a sharp pang in her chest. Simon's voice carried a pain she couldn't ignore, and the unspoken accusation lingered heavily between them. There was a story here, one thick with history and loss. Her eyes darted to the sheriff, seeing him in a new light. What could he have done to cause this man so much anger and grief?

"You know what happened back then," Simon continued, his tone heavy, almost pleading. "She deserved better than what she got." His eyes lingered on Elanor as he spoke, and a chill swept over her as if he was seeing someone else in her place—someone lost and beloved.

The sheriff's voice was barely audible, the burden of his past reverberating in every word. "I know, Pop. I've carried it with me every day."

A tense silence hung between them, broken only by the faint breeze whispering through the rocks. Simon's face softened, the harsh lines carved by anger and regret easing as he looked at the sheriff—his son. He took a steadying breath, seeming to search for the right words, but his voice was low, almost fragile when he spoke.

"You know I was among the ones who drove you out, don't you?" His eyes darkened, the memory of that day casting a shadow over his face. "Your own father, believing you were to blame for . . . for her death. I thought . . . we all thought you'd betrayed us, betrayed her. That you'd just let her go, that you didn't . . . that you didn't fight to save your sister."

Foster's face turned ashen, the pain of that memory flashing across his features. Elanor felt a deep pang in her chest, an inexplicable sorrow welling as she watched him. Something in this story—this loss—

177

resonated uncomfortably close to home. Her throat tightened, the faintest fragments of a forgotten sorrow flickering just out of reach.

Simon's head dropped. His voice was filled with remorse that stretched back over all the years that had passed since. "I chased you out of town, Foster. I was the one who rallied them all against you. I couldn't see beyond my own grief and anger. And you didn't fight back, didn't explain . . . I thought it was because you couldn't, but now I know it was because you were protecting us from the truth."

Foster's hand rested against the rock beside him as he steadied himself. "You'd already decided. My words wouldn't have changed anything," he said, though his voice held none of the bitterness Elanor might have expected. Instead, there was only sadness.

Simon gave a slight nod, acknowledging his son's words. "After you left, I . . . I thought it would all go away. I thought losing you would bring some kind of justice, some relief. But the silence only made it worse." He looked directly at Foster, a flicker of raw vulnerability crossing his face. "I went to Tawa not long after you left. I thought . . . I don't know what I thought. Maybe that he'd confirm I was right, that it would somehow make it easier to live with it all. But he showed me the truth—that you'd tried to save her and done everything you could."

He paused, his voice breaking as he peered at Elanor. "He showed me that it was her time, that sometimes . . . sometimes we can't hold on to those we love, no matter how much we fight for them."

The sheriff's face softened, pain glimmering in his eyes. Elanor watched him closely, a knot tightening in her chest. She couldn't help but feel an ache that resonated deep within her heart, a vague but persistent sense of loss, of something—or someone—she hadn't been able to save, a memory she couldn't quite grasp.

"You couldn't have known," Foster finally said, his voice rough but steady. "No one did. And I didn't have it in me to defend myself against . . . against you. I loved her as much as you did."

The quiet admission stirred something in Elanor, and her eyes stung, the rawness cutting through the night's chill. She looked at Weston, who held her gaze with understanding, as if sensing that this story wasn't just about the sheriff.

Simon inhaled deeply, his voice barely audible. "I've carried this guilt ever since. I never thought I'd get the chance to ask your forgiveness."

Foster's hand moved slightly, a tremor of emotion passing through him, and he looked at his father, his expression softening with something close to acceptance. "I don't know if forgiveness is what matters. What matters is that we've come together again after all these years."

A silence stretched between them, filled with unspoken words, years of separation and sorrow gradually easing through understanding. Simon nodded, accepting the words with the quiet dignity of someone finally coming to terms with his faults.

Elanor's pulse quickened, every piece of this moment stirring an unresolved grief in her. She felt it there, a pulse beneath her pain—an old wound, as if she, too, had once been left to carry such loss and blame. Her own sister's face flickered in her mind, a fleeting, half-formed memory that disappeared as quickly as it came, leaving her shaken and confused. She couldn't place it; the memory was hazy and blurred, but the feeling—the ache—was unmistakably genuine.

For a moment, she looked down, her hand curling around the edge of the rock beside her as the ache intensified. It was as if her body reacted to something her mind refused to let in. She sensed the same grief in the sheriff's story, mirrored in her heart.

As Simon spoke to his son, the words blended with her fractured memories, pulling at the deepest parts of her.

Weston shifted closer, his arm brushing hers as he leaned in, his eyes steady and concerned. "Everything okay?" he murmured, his voice a quiet thread that grounded her.

Elanor nodded slightly, swallowing the knot in her throat. "It's . . . it's just so much," she whispered. "Hearing it all . . . it's like it's reaching somewhere I can't explain." She looked up at Weston, his eyes full of understanding, and then quickly back down to hide the moisture in her eyes. She felt the delicate edges of something slipping just out of reach—like a memory she could touch but couldn't hold.

Simon's voice brought her attention back. He was staring at Foster with an intensity that made it clear he'd held on to this guilt and need to reconcile for years. "You don't have to carry it alone anymore," he said.

"I didn't understand back then. But now . . . I can see what I missed, what I closed my eyes to. And it was my own pride that cost us both all these years."

Foster nodded, his eyes distant as if seeing through the years. He offered a faint smile, the kind born from knowing that even the heaviest burdens could be lightened, if only by sharing them. He looked over at Elanor, and something in his expression softened.

"You know," he began, his voice softer as his eyes met Elanor's, "sometimes you carry something for so long, it starts to feel like it's a part of you, even if it shouldn't be."

Elanor felt an unexpected sting at his words, their truth striking her more deeply than she had anticipated. She gave a slight nod, unsure what to say but feeling his words settle in a place deep within her that had been empty for too long.

The silence settled thickly around them, heavy with the emotions left unsaid. Elanor glanced between the sheriff and his father, the weight of their reconciliation stirring a familiar ache within her—a quiet reminder of her unanswered questions and lingering regrets.

Breaking the silence, Weston said, "Simon . . . you mentioned you went to Tawa. You've met him?"

Simon nodded slowly, looking to the distant horizon. "Years ago," he said, almost reverently. "My pal, Cole, took me to him when I was too blind to see the truth for myself. Tawa . . . he didn't judge, didn't lecture. Just guided me to where I needed to go. Changed everything."

The mention of a journey to Tawa ignited a flicker of hope within Elanor. This journey had always been about finding him and getting answers she could barely articulate but needed nonetheless. The stories surrounding him painted Tawa as something beyond just a man—a guide, a healer, someone who could pierce through the obscurity of one's soul. And now, with Simon here, they had a real lead to him.

Weston nodded, his focus never wavering. "Would you be able to lead us to him now?"

Simon turned to Foster, searching his face for something unspoken. The sheriff, his expression softening, gave a slight nod. "What do you say, Pop? We could make up for lost time . . . together."

The question hung in the air, laden with old wounds and unspoken forgiveness. Elanor's chest tightened as she watched the two men. She felt something resonate within her, a stirring at the core of her being. A whisper of regret and guilt over someone she couldn't fully remember, like pieces of a puzzle just out of reach.

Simon finally nodded, glancing at Elanor. "If this is the road you're set on, I'll take you to him. But understand this—Tawa isn't easy to find. He's not bound to any one place. If he doesn't want to be found . . . he won't be."

Elanor nodded, grateful for Simon's help. "Thank you," she murmured. This was the path she'd started on, and she wasn't turning back now.

Simon turned his horse toward the distant horizon. The sheriff exchanged a small, relieved smile with Elanor, a glint of hope in his eyes. "Well, Miss Elanor," he said, his voice lighter than before. "Let's see if we can finally meet the man who started all this."

Elanor's breath caught in her throat, a pulse of determination surging through her. Tawa was more real now than ever after all their hardship, endless trials, and close calls. The thought of meeting the man who held answers to all her questions stirred something in her—a mixture of anticipation and fear. She nodded at the sheriff, a silent agreement that she, too, was ready to face whatever laid ahead.

Weston, catching the moment, broke the silence. His attention shifted to the darkened path they'd taken to reach their hiding spot. "If Merrick's men swing back, we'll want to be far from here," he murmured, glancing at Simon, then to Elanor, who steadied herself with a slow, determined breath. "Best we get moving."

The sheriff's father gave a solemn nod, his presence a grounding force among them.

Elanor underestimated the length of the journey through the rocky desert, feeling the strain of past days with each step of the horse's hooves. The path ahead was dimly lit by moonlight, casting eerie shadows on the canyon walls. Though her eyes strained to stay open,

Elanor focused on the movement of Simon's form, willing herself to keep up and ignore the ache settling in her bones.

The night air was dense as they pressed forward, the faint silhouettes of distant peaks breaking against the dark horizon. Elanor's muscles ached with each mile, her eyes barely staying open. Even the steady rhythm of hooves over gravel and sparse brush was muted in the early dawn.

As the first streaks of morning light began to bleed over the horizon, casting a soft glow over the desert landscape, Elanor spotted a lone, coiled juniper tree, its branches like dark fingers reaching skyward, marking their meeting point near the Joshua tree grove. Muted pink and gold hues washed over the land, illuminating the grove in a soft, surreal, foreign, and familiar light.

Relief surged through her as they closed the last stretch, and she saw Nora's figure, casually leaning against the tree. Her regard was as sharp as ever, catching sight of them the moment they approached. Boone stood a little to her left, hat tipped low, but his posture tense, fingers drumming restlessly against his belt in a rhythm that betrayed his antici-pation. The sight of them standing watch was an anchor, a reminder that, despite everything, they weren't facing this alone.

As they neared, Nora's lips curved into a slight grin, her tone dry as she called out, "Thought you lot had lost your way. We were about to head in and rescue you."

Boone looked up, giving the group a lazy salute before crossing his arms. "Figured we'd at least get a few minutes' rest before you showed up—but hey, dawn waits for no one, huh?" He tilted his head, shooting a glance toward Simon. "Now, who's this new addition? Thought we were done pickin' up strangers," he said with a teasing grin, his eyes holding a glint of curiosity.

The group reined in their horses just a few yards away. Elanor swung her leg over the saddle and slid down with a soft grunt, her boots crunching against the dusty ground. The sheriff dismounted next, his movements slower, more deliberate, the thought of introducing Simon settling in his shoulders. Weston followed, keeping a steady hand on Elanor's arm as she adjusted to the ground beneath her feet, while Simon eased himself down with a stiffness that hinted at his older age.

The sheriff nodded toward Simon. "Nora, Boone, this is Simon, my pops." He cleared his throat, glancing between his father and the rest of the group. "Turns out he's got a better idea of how to get to Tawa than we ever did."

Nora raised her eyebrows, looked at Boone, then turned back to Simon. "Seems we're collecting guides as we go," she said with a laugh, her expression softening as she nodded to the older man. "Well, then, welcome to the crew."

Simon gave a slight nod, taking in each of them with a measure of respect before he spoke. "You all have a hard trail ahead. But I know the way to one of his spots. He'll appear to you if he knows you're good people." His voice held a steady certainty, which made Elanor feel a flicker of hope, despite the weariness seeping into her bones.

"Good," Weston murmured, shifting slightly as he adjusted his saddle. "The sooner we move forward, the better. We're too close to Leto to risk anyone else coming after us."

Boone smiled, briefly tossing his hat in the air as they all nodded in agreement. "Tawa better have some answers or at least a good stash of whiskey for all this trouble."

Nora nudged him with her elbow, smirking. "I think answers are what we need more than your idea of refreshments."

A faint laugh escaped Elanor as she watched them banter. The camaraderie among them, though laced with weariness, was grounding. She had grown to care for each of them in ways she hadn't anticipated—especially Boone's wild stories and Nora's fierce spirit. Her eyes lingered on Weston longer than she intended, the warmth of his earlier concern still settling like a balm over her. And despite the warmth toward her friends, Elanor's eyes became heavier as she glanced around.

The sheriff spoke up again. "With Simon leading, we should make good time, but it'll still be a long stretch through harsh terrain. Let's stay close, avoid any side trails, and—"

But before he could finish, a wave of dizziness washed over Elanor, the edges of her vision blurring. She shook her head, trying to clear it, but the exhaustion she'd been pushing aside clawed its way back with a force she couldn't ignore. The ground swayed, her limbs growing heavy.

Weston's voice cut through the haze, his concern evident. "Elanor?"

She opened her mouth to respond, but the words wouldn't come. As she slipped away, her legs buckled beneath her, causing the world to tilt and the voices around her to fade to a muffled blur. The last thing she felt was Weston's strong arms catching her before the darkness took hold.

CHAPTER EIGHTEEN

Elanor's senses stirred before her eyes opened. A warmth settled beside her, a steady pressure on her shoulder—Weston's hand. The familiar scent of dust and sage floated around her, mingling with the earthy aroma of the ground beneath her. Slowly, voices filtered in, low and gentle, mingling with the distant sounds of crackling fire. She opened her eyes a fraction, blinking against the dim glow.

The blurred outlines of her friends came into focus. Weston was leaning close, his eyes fixed on her with worry and relief. He gave her a small, gentle smile, the corners of his mouth softening as he met her gaze.

"Hey, you're back with us," he murmured, his voice warm, each word reassuring.

Her lips curved in response, though she was too tired to say anything. She peered around, noting the others' quiet presence: Nora kneeling beside her, handing her a canteen; Boone off to the side, resting on his haunches, watching her with a teasing grin, even as relief softened his expression; the sheriff sitting a few feet away with Simon, his eyes fixed on the horizon but occasionally flicking over to Elanor, a silent guardian.

"You had us worried there, Elanor," Nora said gently, her voice holding a warmth that matched Weston's, though her eyes betrayed an underlying worry. She handed Elanor the canteen, which she took gratefully, savoring the cool water on her parched throat.

Elanor managed a faint smile, her words a mere whisper. "Didn't mean to scare anyone."

Boone let out a chuckle. "Well, reckon we're all a bit scared, but if anyone's got a habit of keeping things interesting, it's you, Elanor." He tipped his hat in mock respect, a playful glint in his eyes. "Keeps us all on our toes."

The group laughed softly. As the laughter faded, Weston's voice drew her attention again. His face softened as he studied her. "You need to rest more. We'll stay put until you're steady on your feet."

Elanor shook her head faintly, struggling to keep her voice firm, despite the fatigue in her bones. "I'm okay . . . I just . . . needed a moment." She tried to sit up, but a wave of dizziness forced her back down, Weston's hand steadying her gently as he adjusted his grip to keep her upright.

"We've already relocated. We're in no rush," he said softly, his voice like a balm against her frayed nerves. "Not until you're ready."

Her cheeks flushed under his steady gaze, and a subtle pang stirred in her chest at the quiet protectiveness in his voice.

As Elanor settled back, she sensed the group beginning to relax around her

Nora stretched her legs out, rubbing her sore shoulders with a weary smile. "Feels like we've been traveling for months," she said, her voice light but filled with the underlying exhaustion they all felt. She gave a small laugh. "Good thing I packed a lifetime's worth of patience."

The sheriff grunted in agreement, settling down beside her. He took off his hat, running a hand over his forehead, a gesture that made him look older. He caught Elanor's gaze and gave her a reassuring nod. "Still strong enough to keep going, thanks to you all. Couldn't have done it alone."

Boone nodded thoughtfully. "Not that I'd ever admit it too often," he joked, but his eyes were sincere as he looked around at each of them. "This lot's not so bad to have by your side."

They exchanged weary smiles, and for a moment, there was a shared silence as they each took a mental inventory of their visible and hidden bruises. They'd survived deserts, mountains, bandits, and their internal battles. In the depths of their shared glimpses, there was an unspoken promise to protect each other, to hold on.

Nora's expression softened, and she looked at Elanor with a depth hinting at her inner reserves. "You know," she began quietly, "sometimes the hardest part of a journey isn't the steps we take but the things we leave behind. I think . . . I think it's okay if we feel scared or uncertain. That's part of how we grow."

Elanor listened, feeling Nora's words resonate deeply, though she didn't fully understand why. There was something in Nora's tone—a layer of rare vulnerability, even as it brought a sense of comfort.

Boone cleared his throat, a rare seriousness coloring his voice as he looked at each of them. "Well, whatever comes, I reckon there's no better crew to face it with." He shot them all a lopsided grin. "Could be worse—we could be back in that forsaken town, chasing our tails in circles."

Weston chuckled, leaning back beside Elanor. "Wouldn't trade this lot for any other," he said, his eyes soft as they met hers.

After a few moments of quiet, Nora cleared her throat, looking out as if she could see beyond the mountains, past the trail that had brought them here. The flicker of firelight danced in her eyes, shadows softening the hard lines of her face. She let out a slow breath, almost as if testing the strength of her voice.

"You know," she began, her tone softer than usual, "there was a time I didn't think I could make it through a day without feeling like I was about to drown. It was right after . . . well, a rough loss. Someone close to me." She looked around the group, each face reflecting the quiet anticipation and understanding that this was something Nora rarely shared. "At first, it felt like I couldn't breathe. Couldn't think past what happened."

Elanor watched Nora's expression closely, feeling a strange pang of empathy—something about Nora's loss resonated with her. As she looked at Nora, a flicker of something half-remembered brushed against her thoughts.

"But there came a time," Nora continued, her voice steadier, "when

I had to make a choice. Either let the weight drag me under or find a way to swim up for air." She paused, a faint smile touching her lips. "So, I took on a challenge—a stupid, foolhardy challenge I thought would make me feel strong again."

Boone, sensing the moment's gravity but unable to resist a grin, muttered, "Sounds like the Nora I know—only satisfied if it's life or death."

Nora shot him a wry look. "You're not wrong," she admitted. "There was this woman in my town, powerful and mean. Thought she owned the place and everyone in it. I figured if I could stand up to her, I'd stand up to anything. It terrified me," she admitted, almost reluctantly. "But I knew if I didn't face her, I'd be letting that fear define me."

The sheriff nodded, his expression one of deep understanding. "Standing up to someone like that . . . it takes more than courage. Takes belief that you're worth defending."

Nora's eyes softened, a flicker of vulnerability crossing her features. "Exactly," she said quietly. "I didn't think I'd find that belief. But I had to dig deep, pull it out from somewhere I didn't even know existed. And afterward . . . well, I felt a little less like a ghost, a little more like myself."

Her words settled over them, filling the quiet space. Elanor's chest tightened. There was something hauntingly familiar in Nora's story.

Nora glanced at Elanor, her expression softening. "Guess what I'm saying is, it's okay to feel lost sometimes or to not have all the strength you think you need. Strength doesn't mean you're never afraid or never uncertain—it just means you keep moving forward, anyway."

Elanor swallowed hard, blinking back the moisture gathering in her eyes. "Thank you, Nora," she whispered, feeling gratitude settle in her chest. "I think I needed to hear that."

Nora gave her a gentle smile, the kind of smile that carried years of experience and strength. "We all need a reminder sometimes. Life doesn't exactly hand out instructions."

Boone, never one to leave a serious moment hanging, cleared his throat with a dramatic flourish. "Well, here's to being lost and found again. Now, someone pass me a flask before I start crying, too."

The group chuckled, and the atmosphere around the firelight softened. Nora's story had reached each of them, binding them tighter as they prepared for the next leg of their journey.

The fire crackled softly, filling the quiet as Nora's words lingered in the air, casting a warmth that was more than just physical. Each group member sat absorbed in their thoughts, processing the story Nora had shared. It was a rare moment of calm.

Elanor's attention settled on Weston, who was staring thoughtfully into the fire, his expression contemplative. He looked up and met her eyes, a subtle warmth there, a shared understanding that didn't need words. She gave him a faint smile, feeling a sense of grounding in his presence, a reassurance that had become as essential as the air she breathed.

The sheriff stretched his legs, settling back against his saddle with a sigh. "Sometimes it takes a night like this," he murmured, almost to himself. "A reminder that there's more to the journey than just where we're headed."

Boone leaned forward, tossing a twig into the fire and watching the embers rise. "That's the thing, ain't it?" he said, his voice uncharacteristically soft. "You don't always know what you're searching for until you've already found it." He caught Elanor's eye, and she noticed a hint of sincerity beneath his usual playful demeanor.

Nora nodded, looking out at the vast expanse of desert beyond their small circle. "And sometimes the hardest part isn't the journey—it's finding the courage to start it again, no matter how many times life knocks you down."

The fire flickered lower, casting the group in a gentle twilight, drawing strength from one another. Nora's story had reminded them of something vital: They were each empowered to keep going, even when the path was uncertain. For Elanor, it was a reminder that the journey wasn't just about reaching Tawa or uncovering some hidden truth—it was about finding a way to carry forward, to embrace the unknown with a steady heart.

The group settled down to rest one by one, the day fading to cool night. As Elanor closed her eyes, a deep sense of calm relaxed her, reassuring her that, even in the darkest moments, they could find the light together. The night settled around them, silent and still, as they drifted into a much-needed sleep.

The first blush of dawn crept over the desert, casting a gentle light across the camp as the group stirred awake. The air was still and cool, the quiet moments before sunrise lending a sense of calm and purpose. Elanor stretched, feeling the lingering aches of yesterday's exhaustion but also a subtle strength, as though Nora's story had breathed new life into her.

Weston moved quietly, already packing his gear. He glanced over at Elanor, a hint of a smile playing at the corner of his mouth. "Looks like you got some decent rest," he remarked softly, the warmth in his eyes encouraging.

Elanor nodded, her quiet smile mirroring his. "Yeah, I needed it," she replied, glancing at the others, who were also beginning to pack up. Nora shot her a slight grin that conveyed both pride and support, and Boone offered an exaggerated salute as he strapped his saddle.

With a dramatic sigh, Boone hoisted his pack. "Just when I was gettin' used to sittin' around, we're off again," he quipped, throwing a grin at Elanor. "Though I reckon adventure waits for no one."

The sheriff chuckled, clapping Boone on the shoulder. "Good thing we've got you to keep us entertained," he said, his tone light as he looked out across the horizon, "but it's time we make some ground today."

As the last of their things were packed, Nora took a moment to readjust her hat, her eyes shifting between the group and the path ahead. "Alright, folks. Let's make our way to Tawa while we've got daylight." Then she glanced at Simon, who was fastening his saddle with a quiet, practiced ease.

"Simon," she prompted, raising her brows with a small, expectant smile, "ready to lead us to this wise man you've been talkin' up?"

Simon paused, then gave a firm nod. "Tawa's place is about a day or two's journey—the path twists around the cliffs," he said, glancing between the group and the distant landscape. "We'll want to keep a good pace."

Nora gave him an approving nod. "Then I say we head out then."

The night had given Elanor clarity, reminding her that each step forward was more than survival—it was a step toward understanding and uncovering her own strength. She reached for her horse, feeling a steadiness in her grip that hadn't been there before.

Weston leaned over as they mounted their horses. "We've got a long day ahead," he said. "If you need a break, just say the word."

Elanor met his gaze. "I'll be alright," she assured him. "Let's get going."

With a shared nod, the group set off, leaving the remnants of their camp behind. The rising sun cast long shadows across the desert, lighting the way as they moved steadily forward.

As the landscape stretched before them, a sense of anticipation, a quiet certainty that they were finally on the right path, took over.

CHAPTER NINETEEN

The group pressed onward through the stretch of barren, rugged desert, their horses picking carefully over rocky terrain. The sun beat down from a cloudless sky, and Elanor felt the relentless heat through her clothes, pressing her deeper into the saddle with each passing mile. Her mouth was dry, and the hot, dusty air left her throat feeling raw. She kept a tight grip on the reins, her knuckles white against the worn leather as her horse shifted beneath her, searching for stable footing.

Ahead of her, Weston guided his horse with steady hands, casting a concerned glance back to check on her. Elanor offered him a weak nod, signaling she could keep going, though her body drew heavier with each passing moment. He was unconvinced but turned his attention back to the endless stretch of desert, his eyes scanning the horizon as he adjusted the strap of his canteen—a reminder of how little water they had left.

"How much farther, you think?" Elanor's voice came out as a hoarse whisper, barely audible above the soft clink of tack and the occasional snort of a horse.

"Can't say for sure," Weston replied, a hint of strain in his voice. "Simon's the one guiding us now, and he says we're on the right track. But out here, there's no telling how long this stretch will go on."

Riding a bit ahead, Simon's posture had begun to sag in the saddle.

Beside him, Nora rode with her hat pulled low, casting a wary look at the path ahead. Even she, who rarely showed signs of wear, looked worn down by the sun and harsh terrain.

"Resources are running low," Weston continued in a hushed tone, almost to himself. Water, food . . ." he hesitated, then added, "and patience." His attention shifted toward Boone, who had fallen behind. His ordinarily cheerful expression was replaced by a scowl as he tugged at his collar.

"If I'd known we'd be crawling through the hottest part of this desert, I might've reconsidered," Boone muttered, wiping his brow and adjusting his hat. "And not a single drop of whiskey to take the edge off."

Nora rolled her eyes but managed a weary smile. "Save it, Boone. Let's keep our focus for when it really counts.".

Foster kept a steady pace near the front, his face set with a look of concentration as he surveyed the land. Elanor wondered if he was carrying his own private worries, the desert mirroring his sense of isolation. The relentless landscape pulled each of them deeper into themselves.

Elanor's horse stumbled slightly as her thoughts drifted, causing her to grip the saddle horn to steady herself. Weston's hand shot out to support her. "Easy there," he murmured, his voice tinged with worry. "This heat's brutal. No harm in pausing."

"I'm alright," she managed, though her voice sounded weaker than intended. The relentless sun was chipping away at her, stirring something deep within—something heavy and unresolved.

Nora caught Elanor's gaze and offered a subtle nod of encouragement, reminding her of the strength she'd forgotten she possessed. The look alone steadied Elanor's heart, a small reminder that they were in this together. She gave a determined nod and shifted her focus back to the path ahead.

Simon spoke up, his voice slightly strained. "There's a rise up ahead. If we can make it there, might be some shade and a chance to rest the horses."

The thought of even a tiny reprieve urged them forward, the horses moving with labored steps as they climbed over the uneven ground.

Every jostle and bump made Elanor's muscles ache, but the promise of shade, however faint, was enough to spur her on. They rode silently, each group member pushing through the exhaustion, hoping for relief a little farther up the trail.

As they pressed on, the terrain grew harsher, rocks and scrub replacing what little patches of softer sand they'd encountered earlier. Each bump and shift in the ground intensified the group's fatigue, and the discomfort of the journey began to erode the patience that had once bound them.

Boone shifted uncomfortably in his saddle, muttering under his breath as he adjusted his canteen, which had been empty for the last stretch. "You know, I didn't sign up to be treated like a pig over a spit." He shot a glare at Simon, his tone edged with irritation. "Tell me again why we're trusting a man who only recently strolled into the fold?"

Simon's jaw tightened, but he kept his focus ahead, unflinching. "I know this area better than any of you," he replied evenly, though a hint of frustration tinged his voice. "And, like it or not, there isn't another way around this desert."

Nora said, "Knock it off, Boone. We don't need another fight—especially not out here."

Boone let out a frustrated sigh but fell silent, muttering something inaudible as he looked away. Elanor saw the resentment in his eyes, and for a brief moment, she felt it too—a nagging question about whether they were all lost, chasing after mirages.

Sensing the rising frustration, Weston cast a steadying look around the group. "Let's keep it together," he said. "We're all feeling the strain, but right now, Simon's our best shot at finding Tawa." His eyes lingered on Elanor, a wordless reminder of their purpose and promise to each other.

Elanor tried to focus on Weston's words, but something about the barren landscape around them tugged at memories she couldn't quite grasp. The feeling gnawed at her as if pieces of her past were surfacing just beyond reach, a shadowy reminder of grief and guilt she had buried long ago. The oppressive heat and her exhaustion only drew it closer, stirring an ache she could no longer ignore.

Lost in her thoughts, she almost didn't notice Foster slowing his horse beside her, his face clouded with concern. "You alright, Miss Elanor?" he asked, his tone softer than usual.

She nodded, though her voice came out shaky. "Just . . . tired. This place, it gets to you."

The sheriff nodded slightly, looking out over the desert solemnly. "It has a way of bringing things to the surface," he murmured. His words resonated deeply with her, reflecting the tumultuous emotions she had yet to confront. She sensed an understanding in his eyes—a recognition of something deeply familiar.

Boone, catching sight of the sheriff and Elanor's quiet exchange, rolled his eyes, though his voice held a glimmer of strain. "If we make it through this desert, maybe we can all sit around sharing secrets. For now, how about we just keep moving?"

Managing a tired smile, Nora said, "That might be the first good idea you've had all day, Boone."

As they pushed forward, the silence that settled was charged, each of them caught in their thoughts as the desert tested their physical and emotional endurance. The vast, unyielding landscape reflected their vulnerabilities, bringing each fear, frustration, and doubt closer to the surface with every step.

As the group rode on, the oppressiveness of the desert pressed down on Elanor, its silence drawing her into a space of uncomfortable reflection. The rhythmic sway of the horse, usually a source of stability, now lullabied her, tempting her into a restless reverie.

Fragments of memories surfaced blurry images and emotions that didn't seem to fit neatly together but still left a haunting impression on her heart. Faces she couldn't quite place flitted through her mind—a warm, knowing look; a laugh both teasing and gentle; and the hollow, echoing feeling of loss. She couldn't shake the impression that all of this was somehow connected to what had driven her here. It was a gnawing, vague, unrelenting thought, as if her mind were working to piece together a puzzle she'd forgotten existed.

A pang of guilt rose within her, the sharp, unforgiving reminder of responsibility. In these flashes of her past, she felt the insistence of someone else's expectations, someone she'd let down. It gnawed at her chest, surfacing memories of another place and time where this weariness settled over her. She couldn't pinpoint the reason, but the pain from these past moments, when she lacked strength or bravery, permeated her present, imbuing every step with a hint of uncertainty.

Then, the image of Weston flickered in her mind—steady, unwavering, always near her side through this journey. Somehow, his presence both steadied her and intensified her guilt. A whisper of a thought crossed her mind, a question she couldn't fully articulate:

Am I just going to let him down, too?

She swallowed, glancing at him as he rode a few paces ahead, his profile etched with the strength and determination she'd come to rely on. He was so confident, so rooted, and it only reminded her of her uncertainty.

Lost in these thoughts, Elanor didn't notice her grip on the reins had slackened until her horse slowed slightly, prompting Weston to look back with a concerned expression.

"You sure you're doing alright back there?" he called, his voice breaking through the haze of her thoughts.

She forced a nod, managing a weak smile. "Yeah. Just . . . thinking."

His face told her that he understood, though a hint of worry remained in his eyes. "If it helps, you're not alone in that. We're all carrying things that weigh us down." His words were simple, but they struck her deeply as if he had sensed the storm within her and offered quiet reassurance.

She straightened, trying to shake off the lingering shadows, but they clung to her, their roots deep and tangled. Whatever held her back, whatever memories laid dormant, she would have to face them sooner or later.

And as the journey wore on, the vague sense of responsibility tightened around her, whispering that her part in this was more significant than she understood.

As the sun dipped lower, casting long shadows across the cracked earth, Simon slowed his horse and motioned to the group to veer left toward a narrow pass half-hidden between two ridges. Elanor exhaled in quiet relief as they crested the rise, a lightness spreading through her. They found a small, secluded oasis between the rocky cliffs—a pool of water shimmering under the fading light, surrounded by sparse, resilient vegetation.

"We can rest here," Simon murmured, his voice subdued but filled with relief. "It's a good spot—hidden from the main trail and well-protected by these rocks."

The group dismounted, visibly relieved to feel the solid ground underfoot and finally see a water source. Elanor's knees wobbled slightly as she stepped down, exhaustion clearly evident in her limbs. Weston, catching the flicker of weakness in her stance, gave her a reassuring look, and she offered him a tired smile in return. Together, they led their horses toward the pool to let them drink, each dipping their hands into the cool water soon after, the relief palpable.

Nora sighed, tilting her hat back as she surveyed the area. "Finally, a break," she murmured, her voice laced with gratitude as she splashed water over her face. "Feels like we've been riding forever."

Elanor crouched down by the edge of the pool, allowing the water to soothe her parched skin. As she leaned closer, her reflection came into focus, and a pang of unease rippled through her. She barely recognized the face staring back at her. Dark circles smudged beneath her eyes and, once rich with warmth, her skin now looked dull and sallow under the lowering sun. Her cheekbones jutted more sharply than before, the hollows beneath them deepened by days of too little food and too much sun.

Her black curls hung limp and tangled around her face, crusted with grit and streaked with dried sweat. The lines of exhaustion etched into her features made her seem older, as if the desert had drained something vital from her. She ran a hand over her face, fingers brushing the rough patches of her dry, cracked lips and sunburned skin.

For a moment, she didn't move, staring at the familiar but foreign reflection. Was this what she had looked like the last time she'd caught her reflection? Or had she deteriorated even more since then? The thought tightened her chest, and she looked away quickly, cupping her hands to drink. The cool water was a temporary balm, soothing her body, if not her mind. She pushed the thoughts aside, focusing instead on the quiet gratitude that they'd managed to find this place, however fleeting their reprieve might be.

As the group settled, a prickling unease stirred at the back of Elanor's mind. The peacefulness of the oasis was almost too perfect, too serene—a strange calm that only amplified the dangers lurking beyond. Looking around, she caught Weston's gaze, and he raised an eyebrow as if reading her thoughts.

"Feels a little too quiet, doesn't it?" he said.

Elanor nodded, scanning the perimeter. The shadows between the rocks deepened as the sun dipped, casting an eerie stillness over the oasis. She hadn't seen any fresh signs of pursuit, but her instincts tingled with the unsettling feeling that they weren't alone.

Boone strolled over, wiping his face with a handkerchief. "What's with the serious looks?" he asked, glancing between Weston and Elanor. "We finally found some water, a bit of shade . . . y'all keep talkin' 'bout water. What's there to worry about?"

"Not sure," Elanor replied quietly, glancing over her shoulder as she spoke. "Just . . . something feels off. Like we've been lucky for too long."

Overhearing, Simon shifted uneasily, his attention turning toward the distant path they'd traveled. "Wouldn't be the first time I've been tracked without realizing it. Merrick's men could be miles back, but that doesn't mean they aren't watching."

The group exchanged uneasy glances. Nora straightened, her hand instinctively moving to her pistol as she scanned the surrounding ridges.

"We'll have to keep watch through the night," she murmured. "No telling if we're safe here, but it's better than being out in the open."

As the group began preparing for a cautious night of rest, Elanor's attention lingered on the shadows between the rocks. The oasis was a reprieve but a fleeting one—a reminder that their journey was far from over and that their enemies lurked just beyond the ridge line.

CHAPTER TWENTY

As the first soft light of dawn began to cast long shadows over their camp, Elanor shifted in her bedroll, stretching off the haziness of sleep. The air was cool, the sky still streaked with the remnants of night. For a moment, a calm settled over her.

But then, she caught a glimpse of Simon returning, his steps swift and purposeful, his eyes alert. She noticed him pause just outside the camp, looking back over his shoulder before he finally made his way to the group, expression taut with worry.

"Tracks," he murmured as he reached the others, careful not to raise his voice. "Not far off, maybe a quarter-mile south. Fresh."

Elanor sat up fully, the grogginess of sleep quickly slipping away as the words sank in. She exchanged a look with Weston, his face hardened.

"They're riding heavy," Simon continued. "A lot of hooves and fast —straight toward us, though it looks like they haven't yet picked up our exact trail."

Weston nodded. "They're close. Closer than I'd hoped."

Elanor's stomach churned, her mind filling with images of Merrick's men riding toward them, relentless and unyielding. There was an unspoken urgency in the air, and as she met Nora's gaze, Elanor's anxiety was reflected.

Nora pushed up from her bedroll, brushing dirt from her hands with a nod of quiet determination. "Well, then," she said, "guess we better be moving."

The group worked swiftly, gathering supplies and securing their horses with an understanding that every second counted. Elanor packed up her things, the slight tremor in her hands revealing the undercurrent of fear she tried to suppress. She tried to focus on the rhythm of her movements, quick and precise, but her thoughts kept returning to the approaching danger.

As she tightened the straps on her pack, Weston stepped up beside her, his eyes reassuring. "We'll stay close," he said, his voice a calming anchor amid her anxious thoughts. "Keep each other in sight and don't lag. Simon mentioned a narrow trail—it's our best chance at losing them."

Elanor nodded, pulse racing as she finished securing her belongings.

"Everybody ready?" Simon asked, looking around to ensure they were set. They each nodded in turn, their expressions a mix of determination and wariness. Simon gestured to the rocky terrain to the west. "This way. Be silent and vigilant."

The morning light grew stronger as they moved, casting long shadows across the land, but it did nothing to warm the chill that had settled in Elanor's chest. She followed close behind Weston, her senses on high alert, every rustle in the brush and shift of sand around them setting her nerves on edge.

With each step away from camp, she cast one final look over her shoulder, a sense of finality washing over her as she observed the place that had given them brief refuge disappear into the distance. The tracks Simon had seen were a haunting reminder of how close danger lingered.

In the silent space between each footfall, Elanor's thoughts swirled. She met Weston's gaze as he peered back, and despite his silence, his slight nod conveyed a powerful message. Whatever laid ahead, they would face it together. And with that shared, silent vow, Elanor steadied her breath and moved forward, following Simon's lead as they left the tracks—and the remnants of safety—far behind.

The morning air grew cooler as the group moved deeper into the rocky paths Simon led them through. The landscape around them twisted and narrowed, jagged ledges and steep inclines forcing them to stay close and step carefully. Gritting her teeth, Elanor felt the strain in her legs and the lingering weakness in her body. The terrain was unyielding, each step through loose gravel and uneven rock jolting her weary muscles.

Beside her, Weston kept a close watch, scanning the path ahead and occasionally checking in on each person in the group. Every so often, he'd offer a quiet word of encouragement as they navigated the harsher patches of ground.

Ahead, Nora led the group with Simon beside her, the two moving with a shared purpose and caution. As they rounded a narrow ledge, Nora suddenly raised her hand, signaling for silence. She dismounted and knelt, her serious face causing the group to halt. Elanor held her breath, following Nora's attention to the path ahead.

Through a barely visible break in the rocks, she saw several figures lying low in the distance, their bodies partially hidden behind boulders and scrubs.

Merrick's men.

They appeared poised, waiting silently, their eyes trained on the trail the group was meant to follow. Merrick's men had prepared their ambush with cold, calculated patience, anticipating their route.

Weston crouched beside her, his expression grim as he studied the scene. "They're not just following—they're hunting," he whispered, his tone laced with anger.

Elanor swallowed, her focus flicking between the ambushers and the narrow ledge they were perched on. A single wrong move could draw attention, and the thought sent a ripple of anxiety through her. Fear clawed up, but she steadied herself, remembering the confidence she had built throughout her journey.

Nora crawled back, her voice barely above a whisper. "We'll need another way around. Simon?"

Simon nodded, glancing back the way they'd come. "There's a path that dips down a bit—steeper, but it curves around their line of sight. It'll be rough, but it'll keep us hidden."

They began backtracking, each step cautious, their movements slow and deliberate. Elanor did her best to keep her breathing steady, every muscle tense as they slipped through the rock-strewn path, hoping they remained unseen.

Navigating around a cluster of boulders, they began descending the steep, winding path Simon had described. The loose gravel made it hard for their horses to keep their footing, and Elanor found herself clutching at her horse's neck for balance. She felt the burn in her muscles as they descended, her body protesting the relentless pace, but there was no time to slow down.

Ahead of her, Nora shot her a glance, nodding in encouragement. Elanor responded with a small, tight smile, grateful for Nora's quiet assurance. Even as they moved in silence, she felt the shared strength of the group—a mutual understanding that kept them pushing forward, step by careful step.

The path wound and felt like it sometimes went in circles before leveling out, leading the group into a small, sheltered clearing nestled between jagged boulders. The early sunlight cast long shadows, softening the edges of their surroundings, and a faint breeze stirred the dust around their feet.

They gratefully paused to catch their breath, each taking a moment to assess the relief of safety. Elanor sank onto a flat rock, trying to steady her breathing, her muscles tingling from the exertion of clinging to her horse on their descent. Across from her, Weston stood watch, his eyes scanning their surroundings.

Boone broke the silence with a quiet chuckle. "Y'know," he began, leaning back against the wall with a sly grin, "this whole mess reminds me of the time I got chased by a one-eyed rooster. Meanest damn bird you ever saw. Thing pecked a hole clean through my boot before I even made it to the barn."

Nora raised an eyebrow, pausing mid-motion as she handed a canteen to Elanor. "A one-eyed rooster? Really, Boone?" she deadpanned, though the corner of her mouth twitched with amusement. "You sure you didn't imagine that one after a few too many?"

Boone feigned offense, pressing a hand to his chest. "I'll have you know, Miss Nora, that rooster was real—and I've got the scars to prove it." He winked, his grin widening as Nora rolled her eyes and whispered something about men and their tall tales.

Nora turned her attention back to Elanor. "The water doin' you good, twin?"

Elanor nodded, offering a small smile as she tipped the canteen back against her mouth. The cool water soothed her dry throat, and she could feel the chill seep down, grounding her. As she sat quietly, her mind drifted to the moments before Merrick's men had taken her, to the people she'd fought to protect. That sense of responsibility, the urge to shield those around her, had always driven her, yet now it was heavy—an expectation she wasn't sure she could uphold.

Lost in thought, she hardly noticed when Weston came to sit beside her. His shoulder brushed hers, a subtle warmth that pulled her back to the present. She turned, catching the concern in his eyes and how they softened as he looked at her. "Quite the journey, huh?" he asked, his hand touching her shoulder.

Elanor managed a slight nod, the emotions swirling within her, challenging to put into words. "Yeah," she murmured. But her voice wavered slightly, betraying her thoughts. "I . . . I keep thinking about what we're all walking into. It's hard not to think I brought everyone here into all this."

Weston shook his head gently. "You didn't bring us here, El. We all chose this. I chose this," he said, his usual Southern drawl softening to match the clearer, more neutral tones closer to Elanor's. "You're not in this alone. And whatever lies ahead . . . we'll face it together." Elanor noticed the shift in his accent, finding the sound surprisingly pleasant, yet her focus remained on the reassurance and conviction in his words.

His words wrapped around her like a shield, easing the guilt gnawing at her. She looked down, her hand brushing against his, and for a moment, she let herself lean into the strength he offered.

Elanor stared at the ground as a memory stirred, faint but unmistakable. She said, "I saw my horse—"

"Where?" he asked plainly, almost as if he hadn't fully processed what she was talking about.

She continued. "At Merrick's camp. I'm sure of it. The same white marking around the left eye. I thought she was dead."

Weston's expression flickered, but only for a moment. "Merrick likes collecting things in this world," he said casually, too casually, as he adjusted the strap on his pack.

Elanor blinked, his words not settling right. "Collecting things?" she echoed, her tone skeptical. "What's that supposed to mean?"

Weston shifted uncomfortably, his hand rubbing the back of his neck. "I just meant—uh—maybe it's not your horse," he said, stumbling slightly over his words, his Southern accent entirely gone. "Could be one with similar markings. Desert horses all start to look alike after a while, you know? It's probably just a coincidence."

Elanor didn't respond immediately, her eyes narrowing as she studied him. Something about his answer was off, but she couldn't quite pin it down. Finally, she nodded, though her suspicion lingered. "Yeah, maybe," she said, her voice softer, though doubt still colored her tone.

Weston gave her a tight smile and turned away slightly, fiddling with his gear. "Let's just focus on getting you to Tawa. That's more important than worrying about Merrick and whatever he has going on."

Elanor nodded again, but the thought stuck with her, nagging at the edges of her mind.

The others had settled back around them, taking in the quiet as they waited for Simon's signal to continue. Elanor felt the stillness deepening, but with Weston's steady presence beside her, the fear was easier to bear.

As they set out again, the landscape around them shifted, morphing from rocky, sparse hills to a more structured pathway that hinted at a well-trodden route. Simon rode ahead, his focus sharp, scanning the ground for signs that had gone unnoticed by the rest of them. His movements grew more confident, and his familiarity with the path became evident as he slowed, finally pulling his horse to a stop. He turned to the group, his voice filled with an intensity that caught Elanor's attention.

"This path," he murmured, gesturing to a narrow, winding trail that veered off into the distance. "I recognize it. It's the same one I took when I went to find Tawa years back. If we stay on this route, I believe we'll reach him by nightfall."

Elanor's heartbeat quickened as a glimmer of hope ignited within her. The closer they drew to Tawa, the more an unspoken pull nagged at her, as though this journey wasn't just about unearthing answers that had lingered just out of reach, but something transformative. A quiet determination welled inside her; this path might hold the truths she had been seeking all along, even if she didn't yet understand why they felt so vital.

Nora caught her look and offered an encouraging smile. "We're getting close," she said, her tone steady, the edges of her words carrying warmth. "Whatever lies ahead, I know you're ready for it, Elanor. This journey hasn't been easy for any of us, but every step has been worth it to get you here."

Elanor nodded, a deep sense of gratitude welling up within her.

Boone broke the silence among the group. "So, what's this Tawa fella like? He some kind of desert sage or just another old coot with tricks up his sleeve?" His tone was light, but genuine curiosity flickered in his eyes.

Simon spoke softly, almost like he was sharing a secret with them. "Tawa's not just a man; he's a guardian of old truths, the kind of knowledge that doesn't belong to one person or even one lifetime," he said, his eyes fixed on the path ahead. "When I met him, I wasn't the same afterward. He has a way of seeing through a person, of knowing what they're carrying, even the burdens they're not aware of."

The others rode silently, absorbing Simon's words, a collective anticipation settling over them. Elanor listened closely, each of Simon's descriptions stirring a sense of awe but also apprehension. Tawa's knowledge was a beacon, a guiding force drawing her toward something profound. The realization struck her with a pulse of anticipation—meeting Tawa wasn't just another step in their journey—it was a culmination of all that had been endured.

Nora looked over at Elanor, her expression serious but kind. "This journey," she said, glancing at the group before returning to Elanor, "it's tested each of us. And we've come out stronger because of it, including you. Whatever we find up there, you're ready for it, Elanor."

The group urged their horses forward, riding toward the sunset. The path unfolded before them as a bridge to whatever truths awaited at its end.

As dusk blanketed the horizon, the group was surrounded by shadows, deepening with each passing moment. Simon slowed his horse and gestured for them to pause. His eyes narrowed toward a rugged, hidden path winding between two towering cliffs. Just barely visible against the dimming sky was an opening sheltered between ancient stone that pulsed with quiet, timeless energy.

"There," Simon whispered, his voice filled with reverence. "That's where we'll find Tawa. We're close now."

A thrill of anticipation swept over Elanor, a pull as if the earth were guiding her toward something that had been waiting for her. But mingled with her excitement was an ache—a hum of fear that she couldn't shake. This was the place she'd been drawn to all along, and now, with the end so close, she wondered if she was ready for the answers it would hold.

Weston rode up beside her, his eyes gentle but focused, sensing her hesitation. He reached out, letting his hand brush hers in a quiet gesture of reassurance. "You've made it this far, El. Whatever happens now, we'll face it together," he murmured.

She turned to him, a soft smile breaking through her worry. "I know. I think . . . I think I've felt you beside me long before this whole adventure. I wasn't sure I was ready to admit to something I had only pieces of the truth to, but now I am."

A glimmer of hope sparked in Weston's eyes at her words, a faint but unmistakable sign of relief. Her emerging memories, the threads of their past perhaps knitting together again, offered him a solace he hadn't dared to anticipate fully.

Behind them, Nora's sharp focus flickered over the rocky terrain ahead, her expression softened with an unspoken pride. "Finally, we're right where we need to be," she said, her words as steady as the resolve they all displayed.

Boone, adjusting his hat, let out a low chuckle. "Well, here's hoping Tawa's got somethin' a little stronger than water for us after this journey. Could use a real drink about now."

Foster rolled his eyes, nudging him with a grin. "Of course. Leave it to you to think about whiskey at a time like this."

The group chuckled softly, the lightness in their voices a welcome contrast to the heavy air around them. A sense of camaraderie filled the moment, a feeling that, despite all the unknowns waiting for them, they were exactly where they were meant to be.

Simon peered back, his attention lingering on each of them, an almost paternal pride in his eyes, before landing on Elanor. "You'll be ready for whatever Tawa has to say," he said.

As the last traces of daylight slipped beyond the mountains, they advanced slowly toward the entrance. The ancient cliffs watched over them, an unspoken promise that whatever truths laid within would soon be theirs. The final stretch was long, every step filling them with anticipation as they prepared to meet the mysterious figure who held the answers they'd come so far to find.

CHAPTER TWENTY-ONE

The group followed Simon into the sanctuary, their horses carefully stepping along the narrow, shadowed path, which was blanketed by towering trees on both sides. Fireflies flitted around them, their faint, golden light flickering like lanterns in the dark, guiding their way deeper into the forest. Overhead, the nearly full moon peeked through the tree-tops, its silvery glow fragmented by the branches, casting shifting patterns on the mossy ground below.

With each step, the air changed, growing cooler and heavier, carrying the damp, earthy scent of untouched wilderness. The barren, cracked soil of the desert was left behind, replaced by a rich green moss that cushioned their horses' steps. Wild ferns and flowers lined the trail, their delicate blooms catching the moonlight like scattered jewels.

Elanor breathed deeply, letting the cool air soothe her dry throat and aching lungs. She looked at the others, their silhouettes softened in the dim light. Their exhaustion eased slightly with the changing landscape, the oppressive heat of the desert a fading memory. Even Nora, who rarely allowed herself to appear vulnerable, sat looser in her saddle.

Simon rode ahead, his posture straighter than earlier in the day. He hadn't said much since they'd entered the forest, but his quiet demeanor was now different—more purposeful, as though he was leading them to something sacred. The lines on his face, usually set in stern resolve, had softened, and his awareness swept over the path with the calm precision of someone who had walked it before.

The path began to wind downward, descending into a secluded valley that was a world unto itself. The sound of rushing water grew louder, a steady rhythm that called to them as it echoed off the trees. The horses' hooves padded softly on the mossy trail, and the dense foliage overhead thickened, shrouding them in shadow. A strange stillness settled over Elanor, a quiet reverence tightening her chest.

As they rounded a bend, the forest opened into a clearing bathed in moonlight. In the center stood an ancient stone structure, half-hidden beneath creeping vines and wildflowers. The stones were etched with symbols, their intricate lines weathered by time yet still visible under the faint glow of fireflies. The air hummed faintly, a subtle vibration in her chest more than an echo in her ears. It was as if the ground they stood on was alive, waiting to welcome them.

Simon dismounted first. He turned to the group, lingering momentarily on Elanor before sweeping over the others. "This is it," he said quietly. "The sanctuary."

Elanor slid from her horse, legs trembling slightly as her boots met the earth. She placed a hand on her horse's neck, steadying herself as her eyes swept over the clearing. The sanctuary was expansive and intimate, existing seemingly outside of time. The rushing sound of water was louder here, mingling with the rustling leaves and the occasional chirp of a night bird.

The others dismounted, each quiet as they took in the scene. Nora stepped closer to the stone structure, her fingers brushing the vines that clung to its surface. Boone let out a low whistle, his usual humor muted by awe. Even Foster, usually stoic and guarded, relaxed slightly as he took in the tranquil surroundings.

Elanor closed her eyes for a moment, letting the sounds and scents of the sanctuary wash over her. The harshness of the desert, the constant threats and losses, began to lift. Here, surrounded by towering trees and ancient stone, something she hadn't allowed herself to feel in a long time took over . . . hope.

The clearing exuded an almost reverent stillness, as if the air held its breath in anticipation. The stone structure's surface was weathered and veined with creeping vines. Symbols were etched deeply into the stone—lines and curves alive in the fireflies' flickering light, as though whispering secrets from long-forgotten times. The sanctuary was untouched, a place beyond the reach of time or decay, its beauty solemn, humbling.

Elanor's breath caught as her gaze traveled over the structure. The carvings didn't resemble any language she recognized, yet they stirred something deep within her, an inexplicable resonance that sent a shiver through her. Her boots pressed into the soft moss as she stepped forward, unable to take her eyes off the symbols. The air hummed faintly, a sound just out of reach, more felt than heard.

Almost as if he'd been waiting for them, a figure stepped forward from within the stone structure. Tawa appeared calmly with an authority that filled the space around him. His dark skin caught the faint glow of the fireflies, and dappled moonlight filtering into the clearing, giving him an almost ethereal presence. His features were striking, framed by long, jet-black hair that flowed over his shoulders like a river of night. He carried himself with an ageless grace, his movements deliberate and fluid, as though every step was connected to something more profound and timeless.

His attire was as commanding as his presence. Tawa wore traditional Native American dress, its intricate beadwork catching the faint light with subtle glimmers of turquoise, white, and red. The patterns on his clothing told a story—woven threads of his people's history, their struggles and triumphs. A fringed leather tunic draped over his tall frame, its edges worn but well cared for, as though it held the heaviness of generations. A sash wrapped around his waist, adorned with more beadwork and feathers that swayed gently with his movements. His sturdy yet graceful moccasins were intricately stitched, each detail a testament to craftsmanship and reverence for the land beneath his feet. Around his neck hung a single pendant—a carved stone, blue with gold specks that mimicked the sky and stars, humming with quiet power—resting just above his heart.

Elanor couldn't help but stare, her breath catching in her throat. His dark eyes held a depth that echoed the centuries; they were watchful, knowing, and filled with comforting and unsettling wisdom. Something familiar reflected at her—not in words or action, but in the shared resonance of skin kissed by the sun. The realization struck her like a quiet thunder, unspoken but powerful, stirring something profound inside her that she couldn't quite name.

She felt an energy radiating from him—a gravity that drew her in while sending a thrill through her chest, as though she were teetering on the brink of a long-sought revelation. In Tawa's presence, the world was both larger and smaller. She thought she might genuinely find the answers she'd been chasing.

The urge to draw closer was almost instinctive, as though some invisible thread connected her to this man she'd never met. An inexplicable familiarity and a strange apprehension set in, like she had been waiting for this moment her entire life without ever knowing it.

The group stood silent as Tawa's gaze swept over each of them. His eyes were deep and knowing, as though he could see beyond the dust of their journey and into the very heart of who they were. His stare was intense, an ageless wisdom tempered by sorrow. The quiet reverence of the sanctuary intensified, and the air grew denser, holding an almost tactile weight as he observed them.

He studied each person individually: Simon, Foster, Nora, and Boone. He paused on Weston, nodding and speaking softly.

"Weston."

And when Tawa finally turned his attention to Elanor, a strange warmth filled her chest, a sensation of familiarity, almost as if she'd been in his presence before. But no memory came—only a deep, inexplicable comfort mingled with the sharp pang of fear.

Tawa inclined his head, gesturing for her to step forward. "Come," he said, his voice calm but edged with authority, the tone of someone who spoke infrequently but deliberately. "We will speak privately, you and I."

Elanor nodded, remembering this was her journey, even if it meant stepping away from her friends. Weston's gaze remained on her, and he gave her a slight nod, almost as if he knew what was to come.

Tawa led her along a winding path deeper into the sanctuary, the thick canopy above casting dappled shadows on the ground. The air grew cooler, and the scent of damp earth and wildflowers intensified, filling her senses and grounding her in the moment. As they walked, she became acutely aware of the trees, trunks wide and ancient, branches coiling overhead in a graceful tangle. Each step was purposeful, as though she were walking into a place that didn't adhere to the rules of her world.

Tawa's voice broke the silence, low and measured, as if each word had been carefully chosen. "This land has seen many lives," he began, his focus fixed ahead. "It holds memories—not only of those who once roamed freely but of those who came after, seeking something they did not fully understand."

Elanor listened, caught between his words' rhythm and the air's energy. The earth itself paused, listening as if the trees and stones cradled the memories he spoke of, bound by time yet untouched by it. The shadows extended over the ground, creating intricate patterns that complemented the whispering leaves, capturing the timeless tranquility of a world in a state of suspension.

Tawa spoke, his voice resonant and calm as it settled into the air. "They spoke to the rivers, the wind, and the stones—not in words, but in understanding. They were part of this place, as inseparable as breath is from life." His eyes, dark and infinite, held something vast and unfathomable. "But time forgets. It erases the threads of what once was, leaving only echoes. Lives ended here—not as they were meant to, but caught in the in-between. Fragments remain, waiting for their turn to find the peace that was denied."

The air around them became heavier, as though the space was listening to his words, responding in a way Elanor couldn't quite place. The trees shifted without moving, and the soft hum of unseen forces pulsed faintly, just on the edge of perception. Elanor glanced at the others back in the clearing, their faces drawn but focused, and then back at Tawa. There was something about him—something in how he spoke, as if he had been here long before the world as she understood it had even begun.

Her stomach twisted uneasily, but she couldn't explain why. She was standing on the edge of an unraveling truth she couldn't yet comprehend. Instead, she nodded faintly at his words, her attention lingering on his face, searching for an answer she didn't even know the question to.

His words hung in the air, stirring something deep within her. A shadow of loss, the echo of something long forgotten. Her throat tightened, unspoken grief settling in her chest. She watched Tawa, wondering if he comprehended what she was thinking and understood the ache that lingered inside her, the same ache that had haunted her since she'd awoken in this strange, uncharted world.

"Tawa," she started, her voice barely audible. "I . . . I don't know who I am. Or why I'm here. Do you have the ability to help me remember?"

He paused, his gaze drifting to the trees as if searching for answers in their ancient branches. "Memory is a delicate thing, Elanor," he said finally, his tone thoughtful, almost reverent. "It is not a tale to be told, nor a mere sequence of events. It is something you must feel flow through you like water shaping the stones of a riverbed." He turned back to her, his expression solemn. "I cannot tell you what you seek, for it would be a shadow of the truth. You must face the depths, the light, and the dark if you are to truly understand and accept what you are currently faced with."

His words were both frustrating and compelling, filling her with a sense of purpose, even as they left her with more questions. She took a shaky breath, his gaze grounding her as she gathered her courage. "Then . . . what do I do?"

Tawa nodded slowly as though he had been waiting for her to ask. "There is a waterfall, a sacred place hidden deep within these lands. It is known as Alo River, a source of memory and truth, guarded by the spirits of those who came before. The water there holds the power to reveal what has been lost, but only if you drink from it willingly, ready to accept the truth."

He paused, his eyes holding hers with an intensity that sent a shiver down her spine. "The next full moon rises tomorrow. Then, you must drink from the waterfall, or its power will slip away, and with it, the chance to know yourself fully. This is a path of choice, and choice alone holds the power to unveil truth."

Her pulse quickened, the sense of urgency threading through her like a wire pulled taut. "Why . . . why the full moon?" she asked, voice trembling.

Tawa's face softened, and a faint, enigmatic smile touched his lips. He whispered, almost to himself, "The moon holds secrets and silently observes the cycles of life. It is only when it is full, when it shines brightest, that it reflects what lies within." He trailed off, leaving an air of mystery that only deepened her curiosity.

A ripple of understanding passed through Elanor, though she couldn't fully grasp its meaning. The waterfall, the moon, the memories —more pieces of a puzzle she had yet to assemble. But one thing was clear . . . she had to drink from the waterfall, to face whatever truths sat within its depths, no matter how painful.

The quiet around them grew thicker as Tawa stepped back, his eyes lingering on her. He said, "Remember, Elanor," his voice barely audible above a whisper, "this path is not about survival. It is about acceptance, about embracing what you have hidden from yourself. Only then will you be free."

His words settled into her bones, a steady pulse echoing through her. She felt his wisdom, the layers of meaning behind his words that would only reveal themselves in time. There was a finality in his tone, a sense that he had given her everything she needed—and now, the rest was up to her.

Tawa's attention lingered on Elanor, his dark eyes holding hers with an intensity that sent a surge of electricity through her chest. "There will be dark entities," he said, calm but laced with an unyielding seriousness, "that look to take you off your path and into a world of darkness, entities I fear you have already encountered. They will whisper lies, twist truths, and offer you solace in shadows. Do not give in—no matter how tempting or familiar it may seem. Hold fast, and you will find what you truly seek. Do not fear, though, light entities have been present along your journey and continue to support your quest now. Allow them to support you in your desire for enlightenment."

Elanor's throat tightened as she processed his words. She nodded, the warning settling over her like a heavy shroud. "Thank you," she said quietly. "For your wisdom—and for everything."

A small, knowing smile tugged at the corners of Tawa's lips. "Your journey is your own, Elanor, but you do not walk it alone."

She hesitated, then asked, "Where do I find Alo River? How do I get there?"

Tawa turned toward the distance, gracefully moving his hand toward the faint outlines of the trees framing the horizon. "Follow the crashing sounds of the waterfall," he said, his tone as steady as the earth beneath them.

Elanor followed his gesture, squinting into the dim light, but shadows and the faint rustling of unseen leaves obscured the path ahead. Her nerves curled in her stomach. "And . . . I will get my memories if I drink from the water?"

Tawa's eyes returned to hers. "You will find what has been waiting for you all along," he said cryptically. "But you must face it without fear, or it will remain beyond your reach."

Elanor swallowed hard, nodding again. She couldn't quite decipher the meaning behind his words, but something told her they were true. She squared her shoulders with one last glance in the direction he'd pointed, knowing the answers she sought laid ahead—if she could summon the courage to find them.

Tawa's voice broke through her thoughts, calm and steady. "I look forward to seeing you again soon." He gave her a faint, enigmatic smile before returning to the shadows.

And then, he was gone.

Elanor took a deep, steadying breath as she stepped away from where Tawa stood, his words still settling into the quiet corners of her mind. She turned back toward the path, the whisper of leaves and the distant trickling of water seeming to guide her steps. The sanctuary's beauty and calm lingered, the ancient trees and wildflowers surrounding her like a protective embrace.

As she neared the grove where the group waited, their figures were silhouetted against the soft, dappled light filtering through the trees: Nora sat on a fallen log, turning a small stone in her hands; Boone paced lightly, his fingers tracing absent-minded patterns in the air; Foster leaned against a tree, his focus distant but calm; and Weston's posture was tense, his focus sharp on the path, as though he'd been waiting on edge for her return.

The group looked up as she entered the clearing. Relief washed over Weston's face, and he stepped forward, his hand reaching for hers as though to steady her, to ground her after her meeting with Tawa. She welcomed his touch, feeling a surge of quiet strength fill her as their fingers intertwined.

"How'd it go?" he asked softly, his eyes searching hers.

She nodded, letting the quiet affirmation settle into her. "Good," she replied, her voice steadier than expected. "Tawa . . . he told me about a river, Alo River. I have to drink from it during tomorrow's full moon."

Nora nodded firmly, her eyes steady on Elanor, while Boone leaned back, a slow, thoughtful grin crossing his face. He sighed in mock relief. "Guess we'll have to ensure Tawa's got the finest waterfall around. It's not every day you go drinking magical water."

Nora rolled her eyes but smiled. "He's right, Elanor. We'll make sure you make it to the river."

Simon raised a hand. "Just a moment," he said. His attention shifted to Elanor, and there was something in his expression she hadn't seen before—a deep calm as though the turmoil that had clung to him was gone. "Mind if we talk?" he asked, tilting his head toward a quieter corner of the clearing.

Elanor hesitated, glancing toward Weston. He gave her a faint nod, stepping back to let them speak. She followed Simon to the edge of the clearing, where the dense foliage of the trees softened the moonlight into a muted glow. The sound of the waterfall was a distant murmur now, a low hum that filled the space between them.

Simon turned to face her, his shoulders squared but his eyes soft. For a long moment, he didn't speak as though weighing his words carefully. Finally, he said, "I've been thinkin' a lot about why I'm here. Why I was brought back to this place." His voice carried a quiet reverence, a vulnerability that surprised Elanor.

Elanor's brow furrowed. "You've done so much to help me," she said. "We wouldn't have made it this far without you."

Simon gave her a faint smile, the corners of his mouth pulling upward with gratitude and sadness. "Maybe that's true," he said. "But there's more to it than that." He looked toward the clearing, his gaze distant. "I've been holding onto something for a long time—my daughter. I lost her a long time ago. Too soon." His voice wavered, but he steadied himself. "I thought I'd never see her again. But now . . . she's waiting for me."

Elanor's chest tightened as she absorbed his words. "Simon—" she began, but he shook his head gently, cutting her off.

"This place," he continued, gesturing to the sanctuary, "it's not just a stop on your journey, Elanor. It's a location where everything completes itself. And for me, I think that circle's just about closed." His eyes met hers. "This journey's complete."

A lump rose in Elanor's throat, and she struggled to find the right words. "But you can still come with us," she said, her voice quieter now, almost pleading. "We're not finished yet."

Simon smiled again, the expression soft but resolute. "You are," he said gently. "You just haven't yet accepted your peace. But me? I have." He reached out, his calloused hand resting briefly on her shoulder. "You don't need me to finish this. You've got everything you need inside you. I can see it clear as day."

Elanor gripped the edges of her shirt as his words settled over her. "Will I see you again?" she asked, the question slipping out before she could stop it.

Simon's smile deepened, his eyes crinkling at the edges. "Oh, I reckon you will," he said softly. "Sooner than you think." His tone carried a mysterious warmth, an assurance that lingered long after the words faded.

Before she could respond, Simon stepped back, his attention lifting toward the treetops. "Take care of yourself, Elanor," he said, his voice filled with quiet pride. "You've got a light in you. Don't let it go out."

And with that, he turned and walked toward the edge of the sanctuary, his steps slow but purposeful. The fireflies followed him, their golden light dancing in his wake. Elanor watched him go, her chest tight with a bittersweet ache. She didn't call after him—somehow, he was precisely where he needed to be.

When Simon's figure disappeared into the shadows, Elanor exhaled shakily, the moment settling into her bones. Oddly, without understanding why, the words "Bye, Dad" slipped from her lips in a faint whisper. Puzzled by her own words, she paused, wondering why she would say such a thing. Perhaps, she reasoned, Simon had been like a father figure to her in some forgotten way. Dismissing the thought as a fleeting mix-up of her jumbled memories, she turned back toward the clearing where the others waited.

Weston stepped forward, his hand reaching for hers, and she took it, feeling the steady warmth of his touch.

"He's gone," she said softly, the words heavy with finality.

Weston nodded. "He found what he was looking for," he replied.

Elanor looked toward Simon's path, her heart still aching but steadied by the certainty of his departure. She took a deep breath, letting the stillness of the sanctuary fill her. "He did so much for me, and I'm not sure he knows how much that means to me. I wish he could have seen this through," she said, her voice carrying a quiet strength that surprised even her.

A faint smile escaped Foster's lips. "He knows," he said.

Nora crossed her arms while leaning against the stone structure. "Well," she said, "can't say I blame him. Losing a child like that . . . it stays with you."

Boone nodded, his usual humor absent. He ran a hand through his dusty hair, fingers lingering at the back of his neck. "Yeah, but it takes guts to face it like that," he said. "To know when it's your time and just . . . let go."

The sheriff remained quiet, hat pulled low over his eyes as he stared at the ground. When he finally spoke, his voice was softer than usual. He spoke simply. "Not all of us get that chance."

Elanor stood at the edge of the clearing, her arms wrapped around herself as she looked toward the shadows where Simon had disappeared. She still felt his hand on her shoulder, his voice when he told her his journey was complete. It wasn't just his words that stayed with her—it was the way he'd looked at her, as though he'd seen something in her she hadn't fully recognized in herself yet.

Weston stepped closer. "You alright?" he asked softly, his voice breaking through the haze of her thoughts.

She nodded slowly, her grip loosening as she exhaled. "I think so," she said. "It's just . . . he was so sure. Like he knew exactly what he was doing."

"He did," Weston replied. "And that's what we all need to hold on to. He wasn't lost, Elanor. He found his way."

Nora pushed off the stone, her attention shifting to Elanor. "And now it's your turn," she said, her voice not unkind. "He was right—you've got everything you need to see this through."

Boone tilted his head, offering a faint, crooked smile. "For what it's worth," he said, his usual teasing tone returning faintly, "I'd say you're doing a hell of a job holding it together."

The sheriff gave a slight nod, arms crossed tightly. "We'll get to that river," he said. "All of us."

The words hung in the air, heavy with promise. Elanor watched each of them, their faces illuminated by the faint glow of the moon and the fireflies: Nora's sharp determination; Boone's youthful humor; Foster's quiet resolve—all of it surrounded her like an invisible shield, bolstering the flicker of courage Tawa's words had sparked within her.

She straightened her shoulders, the heaviness in her chest giving way to something lighter, steadier. "We will," she said firmly, her voice stronger now. "We'll see this through."

Weston's hand brushed hers in a quiet gesture of support. "Together," he said, the single word carrying a depth that made her chest tighten.

The group fell into a comfortable silence, the soft hum of the sanctuary filling the space between them. Elanor let her attention drift toward the horizon, where the faint glow of the moonlight illuminated the edges of the forest. The waterfall was waiting, its distant roar a constant reminder of the truth she had yet to face.

But she was ready.

The sanctuary grew quieter as the night deepened, the fireflies casting soft, flickering light across the moss-covered ground. The air was cool and damp, carrying the faint scent of pine and earth, and the sound of the distant waterfall continued its steady rhythm, a low murmur that kept time with the heartbeat of the forest.

The group settled into a loose circle near the stone structure, their bedrolls arranged in the soft grass. Boone stretched out with a dramatic sigh, hands tucked behind his head. "You know," he said lightly, "this isn't the worst place I've ever spent the night."

Nora snorted softly as she folded her coat into a makeshift pillow. "Considering some of the dumps we've camped in, I'd say that's not much of a compliment."

Elanor grinned faintly, her eyes drifting up to the sky. The canopy of trees above them framed the stars, their faint light shimmering in the darkness like scattered memories.

The sheriff sat apart from the group, his hat pulled low over his face, but the rubbing of his hands showed he wasn't asleep. Weston leaned against a tree, his posture relaxed but his eyes alert, tracking the edges of the clearing as though guarding against unseen threats.

Elanor lingered at the edge of the camp. Her focus shifted to the distant horizon, where the forest faded into shadow. She let out a slow breath, her fingers brushing the silver locket on her chest. The cool metal was grounding, anchoring her in the here and now, even as her thoughts churned.

Tawa's words echoed in her mind: *Memory is a delicate thing, Elanor. It is not a tale to be told, nor a mere sequence of events. It is something you must feel flow through you like water shaping the stones of a riverbed.* The importance of the task ahead pressed on her. Alongside the fear was something else—a growing determination, a quiet resolve she hadn't felt before.

Simon's farewell lingered, too, his voice soft but sure: *You've got a light in you. Don't let it go out.* She could still see how he had walked away, his steps steady, as if he'd known exactly where he was going. The memory brought both an ache and a strange comfort. He had found his peace; now it was her turn to find hers.

Weston's voice broke through her thoughts. "You should rest," he said, stepping closer. "Tomorrow's going to be a long day."

Elanor turned to him, her lips curving into a faint smile. "I'll rest," she said, though she wasn't sure if she believed it. "Just . . . needed a minute."

He nodded, his gaze holding hers for a moment before he looked toward the others. "We're with you, El. All the way."

The words settled over her like a warm blanket, soothing the edges of her unease. She touched his arm briefly, a silent gesture of gratitude. "Thank you," she said softly.

As Weston returned to the camp, Elanor sat at the edge of the clearing, drawing her knees to her chest. The sanctuary thrummed with life, its energy pulsing faintly beneath the stillness. She closed her eyes momentarily, immersing herself in the symphony of night sounds and the fragrance of damp earth and foliage. The waterfall's roar grew louder, more insistent, echoing through the trees like a call she couldn't ignore.

Elanor opened her eyes, her chest tightening as she peered at the near-full moon's soft glow. Hanging high above, its light illuminated the trees in silver, casting long shadows that shifted and breathed. Tomorrow, she would face the truth Alo River held, confronting the memories she had been chasing and the pieces of herself she had buried.

She wasn't sure what she'd find, but she wasn't afraid to look.

CHAPTER TWENTY-TWO

Elanor opened her eyes, blinking against the soft light that broke through the leaves. For a moment, she was suspended in the quiet embrace of the sanctuary.

The sanctuary stirred to life with the first rays of dawn. Golden light filtered through the dense canopy above, casting shifting patterns on the mossy ground. The air carried a calm stillness, dampened by the earthy scent of pine and wildflowers. The distant murmur of the waterfall provided a steady rhythm, lulling the sanctuary into a peaceful wakefulness.

The previous day's events were distant, like a dream fading in the morning glow. But as Elanor stretched and shifted, the ache in her muscles brought reality back to her.

She peered around. Nora was already awake, seated on a fallen log, her elbows on her knees as she stared at the horizon with a contemplative look. Boone snored lightly nearby, sprawled out with one arm across his face, while Foster, seated against a tree trunk, held his hat low over his eyes. Weston was closest to her, still lying on his back, one arm tucked behind his head, his face calm in sleep.

The absence settled over Elanor before she fully recognized it: Simon's space near the fire was empty, his bedroll neatly folded, a reminder he hadn't changed his mind and returned in the night. Her chest tightened, the ache of his quiet farewell leaving a lasting echo within her.

Weston stirred then, his eyes opening slowly as he blinked against the light. He propped himself up on one elbow, his gaze finding Elanor almost immediately. "How'd you sleep?" he asked softly, his voice still rough.

She hesitated before nodding. "Better than I expected," she admitted, though her heart was heavier than her words let on.

He studied her for a moment. "We'll get through this," he said, his voice steady. "Together."

Foster stood, stretching with a quiet grunt before gesturing toward the horizon. "I've taken a look at the trail ahead. We've got some ground to cover, and we'll have to do it by foot. Best we get moving before the sun gets too high."

The group moved silently, gathering their belongings and preparing for the remainder of the journey. Nora adjusted her hat, her movements slow but deliberate. Boone rummaged through his pack, muttering about misplaced items, while Weston checked the straps on his satchel with quiet efficiency. The sheriff lingered at the edge of the clearing, his look distant.

Elanor stood still for a moment, letting the calm of the sanctuary wash over her one last time. The soft moss breathed beneath her boots, the cool, damp air brushing against her skin. She ran her fingers over the silver locket around her neck, the cool metal grounding her.

Simon's words echoed in her mind still. She closed her eyes, inhaling deeply, and when she opened them again, a renewed sense of determination took over. Whatever laid ahead, she would face it—with her friends, and for the memory of those who had brought her this far.

As they moved toward the trail, the clearing faded behind them, the light shifting as the dense trees closed in once more. Elanor glanced back one last time, steadied by purpose.

The morning's tranquility hung in the air as the group moved deeper into the trail's verdant embrace. The distant roar of the waterfall served as a steady reminder of their destination, a beacon pulling them forward. The ground was soft and damp, muffling their steps as they navigated the winding path. Nora led the way, her sharp focus scanning the dense underbrush for any signs of movement, while Boone lagged slightly behind, muttering about the weight of his pack.

Foster trailed behind, his tense posture suggesting he sensed the shift in the air before anyone else. He paused mid-step, hand hovering near the holster at his hip. "Hold up," he said quietly, his voice cutting through the soft rustle of leaves.

The group froze, their breaths catching in their throats. Elanor's pulse quickened. The sound came faint at first—a muffled thud, like distant thunder—but it grew louder with each passing second. Hoof-beats. Slow and deliberate, their cadence steady and unrelenting.

Nora's jaw clenched. "They've found us."

Elanor's pulse quickened as her attention darted to Weston, who stepped closer to her. "Stay low," he murmured.

The hoofbeats were joined by another noise—boots crunching against the forest floor. The sounds moved in a calculated rhythm, closing in from multiple directions. Shadows flickered through the trees, shapes shifting as figures moved with predatory precision.

Boone crouched behind a fallen log, his usual smirk replaced with a grim determination. "Guess they weren't keen on letting us slip away," he muttered, checking the chamber of his revolver.

Foster gestured sharply toward a thick cluster of trees. "Get behind cover," he hissed. The group obeyed, scattering to positions offering what little protection the sanctuary could provide.

Elanor found herself pressed against a moss-covered boulder, her breath coming in shallow bursts as the sounds of pursuit grew closer. Panicking, she looked over her shoulder, catching a glimpse of Weston by her side. "Weston, I need a pistol," she said.

Weston hesitated, clearly conflicted about arming her. "Elanor, I—" he began, but she cut him off with a sharp, insistent tone that brooked no delay.

"Now, Weston!" she demanded, her eyes locking onto his with an intensity that echoed Nora's steely resolve. He nodded, reluctantly reaching into his holster to hand her his spare gun.

The hoofbeats abruptly stopped, replaced by a tumultuous silence. Elanor strained to hear, her ears pricking up the faint rustle of leaves and the occasional snap of a twig. Merrick's men were out there, moving like wolves through the shadows, their presence a dark stain on the sanctuary's serenity.

A voice shattered the stillness, sharp and mocking. "Well, well. Looks like the little mice have found themselves a cozy hole."

The sound of Merrick's voice chilled Elanor's blood. It carried through the trees with a sneering confidence, each word laced with venom. She peeked around the boulder's edge, a jolt running through her as he stepped into view.

Mounted on a sleek black horse, Merrick cut an imposing figure, his dark coat billowing slightly in the faint breeze. His sharp eyes scanned the clearing, his lips curling into a cruel smile. "You thought you could run?" he called out, almost playful. "Thought this entrance to Paradise would keep you safe? You should've known better."

Behind him, his men fanned out, weapons drawn, eyes gleaming with anticipation. Once a haven of peace, the sanctuary was now a trap, its dense foliage and winding paths offering no apparent escape.

Nora's voice came in a harsh whisper. "We can't stay here. We won't be able to endure this."

Boone's hand twitched near his revolver. "Or we give 'em a reason to think twice."

Foster shot them both a sharp look. "Hold your fire. Let's see what he wants."

Elanor's breath hitched as Merrick dismounted, his movements slow and deliberate. He adjusted his coat, eyes sweeping the sanctuary with a proprietary air. "I know you're here," he said, his voice turning even colder. "And I'm feeling generous today. Surrender now, and maybe I'll make this painless."

Weston's hand rested lightly on Elanor's shoulder. He gave her a slight nod, his eyes steady. "We'll handle this," he whispered.

Merrick took a step closer, his boots crunching against the moss. His smile widened into a predator's grin. "Or," he continued, his voice dropping to a menacing growl, "you can make me come find you. But I promise, you won't like how that ends."

The group remained silent, their breaths shallow as they waited. Elanor's pulse pounded, roaring in her ears as Merrick's men moved closer, their shadows stretching across the forest floor. She tightened her grip on her pistol, knuckles whitening.

The silence stretched, taut and brittle, as Merrick's glare swept the clearing. His men held their positions, their weapons gleaming faintly in the dappled light filtering through the trees. Each moved with cold precision, spreading out to encircle the sanctuary. The heaviness of the moment pressed against Elanor's chest, the charged stillness feeling as though it might snap at any second.

Merrick's voice rang out again, sharp and taunting. "I know you're hiding in these woods, Elanor. I can smell you like a bloodhound. You've been running long enough. Time to step into the light."

As Merrick's men edged closer, Eleanor knew there was no avoiding the confrontation.

Nora's voice came low and fierce. "You don't have to do this, Elanor. We've got your back."

Elanor glanced at her, drawing strength from the determination in her friend's eyes. Then, with a deep breath, she stepped out from behind the boulder, her boots crunching against the mossy ground. The forest held its breath as she moved forward, Merrick's attention snapping to her like a predator spotting its prey.

"There you are," Merrick said, his smile expanding even more as he extended his arms in a mocking gesture of greeting. "The woman of the hour. I was beginning to suspect you had lost your composure."

Elanor stopped a few paces away, shoulders squared, chin lifted in defiance. "What do you want, Merrick?" she asked, her voice steady despite the adrenaline surging through her veins.

He tilted his head, studying her with a predatory gleam in his eye. "Oh, I think you know what I'm after," he said. "You see, Elanor, what I seek . . . it's not something tangible that I can simply seize by force."

"You're mistaken," she replied sharply. "You're chasing shadows, Merrick. What you want isn't for you to take claim of."

Merrick chuckled, a low, mocking sound that sent a shiver down her spine. "Oh, I've heard the whispers, the rumors that echo around you. It's not merely about what you possess—it's about what you are."

"You're wrong," Elanor countered, stepping closer, her voice rising with anger and defiance. "I'm not an item to be claimed, Merrick. Whatever you think you'll achieve, it won't be through me."

Merrick's smile faded, his expression hardening. "You think you can stand there and tell me what I can't have?" he snapped. "You don't understand the stakes here, girl. You're playing with forces you can't begin to comprehend."

Elanor's hands shook, but she kept her eyes steady. "And you think you can just take what you want? That you can manipulate people into giving you whatever you desire?"

The words resonated deeply. Merrick stepped closer, his boots crunching against the ground as he loomed over her. "You don't get it, do you?" he hissed. "This isn't about fair play or morals. It's about who's strong enough to claim what they need. And I won't let some naive girl and her band of misfits stop me."

Elanor's breath caught, her pulse roaring in her ears. But then, Tawa's words echoed in her mind: *There will be dark entities that look to take you off your path and into a world of darkness, entities I fear you have already encountered. They will whisper lies, twist truths, and offer you solace in shadows. Do not give in—no matter how tempting or familiar it may seem. Hold fast, and you will find what you truly seek.*

She squared her shoulders, her voice steady as she said, "You don't scare me, Merrick," her words piercing the tension like a blade. "Your power comes from fear, from controlling others. But that's not strength. It's weakness. I will not surrender to you; I think that's what you want me to do. I will not do it."

Merrick's expression faltered for a moment, a flicker of doubt crossing his face. But it vanished as quickly as it came, replaced by a sneer. "Bold words for someone standing in the shadow of her own grave," he said, his voice dripping with venom. "You have two choices, Elanor. Surrender yourself to me, or watch your friends pay the price for your defiance."

Elanor glanced back at the group, their faces resolute despite the danger. Nora's hand hovered near her revolver, eyes blazing with determination. Boone gave her a subtle nod. Weston stood tall, as if daring Merrick to make his move.

Turning back to Merrick, Elanor met his gaze head-on. "I'm not giving you anything," she said firmly. "And neither are they."

Merrick's sneer deepened, his hand twitching near the gun at his side. "So be it," he growled.

Elanor's breath caught in her throat as Merrick's hand drifted closer to his gun. Her friends spread out behind her, each moving with silent precision, finding cover or drawing their weapons in preparation. The sanctuary, so serene and sacred just moments ago, was now the stage for a battle it was never meant to host.

For a long moment, nothing happened. The two sides stared each other down. The only sounds were the waterfall's distant rush and the faint leaves rustling in the breeze. Elanor's heart thundered, her grip on her pistol tightening as she looked toward Weston. He gave her a slight nod, his eyes steady and relentless, grounding her amid the rising chaos.

Then, like a spark igniting a flame, a single shot rang out from one of Merrick's men.

The sanctuary exploded into chaos. Merrick's men surged forward, shouts and gunfire tearing through the tranquil morning. Elanor ducked instinctively, the crack of bullets ricocheting off nearby rocks and trees. The acrid smell of gunpowder filled the sharp, suffocating air as the group scrambled to hold their positions.

"Nora, left flank!" Foster barked, his voice cutting through the cacophony as he fired a precise shot, dropping one of Merrick's men. Nora moved quickly, her revolver steady in her hands as she returned fire with deadly accuracy, her movements fluid and controlled.

Boone whistled sharply as he darted behind a fallen tree, far from the town drunk Elanor met in Bodie. He drew the attention of two of Merrick's men. "Over here, you sons of—" His taunt was cut short as he ducked low, a bullet splintering the branch above his head. He grinned despite the danger, his laughter ringing out like a challenge. "Come on, is that the best you've got?"

Elanor crouched behind a boulder. She peeked over the edge, eyes scanning the chaos as she tried to focus. Merrick stood at the center of it all, his movements calculated as he directed his men, his sharp eyes darting across the battlefield like a hawk. He was calm, as though he was savoring the destruction.

A sharp crack of gunfire snapped Elanor's attention back to the fight. She raised her pistol, hands trembling slightly as she aimed at one of Merrick's men advancing toward Weston. The shot rang out, and the man stumbled, clutching his leg as he fell. Elanor's breath hitched, adrenaline and shock surging through her.

Weston caught her gaze and gave her a slight, approving nod before returning fire, his stance solid and unyielding. "Nice shot, El!" he called over the noise.

Nearby, Foster moved with a new confidence, his revolver blazing as he covered Nora. They held the right flank together.

Amid the chaos, Merrick's voice rang out, sharp and commanding. "Push them back! This is our fight, and we will win it!"

His words sent a surge through his men, who pressed forward, their attacks becoming more coordinated. A wave of panic rose in Elanor's chest as their line began to falter. The sanctuary's once-impenetrable calm was now a battlefield littered with broken branches and churned earth.

Tawa's words echoed in her mind again: *This path is not about survival. It is about acceptance.*

She took a deep breath, grounding herself. Her voice cut through the chaos, steady and unwavering. "Merrick!" she shouted, drawing his attention. "You think you have power here, but you don't. All you have is fear—and it won't work anymore."

Merrick turned toward her, eyes narrowing as a slow, predatory smile spread across his face. "Feelin' weak, are you?" he sneered. "Do you think your little speeches will save you?"

"They're not just words," Elanor shot back. "This place doesn't belong to you, and it never will. You can't take something that's meant to be given freely. You can shoot me, but I will never belong to you."

Merrick's smirk faltered for a moment, but it was enough.

A surge of determination took over as Elanor stepped forward, her fear melting away. She could see it now—Merrick's power wasn't real. It was built on intimidation, twisting truths, and manipulating those around him. And it could be undone.

The group, sensing her resolve, rallied. Nora's shots rang out with renewed vigor, her aim precise as she forced Merrick's men back. Boone let out a whoop as he vaulted over the fallen tree, taking out another attacker with a well-placed shot. Foster and Nora coordinated their movements flawlessly, maintaining the line.

Weston stepped up beside Elanor. "We've got this," he said. "Keep pushing."

Elanor nodded, her grip on her pistol tightening as she focused on Merrick. "This ends now," she said. "You don't control me, and you never will."

The situation started to shift. Merrick's men, once so confident, started to falter under the group's coordinated efforts. The sanctuary rose against them, the dense underbrush and towering trees becoming obstacles that hindered their retreat. Now visibly frustrated, Merrick barked orders, but his men's resolve was crumbling.

Merrick's sneer deepened as the skirmish began to die, his anger boiling over. "This isn't over," he growled, his hand twitching near his holster. But before he could act, Elanor stepped forward, shooting a warning shot that nicked his arm before training her pistol on him.

"No," she said firmly. "It is over."

Her words hung in the air, causing the clearing to fall silent. For the first time, Merrick was resigned, his bravado cracking as he stared her down.

Elanor held her ground.

The clearing grew eerily still, the last echoes of gunfire fading into the dense forest. Elanor stood tall, her breath coming in shallow gasps as she held Merrick's attention. He was no longer the commanding, confident figure who had stormed into the sanctuary—now, something fractured in his expression, a crack in the armor he'd worn so brazenly. His shoulders sagged slightly, his wounded arm hanging at his side, blood staining his sleeve.

"You think this is a victory?" Merrick spat, his voice laced with venom but lacking the force it once carried. "You think defying me changes anything?"

Elanor's grip on her pistol remained firm, though her voice was calm when she replied. "It changes everything. You don't have power here, Merrick. Not over me, not over this place." She stepped forward, her words steady and deliberate. "You can't control what isn't yours. I, and this sanctuary, do not belong to you."

Merrick's sneer deepened, but the uncertainty flickering in his eyes betrayed him. "You're just a girl," he said, though his tone was less sure. "You think you can stop me?"

Elanor squared her shoulders, the weight of Tawa's words grounding her. "You've already lost," she said. "Because you've built your power on fear and lies. But I'm not afraid of you anymore."

The sanctuary responded to her words. A soft breeze rustled the trees, the sound like a whispered affirmation. The mossy ground was solid and alive, like the earth was standing with her. The faint hum of the waterfall carried on the wind, its presence steady and unwavering, a quiet reminder of the truths she was coming to understand.

Merrick faltered, his demeanor crumbling further as he scanned the clearing. His scattered, wounded men were no longer the unified force they'd been when they arrived.

Nora, Boone, the sheriff, and Weston stood resolute behind Elanor, their expressions a mixture of exhaustion and determination, an image that mirrored Angelina and her deputies in Leto. The sanctuary, though battered, still radiated an unshakable strength, as if it had absorbed the chaos and come out stronger.

"You're done, Merrick," Weston said as he stepped up beside Elanor. "Walk away while you still can."

Merrick hesitated, his hand twitching near his holster. But before he could move, Judah stepped forward, his hands raised in surrender. His broad shoulders slumped, and his face was etched with desperation. "Please," Judah said, his voice raw and strained. "Enough blood's been spilled. Let us go. I swear . . . we'll leave and never come back."

Elanor studied Judah. The sincerity in his voice resonated with a palpable urgency, and the anguish etched across his face left no room for doubt. He wasn't merely pleading for Merrick's life; he was begging for an end to the cycle of violence, for a way out of the darkness that had trapped them all.

She turned her attention to Merrick, catching a fleeting glimpse of betrayal flicker across his face. It was a raw, unguarded moment that revealed his shock at Judah's defiance.

"Take him," Elanor said after a long moment. "Take your men and leave this place. If you ever come back . . ." She let the warning hang in the air, its importance unmistakable.

Judah nodded, his relief palpable. He moved to Merrick's side, gripping his arm to steady him. Merrick glared at Elanor, his anger burning hot but his defiance muted. He opened his mouth to speak, but Judah shook his head, a silent plea to let it go. With a growl of frustration, Merrick turned away, allowing Judah to lead him into the shadows of the trees.

The remaining men, battered and defeated, followed silently, their faces cast downward. As they disappeared from view, the oppressive weight hanging over the clearing began to ease, the air feeling lighter with every step they took away.

As the last of them disappeared into the forest, Elanor released a shaky breath. Her shoulders sagged, and the pistol slipped from her hand, landing softly in the moss. The adrenaline that had propelled her through the confrontation subsided, resulting in a profound fatigue.

Weston placed a steadying hand on her shoulder. "You did it," he said quietly, his voice filled with pride. "They're gone."

Elanor nodded. She looked around the clearing, taking in the faces of her friends—each tired, their expressions marked by relief and sorrow. The sanctuary bore the scars of the skirmish, but its quiet strength remained.

The waterfall's hum grew louder, filling the space with a soothing rhythm. Elanor tilted her head toward the sound, the promise of Alo River pulling her attention forward.

The group gathered slowly, each member finding a place to sit or lean, their movements marked by fatigue. Nora rubbed her shoulder where a grazing shot had torn her jacket, her expression pensive but calm. Boone slumped against a tree, his usual grin replaced with a thoughtful silence. The sheriff paced a short distance away, his steps deliberate, as though trying to shake off the tension that still clung to him.

Elanor looked around at each of them, her chest tightening with gratitude and sorrow. The people surrounding her—these unlikely companions—had risked everything to protect her and this place. They had fought for her journey and the sanctuary itself, a place they had come to understand as sacred, even if they couldn't fully explain why.

Her eyes fell to Weston, who watched her with that same quiet intensity he always carried. "It's not over yet," she said softly. "The waterfall . . . Alo River . . . it's still ahead."

Weston nodded. "We'll get there," he said, his words carrying a certainty that lifted her spirits. "We've come this far. We can finish this."

A surge of determination rose within Elanor. The fear and uncertainty that had once dominated her thoughts were fading. She had faced Merrick and the darkness, and she had come through stronger.

As the group gathered their belongings and prepared to leave, Elanor took one last look at the sanctuary. The scars of the fight were there, but so was the sanctuary's enduring strength, its beauty untouched in the ways that mattered most. A strange sense of peace settled over her, a quiet promise that this place would carry the memory of what they had fought for.

Together, they returned to the path. The forest closed around them, the light filtering through the leaves a reminder of the sanctuary's quiet blessings.

As they moved deeper into the trees, her friends' strength surrounded Elanor, guiding her toward the truths that awaited her at the waterfall.

CHAPTER TWENTY-THREE

Midday light streamed through the trees, casting golden beams across the narrow trail. The air was cool, carrying the lingering scent of moss, earth, and the fresh tang of leaves warmed by the sun. The sanctuary, now bathed in sunlight, stood silently in the background.

Elanor walked deliberately, her focus firmly on the winding path ahead. Occasionally, her fingers brushed against her locket, drawing small comfort from its familiar pull against the uncertainties before them.

Walking beside her, Weston provided a steady presence that grounded her in the moment. The quiet between them was reflective, not uneasy, filled with thoughts of their recent encounter with Merrick and his men and the challenges that awaited them at Alo River.

The trail climbed gently, weaving through ancient trees whose branches arched overhead, creating a canopy that dappled the ground with shifting light patterns. With each step, past events—the battle, the dangers of the desert, the sacrifices made—pressed heavier on Elanor's heart.

She looked at Weston, noting the quiet determination on his face. His furrowed brow and clenched jaw hinted at an unspoken strain, a guarded resolve that seemed to echo the unease stirring within her.

The path grew steeper as the trees thinned, giving way to rocky outcroppings that jutted out like ancient sentinels. Below, the forest canopy stretched endlessly, broken only by the sanctuary's clearing, now a fading memory.

"It doesn't feel real," she murmured, her voice barely above a whisper. She perceived the scene's peacefulness as if she were looking through a glass window. "After everything . . . it's like the world shouldn't be so peaceful."

Weston turned to her, his blue eyes meeting hers with a quiet intensity. "The world keeps moving," he said softly. "Even when we feel like *we* can't. Maybe that's how it's supposed to be—like it's reminding us there's still something worth fighting for."

His words washed over her like a balm, soothing the raw edges of her grief. She nodded, looking back toward the horizon. The river was waiting, its allure both promising and daunting. Tawa's words echoed in her mind, propelling her forward. She tightened her grip on the locket.

Behind them, Boone whistled a low, meandering tune, the sound lightening their journey. Nora led the way, her sharp eyes scanning the path ahead, while the sheriff trailed behind.

As the path narrowed, the terrain grew treacherous, rocks protruding at odd angles, demanding careful movement. The air cooled further, and the faint sound of rushing water grew louder, reaching their ears and heightening Elanor's anticipation and apprehension with each step.

"We're close now," Boone said, his voice uncharacteristically quiet, as though the place demanded reverence. His attention flicked ahead, where the sound of water grew louder, its rhythmic roar beckoning them forward.

They rounded a bend, and the trees and rocks opened up to reveal a breathtaking sight. Alo River stretched before them, its waters glimmering with an otherworldly light. The current was swift, the surface reflecting the sky above in shifting hues of blue and silver. On the far side, a waterfall cascaded down a series of jagged rocks, its roar filling the air with a steady rhythm that pulsed in time with Elanor's heartbeat.

The sight left the group speechless. Weston's hand wrapped around

Elanor's waist, steadying her, but Nora's soft exhale of wonder broke the silence.

"Well," Nora said, her tone tinged with awe. "That's . . . something else."

Boone stepped forward. "Damn. Ain't every day you see a place like this. Makes a fella feel small, doesn't it?"

Foster didn't speak, his eyes fixed on the rushing water.

It was more than just a river; it was the culmination of everything they had fought for and endured. And now that they stood on its banks, the enormity of their journey almost overwhelmed Elanor. She swallowed hard, her voice barely audible as she said, "This is it. This is what we've been searching for."

Weston nodded beside her, his blue eyes intensely fixed on the river. "It's more than that," he said thoughtfully. "It's what's been waiting for us."

The air around them was charged, like the river was aware of their presence. Elanor took a deep breath. Alo River wasn't just a destination—it was a reckoning. And as she stepped forward, she knew there was no turning back.

Boone crouched near the edge of the clearing, trailing a hand through the cool, damp grass. "Reckon this is the kind of place that gets under your skin," he said quietly. "Not just something you look at. Something you feel."

Nora crossed her arms, nodding faintly. "Yeah," she murmured. "This place changes you. Feels like it's already started."

Standing a few paces back, Foster adjusted his hat and let out a slow breath. "You can see why my father talked about it like it's something sacred. It's not just a river. It's . . . something more."

Elanor looked at her companions, a wave of gratitude and sadness washing over her. They had brought her here and supported her through every battle and hardship. And now that they stood together on the edge of this great unknown, she reflected on how much they had given and sacrificed to get her here.

Weston broke the stillness, murmuring, "This place will heal, El."

She offered him a faint smile. "I hope so," she said softly, her fingers lingering on the moss before joining the others. Together, they stood at the river's edge, the sound of the waterfall filling the air.

Foster stood a short distance from the group, his tall frame leaning casually against a boulder at the trail's edge, hat pulled low, hands resting loosely at his sides as he glanced at the winding path ahead. His expression was hard to read, but there was a gravity to his stance, a sense that he was carrying something heavier than the rest of them could see.

Elanor approached him cautiously. "You alright?" she asked.

Foster lifted his head slightly, his eyes meeting hers. There was a flicker of something in there—regret, maybe, or gratitude. He nodded slowly. "Just thinkin'," he said. "This place . . . these woods. Feels like they hold onto everything we've been through."

Elanor nodded, understanding more than she could put into words.

The group moved silently as they worked their way down the trail, each person lost in their thoughts. Boone walked ahead, tossing small pebbles into the underbrush as he went. Nora kept pace with Elanor, her sharp eyes scanning the trail ahead, her movements purposeful as always. Weston and the sheriff trailed behind, steady and deliberate

Nora removed her hat, swiping a hand across her brow as she paced beside Elanor. "Mind some company?" she asked softly, stepping closer.

Elanor smirked faintly. "Since when do I mind you hanging around, twin?" she replied with a wink, patting Nora on the shoulder.

For a moment, neither spoke, the silence stretching between them as they watched the dappled light shift across the trail. Nora's presence had always been a sharp and unyielding force, but now, there was a softness to her.

"It feels like I've been chasing you through this whole journey," Nora said, "keeping an eye on you, making sure you didn't get into too much trouble."

Elanor chuckled softly, a slight ache tugging at her as she heard the words. "I guess I've given you plenty to chase after."

Nora's smile broadened, her eyes softening. "You've definitely kept me engaged." I've enjoyed it, and I've gotten the excitement I was looking for. But, Elanor . . . you've grown more than I ever expected." Her voice dropped to a quieter, more serious tone. "Out here, you've truly found your strength. You're stronger than you know—stronger than I think even you believe."

Elanor looked down. "I don't feel strong," she admitted. "Most days, I feel like I'm just barely holding it together."

Nora reached out, her hand resting on Elanor's arm. "That's the thing about strength—it doesn't always feel like it. Sometimes, it's simply about stepping forward, even when you doubt your ability to do so. And, Elanor . . . you've done that every step of the way."

Elanor felt a wave of sincerity in Nora's words, warming her chest as her throat tightened with emotion. "I couldn't have done it without you," she whispered.

Nora shook her head. "Nah. I might've helped, but this journey? It's always been yours. You're the one who's carried it. You're the one who's going to see it through."

Nora's words hung over Elanor, bittersweet and heavy. The unspoken truth in them hung over her, not as an immediate goodbye but as a quiet acknowledgment of the inevitable. Nora wasn't just offering encouragement—she was preparing Elanor for the moment they would part ways.

"You're thinking about the waterfall, aren't you?" Elanor asked, her voice faltering slightly.

Nora's smile softened, a hint of sadness in her eyes. "Yeah," she replied quietly. "It's coming. And when you get there . . . well, you'll see." Nora paused, taking a deep breath before facing Elanor directly. "I've got to head back, twin," she said. "I won't be here once you drink from the fall, so I've got to say my peace now."

Elanor furrowed her brow, confusion clouding her features. "What do you mean? Why won't you be here?"

Nora's expression remained gentle yet resolute. "All of your questions will be answered when you drink from the water," she assured her softly. "It's important, Elanor. Trust me."

Elanor's smile faltered, a sinking feeling settling over her at the news. "I was hoping you'd stay with us a bit longer, finish this out," she admitted, her voice carrying a note of disappointment.

Nora gave her a reassuring look, squeezing Elanor's shoulder gently.

"I know. But you're ready for what's ahead. I've seen you grow, take charge, and overcome. You don't need me watching over you anymore. Besides, other people need my help, too."

Elanor nodded, understanding Nora's duty to her life back home, despite her reluctance to see her go. "I guess I just got used to having you by my side," she said, managing a small, grateful smile. "Thank you, Nora, for everything."

Nora pulled Elanor into a tight embrace. "Don't thank me. Just promise me you'll keep being the fierce woman I know you are. And remember, I'll never be too far."

With one last firm nod, Nora adjusted her hat, turned, and started back the way they had come, her strides confident and purposeful. Elanor watched her go, the reality of her departure settling in.

Feeling a sudden need to pause, Elanor stopped walking, and the rest of the group halted. She sat on a nearby log, Nora's goodbye pressing down on her. Weston sat beside her, offering a silent presence of support, while Boone and Foster remained standing, giving her space yet staying close.

"The path seems a bit lonelier without her," Elanor murmured, her eyes tracing the trail Nora had taken.

Weston placed a gentle hand on her back. "It might feel that way now, but she's given you—and all of us—so much. We carry that with us no matter where we go."

Boone approached Elanor, his characteristic swagger slightly subdued as he closed the distance between them. Next to Elanor, he traded places with Weston. His hat tilted back to reveal a contemplative expression uncharacteristic of his usual cheerful demeanor.

"Well, well," he drawled, his voice a mix of warmth and something more somber. "If it ain't the fearless leader herself. Hate to ruin the moment more than it already is, but I've been doing some thinking . . . 'bout when to say goodbye. And I hate to say it, but I think it's time for me to head back with Nora. Don't want to let things get too far 'fore I have to disappear."

A pang of disappointment washed over Elanor. "You're leaving, too?" she asked.

"Yeah," Boone replied, his voice gentle. "It's not an easy choice, but it's the right one. This journey . . . it's changed me. But you've got to do this next part without me."

Elanor crossed her arms, trying to mask her vulnerability. "I don't understand why you both have to leave."

Boone had a mischievous twinkle in his eye. "Well, Elanor, we're like outlaws on the run—best to keep movin' before the dust settles." He watched her reaction, gauging whether the humor landed.

"Why do you always have to joke at times like this?" she asked, her voice tinged with frustration.

Boone's smile faltered, giving way to a more sincere expression. "Because if I didn't joke, we'd never stop feeling the intensity of what we're up against. And that can crush you if you let it."

She nodded, understanding his ways a little better now. "I'll miss you, Boone. Your jokes, your lightness . . . they've helped more than you know."

Boone scooted closer, offering a rugged, heartfelt hug that Elanor returned tightly. "You're going to be just fine, you know that? You're ready for whatever that river throws at you. And hey," he added, pulling back with a wink, "don't forget to laugh sometimes. It's important."

With that, Boone picked up his gear, tipped his hat one last time, and started back toward the town. Elanor watched him go, feeling the finality of his departure. As he disappeared from view, she turned back to face Weston and the sheriff.

Weston moved to her side. "He's right, you know. You're stronger than you think," he said quietly, giving her a moment to collect herself.

Elanor took a deep breath, looking between Weston and the sheriff, and nodded. "Let's keep moving," she said. "We need to get to the base of the falls."

Foster stepped before Elanor and Weston, his usually stoic demeanor softened by a rare, lighthearted grin. "Hold on, now," he said, his voice mixed with seriousness and jest. "Can't let you all leave without saying my piece. Looks like I've got to head back, too—make sure Boone and Nora don't turn this place upside down without me."

Elanor felt a deeper sense of dread, unprepared to face another farewell so soon. "You, too, sheriff?" she managed to ask, her voice tinged with disbelief and a hint of sorrow.

Foster nodded, his expression turning solemn. "Afraid so, Miss Elanor. This journey . . . it's been more than I signed up for in the best ways possible. But my place is back with the rest of those looking to go on a journey to find themselves. I think I've found a knack for this."

He stepped closer, placing a hand on her shoulder. "You've grown fierce and strong. You're ready to face whatever lies ahead at that river. Remember, the strength you've built up here—it's yours, built by your actions and the trials you've overcome."

Elanor looked up at him, her eyes welling up with tears, but she nodded, understanding the necessity of his departure. "Thank you, Foster," she said, her voice breaking slightly. "For everything—your guidance, your protection, and your understanding."

Foster gave a short, hearty laugh. "Ah, don't mention it. Just make sure you keep this one in line," he said, nodding toward Weston. He tipped his hat one last time, a gesture filled with respect and a touch of sadness. "You'll do great, Elanor. I'm counting on it."

With that, Foster turned and began his journey back, leaving Elanor with Weston and the path forward. Elanor watched him go, each step reinforcing the finality of his departure.

They resumed walking, the path underfoot crunching softly with each step. The silence was heavy with reflection as Elanor processed the goodbyes to her three friends—Nora, Boone, and now Foster—who had been with her from the start. Each had left a mark on her, shaping her into the leader she had become.

A profound sense of solitude and empowerment settled in. Their belief in her was a testament to her growth and capability. The path ahead was hers to forge, and though she lamented their absence, she also had their strength, humor, and wisdom.

The forest and river around them acknowledged her transition, the light filtering through the trees, casting long shadows that danced around her feet. Elanor took a deep breath, the air fresh with the scent of pine, earth, and moss, grounding her. "They believe in me," she whispered.

The journey to the waterfall and beyond was no longer just a path to follow—it was a challenge to embrace, a chance to prove that she was indeed the leader her friends recognized her to be.

Elanor's stride grew more confident, her eyes fixed on the horizon, ready to face whatever awaited her with the strength of her departed friends echoing in her heart.

CHAPTER TWENTY-FOUR

Water cascaded over stone, filling the space with an almost sacred energy. The waterfall glistened in the dusk light, soft rays catching on each droplet and transforming them into flecks of blue as they pooled into a deep, glassy basin below. Elanor took a tentative step forward, her eyes locked onto the water, her pulse racing as Tawa's words echoed in her mind: *The water there holds the power to reveal what has been lost, but only if you drink from it willingly, ready to accept the truth.* For a brief moment, Elanor could have mistakenly believed Tawa was standing across the river, watching with encouragement.

Her nerves ignited, trembling between anticipation and fear. The weight of her entire journey settled on her shoulders, mingling with the ache of parting from her friends and the hope of finally finding answers. The closer she drew to the water, the more the world around her shifted and blurred. She felt herself standing on the threshold of something immense that had always been waiting for her, just out of reach.

She sensed Weston's steadying presence beside her, a quiet strength she could lean on. Though she wasn't looking at him, his support was palpable, grounding her in the moment. His presence carried a silent encouragement that urged her forward. Without a word, she understood he was giving her space—this was her step, and he recognized it as much as she did.

Elanor stopped at the water's edge, her breath catching as her reflection appeared. The face staring back at her was starkly different from the one she'd seen before—no hollow cheeks or tired eyes, no sun-darkened skin etched with exhaustion. Her complexion was smooth and vibrant, black curls shining and full, framing her face with a vitality she hadn't felt in ages. She barely recognized herself, not because of unfamiliarity, but because this was her—her true self, unburdened by the harshness of the journey.

She took a deep, shaky breath, letting the cool, damp air fill her lungs as she knelt beside the pool. Her hands trembled as she dipped them into the water, the coldness biting into her skin. It grounded her, pulling her entirely into the present as though the reflection reminded her of the strength and wholeness she had carried all along, even in the absence of her friends.

Closing her eyes, she cupped her hands and brought the water to her lips. The taste was fresh and clean, unlike anything she'd ever experienced. As she swallowed, an intense rush surged through her—a torrent of memories, images, and emotions flooding her mind with a force that nearly knocked her breath from her.

As a strong memory took hold, the scene around Elanor shifted, the sound of the waterfall fading into the chirping of crickets and the distant hum of cicadas on a warm summer afternoon. She stood barefoot in the backyard of her childhood home, the grass lush and soft beneath her feet. The old wooden swing hung lazily from the towering oak tree near the yard's edge, swaying gently in the breeze. The sunlight filtered through the dense canopy of trees that bordered the yard, casting golden dapples across the ground. A familiar scent of blooming wildflowers and the faint tang of freshly mowed grass lingered in the air.

She was a young girl again, her hair in two messy braids that framed her face, the strands unruly even in their attempt to be neat. She wore a faded pink dress—her "princess gown"—several sizes too big, its hem stained green from dragging along the ground. The edges were frayed from countless adventures, but it was still magical to her.

Beside her stood Imogen, her sister, her skin a shade lighter but glowing in the same summer light. Her black curls were piled into a lopsided bun, a few strands falling free to frame her warm, mischievous smile. Imogen's laughter was light and infectious as she nudged Elanor, her hands full of dandelions she'd plucked from the yard.

On the other side, Weston stood grinning, his face slightly smudged with dirt from whatever grand quest they'd invented that day. He wore a cowboy hat far too big for his head, the brim tilting forward as he wielded a stick like a sword. His stance was dramatic, chest puffed out, one hand resting on his hip as though he were the hero of an old Western movie.

The three stood together in the golden summer light, their laughter ringing like music. The scene radiated warmth and simplicity that Elanor hadn't experienced in years—a piece of a life that had once been infinite, now held in the fragile hands of memory.

"Princess Elanor Foster, the Wild West Duchess," her sister proclaimed in a grand, dramatic voice, "your kingdom awaits!"

As they played, a familiar voice called out from the porch. "Lunch is almost ready, you wild outlaws!" Miss Billie shouted, shaking her head with a smile.

"No, just a little longer," Elanor pleaded, spinning in her oversized dress.

Miss Billie laughed, leaning against the doorway. "If you two keep playing Wild West all the time, I might as well start calling you Boone and Wiley. Alright, twenty more minutes!"

"Thank you, Miss Billie!" Elanor and Imogen chorused, their voices filled with glee.

Elanor let out a peal of laughter, spinning around as if her dress were a magnificent ball gown, her imagination blending tales of far-off kingdoms and dusty trails. The three of them had invented their own world—where Elanor could be a princess and a fearless outlaw at once, unbound by any limits.

As she spun, Elanor laughed, her voice rising in a lilting, exaggerated tone. "Perhaps I shall decree this kingdom to be the grandest in all the land," she announced, her words dripping with theatrical flair.

Weston chuckled, his smile soft and amused. "Darlin', your accent's slippin'," he teased, tilting his oversized cowboy hat back as he watched her. "Where'd all that Southern charm go?"

Elanor smirked, tossing a playful look over her shoulder. "I don't like having a Southern accent," she said with a mock haughty tone, raising her chin like royalty. "I'd much rather sound like a princess from France."

Weston laughed, shaking his head. "Well, Princess, you're in the wrong kingdom for that. You'll have to trade dusty trails for cobblestone streets and tea parties."

Elanor paused mid-spin, a playful glint in her eye. "You know, we could go there," she said suddenly, the mischief in her voice carrying a spark of sincerity. "You'd make a fine prince in a palace. We could run away to France."

Weston leaned on his makeshift sword, smile widening as his face turned soft and fond. "Darlin'," he said with an exaggerated drawl, "I could never leave the West. Too much dust in my soul."

Elanor rolled her eyes with a laugh, but the warmth in her chest spread at his words. She spun back to face Imogen, who had been watching them both with a knowing grin. "Princess Elanor Foster," Imogen proclaimed again, tossing her dandelions like confetti, "the Wild West Duchess and her cowboy prince!"

Their laughter echoed into the golden light, and their world of imagination wrapped around them like a comforting embrace. It was a memory filled with joy and longing, a moment Elanor would carry with her forever, woven into the very fabric of her being.

She watched her younger self look at Weston, a spark of admiration in her eyes as he puffed out his chest, playfully embodying the role of her "loyal cowboy protector." He pointed his stick sword to the imaginary horizon and declared, "Ain't nobody messin' with the Duchess while I'm around!" His tone was playful but filled with an innocent sincerity—one that struck Elanor even now, years later.

She watched how he'd look over his shoulder, checking on her, making sure she was safe even in their pretend world. That small act made her feel like a princess worthy of protection.

The memory wove on, Weston leading her on a grand "journey" around the yard, her sister narrating their every step. Together, they wove an intricate tapestry of fantasy, blending knights and cowboys, fairies, and sheriffs, creating a unique world. She could see now how Boone's wild tales of duchesses and outlaws had mirrored these moments. His stories, so full of life and imagination, reflected her childhood memories, exaggerated yet filled with that same magic. Even now, she could almost hear his voice, carrying her forward with that infectious humor and optimism.

As she watched her younger self bask in that innocent joy, a pang of longing surged through her, a bittersweet ache for a time when life had been simple, carefree, and full of laughter. Those days with Weston and Imogen had been among the happiest of her life. They were reminders of a time when her heart was whole, before loss and guilt had clouded her spirit.

Her younger self turned to Weston, her laughter echoing, and the memory faded. Yet the warmth of it lingered, filling her with a renewed sense of purpose. She understood now that Boone's tales, laughter, and wild imagination had been a mirror of her own life. He had helped her remember the innocence she'd lost, reminding her that even in the darkest times, the joy and playfulness of her spirit remained within her.

Another memory surfaced gently, like a page-turning in a well-worn book. Elanor and Imogen stood side by side in the small kitchen of their childhood home, the late afternoon sunlight slanting through the lace curtains, pooling on the floorboards beneath their bare feet. On the counter, a broken ceramic bowl lay in jagged pieces, the remnants of a hasty, ill-fated attempt to "help" their father by cleaning up after lunch.

Simon Foster loomed over them, his tall frame casting a shadow across the room. His pale skin, freckled from hours spent outdoors, was flushed slightly with frustration. The fine creases around his blue eyes deepened as he gave them both a pointed look, hands firmly planted on his hips. "Elanor," he said with his thick Southern accent, "you're the older sister. You should know better than to let something like this happen."

Elanor's cheeks burned with embarrassment and guilt. "I didn't mean to, Papa," she mumbled, her eyes fixed on the floor. She wanted to clarify that Imogen had the idea to stack the dishes so high, but the words stuck in her throat. Imogen's wide-eyed, innocent look stopped her from blaming her little sister.

Simon sighed heavily, rubbing a hand over his face. His broad shoulders slumped slightly, a gesture that softened his imposing presence. "Both of you need to be more careful. We can't afford to replace things like this every time one of you decides to play kitchen." He pointed to the mess on the counter. "Clean it up, and Elanor, next time . . . think before you act." With that, he turned and walked out of the room, his boots clunking against the floorboards as he disappeared into the hall.

Imogen turned to Elanor when the door clicked shut, her face breaking into a mischievous grin. Her lighter brown skin and curly hair caught the sunlight, highlighting the stark resemblance between the two girls, despite the subtle difference in their complexions. "I told you I wasn't good at stacking dishes," she whispered, biting back a giggle.

Despite her best efforts to remain serious and narrow her eyes at her sister, Elanor's mouth twitched upward, betraying her. "You're lucky I didn't tell him it was your idea," she muttered, though her tone was more teasing than scolding.

Imogen nudged her gently. "That's why you're the best big sister." She crouched down to pick up a piece of the broken bowl, then added with a mischievous sparkle in her eye, "Besides, it's just a bowl. You'd think we knocked over the whole house."

That did it. The two of them burst into quiet laughter, muffling their giggles behind their hands as they carefully swept up the shards. The kitchen filled with their laughter, the stress melting away as they shared the moment. Even as they cleaned up the mess, Elanor couldn't help but feel grateful for Imogen's ability to turn their father's scolding into something lighthearted. This small, shared rebellion was uniquely theirs.

Simon's heavy footsteps sounded faint from the next room, a reminder of his sternness, that behind his frustration was the love of a man who carried the weight of his family on his shoulders. She thought briefly of her grandmother—his mother—who had often spoken about her son's determination to succeed, despite a world that viewed him differently because of his love for someone of another heritage, especially as a man from the Deep South. Even then, Elanor was struck by how Simon's fair skin shielded him from much of what his wife had endured, which was not too different from the experience she and Imogen would someday face.

For now, though, none of that mattered. At this moment, all that existed was the laughter they shared, a reminder that they could face anything together.

The warmth of her second memory faded, replaced by an unsettling chill in Elanor's chest. She blinked, finding herself in a different place, and the world's colors dulled. She was back in her childhood home, in the living room, on an ordinary, sunlit day. Her sister was nearby, her laugh soft and familiar, her presence comforting yet somehow distant.

The scene shifted, and a wave of dread washed over Elanor as the memory sharpened into focus. Her sister, only a few steps away, had climbed onto a low ledge by the stairs. She was laughing, playful, trusting. Elanor saw herself, younger and carefree, urging her sister to be careful, but her sister had only smiled, reassuring her that everything was fine. But it wasn't. In one brief, heartbreaking moment, her sister's foot slipped, and everything changed.

Elanor froze, rooted to the spot as her sister fell, the shock seizing her, rendering her immobile. The awful sound of her sister hitting the ground crescendoed through the house, and then the world went silent.

Her surroundings shifted again, and she was in a hospital room, sterile and cold, as doctors moved swiftly around her sister's bed. Elanor's younger self stood outside the room, clutching her arms tightly around herself, helpless. She felt as if she were separated from reality by an invisible wall, able to see but powerless to act, unable to reach out or help. She could barely breathe.

Then came the voices. Whispers first, subtle and insinuating, growing louder over time. She dreaded how neighbors looked at her, the pity in their eyes tinged with something darker, sharper—blame. She overheard one woman say it outright, a neighbor who had known her mother for years: "If only Elanor had been watching her more closely." Another murmured, "She's the older sister; she should have known better."

The words burrowed into her, coiling into a knot of guilt and shame that grew heavier each day. Her friends, sensing the change in her, began to drift away, their warmth turning cold and distant, as though her grief were something they couldn't bear to face.

She recalled the day her parents pulled her aside, their voices filled with pain as they assured her it wasn't her fault. Her father's pale skin was even more stark against the dim light of the room, his freckled hands trembling slightly as he tried to comfort her. Her mother, with her deep brown skin and dark, soulful eyes, knelt beside him, her expression a mixture of pain and quiet strength. But their eyes betrayed them, and deep down, Elanor wondered if they held her responsible. It was subtle, but it was there—a hesitation in their touch, a quiet distance that had never existed before. She withdrew, wrapping herself in her guilt, a constant ache that never faded, an emptiness that became part of her.

The memory shifted, and she was alone in her room, hugging a pillow tightly against her chest, grief pressing down on her like an anchor. She was isolated, ostracized by her own heart. She could never forgive herself, and that knowledge had become a quiet, persistent shadow that followed her everywhere, even now.

Elanor's thoughts returned to Foster's story, how he'd carried a similar guilt for the loss of his own sister, ostracized by his community and haunted by whispers of blame. She understood, in a way she hadn't before, that he had reflected this part of her—the part that had suffered in silence, carrying the burden of a loss she could never fully articulate.

As the memory began to dissolve, its ache shifted within Elanor, no longer just a source of pain but a bridge to understanding. She felt her sister's presence, a lingering warmth, and the slightest glimmer of acceptance. Foster had never truly forgiven himself, but maybe, just maybe, she could begin to forgive herself now, recognizing that Simon, her father, was guiding her toward forgiveness and understanding.

As the grief and guilt from the last memory faded, Elanor found herself back in yet another scene, one that exuded a sense of quiet defiance, the kind that demanded courage. She was standing in a familiar and foreboding room, its walls lined with heavy bookshelves and framed certificates—a study she'd entered countless times, each visit accompanied by a sense of dread.

Across from her stood her mother, arms folded, eyes sharp and penetrating. Her presence filled the room, not with the warmth Elanor had once clung to but with an authority now tinged with disappointment. Her mother's words were measured deliberately, and though they lacked outright harshness, they pressed down on Elanor just the same. For most of her life, her mother's approval had been her compass, her validation. She had been the one to guide Elanor through her childhood with firm love, and the one whose expectations were impossible to meet.

Her mother had always carried herself with dignity. She was a respected figure in their community who never faltered in the face of hardship, especially after Elanor's father died when she was in middle school. Elanor admired and tried to emulate that strength, shaping herself into what she thought her mother needed her to be: obedient, quiet, and reliable. But now, standing here, that dynamic was different. Her mother's grief—over losing her husband and Imogen—had hardened her, and that quiet blame was laced into every look, every word.

Her mother's voice was calm but unyielding as she questioned Elanor's decisions, her tone laced with doubt. She was challenging Elanor's choice—one that strayed from what her mother believed was right. The specifics of the moment were blurred, but the feelings were sharp and unmistakable: the tensity of being questioned, the subtle erosion of her confidence, and the implied disapproval that had long followed her.

But Elanor wasn't the same person she'd been when her mother's approval had been everything. She wasn't the timid child desperate to please. She'd endured too much—grief, blame, isolation. The whispers after Imogen's death, the stares, the hollow platitudes—they had all forged something within her. Standing here now, those experiences settled into something solid and unshakable.

Her mother's words pierced through the air again, challenging her resolve, but something new rose inside her. A fierce, unbreakable spark ignited, steadying her. She straightened, meeting her mother's gaze without hesitation. For the first time, she wasn't shrinking under her mother's expectations; she was standing against them.

"You may not agree with me," Elanor said, her voice steady and sure, "but this is my life. My choices are mine to make, and I will live by them. I don't need you to approve of who I am."

Her mother's expression shifted, flickering between surprise and something softer—perhaps understanding, though it was buried beneath her usual reserve. But Elanor didn't wait for her reaction. This moment wasn't about winning her mother's approval but reclaiming her sense of worth. As the words left her lips, they echoed within her, powerful and freeing.

The memory lingered as Elanor stood rooted in its truth, and Nora's voice whispered in her mind, urging her forward. It was a reminder of courage, of the strength she had found in herself. Nora had told her about standing up to those who tried to silence her, facing fear head-on, and refusing to be diminished. The parallel clicked now—not just in Nora's story, but in her journey. Not only was her mother Elanor's anchor, but she also faced the challenge of finding her voice.

The memory faded, but its impact remained, wrapping around Elanor like armor. She understood now that Nora had embodied the courage she'd needed to uncover within herself—the courage to speak, act, and rise even when the world tried to press her down. And freedom settled over her.

The memories shifted, and suddenly Elanor found herself bathed in soft, golden light. She was back in a moment that shimmered, a memory of warmth and joy. She was sitting across from Weston, a young adult version of him, his face bright with laughter. They were somewhere familiar—a park from her hometown, the late afternoon sun casting long, warm shadows over the grass. She felt the echo of her laughter mixing with his, both of them leaning toward each other as if they were the only two people in the world.

She remembered this day. It was one of those perfectly ordinary moments that lingered in memory simply because of how it made her feel. They'd spent hours talking about everything and nothing, hands brushing against each other's, voices lowering to a whisper, even though no one else was around. And then, in a burst of courage, she'd reached out, interlacing her fingers with his. He had smiled at her, his eyes soft with a depth of feeling that still sent a rush through her, even years later.

"You'll always have me," he'd said, his thumb brushing gently over her hand. "I'm here, El. Always."

The nickname, spoken with such quiet conviction, was intimate beyond words. It was as if he understood her soul, able to see her fears, dreams, and hidden thoughts with startling clarity. And in return, she sensed she'd known him forever—as if they'd been drawn to each other across lifetimes, two hearts destined to intertwine.

A different memory flickered to life, sharp and sudden. Elanor was in the passenger seat of Weston's Toyota 2000GT, a gift from her father when he upgraded to a new car, fields and forests blurring past as they sped along a seemingly endless road. Weston drove, his hands firm on the wheel.

As the landscape rolled past in a blur of greens and browns, Elanor's frustration grew from an ongoing argument. The road signs were infrequent and unhelpful, deepening her suspicion that they were hopelessly lost. She glanced over at Weston, who seemed uncharacteristically stubborn as he gripped the steering wheel tighter.

"Are you sure we're on the right track? We've been circling the same area for hours," Elanor pressed, irritated.

Weston navigated another curve. "I know where I'm going," he asserted, though his voice betrayed a hint of doubt. "Just trust me, okay?"

"But it doesn't feel right, Weston. We should have reached the motel by now," Elanor argued, her worry morphing into annoyance. "Can we at least check the map or stop to ask for directions?"

"There's no need for a map. I've got this under control," Weston replied, his tone sharp. The car's interior was stifling, the silence growing heavier with each passing mile as if the unspoken words between them filled the space.

Elanor huffed, turning away to hide her growing exasperation. Moments later, driven by defiance and desperation, she reached for the glove box and pulled out a map. The map unfolded with a crisp snap, revealing their meandering path and clearly showing they had missed a crucial turn.

Seeing the route marked so clearly, Elanor's voice softened but carried a note of vindication. "Look, Weston, we should have turned twenty miles back. We are lost."

Weston's expression tightened as he glanced briefly at the map, his pride stung. "Wish we had that earlier," he muttered, his words edged with sarcasm, trying to mask his frustration at being wrong.

The rest of the drive passed in a heavy silence, both nursing bruised egos until they reached the motel just as the sun set. The air slowly cleared inside their room as the familiar scenes from *The Searchers* flickered on the television screen, providing a backdrop for reflection.

After her shower, Elanor reentered the main room, the dampness of her hair adding a coolness to the air that contrasted with the warmth of the motel room. Weston turned off the television as she approached, his expression serious and thoughtful.

"I'm sorry about earlier, Elanor," Weston began, his tone earnest. He motioned for her to sit beside him on the bed. "I was wrong—not just about the directions, but about how I handled my frustration. I ignored your concerns and dismissed the idea of checking the map when it could have saved us both a lot of time and stress."

Elanor sat down, wrapping a towel tighter around herself, her posture open, encouraging him to continue.

Weston took a deep breath, his eyes meeting hers with a vulnerability she hadn't often seen. "I let my stubbornness and pride get in the way of us working together. It's something I've been struggling with, and I realize it's not just about getting lost on the road—it's about respecting your input and admitting when I'm wrong."

He reached for her hand, squeezing it gently to convey his sincerity. "I want to get better at this, at acknowledging when I make mistakes and addressing them sooner. It's important to me that we don't have these kinds of unnecessary arguments. You deserve a partner who listens and values your perspective, especially when you're right."

Elanor's expression softened, touched by his honesty and the effort it took for him to admit his faults. "Thank you, Weston. That means a lot to me. Knowing we can talk about these things openly—it helps me trust that we can handle whatever comes our way."

Weston nodded, his eyes reflecting a mix of relief and newfound determination. "I promise to do better for both of us." He leaned in and kissed her gently, a kiss that spoke of reconciliation and mutual respect.

As he pulled her into his arms, rolling gently so she was nestled beneath him, the earlier tension seemed a distant memory. Their connection deepened through their physical closeness and the emotional bridges they had built in that quiet motel room.

The memory shifted again, and she witnessed flashes of their life together—the countless walks, the shared secrets, the hurt and loss, the late nights spent talking about things that mattered and things that didn't. Elanor was always at Weston's place, wearing his baggy clothes around the apartment to savor the smell of him when he was out. Weston had been her anchor through everything, the one person who made her feel like she could be entirely herself without pretenses or walls. He had always been there for her, steady and unwavering, offering his love and support without hesitation.

A different memory surfaced, one filled with sunlight and the scent of fresh hay. They were at a horse ranch in upstate New York, the lush green fields stretching around them like a promise. In the distance, a white farmhouse stood as a quaint silhouette against the vivid blue sky, its windows catching the light and shimmering like distant stars. Nearby, a wooden fence meandered along the property line, enclosing them in this idyllic setting.

Weston was mounted on a sleek black mare, the animal's coat gleaming under the sun, starkly contrasting the bright, open field. Elanor rode a dusted horse with a distinctive white marking around its left eye, its playful trot kicking up clumps of grass and earth. They rode side by side, the wind whipping through Elanor's hair, their laughter echoing across the fields and mingling with the calls of distant meadowlarks.

As they slowed the horses, Weston turned to her, his expression serious yet full of hope. "I spoke to the owner yesterday," he said, his voice carrying over the soft clopping of hooves. "They agreed on a price for the house and the property."

Elanor looked around, the beauty of the place sinking into her bones. "Really?" she asked, excitement mingled with a touch of fear coursing through her.

"Yeah," Weston smiled, gently patting her horse's neck. "So, what do you think? Would you live here with me?"

Without hesitation, her answer came, strong and sure, "Yes." It was a moment of pure connection; their future suddenly laid out before them, full of possibilities.

But then, with a suddenness that cut through her, came the ache of losing him. The day he was gone. The screech of tires, the sickening crunch of metal, and the suffocating panic as everything went dark. She had been in the car with Weston, the memory overwhelming her like an unstoppable wave. Faint whispers on the edge of consciousness, the feeling of slipping away, and the overwhelming light flashed before her. And then . . . Bodie. She had been there before, walking its streets with him, seeing the confusion and sadness in his eyes as she left him behind. But she had been pulled back, dragged away from him and the quiet stillness of this place, returning to a world without him.

Agony flowed through her as she woke up alone, her body battered but alive, while he remained behind, his voice and presence lost to her. The world had been empty, and all color and sound had been drained. The laughter, the warmth—all of it had vanished instantly, replaced by an unending silence. She had lost him too soon, and the world was a hollow shell without him.

And now she understood—it wasn't the first time she had faced losing him. Only this time, she wasn't being pulled back. This time, she was staying, and Weston was still here, waiting for her.

And yet, Weston was here with her, had been here all along, guiding her through the strange, surreal landscape that mimicked their child-hood adventures. His steady presence, his unwavering support—he was helping her navigate this journey between life and death . . . her journey. This wasn't just a memory; it was his spirit, his love, reaching across whatever boundary separated them, keeping her grounded, urging her to face the truths she'd buried deep inside herself.

Elanor was overwhelmed, a mixture of sorrow and peace flooding through her. She was beginning to understand and accept the journey she had been on.

Elanor's memories of the waterfall, her companions, and Weston dissolved into the dense, rain-soaked cityscape of New York City. Her senses abruptly filled with urban sounds and scents—distant car horns, footsteps echoing off narrow alleys, the sharp chill of rain-dampened concrete beneath her shoes.

The city lights stretched out in muted streams through the misty haze of late night. Street lamps flickered, casting pools of yellow across the wet pavement, each puddle reflecting fractured fragments of the towering buildings overhead. She wandered, her hands tucked in her coat pockets. Her mind was heavy and clouded, weighed down by a sorrow she barely comprehended. The world was distant, as if she were walking in a dream.

As she moved, she clutched a delicate silver locket around her neck, which grounded her in the chilly night air. It was one of the last mementos she had of Weston—of the life they'd once shared and the warmth that now belonged to another lifetime. Her fingers traced the familiar outline of the locket, her thumb brushing over his engraved initials inside, next to his photo, with a tenderness that mirrored her memories.

Her pace slowed as she crossed over an empty intersection, the buildings around her towering and indifferent. Her footsteps echoed in the silence, each step a hollow beat in the rhythm of her lonely heart. She hadn't understood how far she'd wandered from the life she'd known—literally and figuratively. The quiet of the street was almost surreal in the city that never truly slept, yet tonight, it matched her lonely state of mind, an emptiness too vast to fill.

In the distance, she noticed headlights piercing the darkness. A car was approaching, its lights bright and blinding against the muted backdrop of the rainy night. She blinked, feeling momentarily frozen as the reality of the present caught up with her. Time slowed the world around her, narrowing to that single set of headlights cutting through the mist.

A sound—a horn blaring—broke through the fog in her mind. She looked up, the rain streaking her face, her gaze meeting the oncoming light, unable to process the danger in time. In that fraction of a second, she drifted away from her pain and grief. The brightness wrapped around her, the din of the city fading into silence as her body lifted, weightless, like a leaf caught in the wind.

But at that moment, as the city's noise quieted and her vision dimmed, a profound peace settled within her. She wasn't alone. Weston's face appeared in her mind, his eyes soft and understanding, his smile a balm to her pain. The sorrow of her life, the love she'd lost, the regret she carried—it all lifted, replaced by a sense of acceptance. A warmth she hadn't felt in so long bloomed within her, spreading through her like a promise kept.

As the world faded, she surrendered to that warmth, a quiet certainty filling her. This journey—her last—wasn't about holding onto the past but about finding herself again, reconnecting with the parts of her that she thought had been lost forever. In that final breath, she let go, trusting in the love and memories that had carried her, knowing they would be enough.

CHAPTER TWENTY-FIVE

The world around Elanor began to solidify, drawing her out of the cascading memories. The warmth of the setting sun blushed on her skin, gentle and grounding, like an anchor that pulled her back into the present. The sound of the waterfall echoed nearby, its endless flow a reminder of the continuity of time and memory as if whispering that each moment she had just relived was now etched into her being forever.

She inhaled deeply, breathing in the scent of the wild earth and faintly sweet grasses surrounding her. Gone were the sounds of bustling New York, the piercing sirens, and the blaring horns. Instead, she found herself in the familiar, raw beauty of the mystical landscape, where her journey through the Wild West had led, and where she now understood it was destined to end.

Weston knelt by her side, his hand resting on her arm, his eyes filled with something she hadn't noticed before—a soft, gentle hope intermingled with an unmistakable depth of understanding. His presence was more real, more tangible than ever. It was as though, in knowing the truth of who she was, she could finally see the truth of who *he* was, too.

"Do you remember now?" His voice, filled with quiet reverence for the moment, was barely audible. His question was soft but weighted, as if he were giving her permission to recognize everything she had kept hidden, everything she'd been searching for. His question lingered, reflecting the hope and fear he must have carried with him throughout this journey.

Elanor's breath caught, her hand instinctively going to the silver locket around her neck. She was clutching it, but now, with trembling fingers, she found the latch. It clicked open quickly, as though it had been waiting. Inside, a delicate photo stared back at her—Weston, his face familiar yet younger, filled with the same warmth she had always seen in him. Next to the image, engraved into the metal, were three initials: *W.A.C.*

Her voice trembled as she read them aloud, her chest tightening. "Weston Alexander Charles," she whispered, her eyes lifting to meet his. The words unlocked something deep within her, a recognition far beyond the locket or its contents.

Weston's smile softened, and he gave a slight nod. "That'd be me, Elanor Nora Foster," he said, the depth of his emotion barely concealed.

Elanor's tears spilled over as she clutched the locket, her attention returning to the initials and the photo. "Weston," she murmured, the name carrying all the influence of her love, her grief, and the overwhelming realization that this moment wasn't just about understanding—it was about accepting, as Tawa had advised.

Nora, Boone, and Foster weren't just people she had met along the way—they were parts of her. They were her courage, humor, and strength, manifested in ways she could see and hold onto, reminders of her humanity. Each of them had been by her side, helping her confront what she'd buried deeply and guiding her back to herself.

"They were . . . pieces of me," she murmured, her voice filled with awe and gratitude. The realization brought tears to her eyes, releasing all the fear and grief she had carried alone for so long. "Nora, Boone, Foster—they weren't just friends. They were me. They were guiding me back."

Weston sat down, wrapping his arm around Elanor's waist. His gaze never left her face, watching her, giving her the space to feel everything without rushing her to explain or understand it fully. In the quiet between them, something she hadn't allowed herself to think in a long time rose to the surface—acceptance.

The waterfall's steady rhythm beside her synced with her heartbeat. The journey had led her here, not to seek out some external truth but to reunite with these lost parts of herself. With Weston beside her, she felt whole, connected to a strength she'd once doubted, a strength she could now see was always within her.

As Elanor looked up at Weston, a deep sense of gratitude filled her, extending to everything she had lost and found. Weston guided Elanor to a flat rock beside the waterfall, its surface warm under the sun's touch. The cascading water shimmered like liquid light, casting soft reflections around them. For a moment, the world appeared to pause, as if it was waiting for their words.

Elanor pulled her knees to her chest, wrapping her arms around them. She took a steadying breath, then looked at Weston, her eyes reflecting the turmoil within. "Is this real, or has this all been inside my head?" she asked, her voice wavering slightly.

Weston responded with a gentle, reassuring smile. "Everything in life lives inside our heads, one way or another," he said softly. "That doesn't mean it isn't real."

Elanor hesitated, then voiced the lingering doubt in her heart. "And what about Nora, Boone, and Foster? Were they . . . real?"

"Of course they were," Weston replied with certainty. "They were your guardian angels and reminders of who you were."

"And Simon? Was that my father the whole time?" Elanor's asked.

Weston met her gaze, his expression soft yet profound. "I think you already know the answer to that question," he said gently.

She did. Now, it was undisputable that her father was along for the ride to ensure his daughter made it to Paradise.

Encouraged by Weston's words but still grappling with her emotions, Elanor confessed, her voice raw and trembling, "I'm scared. Of losing you again. Of losing everyone again. I don't know how to go on without them." Her words evoked a sense of relief, yet they also revealed a vulnerable aspect of her. She blinked away the sting of tears she'd been holding back.

"How do I hold on when it feels like everything just slips away?" she asked.

Weston reached out, covering her hand with his. His warm touch grounded her against the overwhelming fear and grief that threatened to overtake her. "I'm here," he said, his voice a steady anchor. "I've always been with you. And I always will be." He shifted closer, their shoulders nearly touching. "Love doesn't just disappear, El. It doesn't fade, even when everything else changes. It's a part of us—it's you, it's me, it's them. It stays."

Elanor's brow furrowed, and she turned to Weston, her voice rising with frustration. "Why didn't you say anything? Why didn't you tell me what this was—what this all meant?"

Weston's eyes softened his expression, a mixture of understanding and regret. "I did tell you, El," he replied gently. "But every time I did, it was like this world took those memories away—like it reset. There must be some rules to this world that I don't fully understand."

Elanor tried to focus, her mind straining against the gaps in her memory. Fragments began to resurface, images and conversations piecing together in her mind, though not yet fully formed. "I remember being in Bodie before this journey," she murmured.

Weston nodded, his face solemn. "Yes, you were."

Elanor's eyes met his, a spark of realization dawning. "So, I was the girl that got away from this place—the one you were talking to Nora about?" she asked, her voice a mix of hope and apprehension.

Again, Weston nodded. "Yes, Elanor. That was you."

The pieces of her past began to click into place, though they were still jagged and rough around the edges. "You could have tried again, told me one more time," she said, her voice edging with anger and a pleading undertone.

"I could have," Weston admitted, his voice steady. "But it seems that in this world, your journey to remember had to be triggered by your own experiences, not just by my words. It's about discovering it on your own, reaching an understanding and acceptance—not because someone gave you the answers, but because you found them through everything we've faced together."

"And Tawa?" she asked. "Did you know how to get to him this whole time?"

Weston shook his head. "No. I . . . I think the memory thing worked on more than just you. I didn't even recognize you when I first saw you

— it took me a minute to wake up. The fact that I couldn't recall how to get to Tawa was extremely frustrating, as it could have saved us a significant amount of time."

Elanor's shoulders sagged as her frustration ebbed into a quiet sadness mixed with emerging clarity. She turned back to the rushing water, her thoughts swirling as she let his words and the returning fragments of her memory settle over her. It still hurt, but a small part of her recognized he was right. And in that knowing, something in her began to shift—slowly but undeniably.

Elanor's eyes met his, deepened with his own pain that mingled with the unwavering love that had brought him here. "Letting go feels like losing everything all over again," she admitted, her voice breaking. "I don't know if I can."

"You can," Weston said gently, his eyes never leaving hers. "You're stronger than you think. And the ones you fear letting go of, they're still with you in everything you do. You don't have to be alone, El—not now, not ever."

They sat in silence, the only sound the rush of the waterfall. Unbidden memories of their life together flooded back, including late nights filled with laughter, quiet mornings spent side by side, and the feel of his arm around her shoulders. The ache of what they'd lost and the warmth of what they'd shared settled in her. It was all still there, a part of her.

Slowly, she let herself lean into him, feeling the solidity of his presence. She closed her eyes, allowing herself to feel the depth of her grief but also the love that had always been there, binding them together even through the harshest moments. She whispered, "Thank you. For staying."

"Always," Weston murmured, pressing his forehead to hers. "No matter what."

Something shifted within Elanor—like a wound finally beginning to mend. She lifted her head, meeting his eyes, and in that moment, she was ready to let go of the past. It would always be a part of her, but it didn't have to consume her. Together, they could carry the memories and the love forward.

She reached for his hand again, holding it firmly. "I'm ready," she said, her voice stronger than before. "Ready to move forward." The water continued its endless flow beside them, a reminder of life's persistence and the power of renewal.

The magnitude of it all settled on Elanor, but it didn't feel unbearable this time. It was real—part of her story, not something to run from. "I know who I am now," she whispered, her words more a promise to herself than anyone else. Weston's eyes softened, filled with pride and something more profound—love that had endured.

The two sat in comfortable silence, the steady rhythm of the waterfall offering a soothing backdrop. Elanor's mind drifted over the journey that had brought her here, each challenge, each goodbye now a part of her, woven into the person she had become. The ache of parting from her friends remained, but a newfound strength and clarity tempered it.

Weston stood first, offering his hand to her. She took it, their fingers intertwining, a connection both timeless and present. He asked softly, "Shall we?"

Elanor breathed in deeply, her chest rising with hope, and the remnants of her tears glistened in the sunlight. "Yes," she replied, a small, determined smile breaking through. Together, they took the first step away from the waterfall. The path forward was uncertain, but was one they would face side by side.

As they walked hand in hand, the wind rustled through the trees, and the sound of the waterfall faded behind them. The world was vast and intimate, filled with possibilities and echoes of the past. Elanor felt lighter, her resolve stronger. Whatever awaited them, she was no longer defined by her fear or regret. With Weston by her side and the enduring presence of her friends in her heart, she was ready to embrace whatever the future held.

CHAPTER TWENTY-SIX

The evening air was crisp as Elanor and Weston began their ascent toward the mountaintop, the path ahead shrouded in the soft light of dusk. Their steps were deliberate, and though each distinctly felt the gravity of their journey, an undeniable sense of purpose guided them forward. The terrain was rugged, the rocks jagged and uneven beneath their feet, but neither wavered. Hand in hand, they moved as one, their silent understanding filling the spaces between words.

As they walked, Elanor's gaze swept over their surroundings. The trees that had sheltered them in the forest gradually gave way to rocky outcrops, the transition reflecting her journey—from the tangled confusion of her past to the clarity she sought now. The wind carried the scent of pine and wildflowers, mingling with the earthy aroma of the trail, and she breathed it in deeply, letting it ground her in this moment. Every crack of a branch underfoot and every distant bird call was a heightened reminder of the life and loss that had led her here.

Elanor's memories pressed gently against her chest. She thought of Nora's fierce determination, Boone's humor that never failed to lighten the darkest moments, and Foster's steadfast resolve. Though they had stayed behind, their presence was still tangible, guiding her forward. She almost felt her father's quiet strength lingering like a whisper carried on the wind. Their faces flickered before her, as vivid and real as if they walked beside her now. She swallowed, her throat tight with both gratitude and longing.

Weston squeezed her hand gently, drawing her back to the present. "They're with you, El," he said softly, his voice a comforting balm to her turbulent emotions. She met his eyes, finding the strength and love that had kept her anchored through so much. "Always," he added, a small smile on his lips.

Elanor nodded, her smile bittersweet. "I know," she whispered, feeling their presence not just in memory but in her heartbeat and the courage that pushed her forward. She held that feeling for a moment, letting its warmth sink in before she released it to the wind. Their spirits were woven into her own, a reminder of who she was and still could be.

With one last glimpse over her shoulder at their path, Elanor turned her eyes back to the mountain ahead. There was no telling what awaited them at the summit, but she wasn't walking alone. Together, she and Weston pressed on.

The summit stretched out before them, a broad expanse of rock that crowned the mountain they had climbed. Elanor and Weston walked side by side, their hands intertwined, as they took in the vast view. Below, the forest stretched endlessly, a sea of green painted gold and amber by the sinking sun. No desert, no barren wasteland remained—only life, lush and vibrant, untouched by the harshness they had endured. The air was cool and crisp, carrying the faint scent of sap and lavendar, starkly contrasting the dry, searing heat of the world they had left behind.

The full moon rose higher above, a pale glow against the darkening sky—a duality of light and shadow that mirrored Elanor's journey. She let out a breath she had been holding, their past fading like a distant echo. The horizon ahead was open and full of possibility, untainted by the struggles that had shaped their path.

They sat together on a flat rock, the wind gentle but cool against their skin. For a long moment, neither spoke. The silence was sacred, a shared acknowledgment of everything they'd lost and gained and the unknowable path ahead. As the sun sank behind the far-off mountains, it ignited the horizon, transforming everything into hues of crimson and gold.

Elanor closed her eyes for a moment, the warmth of the sun on her face reminding her of every fleeting moment of joy, every loss, every step that had led her here. She turned to Weston, finding comfort in the familiar lines of his face, the quiet strength in his eyes. He was her anchor, the one constant through the storm of memories and pain.

"Thank you," she whispered, her voice soft but firm, carrying her gratitude. "For being my person."

Weston reached out, his fingers brushing her cheek. "There's nowhere else I'd rather be," he said, his words simple but deeply felt.

Elanor took a deep breath, letting the crisp mountain air fill her lungs. She thought of her father and sister, knowing she would see them again soon.

As the final rays of sunlight reached the horizon, Elanor looked at Weston, her voice soft but steady. "Do you think we've come far enough?"

Weston smiled, his fingers squeezing around hers. "Far enough to find what we needed. And far enough to know that wherever we go next, we'll be alright."

Elanor's lips curved into a small, tender smile. "As long as we're together."

He leaned closer, his temple resting gently against hers.

For a moment, there was no more fear—only love and the warmth of his presence. They leaned into each other, a soft, lingering kiss that spoke of both endings and beginnings. When they broke apart, Elanor was stronger, the shadows in her heart tempered by the light they shared.

The moon continued to rise, casting silver light across the summit, bathing them in its glow. Elanor stood, her hand still in Weston's. The path down the mountain, and whatever it led to, was shrouded in darkness. But she was no longer afraid. With Weston by her side, she would face whatever came.

As they prepared to leave, she took one last look at the sky—the sun's final embers fading into darkness, the full moon shining bright. It was a fitting reminder: endings and beginnings, light and dark, loss and renewal. She turned to Weston, her grip tightening.

Together, they stepped forward.

Thank you for taking the time to read *Where the Sun Dies*.

Please remember to leave a review with your thoughts on GoodReads and Amazon! Reviews are the best way to support an author's growth and success.

Happy reading!

Goodreads

Amazon

ABOUT THE AUTHOR

Farleigh Collins graduated from Hunter College in New York City, where he refined his diverse writing talents, which include screenplays, stage plays, and fiction. His debut novel, *Where the Sun Dies,* was inspired by the classic *The Wonderful Wizard of Oz* and explores the challenges of navigating an unfamiliar world and the quest to find one's way home.

Born and raised in Iowa, Farleigh has lived all over the United States —from the vibrant streets of New York to the eclectic atmosphere of Austin, Texas, and the peaceful drizzle of Seattle, Washington. His love for the outdoors shines through in his enjoyment of hiking and kayaking, activities that provide him with both solace and inspiration during the sunny months.

Farleigh's writing is marked by detailed descriptions, introspective monologues, and the creation of intense atmospheres, all supported by realistic dialogue and symbolic undertones. Through his narratives, he seeks not only to entertain but also to resonate deeply with his readers, encouraging them to discover the subtle messages woven into the fabric of his stories.

As a seasoned traveler, Farleigh draws immense inspiration from his encounters with various cultures and their histories. These experiences enrich his storytelling with broad perspectives and authentic experiences. He hopes his readers will find joy in his tales and appreciate the hidden gems that hint at the broader messages he seeks to convey.

 instagram.com/farleighcollins